Betsy's War

Eliza Morton was born in Liverpool and worked as an actress. She is known for playing Madeline Bassett in *Jeeves and Wooster* and Lucinda in the Liverpool sitcom *Watching*. As well as TV, she has also worked in theatre and film. She trained at Guildhall School of Drama and with the Royal Court Young Writers' Group. She is an award-winning short story writer and has also written drama for TV, film and theatre. In her formative years at convent school, she spent her weekends playing the piano accordion in northern working men's clubs. She lives with her husband – the actor Peter Davison – in Middlesex and is the author of *Angel of Liverpool*, *The Girl from Liverpool* and the Liverpool Orphans trilogy.

By Eliza Morton

A Liverpool Girl
A Last Dance in Liverpool
Angel of Liverpool
The Girl from Liverpool

The Liverpool Orphans Trilogy
The Orphans from Liverpool Lane
The Children Left Behind
Betsy's War

Eliza Morton

Betsy's War

PAN BOOKS

First published 2025 by Pan Books
an imprint of Pan Macmillan
The Smithson, 6 Briset Street, London EC1M 5NR
EU representative: Macmillan Publishers Ireland Ltd, 1st Floor,
The Liffey Trust Centre, 117–126 Sheriff Street Upper,
Dublin 1 D01 YC43
Associated companies throughout the world

ISBN 978-1-0350-1524-5

1 3 5 7 9 8 6 4 2

A CIP catalogue record for this book is available from the British Library.

Typeset in Sabon by Palimpsest Book Production Limited, Falkirk, Stirlingshire
Printed and bound in the UK using 100% Renewable Electricity by
CPI Group (UK) Ltd

Visit **www.panmacmillan.com** to read more about all
our books and to buy them.

For Louis

Prologue

May 1941

James Swann was approaching Stanley Dock, knocking on doors of the houses that still had their lights on, when he heard planes growling overhead. Within seconds, there came the deathly thudding sounds and the sky lighting up as if it was on fire, followed by the horrible clanging of ambulance bells. Word reached them quickly about the bomb that had hit Mill Road Hospital. James, still shy of his twenty-first birthday, along with those who were available, raced over to Everton Road. When the fireman saw James's tin helmet with ARP on it, he stood aside and nodded James towards the direction of the blaze. A man was pleading with them to point the hoses at his pub that had caught alight, but they needed all the manpower they could get to try to stop the fire moving up the sides of the hospital building.

James immediately joined the human conveyor belt passing spades, handed down from a truck, along the line. They all knew what the spades were for – to dig out the injured and the dead – but nobody said anything. Water from a gushing hose flooded the street and splashed over the cobbles and onto his boots. Outside a nearby dance hall, a fire burst into life after sparks from falling timber set a dustbin alight. The nurses, helped by those patients who could walk, had wheeled the beds out into the forecourt from the front of the building. A woman was wailing and clutching her head, making a strange, unnatural sound.

More patients, numb and dazed, faces black with soot and ash, were being put into ambulances. James broke away from the line when someone shouted at him to help push one of the beds over the kerb. How cruel, he thought, with so many casualties of the war already here on the wards trying to recover from God knows what, and now this. But he tried to keep a level head.

Meanwhile, a nurse stood at the door and rushed through those that could still walk, one after another. 'Betsy, Donna Marie, Mrs Marco, Mrs Wright, come on. Don't just stand there like Lewis's dummies. I know what my job is. Let's go. Let's get you out of here.'

When the nurse counted the last, she followed them outside, picking through the rubble, not daring to look back. But then something stopped her in her tracks. The soft sound of mewling. A baby? A life? Hope.

'Go on ahead, ladies,' she said. 'Go on, I have something I still need to do.'

James rushed over. 'That joist is about to collapse, Nurse . . .'

'I need to go back inside. Can you wait here for me to come out? Another ambulance is arriving any minute,' she said.

2

'The joist!' cried James.

But she was gone and all he could do was stand under the sickly orange sky, breathe in the noxious fumes of sulphur and smoke, and wait.

Chapter 1

Fourteen months earlier

March 1940

'*Now*, Deirdre!' hissed Betsy Drew quietly. The rest of the girls in the class were all following the nun's lead, kneeling at their desks and joining their hands in prayer. But Jesus was losing his attraction for sixteen-year-old Betsy and her friend Deirdre. Lately their heads were full of dance halls and dreamboats in the *Picture Post* and there wasn't room for much else. The nun had her eyes shut and was murmuring through the Angelus. Betsy and Deirdre took their chance, jumped up, and darted out of the classroom and down the corridor. They shot out of the door to the nuns' grotto, parting the branches of a magnolia tree, heavy with pink fleshy flowers. Diving through a gap in a privet hedge, they both collapsed against the stone wall on the other side.

'We're for it if they find us here. And in our indoor shoes,' said Deirdre.

Betsy laughed. 'Who cares,' she said, taking out a mess of woollen thread from her tunic pocket and untangling it. She began to rhythmically loop the wool between her fingers.

'Betsy, if you could marry anyone in the world, who would you choose?' said Deirdre, idly watching Betsy fashion the cat's cradle.

'Alvis Dooley,' she replied, carefully transferring the weave to Deirdre.

Deirdre spluttered. 'I meant *anyone* . . . like a famous person . . . Gary Cooper or Bing Crosby. I didn't mean someone who lives in the tennies with us. And especially not that soft Olly. The boys around here are all useless.'

'Alvis is not. He's my one true love.' Betsy sighed mournfully. 'Anyway, it doesn't matter, he doesn't even look at me. He's eighteen. And I'm sixteen. He probably thinks I'm a baby. He once called me daft as a hen.'

She grimaced and sucked the end of a piece of her messy straw-coloured hair tangling over her blue eyes.

'Don't do that. You'll make a big ball of it in your stomach and die. I'm glad Alvis doesn't like you. You stay well clear of him. Bing Crosby's better than that useless lump. And safer.' Deirdre unwound the wool from her fingers. 'Shall I test you on your spellings? You don't want another detention tonight. *Gone with the Wind* is on again at the Coronet later and you'll be stuck here doing yards of flipping lines – *Beloved Mary Mother of God* five hundred times until your wrist aches.'

Betsy groaned. 'Why is it always me?'

'You've got to stop daydreaming, Bets. You're always staring out of the window. What are you thinking about when you drift off?'

'Escape . . .' murmured Betsy.

'You have to at least look as though you're listening. And you do all those stupid things, hanging from the ceiling bars, and throwing the board duster around. And mooning over eejits like Alvis Dooley.'

'I prefer maths to spelling. I love fractions,' she said with a sigh.

Betsy had always felt confident with numbers. Maybe because she liked certainty in life, not vagueness. She had enough of that at home. *Your da might come back one day. If we win the Pools, I'll buy you a new dress. Your brother likes you really, you'll see when you're older.* Or, *That fella Hitler wouldn't dare drop his bombs on Liverpool.* With words, the rules seemed to change all the time. I before E except after C, but not if it's neighbour, or weight, or a whole lot of others. With maths, two plus two was always four and it was beautifully immovable. That's what she needed more than ever lately. She had such a creeping sense of worry and the feeling that everything was changing. There was nothing certain about the world these days. One minute there was going to be a war and they had built a shelter across the road and the sirens were going off every night and there were soldiers on every corner, they were all bumping around in the dark, but now it was just a phoney war.

'Go on . . . Immaculate Conception . . . and the definition . . .'

Betsy spelled it out carefully. 'Double M . . . Conception with a C, not an S . . .'

'Definition. Up the duff when the fella does a runner,' said Deirdre, laughing.

Betsy tipped her head to one side. 'Why does Sister

Bernadette always bring God into everything? Immorality, sinfulness, transubstantiation . . . Why not ask us to spell pneumonia or Wednesday?'

'Because they spend so much time telling us not to think about boys, but actually they're *obsessed* . . . and now it's all we can think about. Virginity, conjugal rights, *sin* . . . We're obsessed . . . Just like they are . . .'

'I'm obsessed with Alvis,' Betsy laughed. 'A real person with real hair and real skin and real lips. Not Gary Cooper in your *Picture Post*.'

'I sometimes go to sleep with Gary's page open on my face. Then I dream of him all night long and it's the next best thing to real.'

'Don't you get disappointed when you wake up and he's not there?'

'Aye. When I roll over and see my snoring little sister on one side, and her ratty twin on the other, yes. But you should try it and stay away from that fool, Alvis. The only person he could ever love is himself. He's not worth it, Bets. You hear?' And then she tilted her head. 'Cave! Sister Bernadette coming up the path!'

An hour later, Betsy stood with her heart thumping like a drum in front of Sister Bernadette, who was sitting at her desk.

'So, Betsy . . .' she said, steepling her slender fingers.

'I'm sorry,' she blurted. 'We won't do it again.'

The nun looked confused. 'Why do you think I've brought you here?'

'Because . . .' She faltered, convinced someone had seen her crawling through the hole in the privet.

'Betsy. A woman from Cunard's has been to visit.

They want girls to work in the accounts department. With so many of their men joining up because of this wretched war, they need girls who are good at maths. I suggested you.'

Betsy felt her heart stop.

'I know you're halfway through your exams but you're sixteen now and I don't see any point in furthering your education whilst we all pull teeth trying to get you to recite the "Ancient Mariner" and dissect a rabbit. I think this will be a marvellous opportunity.'

Half an hour later, when Betsy had told Deirdre the news, Deirdre punched her gently on the shoulder. 'I wish I was good at maths. You lucky beggar. Do you wear a uniform in your new job?'

'A black dress and neat shoes and tied-back hair. There's a woman from Cunard's who comes to your house before you start to check.'

'Sister Bernadette was kind to get you that job.'

'But she will still give me detention if I don't get these spellings right.'

'Doesn't matter now, does it? You can go the rest of your life spelling Immaculate Conception with one M and an S. I'll miss you, Bets. Promise we'll stay friends?'

'Promise.'

'Amen to that, love. Here's to the beginning of your new life, Miss Betsy. You won't forget me, will you?'

Chapter 2

Five months later and just turned seventeen, Betsy stood hopefully in Alvis Dooley's kitchen, hopping from foot to foot. 'Ma sent this, Mrs Dooley. Her sugar ration.'

Joyce Dooley took it gratefully. 'Ta, Betsy. I'll get the bacon ration for you. How's the job at Cunard's going? Settling in, I heard. You clever girl.'

'It's just counting numbers. Doing the ledgers.'

'Still, well done. Your ma's very proud. Now, where did I put the ration book . . . ? Ah, here you are.' She carefully ripped out the bacon coupon. 'Tell your ma I'll swap my eggs for her bread if she wants next time. Bacon for sugar is grand.'

'What time does the nosh-up start?' said Alvis, who had wandered in stuffing the heel of a loaf into his mouth. As he approached the table to saw off another piece of the loaf with a bread knife, he showed no signs of even noticing her. But Betsy's heart still skipped a beat. In her white dress with a stiff net petticoat bunching up underneath, she was hoping he might say something. She had certainly noticed him. The way he was greedily licking the margarine from his lips.

'You're not going dressed like that, Alvis!' said his mother, bustling around the kitchen, flapping a tea towel and slinging it over her shoulder.

'Why not?' he asked, genuinely puzzled.

'Tell him, Betsy . . .'

Betsy frowned.

'Look how lovely Betsy looks in her best dress. You look a right state. Them sleeves have holes in the elbows. And you've been chewing the cuffs again, haven't you? I've put your brother's jumper on the bed for you.'

'No one cares. I'm not wearing our Tommy's hand-me-downs.'

Alvis's mother tutted. 'Betsy has made an effort. She looks gorgeous. Our Lord Jesus died on the cross for you, Alvis, and you can't even be bothered to change your pully. Father O'Connor'll think I'm a terrible mother if I let you go to church like that.'

He grimaced. 'I'm not going to church.'

'Oh, I see. You're planning to just fill your face with fish paste sarnies, are you? This day is not about Alvis Dooley having the craic on free beer and sticky buns, this is about giving thanks to Mary and all the beauty she brings into our lives.'

Betsy looked around at their cramped kitchen. The doors falling off their hinges, the peeling wallpaper stuck up with pins, the creeping mould and damp. She couldn't see much beauty here. Even her white dress was gaping at the seams in places and splodged with yellow stains.

'You'll go to church before the party. We have to. Maisie Riley is wearing the crown of flowers. And hasn't her mother been going on about it for weeks,' she muttered.

Alvis smiled.

'Maisie Riley. She the one who . . . ?' said Betsy.

'Plays the cello, yes,' she snapped. 'Though there's no amount of practice that will improve those ankles.'

Alvis and Betsy shared a smile and Betsy's heart leapt. It might not have been words they had exchanged, but it was something.

'Now, get ready, Alvis. Look sharp.'

Today was Assumption Day, when friends and family would come together from all over Liverpool, when they would push the tables into the centre of the courtyard of the tenements and float white linen cloths over the top of them, when jugs of warm lemonade and orange squash would miraculously appear along with towers of malt loaf and pink and yellow Battenberg cake. There had been talk from some people about it not happening because of Hitler stomping his boots all over Europe – wouldn't be a nice thing to do when there were those suffering – but the man with the ridiculous moustache wasn't going to stop those in the tenements having their fun and everyone from Liverpool Lane down to the docks would still be taking out their best dresses, pulling on their white socks, spitting on their shoes and Brylcreeming their hair.

'Nosh-up starts after the procession. They have to take Our Lady into the church first. They've already put out the sarnies,' said Donna, Alvis's elder sister, clacking over the linoleum in her high-heeled sandals.

She had wandered in wearing just her slip over her girdle with sunburned cheeks as pink as her lipstick and was now lining up three empty small evaporated milk cans on the table. She went over to the sink and after filling a chipped enamel jug with water she then stirred in a spoonful of sugar from the sugar bowl. After the sugar had dissolved, she sat down and carefully poured the water into the small Pomagne bottle. Betsy watched, mesmerized, as she pumped the crocheted ball at her hair then carefully rolled sticky wet pieces of it around the milk cans. Donna pursed her lips and looked at herself in the cracked mirror she had propped up against the jug.

'I've told you, sugared water on your hair will attract the wasps on a sunny day like this, daft girl,' said her mother. 'Besides, I can't afford for you to waste our precious sugar ration.'

'Fix the back can, will you, Betsy?' Donna said, ignoring her. 'I'll look like Loretta Young when I'm done.'

Betsy glanced at Alvis's mother, who rolled her eyes. She then went over and wrapped a piece of Donna's limp hair around the can.

'Give it a good spray so it sticks . . .'

'Spam, and jam. And jelly, and cakes with icing and hundreds and thousands. Come on, else everyone will eat them,' chanted the youngest Dooley sister, Carmel, dashing in and skidding against the table.

'Will you stop talking about food, all of you! You're making me hungry. And shush . . . Listen, everyone . . .' said Joyce. She patted the air and tipped her head to one side. The room went quiet. 'I can hear the singing!'

Half an hour later, they were all walking towards Scotland Road, which had bunting in the Virgin's colours of Marian blue and gold strung across the streets and fluttering in the gentle breeze. People were already excitedly waiting for the priests to start the procession. When they reached the tenements, the altar boys and a few nuns were processing along the middle of the street to the sounds of 'Ave Maria' whilst the Monsignor in his white and gold vestments nodded at the thrilled crowds that were coming out onto the pavements waving flags. He gazed up at everyone hanging over pennant-decorated balconies, kissed his fingertips and crossed himself. Alvis and Betsy stood under the curved brick arch to the entrance of the tenements and watched.

'Thinks he's the flaming Pope. Thinks he walks on water, that one. I heard he likes a flutter on the gee-gees and a drink like any fella.'

There were long tables covered with white table-cloths and piles of sandwiches curling in the sun and flowers picked from hedgerows that had been stuck in jam jars. A few more altar boys with shiny oiled hair and wearing starched white lace vestments were coming together in a serious group, gripping their polished brass sun-burnished candlesticks, waiting to come into the courtyard.

'Doesn't it look lovely?' said Betsy. She shielded her eyes with her hand to look at the crowds and then up at even more groups of people coming to hang over the balconies, smiling.

A handsome young priest and three serious-looking altar boys walking behind him appeared carrying a plinth on which sat a blue and gold statue of Our Lady, with sprigs of hawthorn and white lilies dripping from the base of it. Behind them followed the procession of more people holding white flowers, nuns at the front, girls in their dresses, singing and swinging purses and twisting ribbons.

Betsy, walking alongside Alvis's mother pushing the baby in the pram with the wobbly wheel and with Carmel dancing about by their side, felt a burst of something. It's like I'm in a dream, she thought. She shielded her eyes with her hand again to look at the scene. Ahead was a huge crowd bunching up under a small tree in the courtyard. Everyone seemed happy. No one appeared worried at all despite the information leaflets being pushed through their doors daily, the nightly blackouts, the sinister crosses on the windows. The world was full of darkness and worry these days. But today it was full of so much light it was making her eyes hurt.

Alvis leaned forward across one of the tables and took a fistful of sandwiches and stuffed them into his pocket. He then grabbed another, sniffed it, and took a huge greedy bite. Betsy was astonished at how much he could eat, and how thin he was. He had an appetite. You could see it in his eyes. Always hungry, always searching for something else to grab or snatch. And that was the way he was looking at her now. Still chewing on a mouthful of Spam and bread, he grasped her hand and pulled her to him.

'Betsy . . .' For so long she had wanted him to just glance in her direction, and now here he was – the voice close against her ear, the hop-sweet warm breath making her heart gallop.

'What?' she asked.

It didn't even sound like him.

He grinned. The sound of the nuns' voices singing lilting hymns to Our Lady would soon turn into the Irish marching tunes, even though they had been told not to sing the bog songs today. Especially with all the talk of invasion and some thinking Ireland was getting into bed with Jerry. They had been told to stay at home. But nothing would stop the Drews and the Dooleys from getting drunk and Davey Slavin fetching his accordion and singing songs about their beloved Emerald Isle, even though half of them had never been to the place. How long would it be before they would fall down the stairs and stagger into the courtyard and start a fight?

'Me ma will stand on a chair and start singing "Mountains of Mourne" in a minute. She thinks your lassie Mary hankering after her precious mountains is the Virgin Mary. This Mary is kind of sneaky and moody.' She looked at him and began to smile. But his eyes seemed to glaze over. 'So come on,' he said.

'Where are we going?' she asked, confused.

'Back to ours.'

'Why?'

He frowned as though he was amazed that she was even asking him the question. 'Just come on,' he said.

She could see Donna, who was carrying a plate of butterfly cakes, glance over at them. Please don't come over and ruin everything, she thought, breathing a sigh of relief when Donna turned away. She felt his hand slide into hers, and he was tugging at her, towing her along, and now he was breaking into a run, yanking her to keep up with him. She felt her heart pounding as her feet slapped the pavements and she gulped air.

They went up to the flat two steps at a time and he looked serious, with a grave expression on his face as though he had a clear idea of what was going to happen next. And one that suggested she should know as well. He pulled her into the kitchen, kicked the door shut with his foot. Outside she could hear the music, but the sound was blurring around the edges. Someone was blowing a tin whistle and another had ruined the nuns' singing with the noise of an accordion and the rhythmic banging of a drum and the shrill sound of a penny whistle. She looked at the framed picture of the Pope above the mantelpiece and squinted as Alvis popped one button of her dress right out of its buttonhole.

'This house is never empty. Never. We're here on our own,' he panted.

And he was right. She had never been with him in a room alone. Straight away his mouth was on hers. She felt his tongue twisting round her teeth as he kissed her. After months, years, praying, hoping he would just notice her, let alone speak to her, or kiss her, she could barely believe what was happening.

He led her into the small, dark parlour. She wasn't sure why, surrounded as it was by shadows, dark with the blackout curtains, apart from the fingers of light coming through the air bricks studded with holes. At first, she was afraid but she had been longing for this moment, night after night hoping he would come to her in her dreams, and as he kissed her harder, she began to enjoy whatever it was that was happening. She could only exist in the moment, the moments when she felt his lips graze hers, felt the softness of his lashes against her cheek, and him now kissing the tip of her nose, then kissing her ears, tracing the grooves of it with his finger.

'What's this? Why are you wearing this daft petticoat?' he asked, pulling up her skirts. Her heart was pounding. Why couldn't she speak? The words seemed to turn to dust in her mouth. But he put his strong hands under her bottom and lifted her right off the floor.

'But what if your ma . . . ?' she managed to finally blurt in a hoarse whisper.

'She'll be singing about sneaky Mary,' he said.

He looked at her and now he had a strange expression as if he wasn't here at all, as if he was somewhere far off, even though he was staring right into her eyes.

'Kiss me, Betsy. Don't be frightened. Are you frightened? Don't be.'

She kissed him back. But the kiss was so much less shocking than his hands moving up her skirt, over her thighs, the rustle and scratching of the white netting petticoat, the snap of his belt buckle, the whole weight of his body on hers as he pushed her against the wall.

And then he shuddered and gasped.

'What's happening?' she asked. 'What are you doing?'

'Don't you know?'

Betsy cocked her head to one side. She was embarrassed to say anything more. She felt stupid and a little alone, but then she took a sharp intake of breath as he fumbled, and she felt herself loosen, becoming loose from the buttons and straps, loose, as it all fell away. Loose. She's loose. A loose girl. This feeling, of becoming free. What was it? As he pushed her harder against the wall, and with his hands underneath her thighs lifted her higher now, right off the floor so that her legs straddled him and clamped to his body naturally and firmly, feet crossed at the ankles, as if she was shinnying up a tree. And then the feeling of something. It started with a sharp pain, and then became something terrifying, but sweetly appalling as he began to move in and out of her, as his breath quickened, as his whole body convulsed and he let out a moan, low and guttural and brutish. She had wanted him, of course she had, she had let him do as he had wished as though she was a rag doll, but had she wanted him to do *this*?

Instinct told Alvis's mother to call out before she entered the parlour. The sound of her voice calling 'Yoo-hoo!' made Alvis spring like a coil towards the door. Then he moved back towards Betsy and pushed her with a shove behind the heavy winter curtain sagging on a wire.

'Jesus! Stay there,' he hissed, hurriedly fastening his trouser flies.

She nodded, feeling her heart hammering at her chest. How long did he expect her to remain like this?

'It's making me sneeze,' she whispered, poking her head out. 'Spiders. I don't like it. Creepy crawlies,' she said.

'Get back behind the curtain! Shush up,' he hissed, hastily rearranging his clothes.

'Alvis? What are you doing in here? The best room? And in your work boots!' said his mother, flinging open the door with a bang as it walloped against the wall. She felt a little sick to see the look on her son's face as he moved quickly away past her into the kitchen. And now he was standing arms folded, obdurate and unashamed, with his back to her, folding his cuffs up his sleeves in front of the sink, feet planted firmly apart. Joyce followed him and tipped her head to one side, looked at him, again, noticed how lately he looked so like a man, his shoulders already broadening from the dock work. He turned around and shrugged and she tried to smile but it was brief and forced. It wobbled around the edges. She noticed his forearms were bulging and veined.

'Getting me cap.'

'Did you need to bring Betsy with you?'

Behind the curtain, Betsy flushed. She could feel the heat rising in her body.

She's still a child, Joyce wanted to say. *And I know you, son. I recognize the hunger, the look. I know that look so well because it's the same one that's in your father's eyes. The yearning for pleasure. Always. It never stops. Maybe because there is so little of it these days you have to take it where you can. But even so.*

'Betsy, I can see you,' she said with a sigh, turning back to the doorway into the parlour. 'I can see your shoes. Come out.'

Betsy stepped out from behind the curtain, cheeks smarting. Loose, I'm loose, a wild girl. Say what you're thinking.

'Come on now. Go back downstairs, both of you. We are going to enjoy ourselves. There's those overseas that have got plans for us not to. But today we won't be afraid, so get out into the sunshine instead of hanging around in the dark. Donna's been stung by a wasp. Mrs Roebuck pulled out the sting but she's still wailing like a banshee. You're missing all the excitement.'

When they all left, her son leading the way – the kind of boy who loved to throw a brick through a greenhouse window and relished the sound of the smashing – she took the key, twisted it firmly and slipped it into her pocket.

Betsy's brother threw his cap onto the table and flopped down into the armchair. 'Did you have a lovely day, Jacky? Did Betsy swap my rations with Joyce? Where is Betsy? On her way?' asked Hope. 'After so much worry these past few weeks about flaming Hitler, it's what we needed,' she said quietly, picking up Jacky's jacket and folding it neatly over the chair.

'Aye. It was the craic. Alvis's sister got stung by a wasp. She sprayed her hair with sugar.'

'What did she expect?' said Hope.

'Too much jelly, though,' he said, clutching his stomach. He burped and groaned.

He plonked his feet on the arm of the chair.

'Get those filthy boots off. Did the O'Reillys turn up?'

He nodded.

'And did Brendan's grandda sing the "Egg Song"?'

'Mebbe.'

'I wish I could have come. Where's Betsy?'

'Here,' said Betsy sheepishly, walking in through the door, her face turned away, eyes cast down to the floor. Mothers could tell when things weren't right. Her mother was a witch even though she loved Jesus, and Betsy moved quickly past her for fear she would read her face or catch the scent of her wickedness.

'You hear Brendan's grandda singing the "Egg Song", Betsy?' she called.

'Aye,' she replied quietly.

'And was it a hoot?'

'I think so . . .'

Her mother cocked her head to one side. 'What's the matter with you? You flew out the door this morning, but you've come back like a dog with two tails.'

Betsy could feel her cheeks going hot. 'Nothing, Ma. Please don't.'

'Doesn't look like nothing from where I'm standing. Are you all right, love?' she said gently.

Betsy nodded and gave a brief, tight smile. 'Grand. I'm grand, Ma. Now can you leave me alone? I'm tired. I'm going upstairs. Don't ask me again. Please?'

Chapter 3

The weeks moved slowly on for Betsy and it felt like winter was on its way and, with it, every day news of another bomb that had dropped. The raids had started quietly, one over the river then another few at the docks by Caryl Street, and then people began to take it more seriously, setting up Anderson shelters in their gardens, running to the local shelters whenever the air-raid warnings started. There seemed no let-up. Soldiers everywhere, more men leaving the city and joining up. Sirens and blimps and blackouts. Serious conversations spoken by serious men in Parliament about the terrible situation in Europe. Once the bombing started in earnest – the Blitz, they began to call it as it worsened – Churchill, chewing on his cigar, began visiting places of devastation in the East End, and now some said he was on his way here.

Sitting at her desk on the top floor of Cunard's Shipping Line and adding up the numbers written out on sheets, putting them into columns, copying them down carefully with a pencil, rubbing them out if she thought she had made a mistake and starting again, Betsy screwed her fists into her eyes. She had been asked to work through to the evening. The files she was working on were top secret and stamped with

PRIORITY, though she had no idea why. It was just columns of numbers to her, but it seemed important.

'Here you go,' said one of the boys, who she recognized from the accounts office down the corridor, also working late. No doubt he was glad of the overtime. She had noticed him these last few days, always giving her a shy smile and a nod as he walked past her office window. He was tall, good-looking with piercing blue eyes, high chiselled cheekbones, clean trimmed nails, and his fair hair was soft and seemed to bounce when he walked. 'Three files to go to Mount Pleasant Street. You all right to keep going until nine?'

Betsy blushed. The day before she had walked all the way to the Mount Pleasant offices, but the weight of the ledgers that she had to deliver to the accountants a few streets away that morning – thick, heavy leather-bound books, pages and pages of watermarked paper – had caused pearls of sweat to break out on her forehead and she had staggered and collapsed against a wall near the Pier Head. When she had got back to Cunard's offices, she had sunk into a chair and one of the secretaries had had to find a glass of water and wave smelling salts under her nose to revive her.

'Let me deliver them this evening,' the boy with the bouncy hair said. 'You don't have to do it. I'm leaving now. It's on my way home.'

This boy was kind. Standing over her in his neat black suit and tie, starched white shirt and polished brogues, he smiled. 'You like arithmetic?' he asked. 'That why they gave you this job?'

Betsy nodded and smiled. 'Comes easy. I don't know why.'

'It's how some people make sense of the world. Mathematics. I rather like that.'

I rather like that. What an unusual way to talk, thought Betsy.

'Where did you learn to do those sums so quickly?'

She shrugged again. She never tired of arithmetic, but she couldn't really remember 'learning' it. It had been Sister Bernadette at school who had noticed how naturally it came to her. Betsy saw numbers and patterns everywhere. Even in church, drifting off listening to the Bible stories with the annotations of the verses and chapters, she would organize the readings in her head according to their numerical positions and amuse herself with finding patterns: how many verses in each chapter, how many lines in each verse, multiplying, dividing, adding. Betsy's mother had been excited and so proud when it had led to Betsy's job. Alvis had come in from next door and whistled through his teeth and nodded in approval.

The boy left, carrying the ledgers. She sat at the desk running her fingers around the edges, moving piles of papers, pencil boxes, a small tin of paper clips, an inch to the left, an inch to the right, wondering if she should engineer passing Alvis's window just when she knew he would be coming home from the pub. 'If I don't see you through the week, I'll see you through the window,' his mother had called out at her the day before on the stairwell. She was so tired, though, and her legs felt so hollow she could barely get out of the chair.

'Fancy a quick drink at The Slaughterhouse? That was a long shift. Still, I'll be able to buy myself some stockings with the overtime,' asked Lydia, the girl from the floor above who she had made friends with. Before Betsy could answer, she had linked her arm and was walking out of the door.

The wailing of the sirens started before the lift had reached the ground floor. Betsy, realizing she was holding her breath, looked round-eyed and worried and glanced at Lydia. When they opened the door, a small crowd had gathered in the foyer.

'Nobody leaves the building. Make your way to the basement to shelter,' Mr Percival was shouting.

Someone yelled back that they needed to go home.

'They've said there should be no one on the streets. Shelter until the all-clear.'

A man rushed in. He stood on the step, patted the air with his hands and shushed them. 'You'll only be directed to another shelter if you leave. So, stay here. We have blankets and tea.'

'And I've got a pack of cards,' cried someone.

They started to move to the staircase. Some muttered, but as the wailing continued, most did as they were told. When they reached the basement, a woman was holding open the door.

'Go in, Lydia, Betsy . . . There's camp beds at the back . . .'

Ten minutes later, after everyone had been ushered in, Lydia turned to Betsy. 'This feels like a bad one,' said Lydia. 'D'you two know each other? Betsy, this is James. James, this is our Betsy. Betsy's the type of girl whose full stop is her smile, isn't it, Bets?'

Betsy looked up. 'I know James.'

'And what would we do without James?' said Lydia.

'He makes a smashing cuppa. Any chance of one now, love? Someone said there's an urn down here.'

James smiled back. Fifteen minutes later the three of them sat nursing mugs, warming their hands and chatting, speculating as to how bad tonight's bombing was going to be and when the all-clear would sound. They took some comfort in the ack-ack guns firing loudly, but the sound was deafening, and it really did feel like a bad one. Lydia was asking James about joining up, and he said he was hoping to volunteer with the RAF. 'Though it's complicated,' he said mysteriously, turning the conversation to Betsy and her mathematical wonders.

'Betsy's a marvel,' he said to Lydia.

'She is that. Ooh, look, you've made her blush,' laughed Lydia.

Half an hour later, just as Betsy's head had fallen back on the couch and her eyes had fluttered shut, someone jumped up and cried, 'Did you feel that? Hear that?'

She blinked her eyes open. No one was asleep now. The ground underneath them was vibrating. You could feel it in your teeth. There was a collective gasp at the sound of a whump-whump.

'Never heard it so loud!' cried Lydia. 'Bloody Hitler!'

Betsy frowned. 'Our Jacky. He's on a late shift at the docks . . .'

'Let's hope he's all right. My ma and da will be in Durning Road. Or Lewis's basement. They've a piano down there and it's becoming a regular party. What about your folks, James?'

'My mother will be fine,' he said, as he ducked

instinctively at the sound of another terrifying roar that made the teacups rattle, and a pile of books slide off a shelf and land with an ominous thud on the floor.

Betsy clutched the side of the bed. Without realizing he was doing it, his hand brushed hers and he squeezed the tips of her fingers tightly.

An hour later, James tipped his head to one side. 'Don't worry. That was it . . . They're turning now.'

'How do you know?'

'The planes sound different when they've dropped their bombs. They're lighter, you see.'

She felt her body relax. This boy made her feel safer. And he was right. As dawn broke, the all-clear sounded and they came blinking out into the light, tired and shocked, with the smell of dust and smoke in the air and small fires still licking into life, but safe. For now.

'James!' called a voice from the opposite side of the road. A man in a chauffeur's uniform was standing on the pavement.

'That man's calling you,' said Betsy, frowning.

James glanced over. And without saying a word, he nodded and, head down, he darted off towards the man without looking back over his shoulder.

'Who sent you?' he asked the chauffeur, breathless as they rounded the corner to the waiting Bentley. 'Mother?'

He shuddered at the thought that Betsy or Lydia might have seen him getting into the car.

'Your Mr Percival rang your mother to tell her you were in the shelter when the sirens went off, Mr Swann.'

He grunted.

'All right, sir?'

'Gordon, call me James, not sir. You've known me long enough,' he said frostily.

They made their way out of the city, driving past one street where a bomb had hit, wordlessly staring at the devastation, two houses reduced to rubble, people picking their way through the chaos, the cara-van of people leaving for the suburbs that always came after an air raid. But as they rolled on towards the countryside, through the leafy suburbs of Blundellsands and Crosby, this part of Liverpool seemed unharmed, and you would never have known there had been bombs falling in the night. Now, birdsong could be heard and a milkman was whistling on his cart and life was going on all around. He leaned his head on the leather strap and looked at the trees ranging in autumnal colours from bright green to dark olive, to patches of yellow, orange and red, each leaf picked out by the sunshine in vivid detail. Forty-five minutes later they arrived at Ince Blundell Woods, carried on out through the other side into fields, and swept through the gates of Mottram Hall – a large red-bricked Victorian manor house. The ruffled silvery surface of the small ornamental lake glittered. As they swung up the gravel drive with the tyres of the car scattering loose stones, James, with a sinking heart, saw that his mother was waiting for him, sitting in an upstairs leaded window, now rising hurriedly to come down-stairs and greet him.

'Mother,' he said, as she bobbed down the steps and stroked his hair and he squirmed away. 'You didn't need to send Gordon. It's embarrassing.'

'I'd come with Gordon to meet you every day after work if I could, dear. You know I would. I'm scared of you working in the city.'

At least he had managed to prevent her from that horror, he thought as he walked past her, shedding coats and jackets and scarves and heading into the drawing room.

'You're scared of everything,' he said. 'You don't need to be.'

'But, darling, was it a terrible night? I was out of my mind with worry. We saw the bombers from here. The sky was lit up all night. Was anyone hurt?'

'One or two lumps of plaster fell but we dodged them.'

'Who's we?'

'A few others who were working late.'

He could feel her overbearing presence watching him from the door, fiddling with the tie on her blouse, so he stopped and sat at the baby grand Bluthner piano. Someone in the shelter had been whistling 'We'll Meet Again' and the tune had lodged in his brain. He began to pick out the notes. He could sense his mother wincing.

'Play a little Brahms,' she said.

'I prefer this,' he said. He knew it would annoy her as his fingers skittered over the keys. He knew she would be disapproving at the way he leaned on certain notes, the spread of the soulful jazz chords. She hated 'dreadful crooners sliding up and down the octaves'.

It irked her when he came in with a new gramophone record, playing it over and over, working out the cadences. Even worse was when he sang along and began 'the awful thumping and heavy left pedal'.

'Tea, dear? I'll find Gordon,' she said.

'Pa would be ashamed of me not doing my bit,' he muttered with a sigh, just loud enough for her to hear as she turned to go.

'You are doing your bit . . .'

'I'm just an ARP man doing a spot of fire watching at the weekends who works in an office. Everyone in the ARP is old. Or they're spivs using their armbands to break into empty houses and steal things. I should be in the RAF. Families like ours *fly*. We're officers, pilots – not clerks.'

He banged down the piano lid.

'You could become a Member of Parliament? Like your cousin, John? There are so many opportunities this war is bringing where you can make a lasting difference. It doesn't have to—'

'*I want to fly!* I want to meet other men my age. Do you know what it feels like to be stuck in the accounts office at Cunard's now that they're all women? I go in and there's just girls, rows and rows of girls doing men's jobs. And I'm still there. Checking the ledgers.'

'You know why you can't . . . It would kill me . . . I can't . . . not again . . .'

'Mother, Father and Teddy died in an accident after the war. And your brother in the Great War . . . It was bad luck he got shot down . . .'

'Bad luck!'

James felt the muscles in his face tightening. The sound of aeroplanes taking off that had so terrified his mother since the tragedy lately had started to come back to James in dreams. He would wake sweating, drenched through. He had thought it was fear, the moment of watching his father crash the Tiger Moth into Mottram Hall wood revisiting him in nightmares, but now he realized it was longing.

'I'll talk to Sister Annunciata from St Mary's about her orphans of the living. Something needs to be done about that. They're desperate. I'm a trustee. You could help. They have committees.'

'Orphans of the living? What on earth are you talking about? I want to fly! I want to fly like Pa did. And your brothers.'

'But look what happened. They all died!' she wailed, her hands curling into fists.

'But at least they *lived* before they died. This way I feel like I'm dying whilst I'm alive. Carrying the ledgers from one floor to another for the girls. I've had it.'

He had sworn to himself shortly after they had come back from holidaying in Sicily that he would go down to the town hall to sign up. Dammit, why hadn't he? he thought. He stood to leave but just as he was about to collect his jacket, a voice trilled outside the door, 'Where is he? Where's James?'

Clementine. His heart sank. He groaned, dropped his head, then snatched up a silk cushion and placed it over his face as he stifled a scream.

'Darling! I heard you were caught in a raid!' she cried, sweeping into the drawing room. She rushed over and kissed him on the lips and perched on the edge of the chaise longue. James's mother sat wafting a fan under her chin.

'Thank goodness you're alive! I came here as soon as Lettice called to say you were home. Was it terrifying?' said Clementine.

James threw a look at his mother. 'It was nothing. We were perfectly safe.' So that was why she had asked Gordon to bring tea on a pretty tray with a sprig of lilac in a champagne flute.

Today, Clementine had more ribbons in her hair than usual, ribbons at her neck, even her shoes were tied with with ribbons. She looked faintly silly, dabbing at the corner of her mouth with a handkerchief.

'I was so scared. But phew, you're safe. By the way, whilst I'm here, I have a question, James. Does this house have ghosts?'

James sighed. Clementine had a habit of speaking in non sequiturs. Out of the blue she would throw something into the conversation that made perfect sense to her but confused everyone else.

'I have no idea.'

'I need to know about the ghosts. I mean, if we're to marry, Jim.'

James frowned. Yes, of course there were ghosts. How could there not be, with so much tragedy in this house? Just not the kind she was talking about.

'If, Clemmie? *When*, we rather hope . . .' said Lettice.

'But it's awfully draughty in here.' Her hands flew to her mouth. 'Oh, please don't tell me there are ghosts. Do you have a grey lady?'

'No, dear. No ghosts at Mottram,' said Lettice quickly.

Clementine looked around and wrinkled up her nose. 'New wallpaper would brighten the place up, James. Those blackout curtains are so gloomy.'

'Yes. It might,' said Lettice.

She was harmless enough, thought James, and he could see why his mother was so fixated on them marrying. But he thought back to Betsy, with her rosy cheeks, tumble of blonde hair and blue searching eyes, who he had sat next to last night whilst the ground shook. This one here seemed to know nothing of life, and she didn't want to, just fluttered around swirling in ribbons and chiffon. And now she had decided she wanted to go on the stage. Another absurdity. He would never be enough for her, he knew that. She craved adulation and love, not of a romantic kind, but an altogether different kind. Love all the way up to the cheap seats. And what would they talk about? Starlets? Hollywood? He wanted to talk about the war and Halifax bomber planes. Good God, once she even seemed to hint at a sneaking admiration for Hitler; he knew she thought his moustache was attractive because she had suggested he should grow one like it.

'James! James? You're daydreaming again,' said Lettice, dragging him out of his thoughts.

'I should go, now that I know my little fire watcher is safe,' said Clementine, pecking him on the cheek.

'I'm volunteering for the RAF,' he said flatly. 'I've had enough of the ARP.'

'Are you? What a relief. I loathe that dreadful tin

helmet you wear,' she said, pulling a face. 'I'm thinking of joining the Wrens. I'm doing it for the lipstick and the sweet little hat. Don't you think I'll look fetching?' She struck a pose with her hands under her chin and head tipped to one side.

He could see his mother frowning.

'They'll have you pinned for an officer in no time at the RAF because you speak nicely,' Clementine said brightly. 'I fancy ENSA. I'd be good at entertaining the troops.' She leapt up and started to trill 'Johnny Get Your Gun'. The noise was dreadful. James winced. Sometimes he wondered if the glassware would crack on purpose.

'James, why are you making a face?' said Clementine.

'Am I? You're a little flat, that's all.'

'No, I'm not. Anyway, I must dash. You'd get your wings in no time. You can already fly, can't you?'

James faltered. 'I would have to be trained to fight a bomber. Those Manchesters are unwieldy things. Even a Wellington would be impossible for me unless I had proper training. Do you know that the Wellington . . .'

But he could see she was stifling a yawn.

Betsy, meanwhile, was making her way back to the tenements. They had moved here five years earlier after her father had jumped from his chair, slapped his thighs and announced he was going to the corner shop for a packet of Woodbines, and never come back. The Corporation had found them a home and they had soon made friends. Little communities would gather on the balconies where the women would smoke Player's and knit and crochet blankets and watch the children playing on the swings in the reccy in the courtyard below, and even though they would moan about not being able to sit on the front step any more or pop next door to the grocer's, they still marvelled at the hot water coming out of the tap and children that came out of the bath clean and shiny and squeaky.

As Betsy came through the arch, Deirdre was waiting for her on the swing. Bored, socks sagging around her ankles, she had twirled the seat and twisted the chains tight and when she saw Betsy, she grinned and let the swing unspin jerkily.

'Fancy the Rialto tonight?' she said, jumping off and kicking the seat away. 'I slept in the shelter last night. Houses all down Liverpool Lane bombed to bits apparently.'

'I'm tired after a night on a camp bed in Cunard's basement, Deirdre. And those bloody ledgers. They've done me in. I had to get one of the clerks to do my job for me yesterday.'

'Ooh . . . was he nice?'

'Speaks kind of funny. The way he says *grass* and *path*, he sounds like the King.'

'I've never really heard the King speak, have you? My ma says he's too shy to speak. Does this fella sound like Clark Gable?'

'James's posh but he's not American.'

'Who cares? Come on, I've got the gramophone all set up. I've been waiting. Come to ours. No one's in. I've got a trifle I made from stale cakes and biscuits. You can have a spoonful. We need to be able to dance better if we want to get a fella. Someone better than the likes of Alvis.'

Betsy smiled. When they arrived at the flat, Deirdre opened the door and pulled Betsy in. Betsy sank into the sofa whilst Deirdre prepared the gramophone and the 45 record. A thin and reedy 'September in the Rain' crackled out.

'Get up . . .'

Betsy didn't have the energy to argue. Facing each other, they began a slow dance, Deirdre turning her around slowly and holding her hands out to grasp her and pull her into her in a twist.

'Why is it so hard today?' said Betsy after stumbling a few times. 'I can't get the hang of it.'

Deirdre took her face in her hands. 'Go with the flow of the music. Imagine we love each other. Well, we do, don't we? So, relax and imagine I'm Gary Cooper and sway your hips like this.' She performed a slow, mesmeric dance, moving from foot to foot and caressing her hips with her hands.

Betsy laughed. 'I love Alvis. I *love* him.'

'More than me? But he doesn't know you like I do.'

'I just love him. I can't explain why. I want to marry him.'

Deirdre spluttered an explosive laugh and bent into her and put her hands flat on her cheeks. 'What is it you're talking about? Love? Really? Don't you just mean you want to eat him up and smother him in kisses? That's not love. For now, can't you just love me and Jesus?'

'No! This is how much I love him. Take your hands and push them against my chest. You can feel my heart beating. It goes fast like that if I just think about him. If I just say his name. Or even if someone else does.

Or if I catch a glimpse of him on his way to work walking past our window. I sit there for hours some days hoping I will. Hoping he might stop and talk to me. He never does.'

She laughed.

Deirdre tipped her head to one side as she moved behind her. 'Until we find someone decent, we've got each other. But you're so soft on flipping Alvis . . . Betsy, you promised me you'd tell me if he came sniffing around. Has he tried to kiss you yet? Don't you go near him. Because I hate to break it to you, he's tried to do the same to me. Lots of times. Everyone knows what he's like. All that "I believe that dreams come true because I met you" nonsense. He's said that to me and to every girl in the tenements. My ma says you can't put lipstick on a pig. She's right. Put him out with the rubbish. Take my hand. Two steps forward. And now spin into me.'

She pulled Betsy to her forcibly and put her hands around her waist. 'You're tiny. I'm so fat,' said Deirdre, moving in closer to her so that their bodies pressed together. She stopped for a moment, frowned. 'But wait . . . lately you're . . . a little rounder . . . in the . . . tummy . . .'

She sounded strange. And then the smile slid from her face. She stood back and took a hard look at Betsy, her eyes dropping and then lifting back up to meet Betsy's.

'Oh, Bets . . .'

Betsy's lip wobbled. Her heart kicked at her ribs. 'I tried to hide it.' A tear spilled onto her cheek.

Deirdre took her hand and squeezed it urgently so

that Betsy's knuckles went white. 'God, Betsy. I know you've not been right. Bit quiet. But I thought it was because your ma had been on at you to help her at the wash-house.'

'No, it's nothing to do with Ma this time.'

'Alvis did this to you, didn't he?'

'I don't know what's happening to me,' Betsy blurted, collapsing on the sofa. She covered her face with her hands.

'What do you mean?'

'Maybe it's just too many pies,' she said forlornly.

'Pies? No one's eating too many pies now. We're all starving.'

'He said I was the only star in the sky.'

'Oh, love. I told you. He says stuff like that to everyone. What are you going to do?'

'What do you mean?'

'If you're pregnant.'

'Pregnant?' She looked shocked. 'We kissed and he . . .' Betsy screwed her handkerchief into a knot. 'I don't know. I didn't know what was happening. I don't know what happened. I still don't.'

'Yes, you do. You just can't face it. Love, this isn't going to end well. You are such a dope. Your mum should have told you about the facts of life instead of going on about being pure for Mary all the time. And I warned you about Alvis. Like I said, I know because he tried to do the same to me. He told me a world without me is like the night sky without the stars. Must have read these cheesy sayings on the back page of his ma's *Picture Post*. I knew you were heading for disaster.'

Betsy shook her head dolefully. 'I'm sorry. Can you help me put it right?'

'That depends. How long without your Auntie Mary?'

'Weeks.' Betsy rolled her bottom lip between her fingers. 'Months.'

'Open your blouse. Let me look properly.'

Betsy dropped her eyes and slowly unbuttoned her blouse. Deirdre gasped to see the rise in her stomach and her full breasts, and her hand flew to her mouth. 'Oh, love. I think it's going to be too late to do anything. When did it happen? Once or more than once?'

'Once. The day of the Feast of the Assumption.'

'And has he kissed you since? Or tried anything else?'

'No. He's not been near me. No, now please just put the music on and dance with me again. And stop saying these things. I don't want to think about it.'

Deirdre looked at her, reached out her hand and placed it gently against her cheek. 'You'd better,' she said. 'You must. Does your ma know?'

Chapter 4

'What is it, Betsy? You look like your face has dropped a stitch. I brought you a banana, look! They were selling them at the pub out of a crate and I had to push to the front of the queue. A banana! Isn't it marvellous? I thought you'd be happy, and you look as miserable as sin. Let me guess. The ledgers? Too heavy again?'

Betsy peeled the skin off the brown-spotted, mushy banana but couldn't even take a bite.

'Deirdre said I should tell you, Ma,' she said flatly. 'I thought it would go away, but she's been nagging me to tell you for weeks.'

'Tell me what?'

'This . . .'

For Hope, first it was confusion, then bewilderment, and then a look of horror and realization as Betsy took a deep breath, smoothed her clothes down over her belly and raised her sad eyes to meet hers. The blood drained from Hope's cheeks and her hand flew to her mouth.

'No! Betsy, you wouldn't have done anything so stupid!'

'I didn't. Deirdre said it was Alvis Dooley that did it.'

The next few minutes were lost to Hope as Betsy

told her tearfully in back-to-front sentences that she had missed three monthlies and that she was so tired, which was probably why she couldn't carry the ledgers, and had been feeling sick every morning.

'Tell me again. I'm in shock,' she stuttered. 'I didn't hear any of that. Oh, Betsy. You stupid, stupid girl! And why do you need Deirdre to tell you who the father is?'

Betsy shrugged. 'I didn't even really know.'

Hope paced the kitchen, in danger of wearing out the linoleum trying to think of a solution. Desperate and exhausted, she flung down the tea towel she was shoving in and out of a glass for no reason, put on her coat and went straight around to Alvis's.

'What d'you mean?' said Joyce angrily. 'Alvis has put Betsy in the club? You can't come here throwing around accusations like that. Anyway, Alvis is not here to defend himself, and have you thought Betsy might be telling tales?' She snorted. 'Alvis has signed up. Merchant navy. Last week. He's on a boat somewhere. God knows where.'

'This isn't about Alvis and Betsy apple scrumping or playing knock down ginger . . .' snapped Hope. 'This is serious.'

Joyce sighed. 'Heavenly Hope, we call you in our house, all the time you spend sucking up to them nuns.' She leaned on the door and sucked coolly on a cigarette and said she would speak to Alvis when he was back, but who knew when that would be. She clutched her hand and said how sorry she was for Hope, how could Betsy do that to her? How ungrateful, she cooed in a patronizing tone, Betsy being lucky to have a mother who was so holy and never missing church and dusting the pews every week.

'This sorry situation remains between us. If I leave Alvis alone, then you must never tell anyone. Do you understand? Not a word about this child? To anyone.'

'Whatever you say,' said Joyce flatly.

Donna appeared with a cigarette drooping from her lip and wearing a dressing gown and hair net, sashaying into the hall to see what the fuss was about. Would Hope really want her daughter marrying Alvis? Would she want to be tangled up with his mother and her children for ever? Weddings, birthdays, christenings, communions and confirmations? No. She couldn't stand it. Turning on her heel, she muttered something under her breath.

'What? What did you just say? I didn't hear you. Say that to my face!' yelled Joyce.

'Your son is a liar and you know it,' Hope said, twisting around to face her. 'Is that loud enough?'

Hope walked home furious. Could anything feel as bad as this? She said the same as she sat with Deirdre's mother, Beryl, tears splashing onto the oilcloth as she swore Beryl to secrecy. Beryl handed her a handkerchief and, trying to stem Hope's sobs, said cheerfully, 'But everyone has babies round here, they just seem to be appearing. Especially with the chaos of this war. The woman across the road had no idea she was pregnant. And she's old enough to know better. We all know Mrs Perkins' baby is not her hubby's. He's been away for months. There's no way on God's earth her jug-eared husband could have produced that pretty child.'

'But how does that help my Betsy? It doesn't. It just makes it even more infuriating. If that Dooley boy walked in here now, I'd take him with my own two hands and I'd wring his neck. And his mother! How could Betsy do this to me? I just want to live in the quiet, and now I have all this noise in my head!'

The following week, with the winter sun throwing fingers of light across the floor, Betsy's mother, like every other day this past week, sat at the table winding thread around a bobbin, more for the lack of something to do with her hands than being useful, and cursed the fact that Betsy was growing bigger by the day. 'I think we need to be practical about this now,' she said. Betsy looked up at her, tears swelling in her eyes. 'I've been around to Alvis's house and still no luck. He's gone. Vanished. I tried to have a sensible conversation with Joyce about Alvis doing the right thing. Again.'

'Doing the right thing?'

'Marrying you.'

Betsy's eyes lit up.

'Hopeless.'

Betsy groaned and rolled onto her side. Hope felt a pang of guilt to see her daughter clutching her moon-shaped belly. Was this her fault? Perhaps if Betsy's da hadn't left? Perhaps if she had told her how babies were made instead of all that nonsense about keeping your knees together whilst living in the image of Our Lady? Some hope round here, though. Everyone was at it.

'So,' Hope concluded to Betsy, over a mug of tea and shortening bread. 'If Alvis refuses to accept that this baby is his, and if anyone asks, as we can't have a real husband, we'll have to have a pretend one just for now. And when you have the baby . . . well, the war will help us. Maybe someone who drowned at sea with one of those German U-boat bombings? Those timings are right,' she said, desperately.

Betsy looked at her, bewildered. 'What if Alvis changes his mind and says he wants to marry me? What if he comes back and I'm lumbered with the pretend husband? What then?'

'Betsy, you're supposed to be clever! Alvis is not going to come back any time soon. Not even for Christmas,' she snapped. 'He's all the way across the ocean. Timbuktu for all we know. Or skulking in Bootle, I bet. Same difference. What about the boy that carried the ledgers? You said he was nice. Would he marry you?'

'Ma, you're crazy. You think I could marry him when all he did is carry the ledgers once?'

Hope crushed her fists into her temples. 'I know. I know. I'm not thinking straight. I thought you liked him.'

'I like Alvis.'

'But he doesn't like you, Betsy, does he? If he liked you, he wouldn't have run off and not answered your letters, would he?'

Betsy felt her cheeks burning.

'I know it hurts to hear the truth,' said Hope. 'And it's only because I love you that I can say it as your mother.'

Betsy whimpered, twisting the cuff of her sleeve. 'Why didn't anyone tell me? I thought he loved me. I love him!'

Hope sighed. 'Is that why you let him . . . you know . . . ?'

'Ma, I didn't *let* him. He just . . .' The sentence tailed off.

'Took what he fancied when he fancied? If I see that boy, I'll give him what for. You do realize this is about the worst thing that could happen to a girl?' Betsy groaned. 'Forget Alvis, love. He's not coming back. No good tramping the streets looking for him. I know that's what you've been doing morning, noon and night. And you're showing so much now. You'll have to stop work. We'll have to think of something to say. Maybe pretend we've been bombed?'

'Ma, stop saying stupid things. I just want to die. I can't stand it.'

Hope banged the table with her fist in frustration. 'And do you think it's been easy for me? Do you think it's been easy for me to tell Sister Annunciata who I do the flowers with every Sunday, clean the church with, polishing the candles, stacking the hymn books . . .'

'You've told Sister? Why?'

'The shame. It's too much.' Her hands fluttered to her face.

'Why have you told Sister?'

Hope drew her shoulders back. 'Never mind. It's too late to look backwards. We need to look forward now. We need to try to think what we should do.'

'Ma, why are you so ashamed of me?'

'I'm not, I'm just . . . And believe you me, if your father was around, he would have pushed you out onto the streets the minute he found out you were having a baby. Betsy, can we not just sit down quietly and have the conversation about what happens next?'

'Thank goodness he isn't,' said Betsy.

The knock at the door was firm and persistent. Her mother got up and answered it. Father Donnelly was standing there. His presence was large and looming and male, and his shoulders seemed to block out the sunlight. He had to stoop to come in through the door in order not to hit his huge head stuffed in a huge hat on the door jamb. What's he doing here? wondered Betsy. He took off the fedora and smiled idiotically.

'Betsy, you're looking grand.'

Betsy glared at her mother. What the flipping heck is he doing here? she tried to ask with her eyes, thankful that the air-raid sirens had just started up and glad of the excuse to race to the shelter.

Chapter 5

Sybil Donaghue trotted through the garden at St Mary's orphanage pushing a pram and shooing the children out of the way. There were just too many of them in this place. Her little girl had just woken up and was rubbing her eyes with tiny fists and she placed her, sitting up, carefully amongst the plump pillows in the pram. The chrome gleamed in the sun. Christmas had been and gone but the tree was still stuck into the ground and there were still one or two sodden paper candle holders stuck onto the branches. She pushed the hood up a little and popped off the cover, so the child was able to lean back and kick her legs whilst gurgling happily.

Just then a pleasant-looking woman in a suit with matching shoes and hat and a man in polished brogues and a linen jacket started walking up the gravel path, as sunny and hopeful as the winter rose bushes. She folded her arms over her chest and glared at them from under the fringe of her rich brown hair cut into a severe bob. She knew straight away what they were here for, but they wouldn't be coming for her baby with her little squashed ear – just the tip of it, enough to make people peer into the cot and ask what was wrong with her. Sometimes she squeezed it at night, hoping the fold would stay until the morning, and sometimes she had taken a tiny peg from the laundry and clipped it. Her baby hadn't even cried, she didn't seem to mind. It was only the tiniest crinkle and it would smooth out. But for now, as people leaned in to inspect the ear that Sybil sometimes said explained why the baby couldn't hear properly, they frowned, smiled politely, and moved on to the next cot.

Sybil didn't see Sister Annunciata come up behind her. 'Go and get out of that uniform and put on a dress and wash your hands. We're going to see someone. A girl. I need you to be on your best behaviour.'

'Who?'

The nun took a deep breath and sucked in air through her teeth. 'Another girl who won't listen to her mother. Stubborn. I expect you two will have a lot in common. I want you to tell this girl that giving her baby up means happiness for another woman – what greater gift is there than that? And the girl, she'll be walking through the gates of heaven. Because when you do something good in this world, it makes it so much easier to get into the next.'

'Jumping the queue, like?'

'That's an ungodly way of putting it, and I wouldn't expect anything more of you. I'll give you a shilling and a pack of playing cards if you say yes?'

'Can I have tomorrow morning with my baby instead?'

The nun threw her a sharp look. 'Very well. However, Sybil, we allowed you to stay here to help with the laundry, but it won't be long before your baby will be adopted. Remember what we told you. Don't be getting too attached. It doesn't do, not for you, and it doesn't do for the child.'

Betsy felt soothed sitting in front of the mirror counting the blots of rust as Hope brushed out the tangles of her long blonde unruly hair. The tingle of the bristles against her scalp, the gentle pull and scrape was comforting, but this feeling of dread she couldn't shake. It crept like the tide. And though all around there was bombing now, no let-up, and even worse over Christmas, and people running to the shelters and announcements on the wireless, she still had the strange feeling that however terrible things were outside this house, they were even worse within these four walls.

'I'm a failure, Ma. What will I make of myself? Nothing. Cunard's didn't even care when I told them I was leaving. That boy was kind, James, the one you wanted me to marry, and he brings me tea most mornings, but everyone else just shrugged.'

Her mother's face screwed up into sadness. 'Betsy, once we have this problem sorted, everything will go back to how it was. The boy will be bringing tea again before you know it.'

'No, he won't. He wants to join the RAF. Why can't I keep this baby? You said we could find a pretend husband.'

'Where from? Betsy, you say that as if they grow on trees. I wasn't thinking properly. Anyway, Father made me think that the orphanage is not such a bad thing. The baby would have a better life than we could give it. The new mum and dad would be so happy. And, love, don't you realize? I want you to be happy as well. I want you to have a life. And a job. A good job. You're such a clever girl. You have a future. A chance to make something of yourself. To have a career. Unlike most of the poor beggars around here, scrabbling to make a living.'

'I don't care about being rich. Is that why we can't keep the baby? Because we're poor? What's a career anyway? Is it one of them cars with the sloping bonnets?'

'Don't be stupid! A career isn't a car. It's a serious job. A for-ever job. Like a nurse or a teacher. And I'm not talking about you being rich. There are plenty of people who have money that are unhappy. All I care about is for you to be happy and to have a future. And I know this baby will ruin that.' She banged down the teapot she was holding, and it made a fork bounce on the table. 'We should never have moved here to the tenements with the Dooleys.'

Drawing down the window to let the cool air rush in, Hope sighed. The clock ticked on the mantelpiece and in her head. The knock at the door was brisk and firm.

'That must be them. Sister Annunciata is kind. She's asked that I leave you alone with one of the girls. She's called Sybil.'

Sister Annunciata smiled when Hope invited them in. Betsy's eyes flitted nervously from the nun to the girl, Sybil, in her scuffed hobnail boots and sagging brown socks and mustard-coloured pinafore, and back to her mother.

'Did we have a happy and holy Christmas?' the nun said with a smile.

Hope smiled back and nodded. Hardly, thought Betsy. Just hiding and pretending she was ill, so no visitors with presents; just her and Jacky sharing a pudding and a leg of ham before he rushed off to the pub.

'I have brought Sybil to talk to you,' said the nun to Betsy.

Why? thought Betsy. Strange people turning up unannounced seemed to be happening with alarming frequency these days.

'Sometimes it's good for you to know that there are other girls in your situation. You can see that their life hasn't gone down the drain or disappeared in a puff of smoke.'

Betsy chewed her lip then looked back at Sybil with her upturned nose and skew-whiff collar.

'Sybil got pregnant just like you. Sybil and her baby live with us at the orphanage. Whilst she's waiting to have the baby adopted, Sybil is working for us. Your mother and I thought maybe you would like to do the same when your baby comes? It wouldn't need to be for ever.'

Betsy shuddered at the thought of it. Sybil stared dead-eyed at her.

'Girls like you two . . . It's a shame, but God has a strange way of making things happen in this world that we will never understand. Your mother doesn't want the neighbours to see you getting bigger. You look quite large now. That bump is showing. I can see it. You can't just go round saying you've eaten too much or put a football under your jumper. You could come with me now if you want.'

Sybil was twitching now, chewing her nail around the base of her thumb. The nun noticed and slapped her hand away from her mouth. 'Stop it, Sybil. Sybil, tell Betsy. Come here and stand beside me. You're happy about your baby? Happy you have a roof over your head with other children and girls? Happy she will soon be adopted?'

From the kitchen, the sound of the kettle whistling increased in pitch. 'There we are,' said the nun. 'A watched kettle never boils. Turns out it does. I'll leave you two alone. I'm going to speak to your mother. I'll be back in a minute.'

Sybil, when the nun had left the room, sprang like a cat towards Betsy and clutched her hand.

'I'm only here 'cos she let me spend the morning with my wee one. Don't give your baby away to Sister Annunciata. Don't do it, love,' she hissed, directly in Betsy's face.

Betsy looked at her tearfully and in shock.

'Your fella did a runner, did he? Bad luck. That's pretty much my story. Turned out my bloke had a wife and three nippers. What you going to call your babby?'

This girl spoke like she had a train running from her mouth. The questions didn't stop coming.

'You're getting big, aren't you? When the baby comes your ma will change her mind and let you keep it. She seems all right. Say no. Pretend you'll say yes, and then when the time comes, refuse. I wish I had. Say you'll tell everyone about getting up the duff and your ma will be terrified of the shame and pretend it's hers.'

Betsy looked at her seriously. It was a plan, and it made more sense than her mother's – lighting candles at the church or sliding into confession boxes promising to give up her whole life to God if somehow Jesus could magically put things right.

'Who knows you're up the duff?'

'Just my brother Jacky. And my friend Deirdre. And the baby's da and his family.'

'This city is full of secrets.'

'I've got no da, so my ma can't pretend the baby is hers. She's tight with Sister Annunciata. They even brought Father to talk to me about it. He was the one who told my ma it would be a grand idea to give my baby away.'

'Of course he did. They must be desperate to have asked me to come and talk to you, that's all I can say. She said your mother is going wild with grief.'

Betsy smiled. 'My ma's not a bad person.'

Sybil glanced over her shoulder. She leaned in and hissed at Betsy again. 'If your baby does end up in St Mary's, I'll look after it. I've been there a year and no one has adopted my girl yet. She's got a crease in her ear. I put a peg in it when I know the adopters are coming to make it seem worse than it is. I'll do the same with yours if you want, and then you can come back and get the wee lamb when you have a job or somewhere to live.'

Betsy's face flooded with light.

'You'd do that for me?'

'I'd do it for you and your babby.'

Hope surged through her for the first time in months. Could she really give her baby away and then take it back? When she had a job again, perhaps back at Cunard's? Maybe she could get a little flat? Sybil didn't think it was a bad idea. And neither did she. Hope. It had been so long since she had felt hope. But this girl with the brown hair and the smiling mouth with the gap in her front teeth had given her that.

'Chin up, chicken,' said Sybil. 'It's us against the world. But we can fight back. I promise. Anyway, names?'

'If it's a girl, May. If it's a boy, Vernon.'

'Vernon? After Vernon's Pools? Nifty. Might bring your baby luck. Might bring all of us a bit of luck.'

'So how was your chat with Sybil? Was it useful?' said Hope after Sybil and the nun had left.

Betsy shrugged. 'I'm not giving this baby away.'

'Oh, love. You're living in a dream. What choice do you have?' Hope sighed as she moved around the room, sweeping up the cups and teapot, banging them on the draining board.

Betsy thought that her mother was looking more and more as if she had been hollowed out from the inside. She was getting thinner and sadder by the day.

'Sybil said I should keep it.'

'What? She wasn't supposed to say that!'

Hope cleared out the ash pan noisily and angrily then took out her frustration on the copper kettle, spitting and polishing, spitting and polishing. Betsy, meanwhile, had fallen dead asleep on the sofa, dreaming of a future filled with different possibilities. Hope went outside and leaned against the wall, taking a long, slow drag on a cigarette, going over and over what they were going to do next in her head. Betsy wasn't the only one unconvinced by the nun and the orphanage. She expelled a long plume of smoke. Recently she had heard of one woman who had quietly placed an advert in the local paper asking for a couple to adopt her unwanted baby. Should she do that with Betsy's baby rather than put Betsy's future in the hands of this unfeeling nun?

She went back inside. Betsy was sleeping, dead to the world, her face rosy-cheeked and smooth with slumber as if she was a child again. How simple life had been such a short time ago. Not like now, Hope thought, looking through the window across the river and into a starless, moonless night, at a world that was becoming more frightening by the minute.

Chapter 6

As Betsy walked down Liverpool Lane wrapped up in a coat and a shawl, too hot for the beginning of May, she told herself that she was just looking at the soldiers and at the ARP men who were waving her through, making sure she was safe, and not looking for Alvis. But as the months had passed and she had grown bigger, he was on her mind more and more. Now she seemed to think of him every minute of every day. She had hoped he might have come home on leave for Christmas but if he had, he hadn't come to see her. Was he one of those fellows in a tin helmet painted with white letters? Or dressed in khaki uniform and boots? She cared more about finding Alvis than being bombed. As she made her way down Liverpool Lane, she could hear the sirens. She thought of her mother saying to her that if she was having contractions, it must be soon, and she felt a little stab of pain in her stomach.

'Go home, you need to be in the shelter,' said a soldier with a gun slung casually over his shoulder.

The sound of the bombs had kept Betsy awake every night. Just like this city was changing, Betsy was thinking about how her own life had changed so dramatically in what felt like such a short time. And now the numbers were hurtling around in her head. How many weeks since the terrible event? How many more months left? How many days before they would have to prepare the house? The first, second, and now the third trimester. All the counting just seemed to bring more problems. Really, what it meant was how many more days she would have to spend hiding in the house. She had been stuck inside for months, hiding under the table when there was another air raid, holding a tea tray over her head. But the worst number was how many days before Sister Annunciata would come knocking on the door to take the child to the orphanage, if her mother had her way.

The pain was sharp in her side. It had started as a dull ache early in the morning along with a headache, and a sickness in her stomach. But this wooziness was strange and sudden. When she arrived home, she was thankful to see Jacky was home from the docks, sitting at the table eating bread and jam.

'Move. Let me sit down. I don't feel too good,' she said, unbuttoning the large trench coat and then stripping off the jumpers that she had been wearing to hide her bump.

She glanced at the stack of towels set on the sideboard. Now that the decision had been made to have the baby at home, new things kept arriving. They wouldn't be having doctors or nurses, said her mother. She was young, and Hope had always said giving birth to Jacky and Betsy had been like shelling peas. If there was a problem, her cousin – who wasn't a cousin – could come and help.

Betsy thought back to the priest who had said of

course they would never want her to be talked into something that she might regret. He had sounded kind, but she didn't trust him.

Jacky leaned back in the chair, face sooty, and pulled off his muddy boots. 'What's all this stuff? I don't like it.'

Betsy sighed. There were the old towels, which Hope had bought from Paddy's market, and the enamel jug and the chipped enamel bowl, ready for hot water. She had bought a vest and a smock for the baby from the market and nearly cried at its smallness and newness when she had laid it out on the bed.

'For when the baby comes,' replied Betsy. 'Bang the mud off outside. Ma says we have to keep the place clean. Germs.'

He nodded his head. 'Betsy, you look like you swallowed a giant football. You're so tiny and you look so strange. But you're cooked, I'd say.'

Betsy shrugged. 'I have no idea how I'm going to get this baby out. I'm feeling . . . ill . . .'

The words tailed off.

'I'll not judge you. Despite what the fellas at the pub are saying. I went to The Boot, where they don't know me.'

'Oh, Jacky, I'm sorry.'

'Here, I've brought you some cinder toffee. Your favourite.'

Betsy shook her head and sniffled. 'Where did you get that? No, ta.' How she wanted to feel it prickling against her tongue, but she was feeling sick just to look at it.

'Fella at work. I'll have it then.'

'Why can't I keep my baby?' she moaned.

'You know why. You've no husband. You don't want everyone to know you're one of them fallen girls. Anyway, it's not that easy. It's a babby, not a puppy. And I hate the way they're talking about you already. They say things about you. Names. I'd punch their lights out, every one of them. Do you want that for the rest of your life?'

'If I could only . . .' But then she stopped and clutched her stomach and let out a sudden cry.

Jacky looked shocked. 'What's the matter?'

Betsy didn't answer, she just let out another moan.

'What's happening? Is it coming? Don't do this to me, Bets! I'll flaming kill you if it is.'

'Don't ask me. How should I know?' She groaned again.

He was beginning to feel frightened at how round and large her eyes were. A sweat was breaking out over her brow like morning dew. 'Should I go and get a neighbour?'

'No,' she gasped. 'The whole point of me hiding here is so that the neighbours don't know! I've not been locked away here for months for you to go and ruin everything.'

'But you're burning up.' He reached out and put his hand on her forehead. 'You feel as hot as a range. I need to find Ma.'

Betsy reached out and clutched his hand. 'Don't go. I've been bad all day. Sweating. Hot and dizzy. Don't go,' she said. 'Don't leave me.'

He didn't know what to do and he looked towards the door but felt compelled to turn back to Betsy.

'Betsy?' Her eyes seemed to be rolling, eyelashes fluttering, and her arms were limp, her neck lolling backwards. 'Come on, Betsy. Squeeze my hand. You never wanted anyone to beat you at anything. Kick the can . . . knock down ginger. You're going to fight whatever this is.'

'I can't,' she said. 'What should I do?' she whimpered. 'Am I dying? Jacky, am I?'

'Of course not.'

'Then what's happening?'

'I don't know, Bets. I'm a fella.'

He was about to run a towel under the cold tap when the door banged open. 'Am I glad to see you, Ma!'

'Betsy!' she gasped, seeing her daughter's lips purpling, and the whites of her eyes.

'I think the baby's coming. She's awful bad, Ma.'

Betsy blinked vaguely, then tried to stand but started to sway and fall. 'Move out of the way,' Hope said, barging past Jacky and catching her. 'Betsy? Betsy, can you hear me? How long has she been like this, Jacky?'

'I went for a pint, and I came in and she said she wasn't good, hadn't been all day . . . but I don't know . . .'

'This isn't right,' said her mother. 'Run down the road and get your cousin Malcolm to bring his bread van. Tell him we need him to get her to the hospital.'

'But Betsy said no one else should know.'

'I don't care about any of that! And anyway, Malcolm is family. We just need to get Betsy to the hospital. Right now, I don't give a damn what anyone thinks. Come on, Betsy, stay with us. Can you hear me, Betsy?'

Hope pulled up the bottom of Betsy's skirts. Her feet were so swollen, bulging over the straps of her Mary Janes. And she was so tiny. So very small. But now she looked so very big and strange.

Malcolm grabbed his cap and jumped into his small bread van as soon as Jacky told him what was happening. He lifted Betsy into the front seat – awful floppy, he said – and opened the throttle, swerved into Liverpool Lane and towards Mill Road Hospital. Thankfully the sirens that normally went off at this time every night had remained quiet on the journey but there were signs of the terrible bombing the night before and he had to avoid debris in the roads, soldiers waving them along hurriedly, a smouldering heap of rubble being hosed down. By the time the van passed under the Tate and Lyle chute, Hope saw that Betsy was beginning to loll her head to one side and her eyes were starting to flutter shut. Shaking her awake as they approached and pinching her hand, making the shape of crescent moons with her fingernails in Betsy's pale skin, she said thank you gratefully and was relieved that Malcolm, despite his eyes widening with shock when he had arrived at the house and had seen Betsy groaning and whimpering, wasn't asking questions that she didn't want to answer. Betsy came around slightly with Hope and Malcolm propping her up under her shoulders, walking her through the hospital doors. A nurse was standing waiting for them as if she knew.

'Oh dear. How long has she been like this?'

'A few hours. She said she was starting to feel sick this morning. A roaring temperature. Sickness,' said Hope. 'It happened so quickly.'

'Well, you're in the right place. What's her name? Are you the father?' she added, turning to Malcolm.

'Her name is Betsy Drew. And yes, this is her husband,' said Hope. Malcolm's mouth fell open. But she had said it so purposefully, so directly, he didn't respond. 'Please, Nurse, I'm worried.'

The nurse bustled around them, putting a blanket around Betsy's shoulders. 'We'll take good care of her. Leave her to us now.'

'What's wrong with her?' Hope asked.

'Sometimes there's a lot of stress on the heart. She's having a baby. Let's see what we can do. We need to get her temperature down. And then we can see what's what. I'm presuming her waters haven't broken? And what's her due date?'

'Next week.'

Betsy started to stir. Hope mopped her sweating brow.

'Here comes the wheelchair,' said the nurse brightly.

A porter appeared pushing a chair. After he lifted her into it he began to wheel her towards a room that had *Labour Ward* written above the door.

'We'll take over now. You can have a nice hot cup of tea in the waiting room and as soon as we have news we'll come out and find you both. It's a nervous time for new fathers. Please God there will be no bombing tonight. We'll ring the bell when the baby comes. The dads mostly huddle outside smoking but you're both welcome to sit here as long as you like and until we have news.'

Nurse Jennifer Jones left the room, her feet clicking over the polished tiles. Hope sank into the chair.

'*Husband?* Well, well, well.' He laughed and Hope tutted.

'The nurse said it first, not me.' She sighed. 'You can go now, Malcolm.'

'I'll stay for the craic,' he said, grinning.

Hope raised her eyes. Typical Malcolm, she thought. 'This isn't Betsy's fault, Malcolm. Don't you think badly of her. This is flaming Alvis Dooley. If that boy walked in here now, I would take him with my own two hands and I'd wring his neck. Not that that matters now. Say a prayer. Say lots of prayers. For Betsy. And her baby. And not a word about this. Not to anyone. Not to your mother or your brothers. Not ever. Can I trust you, Malcolm?'

'Your secret's safe with me, Auntie,' he said, with an unpleasant wink.

Two hours passed with Hope and Malcolm sitting there in the cold, draughty corridor, Malcolm yawning and nodding off and snoring from time to time, Hope pacing, sighing, pacing. And in all that time there was only one thing that was racing around Hope's head. And it wasn't the fear of the sickly sound of the sirens starting up and the worry of Hitler's bombs, or the shame or guilt of being found out that she had a daughter who was unmarried and pregnant. Or what awful things Malcolm was thinking. Live, she prayed, quietly, over and over again. Please Lord, let my Betsy and her baby live.

Chapter 7

'Good news. You have a son, Malcolm! Congratulations,' said Nurse Jones, smiling and folding the cuffs of her sleeves up her arms. 'And what a bonny little thing he is.'

Hope threw him a look.

'He's beautiful,' the nurse gushed. 'He's an angel. Eight pounds. Wonderful.'

'And Betsy?' said Hope.

'She's doing grand. It was a temperature. Sky-high fever. But she's fine now. Ventouse did the job in the end.'

Hope let out an audible breath. Relief flooded through her. God had answered her prayers.

Betsy was lying on the bed, a sheen of sweat glistening over her forehead and cheeks, holding the child and staring into its face, hypnotized by his long dark lashes, upturned nose, crinkled face and soft velvety head. She had been alarmed at first when the child had finally slithered out from between her legs, all slippery with squashed features and fine downy hair over his shoulders and a scream so loud he had woken those across the water in Birkenhead, Nurse Jones had said with a smile. 'Why is he so hairy?' she had asked Nurse Jones worriedly. The nurse had laughed and said it was because the baby had been in too long, overcooked, and that the hair would fall out over the next few days. Her mother came rushing into the room, flushed and happy, with Malcolm following.

Good grief, so is he my pretend husband? thought Betsy.

'Hello, Malcom,' she said, confused.

'I'll leave you alone for a few minutes. You must be very proud, Malcolm,' the nurse said with a bright smile as she left the room.

'The nurse thinks I'm the da,' he said with a laugh. He made an elaborate show of taking off his cap. 'I'm happy to oblige, Betsy, love. Your secret is safe with me.'

'Shush,' hissed Hope. 'These nurses are sharp as tacks. Oh, isn't he perfect?' she said, checking for five fingers and five toes and noticing he had a little port wine stain birthmark on his right thigh.

Nurse Jones came back through the door carrying a stethoscope. 'Please God it's not going to be another terrible night like yesterday,' she said. 'What a time for this little one to come into the world. And all those poor lads out there. They say this war is about bringing peace, don't they?'

'They said that about the last one,' said Malcolm.

Betsy could see her mother glaring at Malcolm as if she was willing him not to speak at all. *Stop talking, before you say something stupid.* Hope flicked her eyes back to Betsy.

'What part of this mayhem are you, Malcolm? Reservist?' asked the nurse.

'Aye, I work a bread round in my van. Folks still need feeding.'

'I suppose you've had a time of it, haven't you? The streets aren't safe. And driving around in the dark at night in the blackouts. Well, we all have. And we're grateful for what you're doing.'

Why was she asking him all these questions? thought Betsy, twisting the cheap Woolworth's wedding ring that she had been wearing for the past month. She felt her cheeks smarting.

'The baby's sleeping,' said Betsy. 'You should both go, Ma.'

Nurse Jones went to the end of the bed and began folding a linen napkin. 'There's no rush. Stay as long as you want. Don't mind me. I'll be in and out. I have checks to do on the other mums.'

No one said anything. Nurse Jones couldn't understand why Malcolm hadn't even picked up the baby, just leaned into the cot once or twice, stuck his finger out to see if the baby would grasp it. It hadn't. Overwhelmed, maybe.

'Life is a rich tapestry and not all the stitches are even. Oh, look, he's opening his eyes.' She was trying to be kind, thought Betsy. 'Is Dad ready to hold baby now?' The nurse watched Malcolm walk quietly to the edge of the bed. 'Betsy, give him to Malcolm, he won't bite.'

'What if it cries?' said Malcolm.

'Babies cry all the time,' Nurse Jones said, with a smile.

Betsy glanced at him and frowned as the nurse handed the baby to him. He took him in his arms. He was enjoying this, thought Hope. He must know how uncomfortable he was making her and Betsy feel.

'Rock him. Gently,' said Nurse Jones.

Malcolm performed a slow, unsteady rhythmic dance, moving awkwardly from foot to foot.

Imagine being this young couple bringing a baby into the world, thought Nurse Jones. Bombs all around. No one knowing what was happening next with Hitler. And she worried for their future. The baby started to whimper. 'Pat his back and he'll stop crying. It's probably just wind.'

Betsy looked at Malcolm again, standing there holding the baby as if he were a bag of potatoes. But the nurse didn't appear to be bothered, just slapped her thighs, stood, and said she had another mother to see to. And that was that. No one seemed to be asking any more questions. Maybe it was the idea of having bigger things to worry about, like the threat of the bombs. The sirens had been going off all week and there had been terrible casualties already.

'What I'd give for a night without these wretched bombs screaming overhead. You never know what horror is coming to us next. Still, at least these babies give us hope. Let's pray they don't remember this dreadful bombing.'

Betsy's mother smiled and nodded. She was right, babies did give hope. Just some more than others.

'They'll be coming up the river,' continued the nurse. 'This bombing has been so awful and there's so many people without homes now. We have so many casualties here.'

Hope nodded. Just keep talking about the Germans,

she thought, it's really all anyone's interested in. Probably nobody really cared that this baby had been born on the wrong side of the blanket. Strange, then, that she did.

The nurse picked up the towels and left.

After she had walked out of the room, Hope hissed, 'Malcolm, hold the baby properly, for goodness' sake.' But then she moved quietly to the edge of the bed and her face softened and she said gently, 'Oh, but isn't he a beautiful little lad, Betsy!'

It was getting dark and Nurse Jones had sat with the baby trying to urge Betsy to hold him to her breast. The baby was getting tired and Betsy was exhausted.

'Please, can't we give him a bottle?' said Betsy. 'It hurts. And nothing's happening.'

Nurse Jones sighed. If there hadn't been so much going on, she would have made her persevere, but the hospital was too busy, there were too many others to see to. 'I can get one of the nurses to feed him. But he won't go back on the breast easily. Once he has a taste of the bottle, you're done for. Are you sure?'

Betsy nodded. 'I just need to sleep.'

'The ward sister will be along in a minute to help.'

Betsy's head lolled against the pillow. A younger nurse, harried and flustered, burst through the door.

'Sister, I've been told to tell you, purple warning . . . And can you go to the emergency room?'

'Purple?' said Nurse Jones, shocked. 'Yes, of course. But, Nurse, can you take this baby to the nursery and try him on a bottle?'

'Yes . . . And they need help in the emergency room

for a Mr Papafotis. The patient is the fish and chip shop owner from across the road . . .' she called after Nurse Jones. She turned to Betsy as she lifted the child from the cot at the side of Betsy's bed. 'Please God it's not too serious. We all want our fish and chips, don't we? Imagine if Hitler were to bomb our fish and chip shop? That's a crime that would be remembered.'

Betsy smiled weakly.

'There's a good little fellow. Let's get you fed. Don't want you shouting to add to the drama,' said the nurse, as she left the room and Betsy watched her go.

Hope pulled her threadbare coat around her as she got off the tram and made her way back to the tenements along Liverpool Lane. She had ordered Malcolm to go home and forget what he had seen in the past few hours. 'It never happened, understand, Malcolm?' She wanted to go to Marjorie Hallet's to see if she had any cod liver oil she could take to Betsy when she went back to the hospital in the morning. She jogged on, glancing up at the skies. Roadrunner, some of the neighbours called her, when they saw her stooped figure scurrying past their windows. Always going somewhere in a hurry.

The shelter, as she hurried past it, had its door held open by a man in a tin ARP helmet.

'Going to be trouble tonight. Like last night. Go down to the shelter, missus,' he called.

'What?'

'You'll be safer down here,' he shouted. 'Can't you hear the sirens?'

Hope faltered. She thought about Betsy. The nurse

had assured her that Mill Road Hospital had a basement where everyone would be safe if there was an
air raid. But what about if anything were to happen
to Hope? She needed to stay alive for Betsy. Thinking
about this, she went in and sat on the little camp bed.
She worried about Betsy. About Hitler and his bombings.

'What was that?' she cried, at the sound of a soft
thud somewhere far off. 'Too close. Too close. And
getting closer,' she muttered.

Nurse Jennifer Jones looked in the cracked mirror
above the sink and ran a finger across her brow, trying
to smooth out the creases. I'm too young to have this
face, she thought. Downstairs in ward eight, they had
just begun operating on Dimitri Papafotis, the owner
of the fish and chip shop. He had staggered into the
emergency room doubled over in excruciating pain.
Thankfully the ambulancemen had got to him in time
and the doctors would be well underway by now,
thought Jennifer, putting her chapped hands under the
running tap and wiping them on the frayed linen hand
towel. It had taken three of them to lift Mr Papafotis
onto the operating table, and they had used sheets
instead of a hoist, but that was usual now. Since the
Blitz had started it felt like everyone's job here at the
hospital was to make do and mend, not just with vests
and socks, but with human beings as well. Lately so
many had arrived desperately looking for help, casualties of the relentless bombing. But it felt much worse
now this past week.

Instinctively, she glanced up at the blacked-out

skylight above her. For the life of her she couldn't understand why this hospital was still admitting patients. Mill Road, just off the dock road, was right in the line of fire and as Hitler's Luftwaffe loved to make a beeline for the river, where they would open their hatches above the warehouses and shipyards, she worried that it was only a matter of time before one of the bombs would fall right on top of the hospital. Still, she supposed they needed somewhere in the centre of the city to bring the sick and injured. And they had been so busy with casualties. My God, they had been busy. This place was bursting at the seams.

She went out of the washroom and back into the maternity ward, looking around at the women and girls. The girl, Betsy, was sleeping. At least babies brought some hope amidst all this tragedy.

'Everyone out!' shouted an ambulanceman, bursting through the door, his face pale, eyes round and panicked. 'Everyone down into the basement. Quickly!'

Nurse Jones stood up from the desk. 'I thought we might have a night off.'

'On their way. Just got word. Purple code. Sirens about to start up.'

Some of the women had already sat up in their beds, frightened. One of them leaned over and shook the woman in the bed next to hers. 'Wake up,' she said. 'We need to go down to the shelter in the basement.'

'Girls, take your babies. Take your babies out of their cots and follow Ambulanceman Earnshaw. Don't waste any time.'

She knew there were a couple of women with stitches

who could barely move. And some of the babies whose mothers were exhausted were right now being bottle fed in the nursery.

'Sister, I don't have my baby with me. The nurse took him to have his bottle,' said Betsy in a small, urgent voice.

'Don't worry, dear . . .' Why these girls couldn't just put their babies to their breasts . . . And this one had hardly tried. So young, but insistent that she wouldn't be able to do it. 'You'll find your baby in the basement. Everyone is going down there. The nurse will meet you there.'

She rushed the others through the door. It was easier with some. But not everyone was like Betsy, others didn't seem to care, and it seemed unbelievable that after such a short time a few of the younger mothers just swung their legs tiredly over the side of the bed, sighing at the thought of having their sleep interrupted, as if they had grown bored of the bombing already, as though they couldn't imagine it was them who might be in the line of fire next. Maybe it was precisely because they were young. How could anything bad possibly happen to them? They had their whole lives ahead of them. It just didn't seem fair. This girl Betsy was different, though, jittery, and she had got out of bed, pushed her feet into slippers and was pacing as she crushed her fists into her eyes, saying, 'Sister, please, can I go and find my baby? I need to find him.'

'I told you, the nurses will have your little boy downstairs by now. Come on. Get a move on. If any of you have a bedpan under your bed, a clean one obviously, hold it over your head,' she said in a loud voice. She clapped her hands as she watched them shuffling nervously to the exit. 'Keep in an orderly line. No one is going to get out if you're all crowding around the door like that.'

A couple of the babies started to cry and their mothers cradled them, shushed them and held them close to their breasts. The nurse wondered if the babies could sense their panic and that was why so many of them had begun mewling. And meanwhile the rumbling noise was getting louder.

'That was a strong one,' she said as the ground shuddered beneath them and there was the sound of a soft thud somewhere far off. 'Hurry up.'

Betsy paused. 'Can I go and find my baby?'

'Just do what Nurse Jones says,' snapped a girl hurriedly pulling on a sweater.

'Come on, my dear, the babies will be safe. Your baby will be fine.'

It felt like all around them there was roaring now. 'It really does sound like they're right overhead,' said the nurse. 'Let's go, lickety-split.'

'Feels like hell is opening right above us!' said a woman holding her baby to her chest. 'What if we die tonight?'

'That's not helping things, love. Where's your Blitz spirit?' snapped a second woman, elbowing people out of the way.

The nurse scurried over to the window and peeped out across the courtyard through a small hole in the blackout curtains. Everywhere was bathed in a sickly orange glow. The thought of the lives that had been ruined tonight already made her shiver.

She turned to the ambulanceman. 'Can you tell me what I'm supposed to do with the ones who can't move? Should I stay with them? Because . . .' But she didn't get to the end of the sentence before there was another crack as loud as a thunderbolt and a nurse came running in, panic-stricken.

'No time! Get under the beds!' she yelled. 'Get under the beds! Nurse, can you help this mother who can't get out of bed?'

Nurse Jones looked at the young woman cradling her baby, who she knew to be perfectly able to get out of bed but was just frozen in a paralytic terror.

Someone tried to grab one of the bedpans off the table. 'The babies! Look after the babies!'

Fear rose in Nurse Jones's throat. Another nurse came running in. 'Try to stay calm,' she yelled. 'It's close . . . So close . . . Right overhead . . .'

'My baby!' wailed Betsy, wandering around, clutching her hair in fists on the crown of her head. 'Where is he?'

The ambulanceman grabbed both Betsy's arms and spoke directly into her face. 'Calm down. You heard the nurse. Calm down, love. If we . . .'

But his words were lost in another roaring and screeching sound followed by yells and screams. And then what they had been dreading for weeks, months, the unimaginable appalling event happened. The terrific blast lifted Betsy off her feet and threw her against the back wall, bringing air whooshing into the room and a blizzard of shrapnel, and ripping the floor from under her. And then everything went black, as if black ink had been injected into her eyeballs. And then it was deathly quiet, and all life was sucked out of the room.

In the seconds after the explosion, Nurse Jones heard whimpering, yelping, and a low moan and exhalation of pain.

Betsy rubbed her eyes and, groping on her hands and knees, felt dust and heat choking and burning in her throat. 'My baby,' she whimpered. 'Please, please, don't let anything have happened to my baby.'

And then another nurse with blood on her hands, blood streaked over her face, staggered in. 'How many have been hurt?' She was followed by one of the doctors in a white coat with its arm ripped off, smeared in ash and soot.

'How many in here?' he barked.

And then another young man came tearing in, shouting, 'The ceiling! The ceiling. The whole place has been hit. We've had a direct hit. The ambulances are coming. But there's already a good few dead.'

The noise grew to a crescendo, with people calling out for help, the sickening sound of more planes screaming and growling overhead and the sirens, deafening now since the hospital roof had been blown in. It felt like hell had descended. The sound of wailing became louder amidst more shouting, clamouring, clattering and chaos.

'Where's my baby?' sobbed Betsy. 'What's happened to my baby?'

Chapter 8

The silence after the bombers left was always eerie. Hope came blinking into the soft light of dawn with the sound of the all-clear. She hadn't been able to sleep, of course. There had been a smell of sour breath and sweaty bodies and all night the low roaring of planes and the thudding that might have been far off but still made the ground vibrate under her. Curled up on a small camp bed with the sound of sniffling and coughing and wheezing, Betsy had been all she could think about.

'One nurse hit by a lump of concrete from the cornicing at the top of the stairs, killed on the spot.'

The words hit her like an actual physical thump in her stomach. She tried to unscramble them.

'A piece of shrapnel got the ambulanceman,' someone said. 'Right through his chest. His heart probably.'

'What?' she said.

'Mill Road Hospital. Bombed last night. Bombed badly . . .'

'Betsy! Betsy!' she gasped. And picking up her skirts, she ran.

When Hope turned up at the hospital it was still burning – small stubborn fires around the huge crater at the back courtyard where the bomb had landed, and a larger blaze on one side of the roof. Hitler had made latticework of windows and floors and walls. Sheets tangled around lumps of twisted metal flapped in the wind. Firemen were trying to extinguish new fires that kept licking into life. Wild-eyed, Hope ran over to a nurse with soot on her face looking as tired as death, picking through the rubble. She was carrying a clipboard. Like others, she was urging the small crowd to stand back. Weary and hopeless, she scanned the list.

'Betsy Drew?' asked Hope, trembling.

The nurse lowered her eyes. 'Yes, alive. Ambulance took her last night.'

'Oh, thank God. Jesus, thank you . . . Where?'

'Fazakerley Hospital . . .'

'And her baby?' she said, haltingly.

'Name?'

'Name? I don't know. Not yet. He was born last night. He had a small birthmark on his right thigh? Perhaps they just said baby Drew?'

The nun went down the list, running her finger along the margin.

'Nothing. Nothing here, I'm afraid. Most casualties are at Fazakerley. They'll have more information.'

Hope's face crinkled up in anguish.

A woman behind her was barging into her now, pushing her forward.

'Stand back, everyone!' cried the nurse. 'Next!' she yelled, as the crowd clamoured and pushed, and a chimney stack wobbled and crashed and a cloud of dust and smoke rose from the rubble.

*

Seven miles away, the Greek man, when he opened his eyes, was a little confused. After the anaesthetic wore off, he asked where he was and he was told he was in Fazakerley hospital. He asked again.

'Where am I?'

The soft fuzz of a nurse's silhouette and her gentle smile was hard to make sense of, just like her soothing words. 'You were in Mill Road Hospital, Mr Papafotis, on the operating table last night, but there was heavy shelling and we brought you here to finish you off and sew you up . . . The hospital has been evacuated.'

And now he was all stitched up like new. He touched the sewn-up incision. A miracle.

The nurse leaned into him. 'We managed to get you into an ambulance. You slept through the whole thing.'

'Was anybody hurt?' he asked groggily.

'Sadly, yes, a good deal. Ambulancemen, nurses, and patients as well. Women and . . .'

She couldn't bring herself to say babies. She just frowned, and thought to herself again what a bloody stupid place to have a hospital.

James arrived home feeling weary. He pulled off his ARP helmet and slumped into a chair. He had spent the last hours helping uncoil hosepipes from more fire engines and directing more ambulances to the dead and injured.

'What are you doing up? Go to bed, Mother.'

Lettice closed the fan with a snap and her hand fluttered to her face, and she twisted her head away.

He poured himself a sherry from a decanter on the side table and took a sip, feeling the smooth liquid hit the back of his throat and the fuzzy veil of alcohol come upon him.

'It's indescribable . . . what I saw last night.'

'I was worried sick about you . . .' She fiddled with a tassel on the end of her woollen scarf and began pacing. 'What happened?'

'God knows how many have died, women and children, but the wards were badly hit. Upwards of fifty, it's been reported.'

He took another slug. 'I can't put it off any longer. I need to do more than pass spades along lines. I'm volunteering for the RAF. From now on, I don't want another tear shed for me. Save it for these children, mothers, nurses and doctors at Mill Road. Can you do that for me? Please?'

Chapter 9

A week later

'Will there be a funeral for Vernon?' asked Betsy, in a dull voice. Hope, standing at the sink, didn't reply but Betsy saw her back clench.

'They lost so much in the rubble. And your baby was so tiny. But you can't have a funeral without a body, love. Father Donnelly should say mass. A kind of memorial mass.'

'I don't want to go. If they still haven't found him, I don't want to go.'

Hope sighed.

'Don't say it, Ma . . .'

'What?'

Betsy craned her neck and wrung her hands and spoke in a voice that mirrored Hope's. 'Hard as it is, Betsy, isn't it better it turned out this way?'

'I didn't say that.'

'You're thinking it. I know you are.'

Hope sat down with a thump and grasped her hand. 'I said nothing of the sort, but as you brought it up, we didn't know what we were going to do, did we? We had no idea. We knew we couldn't bring your baby home. Don't you see how things could have been so much worse? Wondering where he was? Who was bringing him up? Were the nuns being kind? That would have been so awful. And now it can be your secret, both our secrets. Sister Annunciata was right. The Lord works in mysterious ways. Oh, Betsy, don't start again. Don't start that yelping and squealing. It would be better if you could just cry like a normal person.'

'Why aren't they searching for my baby?' she wailed. 'I want a *funeral*!'

'Because there was barely anything left of the hospital wards. Just rubble and ash. And they have so many other things to do. Whole streets are disappearing. Ships that have just been sunk with barely a mention and all those people drowning. You know the government doesn't like to talk too much of these terrible things. Bad for morale. Everyone is looking for a loved one somewhere in this city.'

'Why didn't they let me go back and search for my baby? I hate them. I hate them all.'

'You were barely alive yourself. They did their best, love.'

Then one day, Betsy read about the funeral of one of the ambulancemen. She didn't tell her mother, just slipped out quietly, lifted the latch and set off to the church and sat in the back pew and silently wept for her child as the coffin went down the aisle. Later, as she walked around for hours willing a bomb to drop on her, hunched and bent into the wind, she wished she wasn't alive at all. She had said that to her mother, who had sniped back at her not to say such evil things.

'Betsy, when I turned up at the hospital and thought

you were dead, I didn't know what to do. And then when I was told you were alive, all crumpled up but alive, it was like I had been given my life back too. So don't you dare say such things. You were one of the lucky ones.'

Betsy felt her breasts prickling, still tender and full of milk. Her mother noticed her wincing and glancing down at her chest. It pained her to see a wet patch seeping through her blouse. Hope knelt down next to her, gently stroked her hair. 'It will pass.'

'So, what now for me?'

There was a pause. 'You could go back to Cunard's. They have already said they would have you back.'

'And what did you tell them? Where did you say I had been?'

'I said we had to move because the house had been bombed. They didn't ask many questions; they were grateful that you might come back. We can go to church, and we can light a candle. Come on, love. Buck up.'

Betsy stood on wobbling legs. She could feel the cold rising from the flagstones through her tattered slippers. It felt as if her thin bones were hollow. It was such an effort. And what was the point? What was the point of anything?

A month later, Betsy sat at the desk at Cunard's trying to add up the figures, counting on her fingers and with her brain hurting. It was so hard. And her mind was whirling. She wondered about the boy with the high cheekbones that could cut glass and the soft hair, James something, where he was, but when she went down the corridor and asked, they told her that he had gone. And like so many other places, the corridors and rooms seemed full of just women now. There was no one to carry the books either. And they were so heavy. Yawning and scratching her head, she checked no one was around and sat down to write.

Dear Sybil,
I don't know if you remember me. But I won't be coming to the orphanage after all. A terrible thing happened. My baby died . . .

Betsy's heart lurched. She screwed up the letter and threw it in the bin. Why would that girl Sybil want to know any of this? And where should she send it to? This was all too hard and she left Cunard's at morning break to do what she always did when she could – walk along the river and kiss a pebble, then throw it into the Mersey in the hope that it might bring her baby back.

Meanwhile, Nurse Jennifer Jones got off the tram and made her way down Everton hill. The address she had was for one of the flats in the tenements behind Liverpool Lane. She took a deep breath after climbing up the stairs and stood outside the green door with the number eighteen on it. Thankfully this visit would be one of the easier ones. In her twelve years of nursing she had seen plenty of babies die, mothers too, but following up and checking in on the bereaved and injured of the hospital bomb was about the hardest thing she had ever been asked to do, so she was glad she would be seeing Betsy and her baby.

A little bit of joy. Some of the names on the list were families who had lost someone – she had already had to speak to the wives of two ambulancemen this morning – but thankfully there were others like Betsy who she just had to confirm had somehow managed to make it home safely to their beds that terrible night and were doing fine a month later. It always felt rude to refuse their tea and biscuits, and now she was desperate to spend a penny. If Hope and her daughter Betsy invited her in for a cuppa, she would accept it gratefully. The baby – boy, it said on her list, eight pounds – she vaguely remembered was bonny.

Hope answered the door.

'Ah, hello,' said Nurse Jones. 'Betsy's mum, isn't it? I'm from Mill Road Hospital. I delivered Betsy's child.'

'Nurse Jones. Of course, I remember.'

'I'm just checking that your daughter—'

'Betsy is not here, I'm afraid,' she said with her foot in the door.

'Shall I come back?'

'I don't see why you need to. You must be run off your feet. Truthfully, Betsy doesn't want to be reminded of that terrible night.'

'Can I ask you what Betsy named her baby? Just so we can make a note and tick them off the list. I remember she was thinking Vernon?'

'Vernon? No, he's George now,' she said.

The nurse scribbled it down. 'Some poor souls, I'm afraid, weren't so lucky. Didn't even name their baby before . . .' The sentence tailed off. The nurse felt something wasn't quite right, but she shrugged it away. 'Still looking for answers when we have none.'

Hope nodded seriously. 'I'm sorry to hear that.'

'And is Betsy's husband well? Still doing his bread round? They were such a young couple. If you need me to come back . . . Are you all coping?'

'Nurse, please use your time to help the others in a worse situation than us. I believe there are still people missing?'

'The hospital was so busy that night,' said the nurse, sadly.

'Our condolences. We can only think God has a strange and mysterious plan for some that we can't hope to understand.'

What an odd thing to say, thought the nurse as she nodded a goodbye and made her way down the hill, wondering if the remaining four on her list would be as easily dealt with as Hope.

Chapter 10

How many times had her mother said lately that they should be grateful to have a roof over their heads after so many had been bombed? Thousands were dead. Thousands more homeless. There was a sound of a siren somewhere far off. Betsy went back into the living room. To think she had wished this child away when she had first realized it had been growing inside her, and now . . . Nothing could feel as bad as this. She would have done anything to have him back. Sometimes she dreamed she had found a little bundle between the towels in the airing cupboard, and it was Vernon sleeping, or he was curled up under the pile of blankets or hiding in the coal hole. There was still a persistent graze underneath her chin and a red mark on her nose from that awful night, but they were turning darker. Would they scar? A permanent reminder whenever she looked in the mirror of the night her baby died.

'Stop picking at it,' her mother said, when she came in.

'It itches,' she said.

'That means it's getting better.'

'I expect you're happy,' said Betsy, spikily.

'Don't be so silly. No one would ever wish a baby away.'

'Maybe Alvis will come back and then we can marry quietly anyway. Maybe we can have another baby.'

'Betsy! What are you saying, stupid girl? Anyway, we haven't seen hide nor hair of him since the moment we told Joyce Dooley it was his child.'

'This is all too *hard*. Everything hurts,' she said, curling herself up into a tight ball. 'Why can't Vernon have a funeral?'

Her mother looked at her and pushed a strand of hair behind her ear. 'We've been through this. You can't have a funeral without a body. There are people fighting over a foot or a finger that turned up in the rubble just so they can have a burial, but we haven't even got that. I'm not sure you're well enough, even if we did have a funeral. I think it would be too much. We could go to church and light a candle?' She took Betsy's hand and traced the pattern on her palm.

'I hate God. After what He's done to me.'

'Betsy, however terrible this feels, however mysterious and painful, have you thought it might be God's way of giving you your life back?'

Betsy looked shocked. 'Ma!'

Hope pulled her hand away. 'I mean, what were you going to do with the baby? We couldn't pretend that Malcolm was your husband for long.'

'You could have pretended Vernon was yours.'

'My head is whirling around with your nonsense. And I told you . . . the timings didn't work. I couldn't suddenly announce I had given birth. Me, thin as a rake. You're supposed to be so clever, but sometimes I think everything you say is so stupid.'

Hope opened the newspaper tiredly. The hospital

tragedy was still on every page inside and out. And now more tragic stories of the people who were being lost in the Blitz every day were coming out. 'Terrible,' she murmured.

Betsy sat sucking a blanket.

'Stop doing that with your blanket. Do you not see what you're doing?'

Betsy looked up vaguely.

'And you're blinking so strangely. Betsy, as you've got the morning off, do something with your hands and make yourself useful. You could help me knit some of these socks for the soldiers like Sister Annunciata has asked.'

Betsy felt the rise again in her throat. A sour taste came to her mouth. The other day her mother had asked her to knit a blanket, but knitting reminded her of babies. How could she be so cruel? Sometimes Betsy wondered if she wasn't doing it deliberately.

Her mother sighed and announced she was going to work. The rest of the morning passed with Betsy wandering around aimlessly, staring out of the window, lying on her bed, boiling the kettle, letting the tea go cold because she forgot to drink it, boiling the kettle again. And so it went on until five o'clock when Hope returned from the wash-house.

But five minutes later, as Hope was bustling around the kitchen, moving around chairs, folding towels, there was a knock at the door. Hope rushed to answer it.

'Don't be shocked when you see her, Deirdre. I've tried everything. I've never known her to refuse a chip buttie, but she didn't even take a bite. I went all the way to Mr Tattersall's. Spent a sixpence on a bag of chips and a barm cake. She barely touched it. She was skinny before she had the baby, but now . . . Will you talk to her?' said Hope in a low voice. Betsy heard every word.

'There's someone to see you, Betsy!' Hope called.

'Oh, Betsy,' said Deirdre, who was smiling, wearing a little pillbox hat perched jauntily on her head that matched her green dress and court shoes, finally bringing some energy into this dismal room. 'Look at you, Bets! So thin! Like a shadow!'

Betsy smiled weakly but she managed to get out of the chair and throw her arms around her friend. 'I thought you were evacuated?'

'Came back. Couldn't stand the smell of the pigs. And the people we were staying with could only speak Welsh. Bets, I swear I could play the xylophone on those ribs and get a tune out of it. You need to get some flesh onto those bones. I've seen more meat on a butcher's pencil.'

Betsy smiled. 'Ma, can you leave us alone?'

Hope left the room quietly.

'My baby died,' Betsy said tearfully as soon as the door closed. She gripped the oilcloth. She could feel sobs forming in her throat, but she swallowed them down. 'It was awful, Deirdre.'

'I heard. All those ambulancemen who died. And other mothers like you.'

'Nurses as well . . .'

'What happened?'

Betsy dropped her head in her hands and crushed her fists into her eyes. It occurred to her that this was the first time she was talking out loud about the detail of that terrible night. 'No one really knows. But the blast was terrible. One minute everyone was shouting and then it all went black. I remember my lungs feeling as if they were on fire when I breathed, and then I woke up in Fazakerley Hospital. Hitler hit us bad. A nurse was taking Vernon down to the basement . . . so we were separated . . . and . . . and . . . Well, do you know what the worst thing is? My ma said it was just as well that my baby died. I know she doesn't mean it, but I can't get those words out of my head . . .'

'Everyone's coming out with such rubbish. War does that to you. My ma calls our neighbour a filthy traitor because he's Italian, even though he's been giving her sausages for thirty years. Thinks he's going to poison us.'

'She says why can't I just move on with my life? It's just God's plan. Like losing a baby is not such a big thing around here.'

'The woman next door to us got the measles and the baby died. They always say that. Jesus's mystery. Or that the next baby you have will be part of the baby that died and such rot . . .'

'Tell me about everything. What's been going on? I've missed you, Deirdre.'

'Well, the Ink Spots have a new record. Kind of dreamy. It's called "I Don't Want to Set the World on Fire" . . .'

'Unlike flaming Hitler, who's wanting to set us on fire every flipping night.'

'And Glen Miller is making a hell of a noise with his band and storming into my heart.'

'What about your Gary Cooper?'

'Gary's still my number one. Look, will you let me take you dancing? The Rialto is busier than ever. They keep going even when the sirens sound. The band mistress just puts a tin hat on and everyone cheers.'

Betsy shook her head wanly. 'I couldn't possibly do anything like that. Deirdre, have you heard from Alvis?'

'No, I haven't. And I don't like it that you're asking. Now, come on. Tomorrow I'm coming to find you and we're going dancing. Even if it's just to knock back a couple of drinks and lean against the rail listening to the music and watching with the rest of the wallflowers. You need to get out of here. Need a bit of a run outside to get you all rosy-cheeked again.'

'I know.'

'And you need to get away from your mother. So, talking of that, I have another idea.'

'What idea?'

'I'll tell you tomorrow. Make sure you put a decent frock on. That yellow one you used to wear with the pink ribbons? I want you out of those drab clothes. You promise?'

Idea? thought Hope, listening behind the door, her ear pressed hard to it. What idea? Ideas were dangerous. She hadn't invited Deirdre here to bring Betsy ideas. She had invited her to cheer her up. What stupid idea was Deirdre putting into Betsy's head?

Betsy and Deirdre stood in the queue that snaked all around the outside of the Rialto. When they finally went inside, they were hit by the sound of music and a veil of smoke hanging low over the dancers moving around to a Glen Miller song.

'Let's get a table. Dandelion and burdock and a sweet sherry?' said Deirdre.

She returned with four glasses wobbling on a tray.

'It's good to be here,' said Betsy, sipping her drink.

'Music helps you forget, love. Drink the sherry through the straw and it gets you drunk quicker.'

'I've missed this. I can't stand it at home. Ma makes me go to church all the time, as if somehow confession will make a difference. It just makes me feel worse. She wants me to say sorry to God for doing it with Alvis, sorry for giving my baby to that nurse. I don't. When I confess, I just tell the priest that I'm sorry I didn't help with the coal scuttle. I would never tell him anything more than that. I don't trust him. I just don't know what to do.'

'I told you I've got an idea.' Deirdre paused for effect. 'I'm going along to Renshaw Street tomorrow. Read this. I brought it for you.'

Deirdre took a pamphlet out of her pocket, unfolded it and pushed it over to her side of the table. 'They need girls. You could be a Land Girl. Or a Wren. The RAF as well. It means you would have to go away.'

Betsy scanned the words: '*Join the Wrens and free a man for the fleet . . . Come and help with the Victory Harvest . . .*'

'You even get paid. It will be our way of getting out of here. Betsy, isn't that what you want? A change?'

'Away? Where to?'

'They could send you anywhere. Gloucester. Or Lincolnshire. But even Morecambe would be far away enough to escape from your mum making you do your rosary and sending you to church to cleanse your sins. Morecambe is by the sea. You could go paddling on your day off. Buckets and spades and pin the tail on the donkey.'

Betsy's eyes widened. She was imagining golden sands and a pier that stretched all the way to the middle of the sea, rippling sand like crumpled washing, and candy floss. She scanned the pamphlet. And straight away she was gripped with excitement. All she could think of was escape. This would change everything. She would never forget the tragedy of her baby but if she could stand on a beach with fresh air and the salt stinging her eyes, maybe, just maybe . . .

'So, we just have to go to Renshaw Street?' she said, leaning forward and sucking through the straw with a new energy coursing through her veins. 'Then I'm coming with you, Deirdre. I'll not tell Ma for now. But I'm coming.'

The following day, Betsy left the house quietly. Her mother had been looking at her with narrowed eyes all morning and she didn't want her firing questions, so she waited until Hope had left for work at the wash-house. Deirdre helped with the forms and took her down to the town hall, clutching her hand in hers. Betsy was amazed at how quickly they were nodded through and told to stand in a line. From there she had to sign a form, and then another. A woman with sturdy legs looked her up and down when she got to the front of the queue. 'You look like you might be a strong girl if you were fed properly. What is it? Land Girls? You come as a pair?'

'Wrens,' Deirdre said hopefully.

'Always the Wrens,' said the woman, smiling. 'Fancy yourself in the uniform? It's the red lipstick seals the deal, isn't it?'

'No,' stuttered Betsy.

'Hoping to get out of Liverpool then? It's not a crime. Plenty of others like you. Wanting to get away from a boy? Your family? Still, if you are prepared to do your bit, what's the harm? Now, you start with quite menial tasks. You won't be going to the same place, though. You do understand? You'll make new friends. But you can't go together. It's not a picnic.'

'I don't care,' said Betsy. 'When can I start? But please, ma'am. It's the WAAF I'd like to join.'

'Oh, really? Why's that? Don't say the hat. Or was it the poster with the handsome pilot – "*Serve in the WAAF with the men who fly*"? I'd like to know who thought that one up.'

'No. I'm good at maths. I worked at Cunard's in the accounts office. This pamphlet says they need girls to be radar and wireless operators.'

'She's a regular boffin,' interjected Deirdre.

'We'll see. Can you get me a reference from Cunard's? If you do that, I'll put you down for the WAAF. All being well, you'll get a buff envelope. OHMS, it will say on the front. Wherever you are posted you will have to do training camp. The WAAFs' camp is in Wilmslow. Good luck, girls. I can't promise you anything. But thank you for doing your bit. This will be an adventure and a change of scenery, that's for sure.'

*

'Where did you go? What are you up to?' asked Hope when Betsy walked in the door.

'Don't be cross.'

'Just tell me.'

'Ma, I went to Renshaw Street. To volunteer.'

'I guessed.' She stared ahead silently.

The words tumbled out about WAAFs and uniforms and fresh starts. 'We just need a reference from Cunard's. Please, Ma.'

Hope shivered. 'But it's so soon after . . .'

'It's what I need. And it's a job. You get paid. Imagine! I can send money home, Ma.'

Hope sighed. 'Is there any point in me saying you can't?'

Betsy beamed and flung her arms around her mother. And it occurred to Hope that it was the first time she had seen her smile in months.

'Are you angry, Ma?'

Her mother stood and took her hand, turned it over in hers and sighed. 'And why would I be angry? I'm proud of you, Betsy. I think it'll be the best thing for you. You can't stay locked in here for ever. We both need a change. You need to get out of here. And it might . . . well . . .'

Betsy screwed up her face. 'Ma, please don't say it'll help me forget.'

Her mother pushed a tendril of her hair behind her ear. 'Love, you'll never forget. But don't you understand? I just want you to be happy. That's all I've ever wanted. I just want you to live your life and be free. Without it being messed up by a man. Please God you'll not make the same mistake again.'

Betsy pulled her collar right up to her chin and dropped her head, sighing audibly.

'I wish I . . . I wish . . .'

'Shush, love. You know, I think it was my fault. If I had told you about what happens when a man and a woman . . . I think that's really the most difficult part. I thought the nuns would take care of it. Maybe with rabbits in biology lessons. But even so.'

Betsy winced.

'Anyway, now you've learned the hard way, so you don't need me to tell you. But Betsy, if you're going away . . . there'll be men, Betsy. Handsome men. And given you now know how dangerous a handsome man is . . . Especially in the RAF. God help us . . . If . . . when . . . things . . . you start to feel . . . like you're getting carried away . . . that's when you say no.'

Betsy put her hands over her ears. 'Stop . . .'

'Good God. I'm just being realistic. Are you listening, Betsy? Men only want one thing. So wait until you've got a ring on your finger next time. I just want you to have a life. Otherwise, you'll be stuck with another Alvis. You deserve better. You deserve someone who loves you. And a proper wedding in a white dress. And you're my daughter. I don't want people looking at you as though you're some kind of slut. Because I know you're not. You're my precious daughter and you're a good girl. You're an innocent girl. Too innocent. It wasn't your fault that that this terrible thing happened to you. I want at least for this new start to be the chance for you to be happy.'

Betsy looked at her mother, whose face was screwed

up in anguish. Her mother who loved her. Her mother who was kind and good and only wanted the best for her.

Six weeks later, after sitting by the door every morning, Betsy picked up the letter on the mat and read the words on the front of the buff envelope that she had been so desperately waiting for. *OHMS. On Her Majesty's Service.*

> *19th October 1941*
>
> *Dear Betsy Drew,*
>   *You have been posted to Wilmslow RAF on 16th November for training. Please find enclosed your train tickets. You will be met by an officer and an RAF vehicle at Wilmslow station. On arrival at the camp you will be given your hat, your number and your rank. You will spend six weeks training and then you will be allocated, according to your skills, to one of the operational RAF bases, from where you will continue your training and see active service.*

She dropped the letter. 'Oh, Ma. This is so exciting.' Her mother paused from sweeping the floor. She came over to where Betsy was now sat in the rocking chair and placed her hand gently on the crown of Betsy's head.

'Freedom, Ma,' Betsy said wistfully as she pressed the envelope to her chest and squeezed her eyes shut.

And she wished her mother too would find peace away from these bombed-out, dust-choked streets and the great sadness that lately, Betsy had noticed, was slowly hollowing her out from the inside.

Chapter 11

James Swann set off down the track, which underfoot he could feel gradually changing from soil to cinder as he approached the woods. The sky was bulking up with clouds, but it was still spotted with patches of blue. The autumn sunshine lit the path. Craning his neck and shielding his eyes, he looked up to see a plane overhead. The distinct buzzing sound told him it was a Spitfire before he saw it. The thought that in less than six months it might be him up there made him bristle with excitement. He moved between the hissing trees that had been planted out in distinct lines. The wind was stronger. Heading back towards the barracks, which were situated at the end of the path, he took a cigarette out of his pocket and dragged on it hard.

James had arrived at the training camp six weeks earlier after two months at Manchester University, having been schooled in classes that had taught him every technical part of flying. That first day he had been excited to stand in line and have the needle jabbed into the top of his arm for his vaccination, and he had happily allowed the doctor to press a cold stethoscope against his chest. Stepping on the scales, he hadn't minded when a young, big-boned volunteer standing next to him smirked; he was used to being called puny by the boys at school. But he wasn't puny, he was just lithe, tall and rangy, and no matter what he ate his body didn't change. At his boarding school – a minor public school on the outskirts of the city – they had thought him effeminate, but he wasn't. Just because he didn't like thrashing a boy younger than him didn't make him a girl. Nor did it make him a girl because he hated the rows of lavatories that had no doors on them, or the cold floors and frozen flannels. It certainly didn't mean he danced up the other end of the ballroom like he was teased. There had been a few lads in line that morning of the first medical in the training camp being checked by the medics who objected to being touched. 'Manhandling me crown jewels!' one lad had had cried and another had started laughing and squirmed away, protesting that he was ticklish.

'You really think you're cut out for this, boys?' The doctor had raised an eyebrow.

They were all volunteers here in the camp. All equal when they arrived, but the exams and tests and fitness checks to progress to flying a plane were not easy. These lads had probably ruled themselves out that first day. There had followed hours of square bashing, lessons and tutorials. James knew the rudiments, you couldn't help picking it up in a family like his – he already knew how to fly his father's Tiger Moth – and after just a week he had passed his exams and quickly moved to the next stage. But it was also the menial tasks that gave James pleasure and he threw himself into cleaning bicycles, tightening nuts and bolts on engines, polishing bits of metal. He hoped he would be pinned for serving as a pilot, though. He longed to get up in the air and be taught how to fly the unwieldy Manchester bombers. He enjoyed the comradeship; he didn't mind the lads ribbing him for his accent. To be free of his mother with her annoying habits – picking up a discarded tie the minute he dropped it or getting Gordon to iron his shoelaces, starch his collar – felt like a weight off his shoulders. He was surprised by how much joy he found in shining his own shoes and washing his clothes or making his bed.

It was early evening and he was making his way down the path, over the field through the camp gate, towards the huts and past the mess. He would have preferred to go back to the hut and swot up for the exam he had to do the following week but the young sergeant had opened the mess door wide. He was hit by the pungent smell of French cigarettes and the sound of raucous laughter. 'Swann! You coming in?' said a corporal who poked his head out and shouted after him.

James faltered. Why not? he thought. 'First Friday night bevvy?' said the sergeant.

He must have seen the surprised look on his face, thought James. It was something that would be noted by the fellows in the hut if he were to skip it. When he went in the WAAFs, dressed in their uniforms, were moving freely amongst the men, drinking, and some of them smoking like sailors. During the day they were mostly kept separate. He noticed a few of them were even sitting on some of the chaps' knees. One had her head inclined into a young airman's chest with her legs astride him as he tried to make a tower of cards on a table.

After buying a half-pint of shandy at the bar, he

made his way towards a small table with two other sergeants. There were small dimly lit lamps with red tasselled shades dotted about on the green baize-covered tables.

The corporal who had called him in came over to him and clapped his hand around his shoulder.

'Pull up a chair, Swann . . .'

James looked at the chair, and the deck of cards on the table, and back at one of the lads who was now patting the seat. There was a pause and when he sat down there was a small cheer of approval.

'What we playing? Gin rummy?' asked one of the sergeants, shuffling the pack.

'Strip poker?' said the corporal.

James looked shocked. The other men laughed. One of them whistled. 'Hey, Swann. Know how to play? It's just like poker, but you wager your clothes. What'll you take off first?'

The lads started to clap and bang the table.

'Ha! Got yer, pal! Your face! Strip poker! We wouldn't get away with that here. In the navy, maybe. Not in the air force. Maybe those bars in Cairo.' He slapped his thigh and guffawed then swivelled in his chair. 'Maybe if you took Swann back to your ma's back parlour, hey, Judy?' he called to the girl serving behind the bar.

'Gerraway with yer!' she joked back.

'Come on. Let's deal. Gin rummy.'

'I'm not sure how to play that. I might sit this one out,' James said with a smile, drinking his glass of shandy in one go.

'Come on, be a sport, pretty boy! What's your party piece?'

'You have to have a party piece,' said a second sergeant with a wide grin. 'Then you can have a place at the poker table.' He leaned into him and spoke into his ear. 'Don't worry, you won't lose the family silver. We only play with pennies.'

'I can whistle through me nose and Jock here can play the bagpipes,' said the corporal. 'Come on . . .'

'I can play the piano backwards,' James offered.

The sergeant snorted. 'Now, that's one thing I'd like to see. Hey, fellas!' He shoved his fingers in his mouth and whistled. 'Swann here can play the piano backwards.'

'Let's hear!' someone cried. Another person stood on a chair and began to clap.

'Anyone got any requests?' James asked. Laughter ricocheted around the room.

'"The Deepest Shelter in Town"!' one of the lads at the back called out.

'Keep it clean, Degsy, there's ladies here.'

'Some of these ladies could make a sergeant major blush,' came the reply.

One of the girls, huddled with three others, threw back her head and smiled, revealing white teeth. 'You play it, I'll sing it. Do you know "Kiss Me Goodnight, Sergeant Major", lover boy?' she said, wandering over to James, pulling up a chair and resting her elbows on the table and her chin in her palms.

He felt himself blushing. Always with the damned blushing.

'Ha-ha, look, he's gone all shy. Come on, let's go over to the piano give it a try . . .'

James stood up and headed over. At first, after slowly lifting the lid, he sat down facing the keys and cracked his knuckles nervously. But then he swivelled around so that he was sitting with his back to the piano and, searching with his hands, found the chords he was looking for and gave a short trill. A shout went up when they recognized the tune.

'That's pretty impressive,' said the sergeant.

Everyone laughed when he played the introduction. The girl then climbed onto her chair, cleared her throat and began to sing. Almost immediately everyone joined in. Some clapped their hands and stamped their feet. One lad at the back had produced a mouth organ from his pocket and began to blow on it. The girl placed her hands on her hips as her voice soared. James smiled. He felt something he had never felt before. What was it? Belonging?

'Go on, Cochrane, give it the full belt. Come on in, everyone. Bloody marvellous, lads! You, young Swann fella, are a diamond!' cried the corporal.

James looked up and smiled at him. But when he lifted his hands again, they hovered momentarily over the keys. Two girls were standing at the back, peering in through the door. One of them was tall with flaming red hair. And the other . . . she was small . . . and . . . blonde . . . He recognized her from somewhere.

'Keep going, pal!' shouted Judy, the girl from behind the bar.

He turned around to face the piano, and by the time he had finished and twisted around again, the two girls had gone. All he could see was a throng of more people pushing to the bar, and he wondered if he had imagined it.

Chapter 12

The morning before she left the tenements, Betsy had looked at herself in the cracked mirror on the hall landing, stained and blotted with rust. Putting a small hat on, she pinned it at a jaunty angle, the way Deirdre had taught her. Deirdre had kissed her goodbye the night before and said, 'Words from the wise. There'll be plenty of dancing at the camps, so don't forget what I taught you about the hips, and use a bit of twig and some soot to draw a line down the back of your legs. The boys go wild for that. They lay bets trying to see who's wearing stockings and who's not. If you need rouge, pinch your cheeks.'

Betsy had replied, 'I'm not doing this for the boys.'

'I am!' Deirdre had laughed.

When she finished getting dressed, she took a deep breath. She came into the kitchen and stood at the door for a moment.

'I'm ready to go, Ma.'

But her mother was standing with her back to her at the sink.

'Ma, turn around and look at me.'

Hope just coughed and said quietly, 'I'm proud of you, Betsy. I am. You've had to deal with such things already and you're so young. But this is the fresh start you need.'

And she continued to plunge her hands into the soapy water and prayed her daughter might find the happiness she deserved.

Eight hours later, a smiling girl in uniform met her off the van that pulled up outside the camp.

'Hello there! It's my job to show you where you're staying for now. We call each other by surnames here so I'm Lovelady, but my first name is Phyllis. Soon you will be Drew and it'll be your rank and six-digit number that everyone will know you by, not Betsy.'

It had been a bumpy ride and Betsy had sat on the bench that ran down the middle of the van, which was the worst possible place to be, as they negotiated potholes and swung violently around corners and along the bends of the country lanes. She had been overtaken by nerves, looking at the list in her pocket repeatedly to calm herself down. Pencil, sanitary belt and towel, toiletries, hairbrush, toothbrush. To add to her worries, Betsy had also arrived a little late – there had been an incendiary on the road outside Lime Street station. The girl that had met her off the bus had told her not to worry, unlike the sergeant taking names who had shouted at her for not being on time. The fresh air filling her lungs as she walked through the gates of the camp had made her feel calmer.

'Come on, let's drop off your bag. Vaccination and medical first stop after that for your FFI. Free From Infection . . .' Phyllis explained. 'And then pick up your uniform and kit bag.'

After leaving her bag on the small iron bed with the three small mattresses that she was told were called biscuits, then hanging her outer coat on a peg and putting her holdall on a shelf, she made her way to the small outhouse for her nit check and vaccination.

'The medics are pretty stern. No place for being bashful either, I warn you, love.' Half an hour later, after having stripped down to her bra and knickers and then been weighed – *bit skinny, aren't you?* – then checked for nits – *good, no dinner dance in this one's head* – Betsy made her way back to the registration hut. She hadn't used shampoo in months, just Omo flakes when she had needed to, and she was relieved to have a clean scalp.

'You were late . . .' said a rather dour, sturdy-looking woman standing at the door of the hut with a clipboard, who handed her a knife, a fork, a spoon, a mug and a large overcoat. The woman was wearing an immaculately ironed uniform. Her shoes were polished and she had a wide belt with a shining silver clasp. Uniforms, maybe because of the nuns' terrifying black habits, frightened Betsy.

'There was an incendiary near Lime Street,' Betsy started to say, wondering how word had got to her.

'I don't want to hear. Don't let it happen again.' Betsy wondered how she could have stopped the delays while the ARP scoured the road with buckets of sand looking for debris from the device. But she supposed this was a lesson in learning not to speak back, and she'd had years of practice of that with the nuns.

'Go to bed. I hear there's larks in the mess tonight, but steer clear as you need an early night.'

Phyllis had waited for her outside. They headed towards the hut. As they passed the far building, the sound of music and laughter rose into the air. 'Have a peek in there,' said Phyllis. 'It's the mess. There's a bit of a do on tonight.' She walked forward and opened the door. Betsy's eyes widened as she saw a few couples swirling around the floor and a group gathered around a fellow at the piano. 'Looks like they're having a good night . . .' Phyllis said, leading her away.

They went into the hut. The room felt welcoming. There were fourteen beds, and a fire at one end. 'Choose which bed you want. Those three are spare and two other girls will be arriving soon.' As soon as she sat down on the edge of the bed, one of the girls came over and offered to show her how to arrange her kit at her station. There were a few girls huddled around the fire at one end. They nodded a hello but were distracted, getting ready to go to the mess. One of them was sticking a knife into the fire and then smearing it over her shoes.

'Trying to make them look like they're patent leather,' Phyllis explained. Another was pulling her belt in as tight as humanly possible.

Phyllis laughed. 'She won't be able to breathe, let alone play tonsil tennis.' Lights out were at ten. 'Tomorrow, they'll show you how to pack a parachute.'

Betsy had a thick wad of papers to read which laid out rules, instructions, a map of the camp and categories of jobs she might be designated for. 'No one reads that. You just go where you're told,' said Phyllis. But Betsy was happy to sit on the bed propped up against the rock-hard pillow stuffed with horsehair and study them. A few of the other girls came over to her on their way out, all friendly, all helpful, showing her how to make her station her own, asking her where she was from. Exhausted, she pulled the thin sheet over her and fell asleep straight away on the small narrow bed.

When she woke up to the sound of a bell ringing, her arm was throbbing from the needle. It was red and sore. The girl in the bed next to hers leaned over.

'Ooh, love. That looks painful. Make sure you hold your arm high, though. Sergeant Spam . . . Look out for Spam, face like a docker's boot – Pam is her first name, but one of the girls came up with Spam because she goes as pink as a tin of Spam when she loses her temper. Anyway, Spam won't hold back from whacking it in square bashing. And you'll want a pair of boots for the marching. But choose the battered ones, not the new ones. They're less likely to give you blisters. They'll be softer.'

Betsy wasted no time and went straight down to the hallway. There was already a queue of girls standing outside Spam's office. One of them was loudly telling everyone that she didn't like the hat that the Wrens wore. 'It wouldn't suit my head. My head's flat at the back. And I don't like the khaki colour of the army. It doesn't match my eyes. I need to wear bold colours. So here I am. WAAF blue's my colour.'

Moving away behind a curtain after she was given her uniform, Betsy ran a finger over the creases of the navy serge, touching the buttons tenderly, pressing her palms against it. She lifted it to her face and breathed in the smell and luxuriated in the newness of it. She could barely remember wearing something that hadn't been darned or stitched, taken in or let out. Her mother even made her wear clothes that her brother had worn, his old grey school jumpers unravelled and then knitted into another old grey jumper that always made her wonder why she had even bothered in the first place. Putting it on, she came out and handed over her civvy dress and shoes to be posted back home, and made her way to collect her heavy lace-up shoes, thankful for the tip. Square bashing was first thing on the rota after a breakfast of lukewarm porridge in the canteen.

'What are you hoping for? Radar? Balloons?' said the girl slurping porridge beside her.

She replied that she didn't know but that she suspected whatever she ended up doing would be something to do with her work at Cunard's.

'It doesn't always work out that way. We had one girl here who was a wizard at touch typing and office work. But they put her to work in the kitchen because she cooked a tasty scouse stew. Once you're done here, they'll send you anywhere in the country. You leave knowing how to salute, all the ranks, parachute packing, square bashing, nuts and bolts, mechanics. Good with your hands, are you?'

'I'll do whatever they ask.'

'That's the spirit. Oh, and they might give you a bicycle. That's how we get around here as it's a pretty big place. If you have to go and fetch some piece of kit or a bit of clobber, it's quite a distance. When you choose a bike, tie a ribbon around it so you'll remember it's yours. You'll like it here. It's a baptism by fire, but if you keep your head down and do what you're told, you'll enjoy it.'

*

Half an hour later, as the girls made their way out to the far corner of the field where they would be going through their drills on the forecourt, all she could think of was to keep her arms shoulder high and stand at the back and hope she would go unnoticed.

'New girl. Come out to the front,' barked the sergeant. She really did have a face like a docker's boot. 'Take your place where I can see you.' Betsy stepped forward nervously. The woman walked up to her and stood as close to Betsy as she could. Betsy could feel her sour breath on her cheek as she shouted, 'RIGHT TURN. By the centre, quick march . . . Left, right, left, right . . . Swing your arms, ladies. Swing your arms shoulder high front and rear. Squad halt! Into line, left turn.' Even though Betsy was feeling timid she tried not to show it, copied everyone as best as she could, spinning on her heel, stamping in time and shouting. When they were dismissed, she felt relieved to have come out of it unscathed. Phyllis took her hand and gave her a squeeze. 'Well done,' she said. 'You got through it. I think she likes you.'

'Thanks, Lovelady,' Betsy replied.

As they headed towards the row of Nissen huts, some of the girls were untangling parachutes in the sunshine outside standing at long, wide trestle tables. The silk billowed as they spread the parachutes all the way from one end to the other. They were to examine them for holes and pass them to another group of girls waiting to stitch them up. As the wind lifted the floating gossamer, Betsy thought how beautiful it all looked, and how fragile. It seemed a miracle that this delicate material was the difference between a man's life and death. Life really was hanging by a thread.

'Rodrigues there, Olga – she came over from the West Indies to volunteer – has a nifty line in making scanties with the left-over parachute silk. You and me are peeling spuds.'

Half an hour later Betsy sat at the bench next to Phyllis peeling potatoes with a bowl between her legs. She noticed some of the girls' fingers were already raw and chilblained.

Rodrigues approached, swinging a trug of broad beans and plonking herself down on the bench. 'Budge up. I'm going to give you some advice, dear.'

'About pea shelling?'

'No, not about peas, Drew. What happens to you next. Decide now what you want to do in the WAAF – radar, wireless operator, telephones . . . Tell them and then you'll have half a chance of knowing where you're transferred. Remustered, they call it. Or at least have an idea. What I really want to do is fly.'

'I didn't know girls could fly?'

'Just delivering the planes from one RAF base to another, but even so. It's my dream. Who knew a little girl from Guyana could have such dreams? What's yours?'

'I don't know.'

'Everyone has a dream, Betsy. That one over there wants to operate the telephones in the head office just so she can spend all day behind the desk making eyes at an officer. Mind you, part of her job will be calling some poor boy's parents to say they should expect to hear difficult news from the top brass. The mothers and fathers all know about that awful call. That's the one they dread. I wouldn't fancy that.'

'Kind of sad. Not worth it, even to bag an officer,' said Phyllis.

'And whilst we're on the subject, don't you go falling in love with any of these airmen, dear. It's all fine and dandy dancing with them and sitting on their knee in the mess. But you fall in love and then that same man you're head over heels with gets sent off to another camp, starts ops and doesn't come back at all. Ever again. And that's awful.'

'Almost as bad, though, is if he does come back, and then a week later he's going to see his fiancée waiting for him back home. Happened to a girl here again last week. She thought her lovely man was going to marry her. She gave up everything for him, didn't she, Rodrigues? If you know what I mean?' Phyllis said and winked at Betsy. 'I'm telling you this because you look so innocent, and I'm already worried for you. Your face is too pretty. That lass gave him her cherry, but he left her with a bun in the oven and a whole lot of heartache.'

Betsy blushed.

'They're just so bloody handsome in their uniforms, that's the trouble. Even the plain ones, and when they're in those sheepskin jackets with the collars turned up, smoking, and all their badges and their wings down their arms . . . irresistible, aren't they? You got a sweetheart at home? If you have, keep it that way.'

Betsy felt her heart lurch. Olga Rodrigues saw it in her face as she shot the peas into the bucket.

'What's the matter, dear? You look like you're

worrying about something. Do you have a secret? What are you running from? A man? Your mother? One dead-end job after another? Don't want to say?'

This one had soulful eyes, Olga thought. They were a little sad. Like some others here, probably escaping from some heartache.

Chapter 13

Betsy had surprised herself settling in so quickly. It was a sunny Friday morning and she smiled as she saw a girl trying desperately to hold on to a blimp.

'Keep it tight. Keep it on the ground!' the sergeant yelled, as she struggled to do so and her feet lifted off the floor. He ran over, laughing, and grabbed the rope. 'Only teasing,' he said. 'It's impossible.'

Betsy smiled to herself. She had soon grown accustomed to the jokes as well as the dry-tasting meals, the uncomfortable hard mattresses and pillows, and the men's trousers they were made to wear sometimes with the tin buttons that pinged off when they sat down. Spam was still calling her out of line and giving her a glass of milk along with all the other young WAAFs to show them all who the teenagers were. And she had made friends with Lovelady and Rodrigues. It was true, no one called anyone by their first names, and she was beginning to feel more like a Drew than a Betsy. Most afternoons she spent in class, and there was an exam every fortnight and each time she had passed with flying colours. It was Christmas Day in two days' time, but the war didn't stop for Christmas – there had been news of terrible bombing in Liverpool – and even though there was a tree and a

116

promise of turkey for lunch, things went on as usual. That evening, after another long day, she sat down on her bed and, like the other girls, began to write her letter.

Dear Deirdre,

Happy Christmas, friend. This is about the best thing that I've ever done in my life. The first week was a bit of a shock, and I spent the whole time peeling potatoes. But they've told me that my job is to untangle the parachutes, and even darn patches where they have been snagged or torn, and after nearly six weeks, though I'm getting used to it, it still feels like a heck of a responsibility. The boys here are as you'd expect – quite dashing, most of them. They smoke an awful lot, and they like a drink. We are all excited to see where we will be sent next – hopefully I will go to an operational bomber station. They've said I might be good on the radar or in the tower because of my work at Cunard's.

I've heard a few stories from some of the girls about the RAF fighter squadrons, and of course the tragedy is always much worse if it's one of the girls' sweethearts who hasn't come back. Wait till you see me in my uniform. We have to keep them so tidy and polish our buttons and shoes with a button stick and Duraglit every night. Perhaps when I come back on leave, we'll go to the Rialto and I'll even get my dance card filled. I hope everything

*is grand in the Wrens and I hope your ma will
forward this letter. Who thought a war would
make me feel alive finally? Is it wrong to say
that, when already so many people have died?
They've told us Liverpool is still being bombed.
You'd think after what happened at Mill Road
Hospital Hitler would be so ashamed he
wouldn't have the nerve to hurt us any more,
but no such luck.*

    *Betsy. Or I should say AC1 – Aircraftwoman
One – 491032*

The next day – Christmas Eve – and James was
standing in the winter sun behind a trestle table on
the forecourt doing something with an engine and a
monkey wrench. He was so engrossed at first that he
didn't see the officer watching him.

'Sergeant Swann . . . We heard you might be playing
the piano in the mess tonight. Christmas carols? I'm
hoping for "Winter Wonderland". I believe you're rather
good. And you can play backwards, I hear. Splendid!'

James squinted up and pushed his hair back and
nodded. The man with broad shoulders and a bundle
of papers wedged under his arm thrust out a huge
hand. James wiped his hand on the oily cloth he had
been using to clean the nuts and bolts of the small
engine.

'If it cheers people up. Gets everyone in the Christmas
spirit,' said James, smiling.

'But you have other talents. I've been informed
you're making tremendous progress. And you've
flown before?'

'My father taught me, sir.'

The officer paused. 'Yes, Officer Swann. We all knew your father. Swann, let's hope this war is over by the time we get you up in the air. But I've a feeling it's going to continue for some time yet. And congratulations. Top marks. I've been watching you. You'll have your wings in no time. We need more airmen like you.'

'Thank you,' replied James.

'We just don't have the numbers to go against Hitler. Bringing them in from the Dominions now, so that helps, but even so. That's why we want to move you to Brough for your elementary training. Then as soon as we can, after that on to Dishforth for ops.' Just then a group of rowdy sergeants came barrelling along carrying rusty rifles under their arms. 'Off you go with your pals. I'll see you later. But you'll be an asset at Dishforth. It's in Yorkshire. Your test scores are all excellent.' He nodded goodbye and walked off in the direction of the operators' huts.

'Winco is obviously impressed with you,' one of the ground crew said, clapping an arm around James's shoulder after throwing an oiled rag at him playfully. 'Is it because you're a toff? As long as you don't think you're better than us erks. We're all the same here, Jimbo. No matter what school we went to. Mind if I call you Jimbo?'

James smiled back. He had had a lot worse insults hurled at him at his boarding school than Jimbo. Gaylord. Jim in the bin. Smelly Eggy.

When he went back to the job of polishing another one of the bolts from the crate the young boy took the cigarette out of his mouth and said, 'See you in the bar later? We've a good night planned.' He started to walk away, then turned back. 'I need you to do me a favour. Can you run the car into the village and get the banjo for tonight's dance? It's at the pub,' he said.

James stood in front of the grey-painted car and lit a cigarette. Inside the shed he could hear voices and the odd clanking sounds of men at work. He knew enough to know the car was an old Austin Eight, but it had seen better days. Eventually a man appeared and walked over.

'Keys,' he said, tossing the fob in James's direction. 'Don't push it too hard, but it'll get you into town.'

James looked at the keys in the palm of his hand, and then over at an impressive red Triumph Dolomite sports car parked a few feet away.

'What about that one?' he inquired hopefully.

'You'll be lucky,' the man chuckled. 'It may look decent, but it's about as much use as a chocolate teapot. Belongs to the wing commander and the big end has gone. He's not too happy.'

'Big end?'

The man looked at him then shook his head and sighed. 'You lot never know anything about the workings, do you? I doubt the wing commander ever checked the oil levels, and without oil the main bearings give out and the piston rods go on a loud trip around the engine block. Then it's goodnight and good luck.'

James nodded sagely. 'Still no idea what you're talking about, but I get the drift.'

Someone inside the shed swore loudly. The man's

tone altered. 'Don't worry, mate. We're all bloody playing at it these days. I signed up to be a pilot myself, but I didn't have your accent.'

James batted the comment aside, stubbed out his cigarette and slid into the car.

Less than three hundred yards away, Betsy was furtively opening the door of the accommodation block on the north side of the base. Her breath swirled in the cold air. She wheeled her bicycle out from the side of the building and climbed on. The saddle was still too high, but she would have to make do. She pedalled around the base perimeter until she reached the gate. The airman on guard raised his hand and slipped his rifle off his right shoulder. Betsy felt the bicycle shudder as she squeezed the brakes.

'You know I can't let you leave the base, miss. Don't know what you were thinking?' He was stern-faced.

'I was thinking I'll be back before anyone notices.'

The airman raised his rifle menacingly. 'I'll shoot you if you try to pass, miss.' They stared at each other for a few seconds.

Unmoved and still astride her bicycle, Betsy smiled at him. 'Be hard to shoot me, Sergeant, when your gun's made of wood.'

The airman lowered his weapon and sighed. 'Ah, play along, Bets? I remember how you never took your shots.' He was grinning now.

'So, how's my pal Deirdre doing?' asked Betsy. 'I just wrote to her.'

'My cousin is alive and well, thank you. At least that's what she said in her last letter.'

'That's good then. Now, open the gate, there's a love.'

He shouldered his wooden rifle and obediently crossed to open the gate.

'I'm off duty in an hour and a half; you'd better be back by then. Some of these fellas take it seriously.'

Betsy lifted the pedal up with her foot, winked at him and wheeled the bike out into the road. She swung her leg over, adjusted the bell that sat on the handle-bars and felt the hard cold brittleness of the leather saddle. Wobbling along, she squinted ahead. It was her turn to buy the tapioca tonight. How you could go from radar training, men's lives in your hands, to buying tapioca in the space of an hour, but she did what she was told.

James whistled as the little car bumped along and swerved around the corners of the lane with its high hawthorn hedges. It was a task, to collect a banjo for tonight's dance, but he didn't mind. Showing willing had got him noticed.

The car rattled over the loose gravel as he put his foot down on the accelerator. When he skidded to a halt, it was not a sudden movement, but more a gradual losing of power as the car began to go up an incline. He jammed the clutch into a lower gear, but it seemed to have no effect. 'Damn it, come on,' he moaned. He tried to rev the engine up. But the more he stamped on the pedal, the more it seemed to chug and splutter, until power was lost, and it diminished to nothing with a whimper.

Tiredly, he got out of the car and opened the bonnet,

sticking his head inside. It was getting dark now and he began to feel a soft drizzle on the back of his neck. Removing one of the spark plugs, he wiped his hand on his trousers and blew on it like he remembered his father doing. 'I thought it might be the big end,' he said, remembering the mechanic's comments.

He was peering inside when he heard a voice saying, 'Sir, AC1, 491032. Would you like me to get help, sir?' He turned round momentarily to see a fair-haired girl on a bicycle balancing with one foot on the ground, saluting smartly.

A little surprised, he nodded and then stuck his head back under the bonnet.

'I can go and get someone from the camp with another car to tow you back. Or is it some petrol that you need? I know a little bit about these cars. What do you think the matter is, sir?'

The girl had a pretty voice, he thought, but what on earth would she know about the workings of a car?

'I'd be grateful if you could get someone,' he replied.

The girl walked round to the front of the car. 'It's usually the carburettor.'

'I thought it might be the big end.'

'If it was the big end, it would have gone caput and ended with a bang. It sounds like it was the carburettor.'

He closed the bonnet and turned to look at her face on. 'You! I recognize you. You're the girl from Cunard's, aren't you? Miss Arithmetic. You did the ledgers. I thought I saw you in the doorway of the mess a couple of weeks ago. It *was* you!'

'Gosh!' she stuttered. 'James.'

For a moment he just stared at her. The last time he had seen her she had been so pale and wan. She was so strikingly pretty now that she had put a bit of weight on and had some colour in her cheeks.

'I'll tell them at camp. Whoever would have thought it?'

'Let me walk down the lane with you. I can still make the pub before it closes. It's not too far. So, Betsy. It is Betsy? How long are you here for?' he said as they walked along.

'Another couple of weeks. You?'

'Been here eight weeks, but I leave soon,' he said, a little crestfallen. 'They're posting me to Brough and then Dishforth to start flying. Have they brought you here because of your maths?'

'I don't especially know. I'm learning how to untangle the parachutes first.'

She was thinking how different he looked in the blue uniform with his brogue shoes and shiny buttons. More serious and handsome. And those little wings that would be soon sewn onto his shoulders.

'Betsy, tonight there's a Christmas dance. Will you be going?'

'Oh, I don't think so.'

He nodded seriously and tried not to show that he was disappointed. Wouldn't it have been wonderful to be walking with her by his side into the dance hall?

'They probably have plans for you, Betsy. And I hope our paths cross again. You look grand in that uniform.'

She blushed. 'It doesn't really fit properly.'

'You'd look grand in anything . . .'

His cheeks pinked.

'Does Dishforth mean you'll be flying bombing missions?'

'Yes. But it's mostly pamphlet drops at first. I promised my mother I won't get killed.'

She laughed. 'That's all right then.' She liked the way he smiled slowly, and his large blue eyes, his expansive hands.

'And I'm the kind of man to keep a promise.'

She nodded again and, head down, hurried off in the opposite direction.

When she got back to the hut, she took out the letter to Deirdre to finish it.

PS I met the boy from Cunard's! Remember, the sweet one I told you about? He looks handsome in his uniform, more like a man now than a boy. I've been warned not to go mooning over any of these fellas, which if you saw him, is a bit like being told not to fall to the ground if you jump off a wall. Anyway, he's leaving, so that's that. Shame. The one that got away.

PPS On another note, the one that ran away, Alvis. You'll be glad to know that the scales have fallen from my eyes. I wrote to him to tell him he should be ashamed of what he did to me, leaving me in the lurch, and denying he was the father of my baby. But of course, he didn't reply. He has a heart of stone. If only

I had realized earlier and listened to you. But I'm wiser now after what I've been through. I wouldn't get myself into such a mess next time.

PPPS And I don't need my mother to tell me how dangerous handsome men in uniforms are!

Chapter 14

Betsy looked around the office after finishing collecting the papers and pamphlets that had been scattered about the briefing room as she prepared to go back to the hut for the evening. She stared at the banks of wirelesses. Someone had draped a piece of tinsel around one. It was exciting to see how you could just plug them into the wall instead of lugging them around. No dragging them across the floor worrying that the battery acid would spill, like she was used to in the tennies. Life was so organized and well run here. The rules were there for a purpose. She made her way to the door, content to spend another night in revising even though everyone was getting excited about the dance.

When she arrived back at the hut, she was surprised to see Phyllis applying lipstick to her mouth that was so bright it looked like a red gash, and with her hair in rags piled up on the top of her head.

'Where have you been? Come on. Get your dancing shoes on for tonight.'

Betsy was confused. Olga, overhearing the exchange, started laughing. 'You thought because of Phyllis's lectures about not going near any of the boys, it would mean we'd be staying in tonight knitting? It's Christmas! Come on, let's get you ready. I've got a frock you can borrow. The neckline is a bit plunging, but we can always pluck a winter rose and stick it down your cleavage to save your modesty, dear.'

'What you need is a hip flask like this,' Maeve said, waving a small bottle and winking. 'You'll save yourself a few bob if you get a little whisky down your gullet. Duffy has smuggled in bottles of the stuff, and we bury them in the back field. Her da works in a distillery. It'll see you through the night.'

'She won't need that. She's pretty enough never to have to buy herself a drink and there'll always be someone there offering to pay for her,' laughed Olga.

Half an hour later they were walking arm in arm down the muddy track to the barrack's mess with Phyllis negotiating the potholes in her teetering heels, and Maeve picking her way between the puddles in her cream slingbacks.

'Look at you, Drew, in your flat shoes. It's a miracle how you seem to be able to look like a movie star without the help of a decent pair of heels. That's natural beauty, that is. A pair of boats on your feet and your legs still look shapely.'

As they stood queuing outside, they could hear a burst of activity as people ahead of them fell through the door. Before they knew it, it was their turn and they were heading to the bar, Phyllis and Maeve and Olga shouting and waving hello to friends they recognized.

The dance was already in full swing. The room was decorated with holly and ivy around the picture frames and paperchains looping across the ceiling. There was a three-piece band playing and a few people had already paired up and were swirling around the floor in time to the music, doing a foxtrot. Betsy thought it was a little like the Rialto, but everyone was better dressed, and the music, mostly Christmas songs like 'Jingle Bells' and 'Winter Wonderland', was less blowsy.

'Hello, lovelies,' said one of the sergeants, who was wearing a yellow paper hat and sitting on a high-back stool with a pint of beer resting on his knee, as they walked further into the throng. As Betsy's eyes became accustomed to the lighting, the silhouettes on the stage sharpened into focus and began to make sense as actual people, with actual features and faces and playing actual instruments. Another song started up. There was the crowd doing some kind of dance clicking their fingers, but then they all placed their hands on each other's hips and began crashing between the tables. Phyllis started to laugh.

'Well, that's ten minutes of my life I'll never get back, giving you all my good advice about steering clear of the posh fellas,' Phyllis said, nudging Betsy. 'What are you staring at? I can see from the way you're looking at lover boy playing the piano, you didn't listen to a word I said. You can't take your eyes off him. Trust me, he's exactly the type I told you to steer clear of. He's not banging out 'My Old Man Said Follow the Van', he's playing all those dreamy Cole Porter tunes. Which means his ma had the money to pay for him to learn. Which means he's posh and he'll be a pilot soon and . . . good grief . . . Is he? . . . Yes, he's looking straight at you, Betsy. I'd say you're done for.'

Maeve laughed, low, throatily and dirtily.

'No,' stuttered Betsy. 'I know him.'

'Even worse. I know him too. That's the fella who plays the piano backwards. You've not been here two minutes and already you have got some future officer making eyes at you.'

Betsy looked shocked. 'No,' she protested.

'Don't worry. No one's going to think badly of you. We're all taking a little bit of joy where we can find it. Devlin over there, she makes a beeline for every one of them smarmy types and I swear it's supposed to be the fellas with the notches on the bedpost. Good job we've got iron bedsteads here. She's awful loose. Still, no one really minds. Not like they would in civvy street.'

'They call this camp Satan's Mess down in the village. Some of them posh lads, they think ordinary working girls are easy. They think we're all loose. But I bet you've never even kissed a boy before, have you? I feel like I need to look after you, Betsy. You're kind of innocent, aren't you? And those big eyes. Your sweetness is something to hold on to. The fellas go crazy for it.'

Betsy was grateful that the room was dark enough not to see her blushes.

'And look! He smiled at you again, I'm sure of it.' Just then, the sheet music slid off the top of the piano and onto the floor. 'See, you got him all discombobulated.'

'Don't be silly,' said Betsy.

She turned away and didn't notice James jumping down from the stage and heading towards her.

'Good God, he's coming over, Betsy. And he's . . .'

Betsy twisted in her seat. He *was* smiling at her.

130

'You're here?' he said.

Betsy blushed.

'She is,' said Phyllis. 'Come on, Rodders, this is my favourite. I'll teach you how to foxtrot.'

'You think I don't already know?' laughed Olga as they both made their way to the floor.

'May I sit down?' asked James. Betsy nodded. 'I'm so glad to see you.'

'My friend Phyllis persuaded me to come.'

He pulled up a chair and placed his drink on the table. 'Terrific. It seems our paths keep crossing. But you disappeared so quickly from Cunard's, and then earlier you scurried off, so I'll have to nail you to that chair, won't I?'

'I had to leave Cunard's because our house was bombed,' she stuttered.

'Badly?'

'Pretty badly. I went to stay with a relative who lived in . . . Chester.'

'That's a nice part of the world.'

She nodded and rolled the plump part of her lip between her finger and forefinger, feeling a little awkward.

'I would have liked to have got to know you more, Betsy. I hope I still can. Perhaps I could take you for a drink at one of the local pubs one evening? Or we could meet up for a walk before I go? Somewhere quieter.'

'I'd like that,' she said. 'But you said you were going soon? To elementary school – Brough? Then Yorkshire . . .'

'Not straight away.'

James smiled. This girl had a sort of beautiful soulfulness with her blue searching eyes and the wild tangle of her blonde hair. But he didn't dare to reach out a hand and touch her even though he was desperate to.

Betsy, meanwhile, dropped her eyes to the table. *You don't know me*, she wanted to say. *And if you did . . .*

But he was standing now. And asking her to dance with him . . .

The next morning, Phyllis rolled over in her little bed, shouted, 'Happy Christmas, everyone!' and kicked her foot from under the blankets so that she was poking Betsy's hunched body. Betsy blinked awake but pulled the bedclothes over her head. She had slept fitfully, pushing the covers off her, hugging the pillow, turning it over onto its cool side, twisting the rough blanket. Now she was exhausted. Phyllis had woken her just as she had drifted off again but not being a girl to take kindly to being ignored, Phyllis picked up a hairbrush and, aiming it carefully, threw it at Betsy's head.

'Ouch,' cried Betsy.

'So come on, we want to hear the full story.'

Betsy drew her knees to her chest.

'What happened to you last night?'

'What do you mean?'

'You were dancing with that fellow all evening. Everyone noticed. He kept leading you towards the mistletoe. And then that was a nifty trick to get you turning over the pages of his music like that. You didn't leave his side.' She sighed. 'I don't blame you.'

'He's leaving,' said Betsy. 'I knew him from where I worked at Cunard's in Liverpool. He's just a friend.'

'That all sounds very mysterious.'

'No, it's not mysterious at all. We worked together briefly. But like I said, he's going soon.'

'That's just even more romantic and desperate. Did he kiss you? How tortuous and delicious.'

'No! Of course not.'

'You're lying. Olga saw you.'

'She's imagining it,' said Betsy, her cheeks flushing red and a heat rising from her toes to her head.

'It's nothing to be ashamed of. Maeve spent the whole night playing footsie and snogging with Sergeant Patterson, didn't you, love?'

Maeve groaned, clutching her head. 'Too many port wines . . . But you only live once,' she said with a yawn. 'Lovelady, you might be saving yourself for your little man in the hardware shop in Runcorn, but the way I look at it, what goes on in camp stays in camp.'

Betsy propped herself up on her elbows. 'Why aren't you taking your own advice?'

'I'm older and wiser and know how to handle a few knee-tremblers. But wait, do you think you'll end up courting blue eyes?'

'I shouldn't think so. Not unless we go back to Cunard's when this war is over. He said he'd put in a good word to get me moved to Dishforth but it's unlikely.'

'Remustered so soon? Jeepers, never heard of that. He's fallen hard and fast for you.'

'You *did* kiss him, didn't you?' said Phyllis, throwing a pillow at her.

'I'm not answering those questions any more,' she said, chucking the pillow back.

133

'There's more to our Betsy than untangling parachutes and peeling spuds. She's a dark horse . . . aren't you?'

Betsy didn't reply.

Half an hour later she made her way down to the courtyard, shivered off her exhaustion and blinked her eyes wide open, ready to square bash. Then she spent three hours sitting on hard wooden chairs, learning about radar and the operations room protocol, although they had no actual equipment to play with, just cardboard mock-ups marked with large, easy-to-read labels, which made the exercise seem rather pointless. Besides, her head was somewhere back on that dance floor, back when James's lips had grazed hers, back when he had pushed a tendril of her hair behind her ear, back when he had asked to meet her today at midday behind the bomb sheds.

'Drew? What's the matter with you this morning? Another casualty of last night's dance. I can always tell the ones. I hope he was worth it. But training camp is serious business. It isn't a holiday camp, or a dating agency. Now you'll come out here and you'll go through the salutes. And you'd better get it right.'

'Come on. We're untangling,' Maeve said breezily, half an hour later. 'But we could do with another pair of hands. My fingers are red raw from pushing a needle through the silk. You'd think it would be easy, the darning and the patching, but it's fine work and when the light goes, it hurts my eyes,' she said to Betsy as they walked across the quadrangle. 'You're awfully young. And I bet you've got a story to tell. In the meantime, that bloody parachute is waiting for us. Doesn't matter that it's Christmas Day.'

There were several outbuildings dotted about the field. Plumes of smoke rose from a few of them. Probably the wood stoves burning inside.

'Let's get our sewing kits and we'll find the other girls.'

A girl had put a few granules of coffee in a pan which she was bringing to the boil on top of the wood stove. She had one of those laughs that seemed to break through the noise of the crowded room and made people smile.

After picking up their sewing kits, they went down into the hangar, where they were laying out the parachutes on long trestle tables, checking for any weak points or repairs that needed doing. The silk billowed as they unrolled and unfurled them from the backpacks, and Betsy could feel air move about as they floated upwards. Removing her slide, she twisted her hair into a coil and re-pinned it. The room was light and airy, and they were helped with a burst of sunlight filling the lofty space. When they held them up to the large windows, the sunlight would show up any snags or tears in the silk. They soon built up a rhythm: unfurling, lifting, floating, folding and packing, and putting aside the parachutes that were beyond repair that they could stitch into silk camisoles and knickers.

'Drew?' said a voice at the door. She turned around. 'Come this way, please.'

It was the commander, Gayle, the one with the sturdy

legs and stern face, but her features seemed to have softened. 'After you've had your turkey and roast taters, we want to take you down to the data room. It might seem dull. But we need girls with an eye to detail. I've heard about your work at Cunard's. You just need to go through the list, checking, and checking again. Do you think you could do that?'

'I wasn't there too long, Sister . . . I mean . . . Officer . . .'

'Did you call me Sister?' She laughed.

'Sorry, Officer,' she replied, reddening.

'You were taught by nuns? We've had a couple of convent schoolgirls here. Butter wouldn't melt in their mouths. Then you find them shinnying a flagpole and hanging their drawers off the top of it. I bet you chucked the odd blackboard duster.'

'I do know some like that.'

She laughed. 'Drew, I don't care what you get up to in your private life and I'm not going to make you say Hail Marys. It's no one's business as long as it's not distracting you. And as long as it's not distracting any of the men here. Just remember you're here to do a job. And you're here to do it well. No mixing with the officers. No romance, not if you can help it. Understood? I know they all look like Cary Grant in their uniforms and those damned sheepskin jackets. God help us, they stride out to those planes like they were designed in heaven to be put on earth to save us. But turn the other way. Imagine them picking their noses or sitting on the privy after Airman Crossley's rock-hard Christmas pudding.'

Betsy smiled weakly.

'You seem a sensible kind of girl, unlike some of the ones around here. Chop chop, enjoy your lunch, then let's get you to the map room.'

An hour later, after turkey and sprouts in the mess, Betsy's finger was sore from running down the margins and her pencil was blunt. She enjoyed the chatter, but the woman sergeant sitting at the front desk tapping a pen on her inkwell would shush them when the talk got louder, and then the room would quieten down again.

'Drew, will you take these down the corridor?'

A minute later, Betsy was walking towards the office. 'James!' she exclaimed, when she saw him making his way towards her.

'Betsy, I found you! Happy Christmas! Listen, I can dip in a few minutes. They've let us finish early. Meet me on the low wall behind the bomb sheds. Far side of the field?'

'All right,' she said. 'Only Gayle, she told me to steer clear . . . of you . . .'

'Me?'

'Well, officers . . .'

He raised an eyebrow. 'So not me, strictly speaking. I'm still a sergeant.'

She smiled. He touched her fingers and curled his around hers.

'Sergeant Swann!' yelled a sergeant striding towards them.

Betsy withdrew her hand as quickly as if she had just stuck it into a fire.

'That's Flight Officer Dixon. We have to go through

feedback after last night's practice raid. He's a good chap but he doesn't half like to joke about and sometimes it's a little distracting. He was giving us his whole Tommy Handley routine last night. *Dis is FUNF sfeaking . . .* You know the radio show, *It's That Man Again?*'

Betsy laughed. '*It's being so cheerful that keeps me going . . .* We used to listen to *ITMA* every week . . . All of the wireless shows.'

'Betsy, I should go. Will I see you by the bomb sheds?'

She nodded.

'Perfect. *After you then, Claude . . .*' he said in a comic voice.

'*No, after you, Cecil,*' she replied, on cue.

This girl, he thought. He had never met a girl like her.

'I'll see you later, Drew,' he said. 'I can't wait, AC1, 491032 . . .'

As Betsy went back towards the hut Phyllis came hurtling around the corner. 'Drew, Spam is on the warpath. She's looking for you. She wants you in her office. Oh, and she said bring your hat.'

'I can't.'

'You'd better. That means it's serious. And she'll chop your arm off and beat you with the soggy end if you don't. You don't want her putting you on kitchen duties.'

No one had joined the WAAF to fry eggs.

Ten minutes later, Betsy tried to concentrate on what Spam was saying as she stood there, arms folded across her chest. 'Drew, the commander wants to see you in his office. I expected you at balloon practice, but he's asked for half an hour with you.'

Rising to her feet, Betsy glanced at the clock, hoping the meeting with Officer Baines would be over in ten minutes. As usual, the feelings of foreboding came flooding back to her in an instant. Had someone seen her with James? She wouldn't be surprised if it was a nun waiting for her, twirling her rosary beads and waving a ruler. But when she went in, saluting and stamping as she entered, there was no nun, just the harried officer telling her to sit down in a kind voice.

'Thank you, sir,' replied Betsy.

He opened his mouth to speak again but then handed her a letter.

'For you,' he said, in a quiet voice.

Betsy opened it and pulled out the note.

'No, Drew, give it me back, I've done this rather badly . . .'

But Betsy had already scanned the first few words. *Betsy, terrible news . . .*

'Drew—'

'Officer?' she asked tremulously. Her eyes flitted back down to the letter.

You need to come home. Ma is very ill. The doctor thinks she might not last the week, I'm afraid. I'm writing this from SS Albany as I sail back to Liverpool. Jacky.

She felt her whole body shaking. *But I can't come home*, she wanted to scream. *I haven't finished my training.*

'Drew,' he said. 'I'm afraid we had a phone call an hour ago. Your mother passed away this morning.'

Betsy felt her heart kick against her ribs. The officer was frowning, stumbling over his words as he spoke about how winning the war is what we want, but there are battles to be fought at home and this was one of them, my dear, and sadly it didn't turn out how we wanted. And Christmas Day, what a day for news like this.

She looked up at him smoking his pipe, fighting tears. 'Go home to your family,' he was saying. 'I'm giving you a fourteen-day pass. You have almost finished your training. You have a good brain, there's no task you haven't been able to do, and we will have you back to move on to the next level when you're ready. We're desperate for girls like you. And you're fearless, Betsy. We've noticed that. So, I want you to go home. And we will write to you in due course about where we will transfer you,' he said with a slow, mournful nod of the head. 'Your cousin, Malcolm, will meet you at Lime Street station – under the clock, he said – at five. We have a bus going there taking a few officers back to Liverpool to see their families. Drew, you have completed everything here that you need to know. So go home. I like you, Betsy, you're hardworking, and you're bright. Your cooking is not much to write home about, it says here, but from your exam results you certainly know how to make sense of some of these sheets of paper coming back from the depot. We will still be here for you. This war is not going to end any time soon, and we won't let you go that easily. Your cousin seemed a decent sort of chap from our telephone conversation. You need to be with your family. Family is important.'

Betsy was in shock. *But the RAF is my family now,*

she wanted to cry. *And as for Cousin Malcolm. Please God, not Malcolm!*

'The bus leaves in fifteen minutes.'

'No, I can't . . .'

'Why on earth not?'

'I have to see someone. On the other side of camp.'

His eyes narrowed.

'Who?'

'Sergeant Swann.'

'Why? Is it important?'

At that moment, it felt like the most important thing in the world, but she opened her mouth and no words came out.

'Go back to your hut and collect your belongings, and I expect you to be on that bus in fifteen minutes. Oh, and Drew. Happy Christmas. Try to . . . well, you know.'

Betsy's mind was racing. Her heart was breaking at the thought of her mother. Dead? It didn't seem true – like a cruel joke. Although as she hurtled out, panicking that there would be no time for meeting James, no exchanging addresses, no fond farewells until the next time, that felt almost as bad. But as she stumbled towards the quadrangle, ready to race off to find him, she was stopped in her tracks by a shout.

'Drew! Where do you think you're going? Come back. Now, get your things and get on the bus. We haven't got time to wait for you.'

Betsy felt her body crumpling. She walked dejectedly back to the hut to get her kit bag. She could feel Spam's breath on the back of her neck, heard the clomp of her boots on the cinder path behind her, following her every step.

Ten minutes later, as the bus pulled out of the camp with a dejected Betsy on the back seat, there was James, sitting on the low wall, puffing on a cigarette, squinting into the distance. Please turn around, I'm here, she willed, beating on the back window. I'm here! But all hope was gone as the bus left in a cloud of dust and trundled out of the gates, crunching over the frozen gravel.

Chapter 15

The bus pulled up outside Lime Street station and Betsy, now a muddle of bags and damp handkerchiefs, debated slipping off in another direction. But there was her cousin, Malcolm, standing on the platform, hands thrust deep in his pockets, a cigarette drooping from his lip, and the minute he saw her get off the train, his eyes locked on hers and he smiled. Hers were swollen with tears and red-rimmed. Because she had cried nearly all the way, not only over the terrible shock of her mother but also at the thought of James waiting for her on that little wall and no one explaining to him why she hadn't turned up. Malcolm walked over to her with his bandy-legged gait. But my God, he was a man now. With hairs on the back of his hands, hairs bursting out from his shirt collar, his nose, his ears, his chin. How could you go from a boy – an argumentative and annoying show-off twerp – to this man, with a gruff voice and a rough look about him as though he had been hewn out of granite?

'Happy Christmas, love. Betsy, look at you in your blues,' he said, grinning. It was the slightest of movements, just his arm on hers, but there was something about the way he touched her that made her shiver.

'You look the part, love. Convinced 'em, did yer?' She couldn't quite put her finger on it, but she knew in an instant that there was an unpleasantness about him, the way he spat tobacco, and something that didn't feel quite right. This was her cousin. And it wouldn't be the first time that a cousin had kissed another cousin but when he lurched forward and put his wet lips on her cheek, she shuddered.

'It's good to see you. Sorry about your ma, Bets. Ma said it was quick and painless. Fell asleep in the chair. Didn't even finish her hot toddy.'

Betsy nodded and leaned her head into the wind. Noticing barriers had been put up around the station, she allowed him to steer her towards the tram and past soldiers who were smoking behind rolled-up barbed wire. 'Where are we going?' she asked as he pulled her onto a tram. Its blackout curtains were drawn as it was getting dark. As it began bumping over the loose gravel that had scattered onto the lines with the bombing, she realized it was taking her in the opposite direction from Liverpool Lane.

'Your ma had been stopping with us. She wasn't feeling right.'

'But I need to go home.'

'Your home is with us for now, Bets.'

'But I can't. The RAF is going to write to me. That's the address they have.'

'Corpy has taken your ma's flat back. Someone else is renting it. Still, your ma brought your milk pan and mangle back to ours. So that's a couple of things salvaged amongst everything lost, eh, love?'

*

When they arrived at Sidney Street, Betsy was still in a daze. Walking into the tiny house, it felt dark and cold and appeared to have shrunk. Or had all her cousins got bigger? She looked at the four boys lounging around the room. Harry, with his hair sticking up in tufts, was sitting on a stool poring over the football results in *The Echo*, and Robert, who always looked a little simple, was staring open-mouthed into space. Eric was splitting bits of tree bark on the range with a pen knife and grunting as he did so, whilst his brother, Dickie, watched. Malcolm, who was now sticking the poker into the range, was the one she didn't trust. He was the tallest, with broad shoulders and a way of standing with his feet firmly apart, daring people to cross him. There was still the same threadbare purple-coloured chenille tablecloth over the table that they had all hidden under as children and where he had offered her a penny to show her drawers, the same high dresser that Robert had dared her to jump off and the same rocking chair that Malcolm had wildly rocked her back and forth in, once making her sick.

'Oh, Bets! Come here, chicken,' her Aunt Winnie cried, dropping the bucket she was holding as she wrapped her up in her arms and squeezed her to her tightly. 'Your poor ma . . . Three years younger than me an' all! She just fell asleep. Tired. We've tried to find your father but no joy. Probably wouldn't come to the funeral even if we knew where he was. Probably tinkering with someone's engine somewhere. I can't believe it's you, Bets. Don't you look smart in your uniform.'

Malcolm snorted. Betsy bit her lip and nodded.

145

Suddenly, the two younger boys leapt up and started chasing her around the table, reaching out and poking her with their fingers as if they were guns and shouting, 'Pow!'

'I'm sorry, Bets, love. This place is a three-ringed circus. The boys are getting bigger and hairier and smellier, and the baby, he cries all night and day long. Your uncle Clive is fighting in Africa, though if he were here, he'd be hopeless as a hankie in a rainstorm.'

'Another baby? A boy?' said Betsy, shocked.

'Yes.' As if on cue, she turned around, left the room, and came back in with a giant squirming baby wedged on her hip. 'Meet Davey. Six boys. What did I do to deserve that! Still, you're here now. So, tragic as Hope's death is, I can't tell you how delighted I am to know there'll be a girl around the house. You and me. Lasses together. Ooh, I've been starved of chat about scent and nail polish. Your ma wasn't much for that with her blessed prayer cards. We two lassies can swoon over the latest heartthrob from America and dance to Glen Miller on the wireless.'

What are you talking about? Betsy wanted to say, swallowing a scream. A girl around the house? She would be leaving as soon as the funeral was over. This place was awful. It was cold, small and cramped, pungent with the terrible smell of boys and wet boots and sour milk. At least her mother had tried her best to keep the flat pleasant, with the oil lamp, and the antimacassars, and the lace doilies that she spent hours crocheting. Betsy had never liked the crucifixes and the yellowing palms stuck in vases and the little holy cards and medals hanging off every doorknob, but still, there was some orderliness to their home. Her feral cousins seemed to have brought their chaos into every corner of this little house. Mouldy conkers, odd socks discarded on the arms of chairs and vests stuffed down the sofa, stained baggy long johns and discoloured nightshirts hanging on an old clothes horse.

'Come on, Betsy. I could do with a pair of hands. The boys are off school until the end of the month, so that's more work for us all. Here, hold the baby, there's a dear . . .'

'Teacher says me and our Eric, we was scurvy elephants . . .' Harry said to Betsy.

'No, she said you were *disturbing elements*. Though yes, scurvy and ratty, probably that as well. God knows how I'm going to cope. Thank goodness you're here, Bets.'

Betsy raised a weak smile as Winnie placed the baby in her arms. He began to cry and howl. Fitting, she thought.

An hour later, after a bowl of soup and a stale mince pie, Betsy was asked to wash the pots overflowing in the sink – 'There's a dear,' said Winnie – then they talked about the funeral. When the boys had gone to bed, Betsy sat up waiting for Jacky's arrival. She could hear the rain dripping from the guttering onto the roof of the lean-to. It was a slow, steady drip, drip, drip but then to her dismay, she saw it wasn't outside, water was coming inside through a crack in the ceiling. She stood to investigate, and at the same time there was a knock at the door. She didn't know what she should do first, either answer the knocking, or put a bucket underneath the leak. She decided on the former, calling out, 'Come in!' When she looked up, Jacky was stamping his feet in the hall, bringing in leaves and a blast of cold air.

'Jacky!' she cried, and fell into his arms, nearly knocking over the bucket.

'Love,' he replied. For a moment they just held on to each other.

'You're all sunburned!'

'Wind on deck, that is. Where is everyone?'

'Gone to bed. I wanted to wait up for you.'

She took off his wet overcoat and put the kettle on, kissing him warmly, and placing a heel of a loaf and margarine in front of him on the table.

Their words tripped over each other as she told him about the shock of hearing the terrible news, he then explaining how he had persuaded his captain to drop him off in Spain, and from there he had sailed back with the merchant navy delivering rubber tyres. In between tears and sniffles and sighs, Betsy said that arrangements for the funeral had been hastily made. They went through the list of the aunties who might come: Auntie Madge, Aunt Dinah, the aunt in Donegal who wasn't really an aunt and whose name they couldn't remember. But as they crossed them off one by one, Betsy began to feel as if she might cry again.

'The worst is, the flat has gone. I didn't even know Ma was living here with Auntie.'

'I did.'

'And we have nothing to remember her by. They said Ma pawned all her jewellery. That pretty brooch. And her wedding ring. The only thing they have is her milk pan and mangle. I can't stay here a moment longer. I'm going back to Wilmslow the minute the funeral is over.'

He frowned. 'Going back?'

'I'm not staying here. My home is in the RAF now. I'm useful there. There's nothing for me here.'

'Betsy,' he said gently. 'You can be useful here. I received this letter . . .'

He sighed and pushed a piece of paper over the table. 'From Auntie Win. Read it carefully. And don't make a fuss until you've read every word.'

Her eyes scanned the page. She gobbled up each sentence in a second.

Dear Jacky,

I'm so sorry about your ma. But things are hard here, believe me. We need a girl to come and look after the baby so I can go back to work at the Meccano factory. I'm proposing Bets moves in with us now the flat has gone back to the Corporation.

She dropped the letter onto the table, meeting his eyes with a look of horror. 'No!'

'Why not? You could look for a job in the evening maybe? You could volunteer for the WRVS?'

'No, my job would be looking after the wretched baby all day and all night. So, I'd be trapped. And anyway, even if she paid me a thousand pounds, I wouldn't do it. She just wants me to do the skivvying. "There's a dear . . ." is what she says all the time. Those boys. They look and smell like the last time

149

they were washed it was by the midwife. They're monsters. Spitting and shoving. The fighting they do.'

Jacky raked his fingers back through his hair. 'Betsy, we are in the middle of a war. Things haven't turned out as we thought they would. Expect the unexpected. On every front. You of all people should know that.'

She glared at him. 'Does she know? Do you think Malcolm has told her?'

'About what?'

Betsy cast down her eyes to her lap. 'About . . . you know . . .' she said in a small voice.

'I don't think so. I haven't mentioned it. It's not exactly something that Ma wanted to share with the family. She was ashamed. I think she had an easier time telling the nuns. *Mea culpa*, we're all sinners and all that. Auntie would be shocked to know you had a baby.'

'If she does, it's Malcolm who has said something, though he promised Ma faithfully he wouldn't tell a soul.' She sighed. 'Any one of our not-real-aunties would be nicer than this one. She'd love it. Gloat, more like. Ma couldn't have stood that.'

'So, what do you think, Betsy? Shall we give it a try, love?'

'No. I'm serious. I'm going back to the RAF. I get paid there. I have a future. I don't need Auntie Win.'

Jacky sighed and lolled back his head. 'Whatever. But you'll have to stay here for now, Bets. Don't forget we have no home. I'm going back to sea after the funeral and when I come back, I can stay at the Seamen's Mission or the Sailors' Home, but that's only for fellas. So even if you did carry on as a WAAF, what about when you come back on leave or when the war's over? Where will you go? You'll have nowhere. Win won't ever have you through that door again if you refuse to help with her baby. Then what?'

'Jacky. It's not just that,' she murmured. 'Can't you see why I can't stand it here? I had a baby,' she said through gritted teeth.

He winced. 'I thought we were never going to talk about that again.'

'It happened and not talking about it won't change that. I *can't* be around babies. Do you not understand that?'

Her brother looked at her. He could see the sadness in her eyes, the desperation as she clutched the edge of the table, and though he felt his heart breaking for her he could say nothing.

'These pots need washing. Help me tidy the place up a bit. And then we can go to bed,' she said glumly.

'I can send you money. Would you like that?'

She nodded tearfully, but it felt strange to be relying on her little brother. He was the one whose nose she had wiped, whose knees she had bathed in iodine and whose mouth she had blown sulphur into. And now he was the one trying to decide what to do about her.

'Anyway, never mind you telling me what to do. The merchant navy. It's dangerous,' she said, sighing. 'Ten ships have already been blasted out of the water in less than a month. And then there's the one that they're still not talking about. The *Arandora Star*. Nearly five hundred people blown out of the water, and we're not allowed to speak of it.'

'Bad for morale, that's all. No one ever talks about

sad things in this city these days. Just sweep it under the carpet. Come on, Bets. We're going round in circles. Let's sleep on it.'

'I'm not staying here a moment longer than I have to, Jacky,' she said defiantly with a thrust of her chin and a toss of her hair.

The funeral – two weeks later – took place at St Anthony's Church. The coffin was lowered into a hole in the earth in the stony ground on a windy hill just behind the church, overlooking the scarred and bleak landscape stretching down to the river. The bitter wind blowing up the valley was stinging. But at least the church had been full. There were friends of her mother from the wash-house and from Mothers for Mary, and she half expected her father to walk in, but of course he didn't. That would have been a miracle, or perhaps a nightmare if he had turned up in a cloud of smoke in an old rattling car.

Jacky had arranged for meat pies and jugs full of beer on the tables in the parish hall, so everyone went back to Winnie's a little drunk and a little maudlin, but feeling slightly happier with full bellies. It hadn't helped that there was still the threat of bombing which kept some away, but there were telegrams from Ireland, and letters and good wishes from sisters and cousins and absent friends. The women from the wash-house made for a rowdy bunch, singing Irish songs, but it was when they were making their way out of the church that Betsy noticed kind Sister David, one of her mother's friends from the convent, hovering in the porch.

'Sister! Thank you for coming.'

'Your mother was good to the Church and to us. How are you, Betsy? I heard you're doing well.'

'Yes,' she stuttered. 'And they want to teach me the radars.'

'Radars?'

Betsy frowned. 'The RAF.'

'Oh, I see. I meant I heard you were doing grand with Winnie's new baby. You're in the WAAF?'

'Yes,' she said, feeling heat rising to her cheeks. 'Radars with the WAAF. Not changing nappies. I'm not much good at that.' There was a silence. 'I'm going back as soon as I can. Sister, I can't . . .'

The nun nodded. And then she took Betsy's hand. She could feel her trembling.

'Can't what? Betsy, you look as if you're in turmoil. And you're shaking. Dear, if you need a place of shelter, or a chat, for an hour, a morning, a night, just come to St Mary's orphanage. Go to the back door. One of the sisters will find me. God bless you and may the Lord comfort you, Betsy.'

Betsy nodded. She was kind, this nun, with the smooth skin and deep brown eyes, but her soft tones and gentle words did nothing to persuade her that the convent was not a cold-hearted place.

Betsy took her coat off and hung it up on the wooden stand in the hall when she got back to Sidney Street. She could hear voices and when she went into the kitchen there was a man sitting at the table, legs splayed, chewing a match, trilby hat perched at an angle. 'Who's this?' said the stranger, raising an eyebrow, sniffing the glass and then taking a slug. Betsy blinked away the worry.

'My cousin. She's a smasher,' said Malcolm.

She flinched, gripping the door handle.

'Hope's daughter. Betsy,' said Winnie, coming in from the parlour, smiling, with a tray full of glasses. Were they really going to have a party? thought Betsy. But then two more women burst in through the door, laughing and waving bottles.

'Betsy, don't go!' cried Malcolm. 'Come and sit down. Sit down on me knee,' he said, glugging back his drink.

Winnie, waving the bottle, grinned and, taking off her feathered hat, laughed.

'Shall we spare Jesus's blushes? Let's put this in the back room,' said a woman with a huge bosom, nodding at the crucifix on a small plinth on the mantelpiece. They all laughed and laughed more when she grabbed it and put it to her forehead and ran around the room shouting, 'I'm a unicorn!'

'Don't,' said Betsy, snatching it off her. 'That was my mother's.'

No one seemed to care, not even Winnie. Malcolm was laughing at his three brothers racing around the room waving the fire tongs. Then he struggled to his feet and stood wobbling on a chair and started singing 'The Rose of Tralee'. He thrust out his empty glass as Winnie passed. Aiming a soda syphon, she snorted when she missed and squirted most of it at his crotch. The room spluttered with laughter.

'Malcolm has drunk too much,' Betsy hissed at her brother. 'The more drunk people get, the more they start to do stupid things.'

'Aye. Like dancing and playing an imaginary trumpet,' said Jacky, nodding at Malcolm doing just that.

'Come on, Betsy, love,' Malcolm whined. 'Where's that sunny smile gone?'

We've just come from my mother's funeral! she wanted to yell. The man stuffed into the armchair took out a mouth organ and started to blow and suck on it. 'You hum it, I'll play it.' His pink cheeks swelled as big as golf balls.

'Hey, Bets. This fella can go up and down those octaves faster than a whore's drawers!' laughed Malcolm.

They all guffawed and snorted.

'They're only teasing, petal. Take no notice,' Winnie called out to Betsy.

Betsy looked at her brother grimly from under her blonde hair falling over her eyes. 'Why are you doing this to me? Making me stay here with Aunt Winnie and all these people? See how awful our cousins are? Those boys stuffing their faces and getting drunk,' she hissed.

'They're just lads. That's what lads do.'

'No, they're wild. The middle one is not so bad, and the youngest one used to be all right, but he's going the same way too. You saw them scoffing everything in sight. Belching and kicking, greedy and rude. Mother has died and they are just here for a party to grab whatever they can. And this house is tiny. Winnie lets them run around like troughing pigs. And she's expecting me to control them! If she tells me to do one more thing and says, "there's a dear,"

I'll scream. And how long before Malcolm tells her about, you know . . . ? If he hasn't done already. Jacky, as soon as I get the letter from the WAAF, I'm leaving. Just so you know.'

Jacky took her aside and spoke into her ear. 'Please, Bets. Everyone gets drunk at a funeral. These people don't mean any harm. Now go to bed. No one will notice. Can't you hear the baby crying?'

A few minutes later, upstairs, she looked at her uniform in the wardrobe. Hanging limply on a coat hanger, it looked like a corpse.

Chapter 16

Eric sat at the table slurping soup Betsy had just prepared and making an unpleasant sound as he sucked it between his teeth. 'Too much salt,' he said. Betsy bit her tongue to hide her temper.

'Grace before meals,' said her aunt, flouncing in and instructing them to all sit down, but when they closed their eyes, Betsy kept hers open. She was startled to see Malcolm wink at her. And when Winnie put down the pie and the tureen of mash and turnips, her heart lurched as she felt him slide his foot underneath the table and rub it against her leg. At first, she thought she had imagined it. But there it was again and though she coughed loudly and scowled, it made no difference; his leg pushed against hers and remained there. She took a mouthful of pie but it felt sour and dry in her mouth.

Malcolm has started on me, she wrote to Jacky. *Touching, leering at me. Why hasn't that blasted RAF letter come? It's been weeks. I've written to them and given them this address . . .*

Are you sure you're not imagining it? he had written back.

'No!' she cried out loud, sitting on her bed in the attic, and she scribbled a letter back, so angry she left

157

an imprint on the blotter. *How could you say that, Jacky? He's a brute!*

Jacky might not believe her but just as she feared, and as more weeks passed, it was every day, every meal, that Malcolm pestered her – the nudging with the knee, the toe stepping on her foot under the table. Then the shutting of the door began when it was just the two of them alone in a room. She found the staring the worst. The awful staring. That bony nose, broken and crooked after a fight probably. She shuddered. The minute she entered a room and smelled his tobacco when he had just left it, the hairs on her body would stand on end. She shrank away whenever he came near.

'Please don't wake Davey. If you wake him now, he won't go to sleep and I'm so tired,' she would say to him every night. He just smiled at her and winked. She could smell the sour odour of alcohol on his breath feet away. And he always just grinned and laughed.

'Suddenly you're picking up the baby now? Every time I come near you?' he said one evening, when she plucked Davey from the bassinet and announced he needed feeding.

Did he know she was using the baby as a shield? As a way of stopping him getting too close to her? He must know. He came over and stood close. It felt like her eyelashes were about to touch his, he was so near to her when he spoke to her.

'It's nice having a lassie like you around in a house full of boys. Are you afraid of me?'

'Don't be daft. I'm leaving soon. But if you come near me again, I swear, I'll tell your ma.'

'What would you tell her? That I love you with a passion? That I love you so much, I'm thinking we should marry. What's wrong with that? There's plenty of cousins that marry.'

'Shut up, Malcolm,' she said and turned around, shocked. She couldn't tell if he was joking or not. He even made Alvis seem like a gentleman.

He reached out behind her and clutched her around the waist, drawing her to him. She felt his fingers curl tight, digging into her through her thin shift dress.

'It says in the Bible that we should only think about things that are pure and spotless. So I've been doing what the Bible says and thinking about you all night and all day and what I want to do to you . . .' he murmured. Then he grinned. 'Go on. Say it. *But I'm not pure and spotless, Malc.* Don't you remember the night at the hospital?'

'You're hurting me,' she stuttered.

He laughed. 'Now, why would I ever do that, seeing as I adore you? And don't worry, your babby – I made your ma a promise. Your secret's safe with me, love.'

She barely took a moment to think what she was going to do next when her body took hold of her senses. Twisting around, she sunk her teeth into his upper arm. But it was like granite. And he threw his head back and laughed.

'I'd like to take a big bite out of you, pet. That lovely little bottom. I see the shape of it sometimes when you're standing by the window in your nightie. It's like a peach. I wonder if it tastes as sweet. God, I'd love to find out.'

'You're disgusting!' she hissed.

He laughed again. 'And you're such a pure little thing, aren't you?' he said, smirking.

Panic shot through her. He just held her gaze and raised one eyebrow.

'Leave me alone,' she said. 'You're a bully and a brute.'

At night when she went to bed, she started to push the chair against the door in the tiny attic room. She would be exhausted, and her eyes would become heavy with sleep, but she would wake every half an hour with a jolt. One night, she woke to see that the door handle was rattling. It was moving, twisting and grinding left and right. She gripped the side of the bed. The handle rattled again.

'Betsy, the baby is crying. Can you get up and see to him? I'm just so tired. Can you get up and give him his bottle, there's a dear?' said her aunt on the other side.

'Auntie, where's my uniform? It was hanging on the back of the bedroom door,' she said, the following week. 'Where is it?' she asked flatly. 'I want to go to Renshaw Street.'

'Still pestering them about going back to the RAF? I have no idea, Betsy, love.' She tipped her head to one side. 'I think the boys borrowed it to play soldiers. They looked so funny. You should have seen them marching up and down wearing your cap.'

My uniform! she wanted to scream. *Do you not understand how precious that is?*

She galloped upstairs to the boys' bedroom. Her

cap was lying on the floor, crumpled. Flung on the bed was her jacket. She noticed one of the buttons was missing. The boys had rolled up the sleeves and it was creased and muddied at the elbows. Picking it up, she felt waves of despair as though she was about to be physically sick. Lightly touching the number sewn on the shoulder, she fought tears and then pressed the jacket into her face. She thought of her mother and what she would say. *Shoving a stick in the spokes is no use. If you don't like it, you need to do something.*

Dear Phyllis, she wrote shakily, half an hour later after she had put Davey in the drawer that was a makeshift cot.

I am forwarding you my aunt's address, which is where I am staying. I've also sent a letter to Spam, but I have heard nothing yet. Officer Baines said he would write to me with a date for my transfer. Would you check with Spam that they received my letter asking if there's any news? I went to Renshaw Street to see if I could enlist again, and they said to go back home and wait. I've heard nothing yet.
Betsy

PS I'm looking after five boys who fight all the time. They destroyed my uniform. It's a right mess. Do you think I can get a new one?

PPS If I don't hear anything soon, I'm coming back. The months are dragging on. I just have to choose my moment. I don't like my eldest cousin. He's got a dark side to him. The baby is all right but I'm not very good at looking after him. He cries all the time and I find it hard to get him to sleep. Still, I'll feel a little sad to leave him.

Your friend,
Betsy

Betsy sucked the end of the pen and tried to think what else to say so that Phyllis would see the urgency of the situation.

'What are you doing? Why don't you ever pick him up when he starts crying?' whined her aunt bad-temperedly, bursting into the room carrying the baby. 'He's howling and it's your job.' She pressed her lips together crossly. 'Betsy, I brought you here and gave you a roof over your head, and you seem so ungrateful. I've noticed you only ever pick him up when you're told to. Who are you writing to?' she snapped.

'No one,' she replied. 'Auntie, are you sure a letter for me still hasn't arrived?'

'No. Can you please stop asking me, Betsy. Davey's crying again. He needs his nappy changing.'

Chapter 17

When James had arrived at Dishforth from Brough, he was struck by the thought that the calm of this gently undulating Yorkshire countryside was the starting place of brutal bombing campaigns and vicious battles fought in the air. The ground crew were going through the checks for the sortie later that night. James was lending a hand, helping one of them put a tyre onto one of the ambulance vans.

'Hey, Swann . . . leave it to the professionals,' said the group commander, strolling by. 'You're a pilot. You shouldn't be doing that. Especially not if you're flying tonight.'

James stood and brushed a hand over his brow. He wiped his hands on a cloth and smiled. It had been a month since he had arrived here after two months at the elementary flying school at Brough, and things had progressed at lightning speed for him. He already knew how to fly the small Tiger Moths and he was now flying Whitleys and Wellingtons and had seventy-two hours in the air and numerous practice sorties. He was fearless. It had been noticed.

'Letter for you, Swann,' said one of the mechanics, jogging over to him.

Walking along towards the huts, James opened the envelope and read the note inside.

Dear James,

   I hope you are well, and you are enjoying RAF Dishforth. I remembered you saying you were heading there after Brough. I'm hearing so many stories about our brave airmen. I am also hoping you remember your words when we were last together. I'm sorry that I missed you. I had to leave the camp suddenly. I can explain why if I do ever see you again, but I expect you're wondering why I'm writing. The thing is, I'm in a tight spot. I still haven't received my transfer papers and the months have dragged on but, long story, I've found myself in a situation. My brother is currently overseas with the merchant navy and when he returns, he will likely stay at the Seamen's Mission. I am at my aunt's but post never arrives on time, and I am wondering if you might speak to one of the officers? I know you suggested the transfer to Dishforth for me, and I don't know how serious you were, but maybe if you might have a word? If I'm honest, I'm pretty desperate to get back to the RAF.
   Yours faithfully,
   Betsy Drew

He folded it in quarters and pocketed it. It was only that morning that they had been talking about how they needed more girls in the watchtower trained in radar. Her arithmetic skills – yes, that's why he should put in a good word. Not because of those lively eyes, her bewitching little turned-up nose, the freckles sprinkled across the bridge of it and spreading over her cheeks . . .

'Officer Kanski?' he said, when he found him reading *The Times* newspaper later in the mess. 'I wonder if I could ask your advice about—'

'Ah, Swann, just the fellow,' Kanski said, interrupting James. 'Pull up a chair.'

James sat beside him at the table in the small alcove.

'Can I ask, have you . . . lost loved ones? Only I heard . . . your father . . . your brother . . .'

James squinted away.

Kanski took a sip of his whisky. 'Sorry, you don't need to answer.'

James paused. 'My father . . . and brother. Not in the war. An accident. It was something stupid.'

Zygmunt Kanski placed his glass in front of him and intermittently moved it around the table. 'Swann, I think you've got what it takes, which means we need to make you fully operational as soon as we can. It's all about strategic bombing now. Pamphlet drops are all well and good, but I think you're ready to fly the new Lancasters.'

James knew the risks. Pamphlet bombers had to dodge enemy flak and it was dangerous, but Lancasters meant the real thing.

'Really?' He hadn't been expecting this.

'So, you're in?'

'Yes. Terrific, sir. All in.'

Kanski shook his hand vigorously. 'Good. Any questions?'

'No, sir.'

Kanski nodded his approval. 'You know, you're like some of the Polish lads we have. My comrades in arms, I suppose, although I never grew up there. They know how to fly, and they'll risk everything because they've seen what Hitler dealt their country. Gives them fire in their bellies. Maybe like you . . . losing your loved ones . . .' He raised his glass and finished off his drink. 'You'll have an excellent team, and I'm sure you'll find the right aircrew. Just need to shore up the tower again. The WAAFs here are well trained and thank goodness they all have level heads. All highly skilled. And they certainly brighten up the place. Just need a few more.'

He was about to walk off when James said, 'Sir, actually, I wanted to ask . . . There's a girl, I know her from Liverpool, she worked with me at Cunard's. And she's good with numbers. Betsy Drew. She trained at Wilmslow. She would be a wonderful radar operator. I've already had a word about her coming here and was told a transfer would be organized but she's heard nothing and I'm wondering if there has been a problem with comms?'

Officer Kanski smiled. 'We're not a dating agency. But I'll see what I can do.'

Still bursting with the news of the possibility of flying Lancasters – everyone was talking about these beasts, how they could corkscrew, how big the bombs were that they could carry; cookies, they called them – James smiled, shook his hand and said thank you.

Later, a group of thirty-five men including James stood around in a field and sorted themselves – randomly – into groups of seven. 'The Lancaster is a beauty, isn't she?' the flight officer said to James as he walked with him back to the NAAFI. They had spent the morning going through safety precautions for crash warnings and landings, crawling through the Lancaster's cockpit and into the Perspex cubicles.

'God help us rear gunners,' someone shouted. 'Not right we have to leave our parachutes in the cubby hole.'

The voice belonged to gunner Mathers, a bank clerk from Scotland, and he was promptly ticked off by the officer about morale, even though he had once been a rear gunner himself and knew to be a Tail End Charlie was the loneliest and deadliest job of a Lancaster crew. The flight engineer was a Sergeant Goodenough with a young, freshly pockmarked face, the nav Gerald Willis, a shy boy who had been a student at Durham University, and the wireless operator, Tony – Toe – Howman, was a farmer's son who had a fondness for drawing comparisons between the Luftwaffe and hens and pigs in a burring Lancashire accent. Front gunner and bomb aimer Paddy Riordan had just left school in Ireland and was planning to work in his father's garage before life had taken this sudden and dramatic turn, and then there was mid-gunner Keith Langham, whose tobacco addiction had earned him the name Smoky. These six men would become James's family, all of them facing death and knowing that only one in three would survive. But they would soon have a bond closer than any family James knew, including his own.

'Did you hear about the officer who knew what he was doing?' laughed Mathers when the flight officer left. 'Neither did I,' he answered.

James smiled. He thought to himself that they had all miraculously chosen to be with six men that would make the very best of a bomber crew and would be entertaining with it.

But it was the thought that he might also be reunited with Betsy that put an added spring in his step as he headed off to catch the bus to Harrogate.

Lettice Swann had arrived in Harrogate the night before, stayed in a small tidy guest house, and was now looking over people's heads in Betty's tea room, excited to see that her beloved son had finally arrived and was hanging his overcoat on a hat stand. When he walked towards her, negotiating spaces between the tables, she thought he seemed taller. He had certainly broadened out. She noticed people's heads turn and look at him as he moved past them. But then another thought crashed into her head and the familiar fear gripped her. He was flying sorties now. Would this be the last time she would see him? Would this be the last snapshot she would have of him? She tried to push the panic down, lifted her hand, smiled, and waved. He came over to the table and she tilted her head and gave him her cheek. He kissed her awkwardly.

'You look well, Mother. That's a striking hat.'

'As do you, James.'

He sat down and as he laid his cap on the table her hands reached out, clasped his and massaged his fingers. 'You look so like your father.'

He didn't want that conversation, not here in the tea room amongst genteel chatter and boiling urns – as always, his mind lurching back to the day of the crash, when he had gone up in the plane with his father just before his brother had with the Tiger Moth stuttering and phutting over the lawn of Mottram Hall, feeling exhilarated and thrilled to see the lush countryside stretching out beneath them as they had swooped over the open green fields, and his father with the wind in his face, turning and smiling and shouting back at him over the roar of the engine, 'In your blood, son!' No one wanted to be reminded of that day. Not today. Not any day. Shocking, how raw it still was. Instead, he talked about being roped in to play the piano at the village hall.

'Shouldn't have told them I can play the piano backwards, Mother. News of it came all the way from Wilmslow.'

'Backwards? That would make Clementine giggle,' she said.

He hesitated. 'Mother, Clementine and I are not courting at the moment.'

It was like a stupid scene in a film where someone spluttered tea. Only this was real and she dabbed at her mouth with a napkin.

'Ma, it was Clementine's idea. She didn't want to be worrying about me every time I left her. And we have to write these goodbye letters, you know, before we fly in case . . . and I thought . . . we thought . . . it was all too much . . .'

'Jum, no!' She clutched the table edge, and he noticed the whites of her knuckles and the pulsating veins standing out like knotted ropes under her skin.

'She's having a fine time in the Wrens. I'm not saying it's over for good, but we are on a pause.'

'A pause?' She frowned. 'What's that? Are there rules with this pause, James? It sounds ridiculous. Are you allowed to dance with another girl? Are you allowed to *kiss* another girl whilst you are *on a pause*? Is *she* allowed to kiss another man? Because people talk, you know, and they know our family and to be honest, if they start gossiping about pauses, it'll get back and you'll be made to look rather stupid.'

'Mother, we're not right for each other. If we were, we would be married by now. There are married people in quarters, you know. Older officers.'

'Yes. I was married to one myself, if you remember.'

'I think the problem is also that Clementine doesn't want to live in our draughty old house,' he muttered.

'Are you saying that our family is not good enough for her? Because we most certainly are. Her mother, Hermione – her name isn't even Hermione actually, it's Pat – she was a dancer, nothing more than a twirly girl, you know, at the Empire. Clementine would be lucky to have you.'

He rearranged the cup in its saucer, twisting its delicate gold handle.

Lettice sighed. She looked at him with a pained expression. 'What about Davinia? Or Cecily? She's doing the season right now and I've heard marvellous reports. She's a wonderful girl. She plays the flute. I could have a word with her mother.'

'Mother, no. Stop.'

She raised her eyebrows and took out a cigarette from her handbag.

'You shouldn't be smoking . . . And not in here.'

'Why not? Stay in the pink with ciggies and drink, that's what they say. Anyway, the doctor prescribed me them after your father died. I'm gasping for a sherry. Do they do spirits?'

He was finding this excruciating. His bus wasn't due until six, but thankfully he hadn't told his mother that.

'Goodness. Is that the time? I must get back. I'm glad to see you looking so well. I'm sorry I can't stay long. Now, choose what you would like. I've heard the Fat Rascal cakes are delicious.'

Chapter 18

Betsy yawned and rubbed her feet. Finally, the boys had slumped into exhaustion and dragged themselves up to bed. She shut the parlour door quietly but when she went over to the bassinet and peered in, she was surprised to see the baby had gone.

'Just you and me,' Malcolm said in a low voice, coming out of the shadows. 'Baby's upstairs with Ma.' He stood there splitting a match between his teeth. He had been smoking that awful cheap tobacco again. She could smell it. His mother didn't like him to smoke around the baby because of whooping cough and she would hit him around the head, but he was too tall now and she would race around the room after him waving the coal brush or the poker or whatever she could lay her hands on, jabbing it in his direction, but here he was, ignoring her anyway.

'My little cousin. We have a special bond, Betsy. We have the same blood. Don't look so horrified. It's not like I'm saying we should get married and have a babby. Just you should be more friendly.'

Betsy banged down the milk pan. For weeks she had managed to avoid Malcolm, picking things up around the room if he came near her, moving away quickly through a door, but this was the first time she had found herself alone with him in a while and her blood ran cold as he shut the door behind him with a kick. "Sides, there's plenty of babies in this family. They're all over the place, aren't they?'

The way he said it made panic shoot through her. But when she tried to move away, he gripped her arm. His hand felt like a manacle, and she could hardly breathe. She didn't dare to. And he was moving her hair away from her face with a finger, pushing it behind her ear, tracing her jawline and the slope of her nose. She tried to turn away but he jerked her head round, holding her chin, twisting it to face him. Why couldn't she say anything? Why couldn't she just tell him to stop? It was like Alvis all over again. Every time she went near him or looked at him, it sent her hurtling back to where she had been two years ago, standing in Alvis's kitchen behind the curtain with her feet poking out.

'I always wanted a sister,' he said.

She shuddered but at that same moment her aunt came marching in through the door.

'Betsy,' she said, yawning. 'Baby's crying. See to him, there's a dear.'

The following morning, Betsy rocked the baby and carefully put him in the pram outside in the backyard. She sighed when she came back in and saw Dickie and Bob hurtling down the stairs and racing around the kitchen table chasing and hitting each other with rolled-up newspapers.

'I thought you'd gone to school?'

'Watch us do a caterpillar!' Dickie held on to his

brother's legs and they tumbled around the room grasping each other's ankles, laughing like drains.

'Stop it now,' said Betsy. This house was too stubby, too cramped for this nonsense. 'You'll wake the baby. Please don't wake up the baby. I've just got him down.'

As if on cue, the baby let out a piercing cry from where he was sleeping in the backyard in his pram.

'Now look what you've done,' said Betsy tiredly, feeling the coldness of the stone floor through her threadbare slippers as she paced the room.

Winnie insisted on fresh air to lull Davey to sleep. She would leave him in the pram outside even in the rain. Betsy remembered the TB ward at Mill Road where people who had polio would have their beds twisted around to face the windows that had been flung open by the nurses, and as Davey yelled she reminded herself that that never worked either.

'Where's Malcolm?'

'Out.'

'Boys, has any post arrived for me that you've forgotten to tell me about?'

Dickie looked up at her and didn't reply whilst Bob and Eric continued to clash the fire irons against each other.

'Betsy, he hit me in the eye!' Bob cried.

'*Enough!* I've had enough of you all!' she screamed, grabbing Eric's pretend sword, shocking them into silence. 'Has a letter come for me?'

But they just shook their heads, open-mouthed and gormless.

*

An hour later she sat down at the kitchen table.

Dear Auntie,

I am sorry to leave so suddenly. I shall forward you the address of Dishforth when I have it.

She faltered. She should have done this months ago. But should she say where she was going? She didn't want Malcolm to come looking for her at the camp. She crossed it out and began again.

Please forgive me. I know I will be leaving you in the lurch with the baby. He is a lovely little boy. But I've been told I could have an important position in the RAF and I can't refuse.

'What you writing?' asked Eric.

'Nothing. Go away,' she said, turning away and slipping the note in her pocket.

Betsy went into her attic room and pulled out the drawer looking for the envelope that she had hidden with her savings carefully folded inside it, now she had made up her mind that she was leaving this squat little house with the musty smell seeping from the walls and the sticky splintering floorboards. Groping in the far corners, when she couldn't find it, she thought maybe she had left it somewhere else. There wasn't much in it, only a few pounds, but it was enough for a train ticket.

Feeling a creeping sense of panic and worry, she started rummaging through the drawer again. Nothing. She walked over to the bed and in desperation she began looking under the straw mattress and turning pillowcases inside out. She flapped the eiderdown and the ragged sheet. With rising panic, she began searching through the laundry basket and finally inside her shoes. Where had she hidden it? She started to feel a little sick. It had been there yesterday. She was sure. And even though she constantly moved it, she checked every few nights.

Treading carefully to avoid making a noise, she crept into Malcolm's bedroom. The small bedside table was pushed up against the wall. She pulled out the drawer forcibly. Her heart was racing. And then she felt it stop. Plucking out an envelope from amongst handkerchiefs and bundles of ties, when she saw the abbreviation OHMS on the front, she felt as if she was going to faint. It was addressed to her and it had already been opened. Shaking, she took out the letter from inside. She was shaking so much it fluttered like a hummingbird's wings.

Dear Betsy Drew,

Please report to RAF Dishforth on 3rd April. Enclosed is a ticket from Lime Street station to York where you will be met by staff for registration and transport . . .'

Weeks ago! The rest of the sentence swam before her. The ticket was out of date, crumpled up and useless. In desperation, she yanked the drawer further, right out of its casing, searching for the money. She didn't care if anyone might hear her. This was too awful. Her fears spiralled out from her, whirling around. She felt as if sparks of electricity were spitting out from her, threatening to set the place alight. Scrabbling in the drawer to see if there was anything else, her fingers trembling, she felt something wrapped in a handkerchief . . . A small metal pin? Her mother's brooch! She gasped when she unfurled the embroidered square of linen. It was confirmed. Her cousin was a thief as well as a lech.

'Malcolm has taken my money, Auntie. It was there yesterday! And why did no one tell me about *this*? It's a letter from RAF Dishforth!' she said, after pelting down the stairs, tripping and stumbling over piles of washing and discarded shoes.

Winnie's eyes widened. 'Stealing money? That's a pretty strong accusation to start throwing around. Did you leave it lying about somewhere that you've forgotten?'

'No, Auntie. And the letter . . . it came weeks ago!'

'There are always letters arriving here. Bills, rent . . . We just stuff them into the back of the nearest drawer and hope we can forget about them. If you helped a bit more with the baby, I could have read them all . . .'

Betsy was about to tell her about the brooch but she expected that her aunt might twist it. There was no point in arguing with liars and she couldn't stay another minute within these sweating walls with these sweating boys and their unfeeling mother.

She waited in the half-light as night drew in until everyone in the house was sleeping. Quietly, taking her uniform out of the wardrobe, she tried to smooth out the creases. Breathing hard and rubbing on the buttons that had become dull and tarnished, she winced, remembering how smart she had looked when she had first worn it, and how crumpled and drab it looked now. Looking towards the cot, the baby was sleeping. That was one thing amongst a sea of troubles.

The child would miss her, though he screamed all day long in a fury as if he hated her. It was no surprise that he enjoyed biting. This child would bite you on the ear, on the nose, your shin. She had tried her best with the little mite but with brothers that would throw him across the room to one another as if he was a football, and with a mother who watched on and thought it was hilarious, there was no hope for him.

'You know I love you,' she whispered to the baby. 'But I have to go. I can't stay here. I fear you'll go the same way as your brothers. Try not to, lovely.'

When she arrived at Deirdre's, out of breath and ignoring an ARP man telling her she should go indoors in case the sirens started up, even though it had been quieter of late, she hammered on the door with her fist. Her heart was beating. She squinted up and saw that the curtains were shut, and the blackout blinds were drawn. Hearing a noise next door, she saw Alf, their crotchety neighbour who used to complain about Jacky playing football in the courtyard, shoving up his window and poking his head out. 'Deirdre is away with the Wrens, and her brother is at—'

'Yes. I know, Wilmslow. But is her ma here?' She could feel spots of rain on her nose and cheeks.

'Gone, love. All evacuated. You shouldn't be on the street.'

The life was draining out of her. Alf banged down the window. She pulled her collar up and headed off. Clouds were bulking up the sky and she felt heavier, pestering rain. Think, think, she said to herself as she made her way down Liverpool Lane, not knowing where she was going. Fury rose in her throat. If Malcolm had not destroyed the tickets, she could have tried to take a train, even if they were out of date, but they were no use now. She thought about the brooch. She could pawn it, but it was a Sunday. Thoughts crashed around in her head. The rain had soaked her through now, and she slumped against a wall and sat on the cold bricks, head bent. And still the rain began to fall harder.

A Mary Ellen lurched towards her dragging her cart, head bent into the bitter wind, on the way back from Paddy's Market. Betsy was embarrassed to be seen like this in her uniform. Not that the Mary Ellen would care, but dressed as a WAAF and hunched up like a beggar, she felt as if she was letting the side down. 'Pride,' Spam used to bark at them. 'It is a privilege to wear this uniform and if you wear it with pride, others will have pride in your service.' Getting to her feet, she brushed herself down. Squinting ahead, she continued down the road against the rain. But then she stopped. She had walked blindly on, tears and lashing rain wetting her face, barely able to see a step in front of her, but at the point of turning back, she realized where she was. *St Mary of the Blessed Angels*, said the gold wrought-iron words set above the brick arch.

Chapter 19

'Jesus and all the saints preserve us! Betsy, whatever is the matter?' said Sister David when she slid open the grille to answer the persistent knocking and saw Betsy standing there, hollow-cheeked with bloodshot eyes, drenched through. 'This is a fine time to be wandering the streets,' she said, unlatching and then opening the door. 'Come on in out of that terrible rain.'

Betsy sniffed and stepped in gratefully. A little pool gathered on the parquet floor and the wool serge material of her uniform was beginning to smell.

'What's the matter, dear? Come in and tell me all about it.'

Betsy followed her into a small room and slumped into a chair, twisting her handkerchief, swallowing down sobs. 'I don't know what to do. I have no money. I need to get back . . . get back . . .'

The nun looked at her. 'Get back where? To your aunt's?'

Betsy shook her head.

'The RAF. I'm in the WAAF now. I need money for my train fare tomorrow morning.'

'I see. I wish I could help you with the money, Betsy. I'm sorry, we have all taken a vow of poverty. I have none. But maybe in the morning I can see what I can do. I can start with a warm bowl of soup and a bed for the night. Will I get one of the girls to bring you some from the kitchen?'

Betsy nodded sorrowfully.

'Follow me and I'll take you to the dormitories first. Get you out of those wet clothes and find you a night-shirt.'

Betsy went up several flights of stairs and down the dark corridor. A perfect circle of light fell onto the parquet floor from the moon shining through a high round window. Somewhere far off she could hear the nuns singing. The candle wax smelled sweet and the freshly cut flowers gave off a heady, musky scent. She had never imagined that finding herself within these walls would be comforting.

'Wait here.'

Betsy sat on the end of the bed in the two-bed attic room dormitory and listened to the voices singing evening prayers. When the door was flung open, she looked up, bewildered, to see a girl with a heavy fringe, smiling.

'Sister sent me along with this and . . .' The girl frowned. 'Wait. I know you. You're the girl who I came to see . . . You were having a baby? Betty?'

'Betsy . . .'

'I'm Sybil! What happened? Did you keep your wee one?'

Betsy looked at her and blinked slowly. 'My baby died. Mill Road Hospital.'

Sybil seemed genuinely shocked and upset. 'Oh no. I'm so sorry. Oh, you poor petal. I heard about the hospital. I'm sorry it turned out like it did. And your little one was one of the casualties?'

Betsy looked at her with sad eyes. She nodded and felt a wave of sorrow rising up from her feet and reddening her cheeks.

'We said a mass for those poor lambs who died.'

Betsy nodded. 'Did you?' Her hands began to tremble.

'So, you're here because you're an orphan . . . or . . . ?'

'No . . .' she replied quickly. 'I'm in the air force. I'm a WAAF.'

Sybil nodded. 'I think that's smashing. Maybe I'll do the same. But I don't trust the nuns, so I need to keep an eye on my baby girl in case they snaffle her, or she gets adopted.'

'Snaffle her? What d'you mean?'

'They snaffle the kiddies and send them away. To Timbuktu. And Australia. Anyway, that's why I'm still here,' Sybil said, grinning.

'I remember you told me about your baby's ear . . .' said Betsy.

'Do you? The peg? In the end it didn't make much difference. But then I tried something else. I point at her bottle and tell her it's a tree. Then I point at the table and tell her it's a ball. The nuns think she's stupid because she muddles up the words. I know she's not. Shame, she's got a little stutter, but it's a small price to pay when the adopters come to pick a baby and the nuns shuffle Belinda to the back.'

'That's . . . well . . . clever . . .' And sad, she thought.

'I can't be split from my Belinda. And leaving here . . . turns out it's not so easy, what with this war raging. But what about you? You still haven't told me what you're doing here.'

'It's complicated.'

'Try me. I'm clever, like my daughter. I can figure things out. I might even be able to give you advice.'

Betsy told her the whole sorry story in jumbled-up sentences and tearful gestures, finishing with how she didn't have any money, not a penny, but how she needed to get to Dishforth.

'Blimey. That's a story and a half. If I met that Malcolm, or Alvis, I'd clobber them both . . .' She sighed. 'Look at us. Both fallen girls. The sisters here think the Virgin Mary will save me if I live a God-fearing life, but it was my Auntie Mary that I needed to save me, and that was never going to happen after that useless lump had his way with me.' Betsy managed to raise a half-smile.

Sybil slapped her thighs. 'Listen, get those warm nightclothes on – that uniform stinks to high heaven – and then come with me. I'll show you something to cheer you up. Let's go and see Belinda. Come on . . . Be quiet. The nuns are saying evening mass, but you still must be careful.'

Betsy, a little thrown off balance by Sybil's deter-minedness and feeling a stab at her heart the way she always did when anyone said the word 'baby', put on the nightdress and allowed her to take her by the hand. They walked a little way down the corridor and when they reached a set of double doors with curtains behind glass panels, Sybil twisted the handle, and they went in. The vaulted room was large and airy with blackout curtains drawn across high windows. There were rows of cots, some with broderie anglaise panniers, others just the bare bars and mattresses. Some had teddy bears tied onto the bars and others had mobiles of balsa wood ducks bobbing above them. Nearly all had a child with a little mop of hair poking out from a blanket. She pointed towards a cot where one was curled up under a sheet. 'That little one's legs don't work properly. And this one's going to the blind school soon. But they're both bonny.' She walked over and leaned into a cot against the far wall and touched the sleeping baby's nose. 'This is her. Isn't she pretty? Can you believe Sister Annunciata won't call her Belinda even though I've asked her? She calls her thingamabob or thingy all the time. It's not kind. What I'm thinking is why don't you stay here instead of the WAAF? You and me? We could have the craic with these kiddies.'

Betsy's face screwing up gave her the answer. 'I don't think I can,' she said quietly. 'Isn't it a bit . . . sad?'

'Not really. Don't feel sorry for me. Not when I'm looking after these little wonders. We'd better go. Singing has stopped.'

Betsy didn't feel like talking much. So she was grateful Sybil was the kind of girl who offered her opinion when it wasn't asked: on the nuns, the food, the weather, the sound of someone's cough, the fall of the curtains.

As they walked back down the corridors, Sybil linked her arm through Betsy's and said, 'I can help you. Sister David might not be able to give you money, but I can. I have five shillings saved. Is that enough?'

*

The next morning, after prayers, Sister David trotted down the corridor with a pile of freshly laundered towels. Sister Annunciata almost collided with her at the bottom of the stairs.

'What are you doing?'

'The girl, Betsy Drew, Hope's daughter, arrived here last night. Bedraggled and in need of a hot bath.'

Sister Annunciata paled. 'Why didn't you tell me?'

'Because I . . .' Sister David stuttered.

'She needs to leave. Now,' she said, sweeping away down the corridor. 'I don't want to see her. But she has to leave now.'

Thankfully, an instinct had already gripped Betsy that she must do just that. After gratefully accepting Sybil's five shillings and not questioning her as to where she got it, she had kissed Sybil, thanked her profusely, scribbled Deirdre's address on a piece of paper so they could stay in touch and she could return the money – *IOU five shillings. If you urgently need what I owe you, my best friend Deirdre will tell you where I am. Deirdre is at Flat 17 Feather Street tenements. Betsy* – and slipped out. Now she was clutching her kit bag and taking a seat on the train from Lime Street station to York. When a woman with a small child climbed in and sat opposite her, she averted her eyes, hoping she wouldn't ask any questions. The child sitting opposite wriggled and squirmed and despite her best intentions, when he grinned at her and waggled his fingers, she couldn't help but smile back.

'Are you going all the way to York?' asked the woman.

'Oh. Yes.'

'Are you going to one of the camps?' The woman had noticed her kit bag. 'You're awfully brave. I think it's marvellous what you young men and women are doing.'

When they reached Preston, a pretty station with hanging baskets on the platform, the woman took out a tin of boiled sweets and unscrewed it. 'Would you like one?' she asked, and Betsy took it gratefully.

There were military personnel on the station when they reached York and to her surprise, a young Wren met her on the platform with a clipboard. 'Where to?' she asked, matter-of-factly.

'Dishforth,' she answered, and she was amazed that when she was pointed to a van and when she climbed inside and took her place on the seat running down the side, no one asked her anything else. There was lively chatter but after half an hour Betsy saw the sign saying *RAF Dishforth* with an arrow pointing down a small dirt track. They arrived at the outskirts of the camp – a collection of a few buildings and outhouses, a watchtower and hangars in the distance – and when she got out she saw a second sign saying *Registration for WAAFs* and a girl with her hair in plaits standing on the door smiling, holding a clipboard and chewing a liquorice stick. She coughed and thumped her chest with a fist. 'I'm trying to give up smoking and I'm using these instead. But they're pretty disgusting. Who are you?'

Betsy was clutching the crumpled letter. 'Betsy Drew.'

'Go inside and see the sergeant in that booth.'

Straightening down her uniform, she nodded and headed over to the sergeant behind a desk. He barely looked up at her.

'You're weeks late . . .' he said, reading the letter.

'Would it be possible to find an officer, James Swann? I'm hoping he might be able to explain.'

'Who's he?' he said, reading the letter. 'Wait here,' he said.

When he came back into the room she started to apologize for her uniform. The sergeant, who was smoking a pipe and had a shock of greased-down black hair, walked over to a filing cabinet and pulled out a folder. Taking out a piece of paper, he nodded up at her as he read.

'You come highly recommended from Cunard's? And Officer Swann requested your transfer? There's a note here from Officer Baines. Oh, I see you completed your training at Wilmslow. With colours.'

'Finished short of a week,' she stuttered.

'Says here you passed with the highest marks attainable in your mathematics exams. I don't need to hear why. Sergeant, take this girl to the dormitory and find her a bed. We've been waiting for you, Drew. Oh, and make sure you pick up a new uniform. You look a state. I'll see you first thing tomorrow.'

She nodded and felt her chest open with relief and finally the heaviness lift from her shoulders.

'Drew? I've been told to find you and give you a new uniform. We're a bit short and they're putting us in the men's trousers for the minute, but you don't mind that, do you? I'm Melanie Lightfoot, by the way.' The girl with buck teeth and a high forehead smiled at her.

Betsy followed her, passing a small room with high glass windows made of small square panes. There was a group of men leaning forward over rows of desks. They held pens above their pads. In the front of the classroom, a man was pointing a ruler at a board.

'We can't go in there,' said the girl. 'And don't look. You'll be shadowing me. It's quite straightforward, just do as you're told. You need to write down all the co-ordinates, then we compare notes after. All top secret.'

Betsy nodded and had a job to keep up. She felt a shiver of excitement. These were real pilots, real men's lives at stake. She had heard how many weren't coming back right now, with one in three planes shot down or crashing, and in some small way she would soon be responsible for them.

'There are perks. If you're in the watchtower and you save the life of one of our airmen, say get them out of trouble if they have a near miss, direct them through bad weather or a tricky landing or a fire – some of them come limping home, you can't imagine – they'll give you a pair of nylons. They get them from the Americans. Have you ever worn nylons?'

Betsy shook her head. Melanie led her back outside and pointed out five large hangars. 'That's where some of the WAAFs learn how to fix the engines and check the tyres and are taught how to read the barometers. Just remember, for the first week you will watch and learn. It will soon be your turn. Betsy, you're not here by accident. You're here in the watchtower because they want to use your brain.'

After Betsy had changed into her new uniform at the service block, Melanie told her to go through to the dormitories. They were the same makeshift Nissen huts covered in corrugated iron as at Wilmslow. When she went in, a girl with wild hair jumped up from lying on her bed, knitting. The others, gathered around the fire playing cards, twisted their heads in Betsy's direction.

'Don't speak!' the girl said, bouncing up and patting the air with her hands. 'We lay bets on where the newbies are from. Just say after me, "Mother's lost her blue bloomers, Mother's lost her blue bloomers."'

'Mother's lost her blue bloomers . . .' said Betsy, falteringly.

One of the girls laughed. 'You a Lancashire lass? She sounds like Gracie Fields, doesn't she!'

Another thumped the bed. 'No. She's one of mine. Liverpool? I knew she was a northern girl, straight away.'

The girl sitting next to her snorted and said in a Scottish accent, 'Liverpool's not in the north. It's in the midlands.'

'Don't be daft, Rosario. Of course Liverpool's in the north. Whereabouts in Liverpool, love?'

'The tenements down by the docks,' she replied in a small voice.

'I know it. Tattersall's fish shop. Does belting fish pies. So, what are you? Green or orange?'

Betsy frowned. 'Oh. We're Catholics . . . But I don't especially bother . . .'

'Never heard of a left footer who doesn't especially bother. I'm an orange. And that's why I'm here,' she said in a low, growling voice with a scowl. 'To fight for me beloved country.' She saluted and stamped her foot.

Another girl grinned. 'Give over. You're here to bag

an officer. Hey, Drew, want to hear our favourite joke? How d'you know if there's a pilot in the NAAFI? He'll come and tell you.' She laughed and then her face changed, and she became more serious. 'We had five men who didn't come back last week. Five. Five girls with broken hearts and with no way of knowing how they will ever mend them.'

'Aye, but do we know for sure if they're all dead?' asked Williams.

'Not definitely. Missing in action. That's the worst. The hope.'

'Let's not upset Drew. She's only just arrived,' said Ross. 'And we had a busy night last night, but they all got home safely. Must be a record. So, there'll be drinking and dancing tonight.'

Betsy realized that this was going to be different to Wilmslow training camp. At the training camp it was mostly drills and square bashing, dances and trips to the village pub. Here you were staring death in the face with sorties nearly every day. One of the girls was talking animatedly about a trainee who just last week had opened the bomb doors instead of the flaps on a practice run, causing it to pick up speed and crash, killing the young pilot – they had just celebrated his nineteenth birthday, she was saying.

Betsy turned away. She mustn't think about death. She had seen too much of that in her own life lately. This was her chance to live again. And they saw her as talented and clever here. However hopeless she was at sewing or how much of an enemy of pastry when it came to baking, that didn't matter. This was her chance to be someone. Or rather, to be someone *else*. And it was these thoughts that were racing about her head as she got undressed and lay in the small flat bed, falling asleep before her head rested on the stone-hard pillow.

'You do nothing but listen and watch and go wherever you are shoved. Come this way, Drew,' said Melanie Lightfoot to Betsy. 'You won't be doing gravel bashing like you did at Wilmslow, but you're still expected to practise your drills. When you're not on duty your job is to get some sleep.'

The camp was much bigger than Wilmslow. Fourteen hundred WAAFs and airmen. There were hundreds of bicycles and even cars to get around, and it felt like a small village with a maze of cinder paths and inter-secting roads. As they walked along one of these paths, ahead was the airfield with the runway in a triangle and she could see a couple of men sitting on upturned packing cases smoking. They were wearing uniforms and the sheepskin jackets that made them look so glamorous.

'It's pretty big here. We'll give you a map. You're staying in HD with the rest of the girls that have arrived this month.'

As Betsy approached the watchtower the door swung back to reveal WAAFs huddled over a map and a few airmen milling around. Betsy had spent the day in classes and tonight, she was told she would be shadowing. There was a sortie that evening, nothing too dangerous, a leaflet run, but it was a good way for her to learn the ropes. In at the deep end, said

Lightfoot. She wanted to ask someone, anyone, about James, and Melanie Lightfoot seemed a sympathetic type, but she had a feeling that she would never be allowed back in the watchtower again if she bothered them with such a triviality.

Betsy, a little embarrassed, made her way down to the end of the room where a small group were gathered.

'Hello, I'm Betsy Drew, AC1, 491032,' she said, smiling, sticking her hand out to the other WAAFs.

'You're young,' said a girl with a broad smile called Carol Rushton, shaking it warmly. 'We had another Scouse lass a few weeks ago, but she got the collywobbles. Left last week.'

Betsy felt a little disappointed. After Cunard's she had thought she had learned to speak without the nasal twang of a Liverpool accent. She had spent so much time listening to the women on the BBC wireless and mirroring them, but obviously not enough.

'There's six of us girls on tonight. We have a rota. And there's no swapping. If you're having a thing with a fella and he's not come back, there's no switching shifts hoping you can wait up until there's news.'

That evening after she made her way down the corridor painted cream on the top half and green below, she peeked into the signals room, and then made her way into the control room. On the wall was the black-painted grid that the WAAFs would have to fill in with the details of each aircraft as it took off and the empty column waiting for the word RETURN to be chalked in. Seven o'clock was the first time she heard the roar of a Lancaster bomber taking off. The deafening sound caused everyone to stop for a moment. The ground shook, the furniture shook, the equipment and instruments rattled. Betsy could feel the vibration in her bones and her chest. It was like nothing she had ever felt or heard before. The smell of the fumes reached her nostrils, the grinding noise, the smell of rubber. It was intoxicating and terrifying at the same time.

'Concentrate and follow me,' said Lightfoot. 'That's S for Sweetie off safely . . .'

Betsy could see from the tower that there were about a dozen men gathered outside on the airfield smoking their last cigarettes. They threw the butt ends to the ground, grinding them into the floor with the heels of their boots, adjusted the collar of their jackets, buttoned them up tightly, and fastened and refastened, loosened and tightened belts before they slung their bags and parachutes, their life vests – or their Mae Wests as they called them – over their shoulders and walked out onto the tarmac.

'Please God it won't be their last cigarette,' Ross said. 'I pray for them every night and every day and I no believe in God, I only believe in Rabbie Burns. But what else can you do? So far, we've only lost seven since I've been here. Richards there, with the wild hair, he's been sent here to train the men. He's wonderful. He knows what to do. Canny. Teaches them to be fearless, but sometimes that means lives are lost when they shouldn't be. Flying too low, too close to Jerry. Michael there reads out the numbers of who's returned and who hasn't as though they're scores on a dartboard. We all want to hear him yelling

Full House! when everyone returns safely. We all hope for that.'

Betsy nodded, wondering in a sudden panic if one of these men who needed to make up the Full House might tonight be James. She jumped when someone blew a whistle. Watching through the tower windows as they began to make their way to the waiting planes, she saw two girls, and men, ground crew – the erks – who were doing final checks with bolts. They looked serious but excited, dashing backwards and forwards with tools, nodding instructions to each other. Airmen stood in their groups of seven, hands deep in their overcoats. One group put their arms around each other and smiled and knelt down on one knee as a photographer took their picture. She had been worried enough when they had been taught how to pack the backpacks of the parachutes if she might get it wrong. One tangled rope and it would be certain death – but this felt far more grave. The men who had been having their photograph taken were now walking towards the plane. Breaking out into a half run, mounting the steps, swinging their legs over the lip of the tiny hatch door enthusiastically, and still smiling. Smiling.

Betsy took her place in the watchtower where men and women now sat at desks wearing headphones plugged into wirelesses and others moved between them carrying papers, looking at the board behind them.

'Here, put these headphones on. I'm guiding them through take-off. I'll give you a list of the call signs. We do it by lights. We don't use the radio from now on, in case the enemy are listening in.'

She could feel her heart pounding as she took the heavy Bakelite headphones and put them over her ears. Collins readjusted the small microphone to meet her mouth. Clive gave her a thumbs up. The lights flickered off and the instruments glowed. The intercom was silent.

'Chocks away . . .' Ross said. 'Take-off clear . . .'

Melanie turned and gave a friendly smile at Betsy and winked and crossed her fingers. Then she turned to the WAAFs sitting beside her. 'Radios off now. Good luck to them. Nice weather for our Skipper . . . Terrific, as he'd say . . .' she added with a grin.

Betsy's heart stopped. There was only one person she knew who said 'terrific' and oh, how much she longed to hear James saying it with that voice, richly textured and kind.

'Come on now. Go to bed. They won't be back until early hours of the morning. I know some like to, but it does no good to be standing there. Counting how many went out and how many come back. That's Richards' job. All we can do is wait.'

Betsy had sat in the tower and watched three planes take off. That was twenty-one brave men whose lives might be lost tonight. Lying in the dark in the hut, staring at the ceiling, she knew Ross was right to send her back to bed. But it was hard being new, and perhaps she would learn in time how not to feel sick with knots tightening in her stomach, her palms sweating and heart racing, though it was difficult to imagine right now. She couldn't do this every night. She would die, she thought.

'Go to sleep, Betsy. Stop tossing and turning. You'll make us all nervous, love. We'll find out in the morning.'

Betsy shut her eyes. Was it James up there, with the radio crackling, the wireless humming and the slow blip, blip of the radar? She wouldn't sleep a wink. When she did drop off, she kept waking, but then she was surprised and confused to hear that someone was clanging the bell, shouting at them that it was six thirty and time to get up. It didn't matter that they were tired and hungry, or those that had been up on duty had crept back during the small hours. The hammering of the bell was loud and persistent. She dressed hurriedly.

'Where are you going, Drew?' asked Lightfoot.

'I just wanted to find out who came back?'

'It was a success. All safe.'

A voice shouted from across the room, 'Knickers day!' A rosy-cheeked girl walked in carrying a basket and handing out silk underwear. 'Ten pairs of drawers made from the finest parachute silk. First come, first served. Some with elastic, some with ties. Gorgeous, they are. Drew? D'you want a pair?'

Later, after sugary tea in the mess, Betsy set off across the quadrangle and went to the watchtower to collect the data sheets and bring them to the office as she had been instructed to do by Ross.

'No running in corridors, Drew!' said a man's voice behind her. 'Stop or I'll have you reported!'

She stopped in her tracks. Her legs buckled from under her. She squeezed her eyes, hardly daring to breathe.

'James!' she said, spinning round. 'I mean, Officer Swann,' she stammered.

'You made it! They said you were here,' he said with a grin. He danced from foot to foot, wanting to hug her, to punch the air, to kiss her.

'Thank you, James . . .'

'Thank you for what? Betsy, I'm so proud of you. You passed out higher than any other person they've had. They've never seen someone like you, your speed and intelligence. Such a large brain in a perfectly formed small head. Terrific.'

'It *was* you! Were you flying last night? I was in the watchtower observing.'

'Were you? Spot of bother on the tail end but we survived. And by God, I'm so glad we did, seeing you standing in front of me. Look at you. You look wonderful. Though those trousers are a little comical. You look a bit like Arthur Askey. Tell me what happened? Where did you go? You're making a habit of this, vanishing. Still, all the sweeter to see you turn up again, just when I thought all hope was lost,' he said, with a grin.

'A family crisis.'

'I got your letter. I would have come to find you in Liverpool but I didn't know where you were. I remembered Chester?'

She nodded and moved the conversation on. 'Yes. It was only ever temporary. So, you've got your wings?'

'I have. They fast tracked me. Two months elementary training camp before here. They're pretty desperate for pilots. They've already put me on ops and I'm an officer now.' He touched the embroidered wings on his shoulder. 'Come on, let's go somewhere quiet where we can talk and have a bimble around. My sixth sortie, can you believe it? Everyone came back. We'll all be celebrating later.'

They walked towards the bomb dumps at the far end of the airfield. Cow parsley was growing and the swaying poplar trees planted in the back fields in the distance were shimmering silver and green.

'So, Betsy,' he asked gently, 'your mother . . . Betsy, I heard . . . is she . . . ?'

'Dead. That's why I left so suddenly.'

'I'm sorry,' he said.

Just then, a young NCO came running towards them. 'Swann! You're needed in the briefing room!'

'Damn it. See you in the mess later?' said James.

She gave a quick nod of her head and was thankful the conversation ended abruptly.

When Betsy went into the mess that evening the girls from her hut were laughing and playing a game of tiddlywinks hunched around a small table. It was full and noisy and someone was playing the accordion.

'Pull up a chair, Betsy,' said Pearl. Betsy sat down and was given a pile of green tiddlywinks.

Pearl glanced over at a fellow standing on one foot with a pint glass balanced on his head. 'Look at my Derek, playing the clown again. He's such a baby. He's a rear gunner.'

Lightfoot smiled and whispered to Betsy, 'They're the ones who pay with their lives.'

Betsy flicked a tiddlywink that bounced off the table.

'For that, they quickly learn more about the facts of life than all the others. Don't they, Glynn?' laughed

Lightfoot. 'If they can persuade their girl they're the ones most likely to cop it?'

'How dare you?' replied Pearl Glynn.

A sergeant stood on a chair tinkling a spoon against his beer glass.

'Chaps! Wheelbarrers!' he yelled.

People stood up and brushed themselves down. The girl whose job it was to remember which officer drank what – she knew all their favourite tipples off by heart and enjoyed walking around the tables and serving drinks on a tray each night – promised a whisky to the winner. A few WAAFs began to tuck their skirts in their knickers. Everyone laughed and clapped as couples gathered at the far end of the room. The girls put their hands on the floor, the men grasped their thighs and hoicked them up around their waists.

'Officer Swann! Find a lassie,' a sergeant yelled across the room.

Betsy turned her head to where James had just walked in and was standing grinning at the door watching the scene. She met his eyes, and he raised an eyebrow.

'She'll do! She looks game!' shouted the adjutant walking round collecting glasses from the tables, pointing at Betsy and nodding at James.

James wandered over and held out his hand. Betsy, blushing, shook her head. But then a chant from the three girls started, 'Do it! Do it!' and others began to join in.

She raised her eyes and laughed, weakened, and allowed him to lead her across the floor to shouts of

'Good on yer, lass!' and 'Show us what you're made of, Swann!'

Lining up, bending down, then feeling his hands clasping her thighs, she was grateful that skirts had been in short supply, and she was still wearing her trousers.

'On your marks, get set, *go!*' the sergeant shouted. As they all began tumbling and toppling across the floor, snorting and honking with laughter, one sturdy girl announced she was exchanging places with her skinny sergeant and carrying him instead. Betsy and James weaved their way through the mayhem, gasping as they fell in a pile over the finishing line. 'Let's get out of here,' he whispered in her ear.

Clutching her hand and pulling her up, they dashed through the doors into the cool night air. Standing under a hawthorn bush in full flower giving off a dizzy scent, they leaned against a tree.

'Betsy . . . can I . . . kiss you? You're beautiful. Jaw-droppingly beautiful.'

Betsy had never heard such a thing. She couldn't believe a man could speak like this. Maybe movie stars in films, but not in real life.

'Of course, Officer Swann,' she said, as his lips met hers under an ink-black sky scattered with stars.

Chapter 20

Lettice Swann felt her little bag of coins going hot in her pocket. When Sister Annunciata used to come around to Mottram Hall to take the collection box, the nun would say the same thing every time. *Every penny helps with Our Lord Jesus's work. Thank you, Mrs Swann.* As the weather grew warmer, more people would make their way across the fields to the small chapel at the Hall, and the collection money for St Mary's grew. But Sister Annunciata had stopped visiting months ago and Father no longer came to say mass. Too busy, too many babies with this blessed war, and Mottram Hall chapel had begun to smell of damp; there were now three buckets on the pews catching the rain instead of two. *Can you come to the orphanage instead, Mrs Swann? I'd like to talk to you about something . . .*

Lettice Swann made her way up the gravel path of the orphanage. She wanted this visit over quickly. The orphanage smelled of musty flowers and beeswax polish. The scruffy girl with the socks sagging about her ankles, Sybil, who she had met once before, was in the garden and opened the gate with a child on her hip.

'Hello, Mrs Swann. I remember you . . . How are you diddling?'

Lettice readjusted the collar on her blouse, turning it over, and winced. 'I'm here to see Sister. Excuse me.'

A nun swept out of the front door. She walked over and shooed Sybil away. 'Lettice. Thank you for coming. How's James? In the RAF, I heard,' she said as they walked off down the winding gravel path together.

'Splendid. I miss him. I am proud. But also terrified. He already has his wings.'

'Goodness. I'll pray for him,' the nun said as they went up the steps and inside.

'Please do. He's brave but headstrong. He ran straight into a fire once.'

'Come to the chapel. We've been so busy trying to place the babies as quickly as we can. But as soon as one comes along there's another sad bundle left on the step or another girl crying at the door. The war, you see. A glut of orphans and the babies all end up here in the nursery.'

'I expect once they start toddling it's impossible. My boys were a nightmare at that age. Some days I would have given them away if you had offered to take them,' she laughed. 'Now, I do have some money for you. That's another thing that has got worse with this war. People's generosity. No one has anything to give. It's not much, I'm afraid.'

'As we say, every penny helps to do God's work, Mrs Swann,' she said, taking the bag gratefully.

Lettice sat twisting her gloves in the pew of St Mary's chapel. She looked around at the drab surroundings. It was all so severe. She was fond of churches with their statues of Our Lady in blue, white and gold and the altar dripping with white flowers and the pews with the red velvet cushions and velvet kneelers – they brought her calm. But this place gave her the shivers with its hard benches and pungent-smelling waxy candles. What was it about some of these nuns at St Mary's? Some were kind but Sister Cyril and Sister Annunciata seemed to think the more pain they had in their lives, the closer they would get to God. They had seen nothing of real pain, she thought bitterly. Nothing. A hard bench wasn't going to make you feel better when you had been through what she had. Besides, she had been to enough ordinations to see the sisters quivering in ecstasy lying face down on the stone floor to know the joy it brought them.

'You know, Mrs Swann, you can enter the order even if you're a widow. Have you thought about it?'

Lettice looked confused. 'Are you saying I could become a nun? But I'm a mother.'

'It might surprise you to know that doesn't matter. It would be unusual but . . .'

It was all she could do to stop herself from laughing out loud. 'I like the good things in life too much. Cherry pie and silk stockings. Sister, can we get to the point? I'm a little late. Why did you bring me here?'

'Come with me,' said the nun, leading her through a door at the side of the altar and down a corridor to another office. The nun opened a cupboard with a key and then carefully laid out papers on a desk. 'Can I trust you?'

Intrigued, Lettice nodded.

'The evacuations. We have been sending some of our children abroad in much the same way. To Australia. Canada. We have been doing this for years.

And it has already been very successful for those children who have settled.'

Lettice looked at her, bewildered. 'And so? Why? What are you asking of me?'

'There are limits on the numbers we can send. You are a trustee here. And with a letter from you, and Mr Worboys, and the other trustees, the Corporation would be much more open to the expansion of our plans. I'm excited. It means a fresh start for more of these children. I can show you. It's grand knowing we are doing God's work. Come with me to the nursery.'

When Lettice stood at the glass door and the nun drew the curtain aside, she was shocked. There were so many children. Some squirming in cots, a few in a playpen, others on the knees of two nurses coaxing them to feed from bottles.

'Run ragged . . .' said the nun. 'You see the problem?'

'Who are all these children? There's so many.'

'Mostly children of fallen girls. It's a shame. Girls have gone feral these days. But this has nothing to do with you, Mrs Swann. Amen to the Lord for that. Who would have a daughter?'

Meanwhile, in the nuns' garden Sybil sat with Belinda on her knees, wrapped in a blanket, dreaming of escape. On the other side of the stone wall she could hear the city going about its business – the echo of the dray horses' hooves on the cobbles, a newspaper boy, the rattling of a dust cart. Sister David bustled up to her.

'Sybil, sometimes I think you're more of a hindrance than a help here. You shouldn't be here in the nuns' garden,' she said, stepping out from behind the bushes.

'What are you trying to do? Get yourself thrown out on the street?' She leaned into her. 'Go inside. And don't let me catch you here again. You'll regret it, dear.'

Sybil made her way back to the nursery. She yawned, picked her baby up and put her in the wooden playpen with two other toddlers. They all giggled together, crawling and throwing their arms around each other and tumbling about, crashing against the bars like new puppies.

'Take her out of the playpen. There's too many of them in there. They'll break it,' snapped Sister Annunciata as she swept through with Lettice Swann.

Stuff that, thought Sybil, she's having fun. She whisked Belinda up but plonked her straight back the second after the two had left the room.

'Sybil. I'm watching you! Did you defy me again? Take thingamabob out of the playpen,' said Sister Annunciata, turning on her heel and coming back in.

'Her name is Belinda. She's got the hiccups,' said Sybil.

'No, she hasn't. Don't lie.' Then she cocked her head to one side. 'How old is your child now?'

'Why?' asked Sybil. Too old for new parents to adopt her, she prayed.

'Never mind,' replied the nun ominously.

A chill ran through Sybil's bones. Something about the way she said it meant the nun was up to something. And Sybil didn't trust her.

Chapter 21

Two weeks had passed since the night of the wheel-barrow race. Betsy hadn't seen much of James since, but he had smiled at her over the crowds of heads in the NAAFI and winked at her when she passed him in the corridor one morning, and reached out and brushed his hand against hers when he had found her on balloon duty, and these moments carried her through each day. At the end of the week when he had waited for her outside her hut at lunch break, he had quietly slipped her a note asking her to meet him outside the bomb sheds, from where they had a pass to go out to the local pub, The Rose and Crown. He met her at the gate, and it was a bus ride and a short walk from the camp to the village lanes, but he held her hand all the way.

'Shall we go in?' he said, when they arrived.

All he wanted to do was kiss her. I want to know everything about this girl, he thought. And I want to kiss every freckle, every dimple, every crease. I want to kiss behind her knees, the back of her ears, the curve of her neck. I want every small part of her to be imprinted on my brain for ever. If I could, I would make a map of her and trace my finger over every part of her, right down to each quivering eyelash. He stood with his hands deep in his pockets as if to stop himself taking her face and planting his lips on hers. When they sat down in a quiet corner with a port wine and a brandy, he immediately reached out across the table.

Betsy smiled, dropping her eyes shyly, but as she did so she noticed someone had newly scratched their name on the small wooden table.

'Peter Nemes . . .' she murmured, tracing her fingers over the name.

'I knew Pete,' sighed James.

'What happened?'

He shrugged and stared into his glass. 'Never came back. He was seventeen. Gunner. They all sign up to be gunners because it's less training. Desperate to get up in the air.'

'Awful . . .' murmured Betsy.

'Skipper almost made it, limped home but couldn't steady the plane. Fuselage just ripped open like a tin of pilchards. It was refused landing twice then burst into flames in the woods. All seven crew, including Peter, died.'

Betsy traced her finger over the deep grooves. 'So young.'

'Yes. Damn shame.' He blinked away, quickly changing the subject. 'Betsy, tell me about you. I want to know every tiny thing. You left with me knowing a little, but I want to know more. I know you're good at maths and you're good with engines. Is there anything you're not good at?'

Lying, she thought as his words tumbled around in her head. She must get better at it now that the real

Betsy, the loose girl she had left behind in Liverpool, was dead and her future was Betsy, charming and innocent. Was he convinced? He wouldn't think she was charming and innocent if he knew the truth, he would think she was grubby second-hand goods, but she quickly shook off the thought.

'I'm not good at cooking,' she said, smiling shyly. 'I'm hopeless. But then so was my mother. I blame her. She spent hours in the kitchen, but she always left it too late before deciding what she was going to cook, and then time ran out, and it just got too cold or it was undercooked. Her liver and onions. It was like chewing an old boot. And I'm not much better. My liver and onions are like chewing an old boot that's stepped in a cow pat.'

He laughed. He liked the way this girl made fun of herself. Too many seemed to take themselves so seriously these days. 'Who are your friends? You said you had a brother?'

Panic rose in her throat and she hesitated.

'I'll make it easy for you,' he said, smiling. 'Likes and dislikes. Let's start with jam roly-poly or sticky toffee pudding?'

'Neither if it's cooked by the chef in the NAAFI. Sticky toffee pudding if it's at Lyon's Corner House,' she said with a shy smile.

He leaned forward, chin resting on his palm. 'Bing Crosby or Glen Miller?'

'Robert Taylor . . .'

He grinned. 'Bovril or sugary tea?'

'Sugary, *milky* tea . . .'

'Your turn to ask me.'

'My turn? I can't think.'

'How about . . . blondes or brunettes?'

'Well, which? Blondes or brunettes?' she asked with another shy smile.

'Isn't that obvious?' he said, leaning forward and kissing her lightly and quickly on the lips. And then he frowned.

'Betsy, I should tell you, I had a fiancée until quite recently. We were over before we started. She was terribly jolly. Loved hats with feathers. Made me sneeze all the time. My mother wanted me to marry her. Unfortunately, I didn't want to.'

'Your mother?'

'Yes, I know it's ridiculous, isn't it? My mother. That's what you're thinking, isn't it? She can be rather suffocating.'

'My ma was the same. She had an idea of how my life should go and then when it didn't turn out the way she expected . . . She had grand ideas for me as well.'

'She would be proud of you, Betsy. What do you mean, didn't turn out like she expected?'

Betsy faltered. 'Oh. I mean, joining the RAF. She wanted me to be a teacher. Or a nurse.'

'My mother wasn't keen either. There's a joke Winco always tells the new officers. *Don't tell my mother I'm a pilot, she thinks I play piano in a whorehouse . . .*'

Betsy smiled.

'You would have made a wonderful teacher. And a *spectacular* nurse.'

'So, this girl, your fiancée? She's probably a nice girl?' She could feel herself becoming hot. She knew exactly the kind of girl she would be. She had met a few in the WAAF. The type that would be pleasant enough and say things like 'jolly good' and 'bravo', but would never glance at a girl like Betsy in civvy street unless it was to ask her to do something for them.

'Clementine's nice enough. But we have nothing in common. She wants to be a singer. And it's all faintly absurd. You should hear her. She sings flatter than a pancake on a billiard table.' He smiled. 'And she's sweet but I will never marry her, and she will never marry me despite my mother thinking she would like us to. Anyway, I don't love her. My mother says that doesn't matter. Clementine is *such fun* and I should stop worrying about love, *you don't know what that is yet, James* . . .' he mimicked. 'I told her the RAF is a quivering hotbed of romance and there's plenty of airmen younger than me who are experts in love, and they'd say there wasn't an ounce of it between me and Clementine.'

'Who are all these experts?'

His voice became more reflective. 'The ones who just know when a certain person walks into the room. The ones who all they can think about is engineering the next moment of the day to be with that person before they have to go on the next sortie. The ones for whom food, drink, sleep become insignificant. The chap whose plane goes into a tailspin and he wrenches her out of it because all he can think about is that person waiting on the tarmac. It's like in the silly films. I know it's all nonsense, but . . .'

He took her chin in his hand and traced a finger

over her full red lips. She froze, and wondered if she might ever be able to move again. Might she just stop breathing and die?

'What's the matter?' he asked.

'Nothing . . . I . . . I . . . But you and me . . .' The words dried on her lips. If she had been able to speak, she would have said, *We're so different. You with your ex-fiancée who loves singing, and the way you talk – using words like rather, terrific – and your mother sounds terrifying, and me . . . me whose world away from here is full of coal scuttles and drab clothes and scouse . . . If . . . if you knew . . .*

'Betsy, that's how I feel about you. I think I might even be in love with you. Can I kiss you properly?'

Glancing around the pub, seeing two sergeants engrossed in building a pyramid of playing cards, a woman fussing over her yapping dog, two more couples – WAAFs and airmen in uniform – staring deeply into each other's eyes, she realized there was no need to be shy of James Swann tenderly placing his hand on the back of her neck and drawing her into him. Was this really happening? she asked herself. And did any of her fears about their differences matter? Certainly not here, in this pub, in this moment, everyone too busy with their own lives to care. Letting her eyelids flutter shut, she felt his mouth on her lips as he kissed her.

James then paused and withdrew and stared deep into her eyes. 'Betsy, it's me next week. I'm flying the Lancaster.'

'Didn't one . . . ? The other day . . . ?'

'Yes, bellyflopped and skidded off the runway into

211

the ditch. It was fine. Don't look so frightened. I can handle them.'

Twisting her sleeve, she smiled, but her eyes said something different.

'Next week we have an important mission . . . I can't say where . . . or what . . .'

'Germany? Letsuke? There's been rumours.'

'Can't say. No need to worry. I know what I'm doing.'

Betsy's dark eyebrows knitted together in a frown. She grasped his hand and squeezed it gently. He returned the gesture.

'Lancasters are safe kites. They're solid and reliable. You can't think otherwise or you're done for. Come on, let's go back. I want to show you something.'

When they reached the camp, it was pitch black. James glanced up at the sky. 'This is the kind of sky we like. Murky with clouds, so we can't be seen by the search-lights, but not so bulked up by fog you can't see where you're going.'

He continued walking across the field, feet mushing through the muddy weeds and then through the longer grass, holding her hand. In the pitch black, the hangar at the end of the runway took shape. When they reached it, he took her around the side to a small door. He knocked and it was opened by a private with a rifle slung over his shoulder.

'Warrant Officer Hughes. Can I come in? Drew here and I need to check something.' He flashed his pass.

The young man nodded. 'Yes, sir,' he replied and went back to his newspaper.

'They'll all be celebrating,' James said to Betsy. 'They had a successful sortie last night. Leaflet dropping in Holland.'

Stepping into the large, cavernous hangar housing two aeroplanes – the four-engine Lancaster he had talked about and a smaller Halifax – he walked over to the impressive Lancaster.

'See what I mean by sturdy? She's beautiful, isn't she? Magnificent. Ever been inside one of these?'

She shook her head.

'Follow me, Betsy.'

He wheeled over some steps and pushed them up against it.

'Are you sure?'

'Yes. I'm a pilot, Betsy. We're allowed.'

Was he really? She doubted that was true. It was more likely he was using that assured voice of his to make young Hughes think he was, but tentatively she did what he said, followed him up, and they both wriggled through the flap. The smell hit her first. Of fuel, and oil, and metal.

'This is where the nav sits. The wireless operator sits there, and the flight engineer next to me in this little cubby hole. And now lie down on your stomach and wriggle through. That platform underneath me is where the bomb aimer looks down and shoots and drops the bombs. But it's the gunner at the tail who has it worst. Bit lonely for him. No room for his parachute, so dicey if he needs to bail. But now this is me. Where I am.' He took her hand and they crawled back into the cockpit. He sat on the pilot's seat and she wriggled beside him, sitting on the flight engineer's seat. 'See how safe it is. I'm snug as a bug in a rug. I rely on my six chaps. Like family we are. But you know, I feel invincible.' He laughed. 'So, no need to worry. You still look scared, Betsy.' He pulled a lever and the seat fell back.

'What about Hughes?' she said in a small voice.

'No one cares. He can't see us up here. Don't panic.'

He put his arm around her. Then he rolled to face her, propped himself up on one elbow. He took her chin, tilted it up and leaned in to kiss her. She kissed him back and she felt his hand on her thigh, his warm, sweet breath on her face.

'Look, I want to show you something . . .' He unscrewed one of his uniform buttons to reveal a tiny compass. Then he produced a silk handkerchief from his pocket. 'Compass and a map of northern France,' he said, smoothing it out on his knee. 'And finally . . . look . . .' He wriggled about a little. From down the seam of his uniform trousers he produced a strong and flexible metal saw. 'We know how to contact the French Resistance, who will help us escape to Spain, so even if I have to bail, I stand a pretty good chance.'

'Of what?'

'Coming back to find you. You won't get rid of me that easily, even if I'm shot at.' He smiled. 'You know, babies have been conceived in these Lancasters apparently, when they were building them at the factory. I wouldn't be the first to bring a girl to the cockpit . . .'

Betsy felt her body stiffen.

He saw her wince. 'What's the matter?' he said, worried as she sat up in a flurry of straightening her skirt and tidying her hair. 'Are you all right? I didn't mean to make you feel awkward or uncomfortable . . .'

Betsy pulled her skirt over her knees.

'We should go,' she said flatly. She could feel her heart hammering. A darker moment in her life came hurtling back into the present. The smell of the musty curtain came rushing back. She thought of her letter to Deirdre. *I know how dangerous handsome men in uniforms are.* And her mother's words. *Men only want one thing . . . You don't want people looking at you as though you're some kind of slut . . .* 'Please. I want to go, James. Now.'

Chapter 22

Since Betsy had disappeared so abruptly, trotting off back to her hut, James had tried to find her every moment he was free, but as the evening of his next sortie grew nearer, he was occupied with the preparations: hours in the briefing room, checks on the planes, test runs, navigation planning. He was still annoyed with himself – he shouldn't have taken her to the hangar, and worse, into the plane. He had scared her, he was sure he had, and had it been too early to kiss her? The way she had left with that steady, determined walk of hers had unsettled him. He had thought about sending a note apologizing, saying he hadn't intended to alarm her, but that seemed unconvincing. Other than that, he couldn't think of anything that might not make the situation worse.

He reread the letter to slip inside his flying manual and leave on the shelf above his bed. It was the one they had all been told they had to write in case they didn't come back.

Dear Mother,
We are being put through our paces but there are some things that are hard and it's not the flying. I'm writing to you in case something

might happen. If this letter reaches you, I know all you will be thinking of is tragedy and death, but I've never felt so alive in my life. So, if this is a goodbye, please understand I died doing something I love.

He should be writing this letter to Betsy, he thought, not his blessed mother. He had tried to distract himself, but he still had not been able to put her out of his head. Soon the plane would be towed out to the end of the runway. He couldn't really think of anything that made him happier than to be up in the clouds with the thrill of the noise and the excitement of wide grey skies and the countryside stretching out below like a green quilt as he headed out over the cliffs of Flamborough Head, on to Holland and towards the unknown. Nothing made him feel whole like flying. Well, almost nothing.

Because now there was the girl with the blue eyes and the blonde floating hair.

Betsy, meanwhile, had also had days of torment. She was embarrassed and regretted leaving the hangar the minute she had done it. The next morning, she tried to find him, but the place was swarming and soon it would be in lockdown. All he had wanted to do was kiss her, and wasn't that what she had wanted as well? But Alvis had come into her head like a ghost, stalking her and ruining everything. She cursed herself that she would be stuck with those flashbacks for ever, hurtling back to the memory of her feet sticking out from behind the curtain. *Come out, Betsy, I can see you.*

The evening came around quickly enough, however. James had spent hours in the briefing room and Betsy had been busy too. More reruns in the wireless communications, going over the instructions and codes on how to bring a plane in, how to direct it towards the flare path. She was still shadowing but tonight she was told she would be in the tower for take-off.

Arriving at the meeting point as she had been told to do, she saw the officers – the 'top brass', as everyone called them – gathering on the roof with binoculars, intermittently raising them to their eyes to scour the sky. All around the airfield were bombers. The three green and grey four-engine Lancasters that were waiting on the tarmac had men crawling all over them – ground crew, riveters, mechanics, all manner of servicemen with a job to do. Out on the field there was a small group checking the tyres, and two men with flashlights that blinked alternately green and red.

'Should be straightforward,' she heard a sergeant say, shouting over the noise of the planes revving their engines for tests.

'Long as the searchlights don't get 'em. Back for breakfast. Piece of cake. Engineers say all tickety-boo with the undercarriage.'

The flight sergeant came in, rubbing his hands. 'Nervous?' he asked, slapping the back of the gunner standing next to him, who was gazing out across the airfield.

The gunner shrugged. 'We lost two last week. The sooner we get more Lancasters up in the air, the better. Those Manchesters are hard to handle.'

'But they'll still do more damage than any of Hitler's Heinkels. There's a new lot coming in next week.'

The bus trundled across the tarmac. A dozen or so men climbed out, which was when Betsy's heart kicked at her ribs. At the back of the bus, making his way between the seats, was James, patting the men on their backs, hiking his parachute over his shoulder.

I'm here, I'm here, she wanted to cry. But he turned away and made his way to the small group waiting on the tarmac near the plane. They would leave as soon as they got the signal. She felt as if her heart was bursting out of her ribcage. After the officer nodded, she watched James walk slowly towards the Lancaster, then stop, turn back, and squint towards the watchtower. She thought she might stop breathing. The rear gunner, Mathers, and the two other gunners and the engineer looked like they were sharing a joke. The nav, the one with the sloping aquiline nose, threw back his head and laughed, clapped his arm around the mid-gunner's shoulders. What was so funny? She wondered how they could laugh at a time like this. But it wasn't her place to answer that. How could anyone begin to put themself in any of their shoes? she thought, as she went inside the building and upstairs to the control room. Facing possible death and facing it again the next night and the night after that.

'Betsy, look sharp,' said Carol, as they went inside and up the stairs.

Betsy took her place on the seat next to her and put the headphones on.

'When we're told, you can tell them to start the engines. I'll give you the nod. You know what to say?'

'All clear. Prepare for take-off,' said Betsy.

'That's it. Simple. Good luck.'

Betsy nodded, her heart racing, palms sweating. Half an hour later, Carol winked at her and gave her the thumbs up.

'B squadron. All clear. Prepare for take-off.' She tried to sound calm, to keep her voice steady.

And though she was shaking inside she must have convinced them because the officer next to her whispered, 'Well done,' as the engines began to make their deafening roar. Out on the airfield the green light flashed.

'Chocks away . . .' said a voice over the tannoy. The smell of gas and oil and fuel filled the air and hit the back of her throat. The air wobbled as the huge tyres rolled and miraculously the plane began to move forward. The sound of the engines grew even louder. Shatteringly loud.

And then it was the vibrating that rattled cups on surfaces and teeth, the roaring and smoke and haze of petrol as the plane lifted. The messages coming through from the cockpit were shaky and muffled until the voices diminished amidst a cacophony of buffeting wind and white noise, which finally dwindled to an intermittent crackling. Her heart thumped and juddered every time she heard a voice.

She noted the distances and speeds down with a shaky hand and measured the ratios. Slowly, moving around the table, she collected the take-off notes and wrote down their coordinates. It was all a blur, but she knew she had to remain focused. She might have been feeling desperately worried about James, but she had a job to do, and she was determined to do it well.

Half an hour later after they had been sent back to the huts, creeping down the corridor, she made her way out of the side door, shivering in the cold air. The only way to calm herself was by counting, multiplying, dividing – distances, fuel loads, heights – whilst fumbling in her pocket for a cigarette. She took it out and lit it.

'Drew! Go back inside! I just told her she needed to go back to bed,' said Janice to Carol, who had followed her. Betsy wanted to argue it was pointless, she wouldn't get even a wink of sleep, she might as well go down and help prepare the teas for the following morning.

'What are you doing hanging around here?' said Carol. Betsy noticed she had reapplied her make-up. She looked startlingly glamorous.

'Oh. I needed a cigarette.'

'Our little Betsy smokes?' said Janice, raising an eyebrow.

She could see the other girl looking at her out of the corner of her eye. 'We've a dark horse here. Caught Drew sucking on a Woodbine outside,' she said, as Janice approached.

'To calm your nerves? You'll be coughing like a miner if you keep that up. Go to bed. We'll find out who has come back in the morning. Second shift are in the tower now. Hopefully all of the boys will be having their bacon and eggs in a while, all a little drunk on rum after they've celebrated.'

Betsy had hoped to stay awake, to wait until she had seen James walking across the tarmac. She wanted to run across to meet him, throw her arms around him and kiss him and say she was sorry for dashing off, but now she had been sent back to the hut and the plane had hours before it landed. Surprisingly, though, she fell asleep the minute her head hit the pillow.

At 3 a. m. she was awoken by the sound of the planes thundering back to the airbase. Blinking her eyes, she scrambled to her feet. Treading carefully, she quietly made her way between the beds. She would say she needed to go to the lavatory if the corporal sleeping in the small room next door woke and noticed her. She couldn't be refused that. Once inside the cubicle, she stood on the seat and pushed open the window a few inches. Squinting across the field, the lights of the flare path were bleeding through the morning mist. Counting each plane bumping onto the runway and rushing towards the copse that marked the end of it, she wondered which one was James's plane. Some of the aircraft were older than others. Some had yellow bombs painted on their noses; others had turrets that were damaged, rivets and sections replaced where they had been hit by flak. As they began to sharpen into focus and take shape, the roaring sound became louder, and the final planes thudded onto the runway, followed by a truck coming out of the hangar. She heard shouting and saw a fire crew race to a plane. Silhouettes of men scrambled out.

'L for Louella in! Looks like bullet holes in the wing. Limping but she'll make it. Send the meat wagon just in case.'

She watched as a group with binoculars searched the expanse of the rose blush of the morning sky.

'M for Misty!' The feeling of dread, and then elation was palpable. And when she saw a WAAF with a blanket nearly collapsing when the pilot got out of the plane, she breathed a sigh of relief as well. But James? Where was James? A little way away she saw the airmen shivering, but no James yet. She felt the knots in her stomach tighten and her heart hammering. But then a voice said, 'S for Sweetie coming in!' She saw Richards waiting on the balcony of the watchtower punch the air. Full House!

'James. You're home,' she murmured. Relief, always the happiest emotion of all, Betsy thought, flooded through her. She came out of the corridor and crept back to the dormitory, hugging her dressing gown around her for warmth.

'Drew . . . what are you doing skulking around out here? I've already told you.'

It was Carol, walking back carrying a tray with shot glasses of rum on it. Those red lips again, looking as glamorous as a movie star to greet the airmen.

'Go back to bed. He's safe. I won't tell anyone. But don't do that again, Drew.'

Chapter 23

The next morning James found her crossing the court-yard. She was carrying the folders with *Top Secret* marked on them that she had been instructed to take to Officer Sweeney's office.

'Betsy!'

'Oh, James!' Flustered, she dropped the top few folders and they slid onto the floor. 'I'm so sorry. I was so rude dashing off the other night like that . . .'

'Stop,' he said, taking her hand and squeezing it. 'I shouldn't have been so forward. I didn't want to . . . I would never want to . . .'

'I know,' she replied, her voice quavering. 'Shush.'

'Some of the men, they give the old story about life and death . . . but you are so sweet . . . the sweetest girl I have ever met. I wouldn't want to . . . Betsy, I'm sorry . . . Do you forgive me?'

'James, it doesn't matter. You have nothing to be sorry for.'

'No, but you're so . . . so . . .'

'James . . . James . . . stop babbling . . .'

'No. I'm sorry. And I love you,' he blurted.

She leaned forwards and, without warning, she kissed him on the lips. For a moment he looked at her in shock. 'It was my fault. Something over nothing . . . Ridiculous of me to run off like that. Now kiss me. Kiss me and never stop. I love you too, James.'

She dragged him behind the low bunker where the hill rose up steeply behind. As her lips met his he felt as if he was the luckiest man alive.

'Time moves differently now, at least since this war started. Betsy, I've fallen in love with you hard. I'm done for. Quicker than the blink of an eye. From the first time I met you I knew you were the girl for me.' He dropped his head. 'The truth is, I'm not experienced. I suppose you think at my age I would be . . .'

'I don't think anything.'

He paused, and then his words tumbled out in short, broken sentences. 'You think I'm a man of the world, do you? But really, I'm not. And I know some of the chaps here would take advantage of a girl like you. But I would never say those things they say, you know, just because I might not come back alive. I couldn't do it to you, Betsy. I mean . . . I would rather wait until my wedding day . . .'

Imagine if he knew that she had had a baby. That she was loose. He seemed to think she was some kind of angel. But would it be a sin to let him think that? Would the truth not hurt him, as well as her? She let him kiss her again as the world around her became nothing and she decided not to worry about it for now.

Two weeks had passed. James was back on his duties but there had been more celebrations when his friend, Fry, had finished a tour of thirty bombing missions. He had had tea with Betsy twice and they had spent their free evenings holding hands walking around the perimeter of the airfield talking about the war and Liverpool and how James planned to stay in the RAF when it was over, and how he had already been asked to talk to them about some of his ideas for design improvements to planes. And they had kissed. They had kissed an awful lot.

'Betsy,' he said breathlessly when he arrived at the hawthorn bush where they had met most nights for the past two weeks. 'I have to go to RAF Speke next week – it's near Liverpool. They're expecting a new consignment of planes from America. They're being driven through the Mersey tunnel on trucks. I have two days' leave and when I told Winco I would be going home to Liverpool, he asked me to take some correspondence to Speke for the Mersey op. I'll get paid for it, so what's not to like? He said I should take an AC1 with me, that I should find someone here who also knows their way around the city of Liverpool. Will you come with me? It's just for one night. A forty-eight-hour pass. I'm planning to see my mother. It's long overdue.'

'Me? A girl?'

'I don't see why not. We're told to travel in pairs in case anything should happen. If the motor breaks down or we get lost. We already know you're a demon under a car bonnet. I thought you might like to make a visit to your aunt's.'

Betsy looked at him and felt her throat go dry. 'They've been evacuated to . . . Wales,' she stuttered.

'Then stay with me at Mottram Hall.'

'What?'

'Come and stay at draughty old Mottram. We've eighteen bedrooms. Choose one. Any one you fancy. It's a chance for my mother to meet you.' She looked shocked. 'What's the matter? Why not? You might breathe a little life into the house. Say yes, Betsy.'

'But I'm . . . Would she approve of someone . . . like me?'

James burst out laughing.

'Someone like you? Beautiful, talented, clever? She will fall in love with you, just like I did, the moment she meets you. Now, stop worrying. I love you. Just be yourself when you meet her. Everything will be all right. If she meets you, then perhaps she will put these stupid notions away of me marrying Clem. You're such a terrific girl.'

Betsy said she would think about it, but by lunch-time, after a conversation with Janice who had told her she would never speak to her again if she refused and she must promise to give her every last detail of the trip to his stately pile, she had agreed. And now James was walking towards the commander's office with a spring in his step and her name written on a slip of paper to hand over to his officer.

Sybil Donaghue made her way quickly down the corridor of St Mary's orphanage, holding the hand of her daughter who was toddling and tripping behind her trying to keep up. She tucked the duster into her belt and turned to Belinda, kneeling down to speak to her directly.

'Don't tell Sister,' she said, slipping a chocolate into her hand.

Sybil had spent the morning dusting vases and preparing the nuns' teas and had managed to steal the caramel cream from the biscuit jars. You couldn't find a sweet in Liverpool these days and yet the nuns had an endless supply because the adopters would bring gifts: sweets, biscuits, packets of coins . . . No one asked who they were for, the children or the nuns, so Sybil had decided to make it her job to redistribute them generously.

She made her way into the nursery. A few nuns were sitting on the armchairs giving bottles to some of the babies. A girl called Ellie was rocking a small boy on her knee.

The sister was waiting for her at the door, arms folded across her expansive chest. 'Sybil, I need a word.'

Sybil faltered. 'Come over here. We know what you've been doing. You've been telling people that there's something wrong with your baby, haven't you?'

'Who said that?' asked Sybil, shocked.

She cast her eyes around and they rested on Ellie. Ellie shrugged.

'Never mind. But there's absolutely nothing wrong with her. From now on, I'll be watching you. And in the meantime, I'm making it a priority to find your daughter somewhere she can thrive. I have already had interest from a couple. Very nice. Mrs Barnes teaches the flute. Is Mary musical? Just think, she could be playing in an orchestra one day.'

'No!' she cried and stamped her foot. 'And she's called Belinda, not Mary!'

The nun sighed. 'Sybil, control yourself. You've been here too long. Of course, you could leave with Mary

228

now if you don't like the idea of Mrs and Mrs Barnes. We don't have locked doors here.'

'But Sister, we have nowhere to go,' she said plaintively.

'Oh, yes. I forgot. Your house was bombed, wasn't it? Your parents died? Then stop being difficult.'

Sybil expelled air in an audible sigh. Then she suddenly threw down onto the floor the headless doll she had been holding with a cry of frustration.

'Sybil! Don't do that! You're like a wild animal today!'

'I am. I know. I'm sorry,' she wailed. 'It wasn't my fault, getting pregnant!'

'Always the way, blaming the men,' the nun said under her breath. 'Calm down. The Lord has given us all self-control. You'd know all about that. Not having any, I mean. Now pick that up. And be grateful.'

'It was a full moon when he did it to me, Sister. I couldn't help it.'

'Tch. What nonsense! Full moon? The dance halls are responsible for all this. Glen Miller blasting away on all those trumpets and it turns everyone feral. It doesn't help all this mixing together for the war effort. More and more girls wearing trousers. Those Land Girls. Hands stuffed in their pockets, smoking and spitting. No better than mules, some of them. The fresh air and the manure go to their heads. Anyway, the good news is that your child has plenty of options for a better future. Not just the Barneses.'

Options? Sybil could feel her heart hammering. What was the nun saying? She had heard the murmurings about the boats. She had seen the children lined up, dressed up in woolly hats and with the suitcases. The girl Ellie didn't stop going on about it. She had told her about the Bible and an apple and a pencil inside the suitcase. She didn't trust the nun. Who were these Barnes people?

'Anything more to say?'

Sybil's pupils darkened. She shook her head and dropped her eyes to the floor. 'Over my dead body and yours,' she said under her breath.

An hour later, after the children were all in bed and she could hear the voices floating up from the chapel, Sybil tiptoed down the corridor. The conversation with the nun had given her fire in her belly and a sudden sense of urgency. What was it that girl Ellie had said? *You'll find everything you need to know in the filing cabinet in Sister Cyril's office.* Would they have more to say about the Barneses? Quietly going through the door, she shut it behind her and pushed a chair up against it. She could feel a sweat breaking out on her brow, but she knew she had to remain calm. She had seen the buff folders being slipped into the filing cabinet many times. Taking a deep breath, she opened the top drawer and began rifling through it. If there was one thing she was certain of, it was that the nuns wrote everything down. They were obsessive about keeping a record of names, dates, addresses, money and gifts received. But going through the first file, there were lists and lists of names. You could have made whole books of them. How many times someone had come to look at the child. Whether they had been interested. Whether they had commented.

There were pages and pages of notes. Folders bulging with correspondence. Receipts, bills. She took a few of the envelopes out, hoping to find something about her daughter and the Barneses. 'Flaming flute,' she muttered.

She found her file quickly and easily thanks to them being in alphabetical order and each drawer being labelled. *Adopters* she went to first. And there it was in black and white. Barnes.

Mr and Mrs Barnes. Hoping for baby but open to having older child on account of nervousness with baby illnesses and deformities and potential ensuing problems. Suggested Sybil Donaghue's child. Lisp and stutter but abating as child is getting older. No obvious defects. Pleasant-looking.

Sybil shook with rage. This was the confirmation she needed. She had to get out of this place as soon as she could. But how? Stuffing the file back in the drawer, she was about to leave, but then something odd caught her eye.

Her gaze alighted on a file that was marked *Confidential* on the shelf next to the drawers. Like a moth drawn to flame, she took it and opened it. She wondered if there would be any names in it that she recognized. Perhaps the wild girl, Ellie. Or the sisters Marcia and Cynthia. It occurred to her that the more wrongs she could find, the stronger argument her case would have. She could tell the man from the Corporation, Higgins. The first few pages she turned meant nothing to her. Names that were just letters being chased off a page, girls who had given up their babies, lists of original names and new names, baptism dates, doctors who had signed off births at the mother and baby homes. But just as she was about to leave, a letter folded in half fluttered out. *Betsy Drew* it said on the front in italicized letters. Betsy Drew? Why did they have a letter about Betsy? she wondered. She'd never been in the orphanage . . . Her baby had died. Hadn't he?

Chapter 24

Betsy and James set off to Speke in the RAF motor car, chuntering up and down the steep hills of the Pennines towards the coast and then down towards Preston and Lancashire. They talked the whole way, all the time with his hand resting on her knee. When he told her they wanted to move him to Norfolk soon to fly Lancasters as part of Bomber Harris's plans, she nodded seriously, and felt a little bit afraid. Stopping at a roadside cafe in a village outside Manchester, they sat on a bench and kissed for an age and watched a robin peck about. Finally, four hours later, they arrived at Speke – an airfield south of Liverpool on the silted-up land of the estuary. It was a much smaller base than Dishforth and it was where they would bring the deliveries of new planes from the factories and train airmen. They got out of the car after being waved through the gates by the corporal. There were already three planes being driven around the airfield.

'Here to see Officer Merrick . . .'

When they were directed to the office, Betsy sat outside. She could hear murmuring from beyond the door. James reappeared quickly, smiling.

'Betsy, Officer Merrick has offered me a run out in a Mosquito. You ever been up in plane?'

She shook her head.

'Then let's go.'

Half an hour later, the plane phutted across the green with James piloting, Merrick sitting beside him and Betsy behind them. The engine roared and the smell of gasoline filled their nostrils. As they took off to a deafening rattling and shaking, Betsy gripped the edges of the seat. When James steadied the plane, he turned and grinned.

'She's marvellous. Beautiful, isn't she?' he shouted.

'Yes. And the plane's not bad either . . .' Merrick laughed.

Betsy blushed. Below them the countryside stretched out and the river widened as they swooped over the estuary glittering in the sunshine.

'Breathtaking, hey, Betsy?' said James, pointing down, shouting to be heard over the noise of the engines.

It really was. They followed the line of the coast out across the city and the docks and then south towards Crosby and Formby with its yellow dunes and rippling marram grass, swooping low over the wide sandy beach and out towards the sea. He nodded over to the lilac smudge of the Welsh hills. For James, the rush of the wind and the thrill of this small light aircraft was so different to the four-engine Lancasters and the unwieldy Halifaxes and after spending time flying sturdy bombers, he was enjoying the fragility of this aircraft and how deftly it responded to his touch.

'What d'you think, Betsy? See why they call her a Mosquito?'

When they arrived back on the ground, landing as lightly as a feather, flushed and excited, he took her hand.

'Are you two in a hurry?' asked Merrick. 'If you have time, I recommend you go for a walk in those woods we just nearly brushed the tops of. There's a pub where you can get a nice pint and a decent ploughman's. Oh, and Drew, if I ask for a transfer back here for you . . . We're short of wireless operators at nearby Woodvale. We would train you up in coding as well. Would you consider it?'

Glancing at James, she nodded a yes, knowing that she could not have replied with a no. This was the RAF.

Half an hour later they walked down towards the Oggie shoreline, arms entwined and holding hands, enjoying the soft sand underfoot. They looked out over the estuary with sunshine dancing off the surface of the water.

'Did you enjoy being up in the air?' he asked.

'I was just a little bit terrified.' She laughed. 'I can see you love it . . .'

'Yes. I do. I feel free up in the sky,' he said, threading her fingers with his. 'I take no pleasure in what we're doing – bombing cities and factories, I mean. I hate it. But it's the flying, Betsy,' he said, kissing the curve of her neck. 'There's no greater thrill than a Lancaster.'

The last part of the sentence tailed off. The numbers were getting worse. It was unlikely a young bomber crew would survive after their fifth sortie. It was a horrible statistic and one calculation Betsy avoided thinking about.

She inclined her head gently on his shoulder. He raised her chin with a finger and kissed her hard on the lips then hugged her close. Feeling grit blowing off the Oggie sands stinging her cheeks, tasting the air, until now she hadn't dared to think of a future with this man who she had loved from the first day she had met him. But the seriousness of what he was saying hit her.

He sighed. 'Betsy, I can't bear the thought of being apart from you . . . But if they're going to be always moving us around – you to Woodvale, me to Norfolk – don't we need something more . . . permanent?'

Suddenly, he got down on one knee, twisted off the thick gold band on his middle finger and held it out to her. She could see he was trembling slightly.

'Will you marry me? Say yes, Betsy. I've never been more certain of anything in my life.'

Betsy was in shock. 'Marry! So soon?'

He blushed, losing confidence. 'You don't want to? Is it a stupid idea?'

'No. Of course not. I love you. And I know with this war everyone is getting married so quickly because . . .' She didn't want to say it out loud: *because if you're flying in RAF Bomber Command you will probably die, so why not marry if it means the world will see your love as more than a notch on a bedpost? Perhaps you will even leave your mark on this earth with a child . . .* How could she say that out loud? Instead, she said quietly, 'But James, there's so much you don't know about me.'

'Like what?'

'My friends. My family . . .'

She shuddered. What would he think of Jacky with his love of betting on the horses, his pub crawls and loud-mouthed pals? And then she felt a little ashamed. Jacky was loyal and kind. But then there was Malcolm. Spitting, grabbing Malcolm, who knew everything about her, every horrific detail. Even Deirdre with her snorting laugh and potty mouth. And Alvis. What if he were to come back and find her? She had heard nothing from him despite writing countless letters to him, and now she didn't want to. But what about when the war was over?

Thoughts thundered through her head. Was this the moment she should tell him about her baby? But it would ruin everything. And after so much sadness, why shouldn't she have happiness like everyone else? Shouldn't she take it by her hands and grab it? She had dreamed of this. To be married. To be loved. And by this man . . .

'Yes . . . say yes . . .'

She opened her mouth to speak and cast her eyes to the floor. And then a wave of energy coursed through her. 'Yes, my love. Yes, yes, yes . . .' she said, her eyes brimming with tears.

He clamped his hands to his temples, then kissed her and lifted her off the ground and whirled her around until she was dizzy. 'I'm the happiest man in the world! Betsy, I love you! I love this girl! I'm the luckiest man alive!' he yelled up at the sky, stretching his arms out and then punching the air.

Betsy laughed. 'You'll frighten the cows.'

'I'll buy you a proper engagement ring. For now, will this do?' he said, pushing the gold band onto her finger. 'My father used to wear this on his little finger. He gave it to me after my first flight. We could get married in our best blues. I just want to be with you for the rest of my life, Betsy.'

'But your mother?'

'I know she always wanted me to get married at the Hall's chapel, and in her mind's eye she saw me with Clementine, but it's you I love.'

Betsy frowned. 'We're so different, though . . . James, your life . . . In ten years I can see you on the steps of your Hall, wearing a suit, a pipe in your mouth, a Jaguar on the drive . . . Me, I don't know . . . I just can't see me in that picture. We're so different . . .'

'We're not different when we kiss, Betsy. We're exactly the same. Aren't we?' he asked as his lips met hers.

'We are. But please, let's not tell your mother. Not yet. Is that all right? What if she doesn't like me?'

The journey out of Liverpool took longer than they had thought. James told her to look for the pretty threepenny-bit house, and soon enough she saw it with its six sides, sitting on the side of the road in the woods. 'Is this your house?' she asked, nervously.

'No, the one up ahead.'

The tree-lined drive from the gates of Mottram Hall up to the house went on for ever. And the lake! She had seen nothing like it in her life. How could two people live in this huge house, in these grounds that were bigger than some villages she knew? What on

earth was she doing here? Standing in front of the
enormous front door with a brass knocker in the shape
of an angel, panic gripped her. Stranger than all of this
was that James didn't seem the least bit unsettled by it.
James. Her fiancé! It didn't feel real. He had been
unwavering in his enthusiasm of her meeting his mother,
and so she didn't want to dampen his mood, but she
was terrified. They were met on the stairs by Gordon.
When they followed him in, she was shocked to see
that Mottram Hall was even bigger and colder than
James had described. The grandfather clock ticked
slowly and deliberately. Grand*mother* clock, James
corrected her in a whisper, when she admired it. Gordon
showed her to her room with the huge four-poster bed.
He offered to carry her bags but when she said she was
fine carrying them herself, James had to lean in and tell
her gently Gordon would much rather do it for her.
'This is the Acorn wing,' he said, gesturing at the rugs
and tapestries, porcelain candlesticks and silver on the
dressers. It all felt like she was in some kind of dream.

Ten minutes later she met James downstairs. Lettice
swept into the room, skirting around the long table
covered in a cream linen tablecloth with silver cande-
labra at each end and a huge tureen in the centre. She
had a cigarette stuffed into a long slim gold holder.

Betsy stifled a sneeze as she sat down and shifted
in the shiny velvet threadbare sofa with feathers
escaping from the seams. A draft wheezed down the
chimney. 'So, my dear, you met when you were both
working at Cunard's, I understand? And now you're
in the RAF with James? What a coincidence,' she said,
rearranging her velvet scarf draped over her shoulder.

Betsy nodded. What would Deirdre think about this cluttered room, browned varnished paintings of men in uniform, shelves groaning with dusty books, every surface apart from the table covered with huge vases, bowls of china eggs and ornate glass candlesticks?

'We don't need to eat dinner in the dining room. I told Gordon we can just have a tray by the fireplace,' Lettice said, though the fireplace was unlit.

When Gordon arrived a moment later with trays on wheels, Betsy looked at the dizzying array of knives and forks, the small pot of jam, the butter in a small dish, the tea strainer and delicate china cups, and began feeling a little ill.

'So, Betsy. What should I call you? Is Betsy short for Elizabeth?'

'Short for Betty,' she said, feeling like her confidence was draining away from her and cursing her mother for that idiocy.

'Is it, Betsy?' said James. 'I didn't know that. Betty's a pretty name as well. Like Betty Grable.'

Lettice's mouth hardened. 'Short for Betty? But it's the same number of letters?' *The world is full of these girls with ridiculously childish names these days*, her face looked like she wanted to say.

Betsy could feel her cheeks pinking.

'Betsy's an absolute whizz with numbers. That's why she's been poached from Cunard's by the RAF. She's so clever, Mother.'

His mother nodded. 'James tells me you are an orphan?' She tipped her head to one side. 'Or are you an orphan of the living? Like my girls at St Mary's,' she asked with a brief, tight smile.

'I don't know what that is,' stuttered Betsy.

'Good God, Mother,' said James sharply.

'Dear, it's exactly what you would think it is. You're a clever girl.' Lettice, being the kind of woman whose wealth shielded her from the need to care, knew she was being unkind.

'Betsy lost her mother when she started her training. It was a shock, wasn't it?'

Betsy nodded.

'Well, you both have that in common. The unexpected death of a parent. What about your father, Betty?' Lettice raised an eyebrow. Had she been born able to do that or had it taken years of practice in front of the mirror? thought Betsy. It had the desired effect and Betsy's teaspoon rattled nervously against the saucer.

'He died when I was eight years old,' she lied. 'The RAF is my family now. And if I can be useful and they'll have me, I'll stick with it. They fast-tracked me. James has helped me.'

'James?' echoed Lettice with a hint of distaste in her voice.

'Yes . . .' she said, with a blush. 'They've said that maybe there will be a place for me in coding eventually,' she added quickly. 'They want me to transfer to Woodvale to see how I get on as a wireless operator.'

'Woodvale? That's the place where Polish airmen train and squadrons go to rest after a tour, isn't it?' said Lettice.

'Yes. They need wireless operators.'

'I told you she was clever,' beamed James.

James's mother peered at Betsy over the top of the

gold-rimmed teacup and again raised an arched pencilled eyebrow. The girl was even prettier than when she had first seen her walking up the steps in her navy-blue uniform and brown shoes, her glossy mane of blonde hair escaping from under her cap – obviously it was this that had turned James's head. But the idea of a serious romance was ridiculous. Whatever he said about her being clever, she had shopgirl running through her veins. You could hear it loud and clear in that blunt, flat accent. No doubt lurking underneath her prettiness was naked ambition. Did she know about Clementine? she wondered. What had he told her? To mention her so soon would be unnecessarily cruel, even for her, but it was important, even though James insisted the romance was over. And good grief, he was now holding the girl's hand. His fingers were intertwined with hers.

Lettice asked another few clipped questions about Cunard's, but she wasn't really interested in the answer. 'Dear . . . your family? Where did you say they lived?'

'Blundellsands,' she stuttered.

'Really?'

A grimace played over Lettice's lips as if to say, if it hadn't been for this wretched war, her son would be sitting here with Clementine, not this dreadful girl, and she would be arranging a wedding and buying a dress from George Henry Lee's and choosing a corsage from Harrods and organizing tea at Coopers with Clementine's mother to talk about table places.

'Has Jum told you about his fiancée, Clementine? Coming-out season is upon us. Did you book your leave, darling?'

Betsy blushed.

'Mother!' he retorted, banging down the cup, which rattled in its saucer, a quick fury rising in his voice. 'She's not my fiancée! And please, don't call me Jum.'

Twenty minutes later they walked circles around the gravel path that threaded through the woodland walk, beech trees stooping and holly bushes prickling through the gaps to find the light. 'She hates me, *Jum*.' A ragged little wind blew. Her eyes flicked away when he tried to meet hers. 'Why does she call you Jum?'

'Because I was so skinny, they used to call me Jumbo. Then it became Jum. Just one of those cruel pet names. I prefer Jimmy. Would you call me Jimmy?'

'Jimmy? Yes. I like it. Jimmy Stewart is lovely. It has a friendly ring to it.'

'She doesn't hate you. Even if she did, I don't care.'

He kissed her on the nose. She shivered. She didn't know much about rich people, but she had read enough books, seen enough films and listened to enough wireless shows to know that she would have to work hard to fit in.

'Betsy, I want to tell her soon that we're engaged.'

'She'd die rather than see you marry someone like me.'

'Someone like you? You keep saying that. You mean, good, kind, beautiful, clever?'

'Poor.'

'I don't care. She can cut me off if she wants.'

'I don't want to come between you. Cut you off . . . ?'

'I don't need this shambolic pile. Look at it. She would be doing me a favour. Betsy, I just need *you* . . .

Let's do it quickly. Shall we? Before one of us gets an actual date to leave for Norfolk or Woodvale?'

Sitting on a bench under a pergola dripping with a sweet-smelling flowering jasmine, he held her hand and kissed the tips of her fingers gently.

'She really hates me,' said Betsy.

'No, she doesn't. She will come round.'

'Come round? She loathes me.'

'Don't be silly. She's just taking a bit of time to get used to the idea that Clementine has gone off with Lionel. It's difficult, but I'm relieved. Clem will be happy, and I'm glad she can make his life a drama instead of mine. Lionel is indulging her in one of her stupid music follies, and good luck to them both. God, Betsy, I love you. You're real, not like Clem and all the other girls my mother has already lined up for me. The season. I can't stand it.'

'What did she mean, "her girls at St Mary's"?'

'Oh, it's one of her committees. An orphanage. St Mary's of the Blessed Angels. Women like my mother don't have jobs so instead they do "good works" to make themselves feel useful.'

Betsy stopped and moved a piece of gravel around the path with her toe. If this was the biggest mistake in her life – not telling him about her own awful connection to the orphanage – she was about to make it. But make it she did, as she silently turned round to face the house and shuddered. It loomed above and seemed to puff itself out. 'This place, it's like something from a fairy tale. It's a castle.'

'No, it looks impressive but it's draughty and old. Last time I was home, hilariously my mother put on a coat and there was a mouse in her sleeve. You might look at it with its turrets and gargoyles and think it's grand, but there are mushrooms growing in the bathrooms because of the damp, and floorboards you have to avoid or you will fall right through them and crash to the floor below, ceilings that the rain comes pouring through. Haven't you noticed the buckets? They're everywhere. The gardens are full of thistles. Look around you. It's all too much. And far too expensive.'

Betsy returned to her room exhausted, her head spinning. One bucket on the stairwell at the tenements was enough. But imagine a hundred buckets that needed emptying each day. She took the ring that she had slipped into her pocket and held it to the light. Engaged. To Officer Swann. It seemed absurd. Her head fell back on the prickly pillow with feathers escaping from the seams. But just as she began to fall asleep, she heard a soft knock on the bedroom door. Opening it, James was standing there dressed in his pyjamas. Burgundy-coloured silk, with white piping. He grinned and shrugged.

'Shush,' he said, putting a finger to his lips. 'Sorry about this get-up. I look like Noël Coward, don't I?' She didn't know who that was. 'Can I come in?'

Betsy nodded and opened the door wider.

'Darling . . .' he said, 'I just wanted to make sure you're all right.'

He walked her over to the bed and sat with his arm around her shoulders. Then, falling backwards, they kissed as he rolled on top of her and they soon became tangled up in the sheets, him tracing his hand gently across the rises and valleys of her body, feeling the heat of her through the thin linen of her nightdress.

She wondered if he knew how much she longed for him. Was he aware of the agonies and ecstasies of this feeling of his skin on hers? Did the sound of her shallow breathing, or the way she jolted every time his fingers touched a new part of her, tell him how much she needed him? She placed a hand on his cheek. 'I love you. How am I not dreaming?'

'You're not. And I meant what I said earlier. If you'll have me, I want to be with you for ever, Betsy. And I don't care who knows. Starting with my mother.'

Chapter 25

Lettice Swann sat in the drawing room pouring tea. Clementine was sprawled on the sofa, nibbling a brandy snap and excitedly talking about how she had a starring role in the ENSA production of the Christmas pantomime. 'I'll be giving them my Princess Rose Petal!' she said excitedly. God help the poor audience, thought Lettice.

'Clementine, I have some uncomfortable news. I need your help with Jum. He . . . has . . . he needs persuading. We were all hoping you two would marry. This RAF has turned his head.'

'If you were still hoping we would marry, then I also have some uncomfortable news. I'm getting married to someone else,' she blurted. It wasn't what Lettice expected.

She had hoped Clementine would persuade James to change his mind over the Betsy nonsense. She had also hoped there was a chance of them rekindling their romance. Utterly horrified when he had told her the morning he had left Mottram – with a broad smile on his face over kedgeree – that he had proposed and Betsy had accepted, she had dismissed it, saying she wouldn't even speak of it to Betsy and that he was out of his mind. He hardly knew her! After a few

247

months. This was madness. *I met her two years ago, Mother. I know I want to spend the rest of my life with her*, was his response. *It's only because the rest of your life might be no more than your next sortie and you're not thinking straight*, she had snapped back, cruelly.

Clementine stifled a yawn. 'I'm sorry. I know you were hopeful that I might marry James, but sadly it's not to be. I feel terribly guilty about James.'

Lettice, flustered, stood quickly out of her seat, turned away and opened the shutters.

'Is this because of his shopgirl – or whatever she is?' Her lips were pressed together in a hard line so that the lipstick on her mouth became a gash.

'I didn't know about that. Is she a shopgirl? If she makes him happy, that's good, isn't it?' Clementine continued. 'I'm not a snob, Lettice. I think that's rather sweet. Besides, he's an earnest sort of boy. And I think he needs an earnest sort of girl. My Lionel. Now, he's a little shallow. He likes a good time. Drinking, dancing, the horses. But you know, with this war, maybe shallow is what will get Lionel and me through. I see where James gets it from – his earnestness. You with your banners and your suffragettes and pamphleting for all those dead and damaged soldiers in the last war. We're all different. I take pleasure from things like fairy rings, and twinkling stars. It might seem girlish, but pearls and mink stoles are such a comfort to me with this war going on. Or maybe a distraction. Who knows? James is the noble sort and maybe the girl suits him.'

'There's nothing noble about her. After the Swann money,' muttered Lettice, banging the shutters, making Clementine squeak.

'Is there Swann money?' said Clementine flatly.

'There's the Hall. Clementine, won't you at least try to persuade him to see sense?'

Clementine sighed.

'Please?' implored Lettice.

As soon as Clementine left, Lettice took a pen and notepad and sat down to write. Her hand began to tremble, with anger probably, and she had to steady herself to stop the words wobbling across the page.

> *Dear James,*
>
> *You have broken my heart. Clementine came to the Hall for tea and we talked about your romance. She's brokenhearted too. I'm asking you to reconsider this Betty girl. James, I will do everything in my power to stop this silly dalliance. Please have absolute certainty also that I will cut you off if you were to do something so stupid as to marry. Can't you see she's a gold digger? Understand that it's because I love you. My entreaties are coming from a place of love. But drastic actions need a drastic response.*
>
> *Why can't you just take the decadent approach? Plenty of airmen have piffling romances. Why do you have to be so serious about everything? I am visiting Dilys's mother today. Can I say you will meet her for tea?*

*Coopers? Your next leave? Will you be home
for Christmas?*
    I love you,
    Your mother

It was almost ridiculous enough to make him laugh
out loud when he read the letter. Cut me off, Mother,
I really don't care, he thought.

'What is it?' asked Betsy half an hour later when
she met him at their usual place on the low wall beside
the row of hawthorn bushes. She had come from the
briefing room, where she had been asked to look at
some of the photographs from last week's sortie and
compare the targets to the actual hits. It was detailed,
methodical work involving reading the coordinates
and Betsy was glad of the fresh air. James was waiting
after having spent the morning doing a test flight.

'Nothing, darling,' he said, kissing her gently on the
nose. 'Nothing at all,' he said, when she pressed him.
'But I've been thinking about the wedding. I've just
had a meeting with Winco. More talk about Norfolk.'

'Oh no. So time is running out for us to arrange
things if you're to be remustered?'

'You mean, we should do it as soon as we can?' he
replied brightly. 'Oh, yes please, sweetheart,' he went
on in a torrent of words. 'That's what I was hoping
you would say, darling.'

Betsy was a little startled. She hadn't meant that,
but now he seemed so excited, so happy.

'But will we need time to get word to your family?'
he asked.

'Why?'

He looked a little puzzled. 'To invite them?'

She froze. 'I have no family who could come. My brother, he's away in France. My aunt . . . no, too busy with her boys.'

'Makes it simpler, I suppose.'

'And Jimmy, what about your mother . . . ?'

'She'll come round. She's not a bad person.'

Of course, he didn't tell her the full details of the letter. It would be too painful for her to hear that his mother had called his beloved Betsy a gold digger and a shopgirl. Instead, he took out a small camera and asked if he could take a photograph of her.

'Why?' she asked, puzzled.

'Because you look so beautiful. Stand under the oak tree. And smile. Smile, Betsy.'

Chapter 26

'Getting married?' squealed Melanie, as she walked with Betsy to the signals room. 'When?'

'Soon. In a few weeks if we can. Before we both leave here. I'm going to Woodvale when they can arrange it. And James to Norfolk, probably. So we want to do it quickly at the village church.'

'Good God, Drew! Quick work.'

Betsy blushed.

'You'll have a night above The Rose and Crown. In the bed with a hollow in it. I'm jealous.'

'It doesn't feel real,' said Betsy.

'You don't seem happy. You seem nervous,' said Melanie. 'Is anything wrong?'

'No. It's just a little rushed.'

'Do you love him?'

'More than you can ever imagine. Melanie, will you be my bridesmaid?'

'Of course!' She kissed her on the cheek.

'James has already spoken to the vicar.'

'Why not do it quickly, though? This is how weddings are now. You snatch them whenever you can. Just imagine, he'll be able to say *my wife* to his crew. They'll take him seriously if he has a wife . . . I can't wait. I'll put rose petals on your bed and find a thimble. And we can decorate the room with flowers.'

Of course, there were plenty who didn't care about being married. Betsy knew that. To hell with what might happen, Melanie had said. If you're left with his baby, at least you have something real of his, not just his blasted tie pin.

Half an hour later, though, the mood changed. The board had gone up that morning and Betsy's heart dropped when she saw that James's name was on it. James jogged over to her, breathless and smiling.

'Jimmy,' she said gently. 'The board. Your name is on it. Weather permitting.'

'Yes, I know. I'm on my way to the briefing.' His eyes drifted to the board and back to Betsy. His face clouded over. 'Betsy. The wedding, is it too soon? Because if it is, Betsy . . .'

'No,' she said, taking the cuff of his sleeve, tenderly stroking his arm. Reaching under her collar, she unclipped the small pin.

'Take this . . . for good luck tonight . . .'

He smiled and let her pin it under his lapel.

'Don't worry about me. Will you ask Lightfoot to be your bridesmaid?' he shouted after her as he walked away down the corridor.

'I already have!' she said with a brave wave.

'You may now light up,' said the group commander. The briefing room murmured approval and smoke filled the air. The curtain swished open when the officer standing with a baton pulled the cord. James sat on one of the benches facing the small stage on which the officer was standing in front of the map of Europe.

Still feeling pleasantly full after a breakfast of bacon, eggs and beans, his hand relaxed on his stomach. He had completed the required air test at midday and the mechanics were doing the final checks. Tonight would be his tenth sortie.

'This is your enemy,' the group commander said, pointing with a ruler at the small crude outlines of aeroplanes. 'Now, listen up, chaps. This will be straight-forward if those clouds don't drift northwards.'

James jotted down notes and scribbled diagrams.

An hour later the commander said, 'Synchronize your watches. All the best. Let's put on a jolly good show tonight.'

The sound of the teleprinters clattered down the corridor as Betsy hurried along, past the control room with the long desk on which the telephones and headphones sat waiting. Bomber Command's final orders had reached the airfield. The Met forecasts were in, and favourable for the mission. They were still waiting for details of bomb loads and bomb heights and more weather reports. No one was allowed out before a sortie but everyone was too busy anyway. Erks – the ground crew – were all over the place. The bomb trains would be loaded up. A large four-thousand-pound cookie bomb was being driven around the airfield. Some knew the many gaps in the fences through which they could slip away, but the pub would be quiet tonight.

Betsy trotted down another corridor. *Careless Talk*

Costs Lives, she read on a poster, and she felt it was speaking to her directly.

Late afternoon and the shadows began to lengthen. The camp would be locked down soon, guards on the gates, no one in or out and with telephones all locked, as was customary before a sortie, but the boy from the post office had pedalled like mad, hoping for a tip, and was grateful he was delivering to Dishforth camp and not knocking on some poor mother's front door. He was only fourteen and to see a mother's eyes fill with tears as they opened the telegram and read it in front of him – often they fainted or howled like an animal if it was bad news – was awful. Sometimes he would put his finger over the blue stamp saying PRIORITY, hoping he could leave quickly. No wonder they called the telegram boys the Angels of Death.

'Telegram for Betsy Drew,' he said to the man on the gates brightly, just as he always did.

'Just in time, lad,' he said.

Meanwhile, Betsy had toyed with going back and waiting outside the briefing room to say good luck to James, but everyone knew this was bad luck, so she had decided against it. She had waited to see him walking across the tarmac to the plane. Glancing up to the sky, seeing the trails of smoke of the two planes that had already taken off, she faltered. When two airmen walked past her she heard low voices talking of flak and how the weather had stopped the planes climbing to a safe height lately, and her heart lurched. Up above, a plane banked and turned. The village would be empty tonight. But plenty would be counting the planes taking off, and those that couldn't sleep would breathe a sigh of relief as they counted the planes coming back.

She looked over to where his Lancaster was lined up with three others at the end of the runway. She thought of the moment when they had lain in the cockpit and he had kissed her and she had pushed him away. Why had she done that? She should have taken every second with him. That was Alvis Dooley's fault. Kind, tender James would never do anything as horrible as Alvis had done to her. They were different in every way, so why would she think they might be the same? Ridiculous of her to run away from James when life hung in the balance every time the board went up with his name on it. His only crime was to love her. A crime that she had long since realized Alvis had never been guilty of. She could hear the wind moaning through the trees and in the distance the revving up of engines as the ground crew tested the engines. She waited for it to slowly build to a crescendo and prayed he would come back in the morning.

'Drew!' called Carol. 'Lad here has a telegram for you.'

'Telegram?' she said, surprised.

It was Carol who slipped five bob in the boy's hand. 'On your way . . .'

The boy nodded his thanks and left, pedalling hard.

'What is it, Drew?' said Carol, looking at Betsy scanning the words.

Dear Betsy, I have news. STOP. When is your next leave? STOP. Come to Liverpool quickly. Cave. STOP. I'm back at tennies. Deirdre. STOP.

Distracted, she pushed the telegram in her pocket. Deirdre, back home? Had she left the Wrens? She wondered if she was getting married too. But she put these questions aside. She would be going to Woodvale soon enough and she could easily take a train out to Liverpool. But for now, all she could think about was James.

'Nothing to report,' she replied. 'Just a friend from home.'

'Come on then. Let's go back to the hut. I've got something to show you.'

When they walked in, Carol went over to her locker.

'Ta-da!' she said, producing a package. 'Stockings!'

Betsy gasped. 'Where did you get those from?'

Carol grinned. 'They're not new, I'm afraid. Borrowed. But you need something borrowed. Even better, instead of wearing your blues, Melanie has seen a wedding dress in the raggy shop in the village. It's made out of a silk parachute and there's satin pumps with a silver buckle. She can take in the dress, give it a scoop and a train. Won't he get such a shock when he sees you walking down the aisle in a white dress instead of your blues? The shopkeeper has put it aside. And here, a white prayer book to carry with the posy I'll make. Isn't that lovely?'

A *white* dress, thought Betsy. And a prayer book.

'What's the matter, love? Is everything okay?'

Betsy looked at her round-eyed and worried. 'Yes,' she replied. 'I'm grateful . . .'

'Then why are you looking like that?' Carol frowned. 'What's happened?'

'Nothing. Just James is flying tonight.'

Carol nodded. She had seen Betsy with James any chance they had, walking the perimeter, talking in low voices behind the air-raid shelter, stealing glances with each other over the NAAFI, plotting, whispering. 'Are you pregnant?' asked Carol, tipping her head to one side. Betsy looked shocked. She blushed to the tips of her ears and didn't reply. 'Is that why you're getting married so suddenly?' pressed Carol.

'No . . .'

'I'm not sure I believe you. Listen, love,' she said, grasping her hand, 'if you are in the club, and things are hurtling forward too quickly because of it . . . well, if you don't want to keep it . . . I know a place. There won't be a fuss. No court martial. They'll just let you go quietly. I know the chief medical officer . . . She can sign a—'

'I wouldn't be so stupid as to get pregnant before we married. I wouldn't do that to James. And anyway, I'd have to leave and the RAF is my life.'

'All I'm saying is, if we knew how to keep the birds and the bees from finishing with the stork, we would, but how could you hold back with lovely James Swann?'

'Stop. I don't want to talk about this any more. You're on the wrong track. I mean it.'

She tried to stay awake, and it was now three in the morning. Finally, just as she was about to say a desperate prayer, through the mist came the comforting, distant sound of engines. Jerking upright, she tipped her head as one after another she could hear them coming in. One, two and then the third roared right overhead. And the fourth. And so there it was. And those others that had stayed awake in the village of Dishforth, hearing the roaring over the rooftops, would roll over onto their sides and finally get to sleep now. In the half-light as the dawn began to break, she imagined his plane flying over the church spire, approaching the red and green flare path of the runway as the lights floated up towards his plane, the wheels clunking as the undercarriage came down. And then in her mind's eye she saw James climbing from the plane, then Carol with her tray of sugary, milky teas and shot glasses of rum. Shifting quietly, rearranging her pillow, with her legs scrunched up to her chest, she felt her breath becoming steadier and finally her body relaxing and her eyes closing. He was safe. Whatever happened next, at least he was home. The words they had all been waiting for would be coming over the wireless. 'Prepare for landing. All men accounted for.' The Lancaster would be roaring, hurtling down the runway. Soon his men would be climbing out of the cockpit, wrapped in long scarves and woollen helmets. Soon her future husband would be making his way to the briefing room, where the air would become heavy with cigarette smoke as they waited around to see their photos and relay their sortie reports and drank rum to celebrate.

But then a niggling thought came into her head. The telegram? She went over it again in her head. *Dear Betsy, I have news. STOP. When is your next leave? STOP. Come to Liverpool quickly. Cave. STOP. I'm back at tennies. Deirdre. STOP.*

Cave? She hadn't really noticed it at first. But wasn't that the silly Latin word they used with the nuns at school? *Beware.* Beware of what?

Chapter 27

A week passed, Christmas came and went with too many serious things to think about, and then as the new year came in, the news that turned all their plans on their head came suddenly.

'Drew. Lightfoot. We're transferring you at the end of next week,' said Sergeant Hargreaves.

Betsy's mouth fell open. 'But I'm getting married on the tenth of February! Here! In the village!' she blurted, and then blushed.

'And I've bought a taffeta dress and new stilettos!' said Lightfoot.

The sergeant looked annoyed at first, but when she saw Betsy's eyes fill with tears, she softened.

'She said I can come back for the wedding,' she explained tearfully to James, later in the mess. 'She'll speak to Winco at Woodvale.'

'Go to Woodvale. I'll arrange for Gordon to drive you back here. Though I could be in Norfolk by then the way things are going. Let's hope if I am, they'll give me leave as well, but it might only be for the day,' said James. 'If we have to postpone the wedding, I can wait, Betsy, if you can.'

No night in the hollow bed! thought Betsy. But they

260

wouldn't be the first to get married in the morning and return to separate camps before the day was out with the marriage remaining unconsummated. She had heard of it several times before. Tragically, one bride was a widow the following morning when her husband's plane had crashed into a lake in the Netherlands, and she had only ever kissed him.

'No. We've planned it. We'll marry whatever happens. Somehow. And won't it be lovely, Jimmy?'

Betsy packed a small bag, stuffing in her toothbrush, her pyjamas, and the other bits and pieces that she had lined up on the shelf. She pushed her worries about the wedding out of her head. There had been more conversations about whether they should continue with it – it was becoming too difficult, too complicated. But the banns had been read. Saying it out loud made it seem more real than ever.

Betsy was delighted that Melanie was also being transferred to Woodvale, and she clutched her arm as they were driven to the station by a young corporal to get the train to York, then Manchester. But when the impressive locomotive pulled into the station at Preston, and the stationmaster blew on his whistle, she thought of James flying more sorties and a fear clutched at her heart.

When they arrived at Woodvale in the small bus Melanie and Betsy were both pleasantly surprised. Nestled between a bypass and the dunes, the camp was fringed by pinewoods and clusters of prickling gorse bushes bursting with bright yellow flowers.

'This place is beautiful,' remarked Melanie. 'Look!'

The small Mosquito planes were dotted around the perimeter. There were two large hangars, and motor vehicles parked in front of the offices, all green. They were met by the adjutant, who took them to their hut.

'Thank goodness. We need you girls. We heard Dishforth has sent their best with you two.'

'That's good to hear,' said Melanie. 'It's grand to be appreciated,' she said with a grin. Though she whispered to Betsy as they passed a group of sergeants taking a wheel off a fire truck, 'Not as handsome as our Dishforth boys.'

Betsy laughed. 'I don't know. Is it just that when they're not in the line of fire, it makes them seem a little less dashing?'

'Why is that, I wonder? Being close to death is sort of sexy, isn't it?'

'Lightfoot!' said Betsy, shocked.

'What? Can you imagine marrying someone on civvy street when you've been with an airman? I can't.'

The sound of the bell woke them early the next morning. When she got to the courtyard she took her place, ready to square bash. After an hour of marching and stamping, she reported to the office. After three hours spent sitting on hard wooden chairs, learning about radar and the operations room protocol – although they had no actual equipment to play with, just cardboard mock-ups marked with large, easy-to-read labels – they were taken to the watchtower. For ten days, Betsy and Melanie were shown where everything was, who everyone was, how it all worked.

On the twelfth day they were left alone to man the wirelesses and practise guiding some of the retired or recuperating squadrons back onto the runway. It all went smoothly. Thankfully, Hitler had turned his attention abroad and Liverpool had been quiet for a year. The biggest problem seemed to be morale and people getting back on their feet again after the terrible damage done by the Blitz. A young WAAF was shadowing her. It was mostly routine manoeuvres, and Betsy felt confident as she moved around, spoke into the wireless speaker, gave instructions and orders.

'Someone to see you, Drew,' Melanie said, as they finished their shift.

Betsy frowned. 'Who?'

'From Liverpool.' Melanie tipped her head. When she had asked Betsy who was coming to the wedding from Liverpool and she had answered no one, no friends, no family, she thought that was odd, so she was intrigued by the mysterious visitor. 'They say they know you . . .'

Betsy gasped inwardly. For one awful moment she thought it might be her cousin Malcolm.

'What did he look like?'

'She. A girl. Pretty. Black curly hair. She's wearing a WRVS uniform.'

'Deirdre?' murmured Betsy.

Betsy jogged towards the hut at the main entrance. It *was* Deirdre! Sitting on a small chair, beaming. 'Betsy, you look smashing. Did you get my message? The telegram?'

'Yes. And I was planning to come and see you when I had a day off.'

'Ma came back to the tennies and she needed me to help with the kiddies. Now the bombing has stopped, I'm home as well. She's gone off again, but I stayed. Still volunteering with the WRVS. Still wearing my little hat. The boys go mad for it.'

Betsy looked at her and nodded. It was like seeing a ghost from her past. 'But Deirdre, I'm on duty. You can't just walk in here . . .'

Deirdre chewed her lip. 'Love, this is important. How about we go somewhere quiet? Is there a tea shop in the village? I have news . . .' She paused again.

'What news?'

'It's a lot for you to take in . . . I've come all this way. My feet are killing me after that walk from the station.'

'Deirdre, can it wait? I'm supposed to be going through the lists for the sorties.'

Deirdre reached out a hand to stay her. 'No, Bets. It can't.'

The sergeant on the desk heard their urgent voices. 'Go on, Drew. I can manage here for ten minutes.'

'Thanks,' said Deirdre.

Betsy faltered. 'What, Deirdre?'

'Walk with me.'

Betsy reluctantly allowed her to take her hand and lead her outside. She could smell the scent of a wild rose that had somehow clambered through a split in the paving stones and up the side of the hut. Deirdre leaned against the wall and squinted up at the sky, then she took both of Betsy's hands and squeezed them tight. 'Betsy, listen to me. This may sound complicated and strange. But your baby . . .' She took a deep breath. 'Your son. He's alive. There, what do you think? A shock, I know. But a nice one, I hope.'

Chapter 28

Betsy looked at her blankly.

'Say something,' said Deirdre, losing confidence.

'I can't . . .'

Deirdre was unnerved by Betsy's ashen face. 'Why aren't you saying anything? I thought you would be ecstatic.'

'There must be a mistake,' she stuttered. Her body had frozen in panic. Could this be true? Or was it just a cruel joke? What did she mean, still alive? 'I don't understand . . . You're wrong. Deirdre, that's a terrible thing to say.' She could feel herself trembling.

'A girl called Sybil came to see me. She said she knows you.'

Betsy paled.

'She said she met you when you came to the orphanage . . . I thought you'd be happy,' said Deirdre.

'But I'm getting married. What is it she wants?' Betsy replied flatly.

'I don't know. But this Sybil, don't you believe her?'

'No. I don't. This is ridiculous.'

Deirdre's eyes darkened. 'It sounds improbable, but it's not impossible from what she's told me. I don't know if I can hold her off.'

'How on earth did she find me?'

'I helped her . . . She tracked me down easily enough. Have you forgotten you gave her my address? She showed me the note you wrote to her. *IOU five shillings. If you urgently need what I owe you, my best friend Deirdre will tell you where I am. Deirdre is at Flat 17, Feather Street tenements.* It *was* you who wrote it?' she asked, wavering.

'Yes, but . . . but . . . *You* helped her!'

'Betsy, I thought you'd be pleased! I wouldn't be surprised if she came here to find you herself if I go back and say you believe me. She's in a state. The nuns want to have her daughter adopted. She thinks you might be able to help her stop that.'

'Me! How?'

'I don't know. But I don't think this is about the money. She genuinely thought you'd be happy to find out your son is alive. So did I. She seems a stubborn kind of girl.'

Son. The word made Betsy shudder.

'He's not my son. My son died. Did you not hear what I said, Deirdre? She's wrong. And I'm getting married.' She paused. 'Is this anything to do with Lettice?'

'Lettuce? What have lettuces got to do with anything?'

'*Lettice.* Lettice Swann. A woman. Has she got to the girl Sybil and made it all up to stop me marrying James? She's connected to the orphanage. I wouldn't be surprised.'

'I don't know what you're talking about. Never heard of Lettice Swann.'

'I'm getting married to her son. A pilot. And nothing will stop me . . .'

'And why would your son being alive stop you? This James, he loves you, doesn't he? You have told him you had a baby?' She paused. 'Oh no, Betsy. You haven't. Otherwise why would you be doing that thing you do when you're upset – squeezing your eyes tight shut? Look at me, Betsy. Tell me he knows about your boy?'

Betsy blinked away tears.

She felt herself shiver and saw her future crashing around her. How foolish to think she could exist in a world where her past – her cousin, her father with the threat of turning up like a bad penny, even her brother Jacky, and most importantly of all, her baby – could be erased. But now . . . how could James love a liar? A fraud?

One dreadful fear was replaced by another. The horror of that girl Sybil turning up at the gates of the camp and shouting her mouth off. The scandal! It was against RAF rules, being pregnant, or being a mother. What if they dismissed her? Low moral fibre, they would say.

She *needed* to tell this girl Sybil that she was wrong. She needed to explain that Lettice Swann was behind it and that it was all ridiculous. And to tell her that her boy died in the hospital bombing and that was the end of it.

And if money was what was behind all this, she needed to pay her what she owed, and maybe a little bit more.

Stupid, *stupid* to think I could have happiness, she thought to herself. Panic gripped her as she watched Deirdre walk away with her head down, her disappointment evident in her small, angry steps.

'Deirdre!' she called.

Deirdre turned.

'I'll come and see you next Saturday . . .'

Deirdre's expression brightened. 'You've changed your mind?'

'No. But I'll come and see you Saturday. This Sybil, I can't risk her coming here. I need to speak to her urgently.'

She watched Deirdre go out of the gates. She had always feared it would be Malcolm who would ruin everything, but she never imagined that it would be Deirdre.

The following week began with meeting the aircrew, a squadron of three crews who were exhausted and battered from completing a thirty-mission tour. Betsy hadn't slept and her hollowed-out eyes, red-rimmed and moist, said so. They attended the briefing room with Winco and she noticed a few of the airmen – still shell-shocked after their tours – fell asleep during his talk. That afternoon they were shown the Mosquitos they would be directing whilst they were here, but the rest of the week passed slowly – mornings in classrooms and afternoons working with the wirelesses in the watchtower. On Saturday, as she had hoped, there was nothing planned as the airmen were given a day to rest.

'It's urgent family business. I have to go to Liverpool,' she said to Melanie.

'Urgent? What? How?'

'I can't say.'

'Why?'

'I will tell you when I'm back. But I haven't time now.'

'Go then. I'll say you went to the village to drop the bicycle off at the repair shop if anyone asks.'

'Thank you.'

'You'll be kissing me next. Go, but come back quickly or someone will notice. Graves has eyes like a hawk . . . If you're not careful, someone will spot that you're not here, and she'll be reporting you as AWOL. Betsy, you do realize that is a crime? They'll also be reading all your letters in and out of this place, so they'll find out soon enough if you're up to something.'

'Yes.'

'When you're back, I want you to tell me all the details of what this is about. Promise?'

'I promise,' said Betsy.

Going back inside the hut, wanting to shut out the noise in her head, she collected her purse knowing she would have to leave now if she wanted to slip away. She wanted quiet. That was all. As long as Melanie covered for her, even if she was late back, the sergeant might believe that she had been locked out. It was serious, absent without leave, but she would find an excuse as to why she wasn't at the camp if she didn't get back in time. She set off down the lane. As she came out into the road, she passed two airmen who were walking back to the camp – one had a limp, and another had a badly scarred face. Both had been injured on their last mission. A boy on a bicycle wobbled past and looked back at them. A man walked into his house with a newspaper wedged under his arm. These were just people living in the present, happy to be alive.

But not Betsy. She had to build her future now and prevent the terrible unhappy twist in her story that threatened to ruin everything with the arrival of Sybil and that blessed telegram.

Chapter 29

When Betsy arrived in Liverpool, coming out of Lime Street station, she was shocked to see how much it had changed. Buildings were boarded up, the familiar landmarks had gone, shops and churches had been bombed out and abandoned and were barely standing. Lewis's frontage was latticework now. The Corn Exchange was gone. Rubble was everywhere. She felt a pang of something. What was it? The connection she had to this place felt as strong as a manacle around her heart. When the door was answered, she was thankful it was Deirdre standing there. Betsy fell into her arms with a whimper.

'Betsy! Come inside. Joyce Dooley is prowling around. Don't let her see you.' The tenement flat felt unusually quiet. Babies just kept coming in this family and she knew there was probably another one that had arrived since she had left, or a stray cousin, or someone who lived down the road, now without a roof over their head because of the bombing.

Deirdre kissed her on the cheek. And then she took hold of her arms, stood back and looked at her. 'Betsy, I'm glad you're here . . .'

But before she finished the sentence Betsy slumped down into a chair and rubbed her temples. 'I've decided

I need to see Sybil. Talk to her. Put these ideas out of her head. I need you to come to the orphanage with me so we can speak to her together. I need to give her the money I owe her. That's what's behind this. I'm sure of it.'

Deirdre nodded. 'Why don't I make you a cup of tea first?'

'No. Let's go. I need to find her and speak to her. She could have just asked me for the money. She didn't need to be so cruel, pretending my baby is still alive.'

'Well, you're in luck, Bets, love.' She turned and called over her shoulder. 'Sybil? There's someone to see you, love . . .'

If Betsy had been standing, she would have fallen. Instead, she felt her whole body go limp. Into the room stepped Sybil with a three-year-old wedged on her hip.

'Do you remember me?' asked Sybil.

'Of course,' said Betsy.

Sybil glanced at Deirdre.

Betsy desperately tried to make sense of the scene. Deirdre's little sister? she thought. But no, she must be six now, and she was back in Wales, and why would Sybil be holding her? Sybil instinctively licked her hand and tried to flatten the child's wild hair against her head, but the piece of hair bounced up again.

'Life of its own . . .' she said.

Betsy frowned. The child was looking at her now with searching blue eyes, sticking her thumb into her mouth. Betsy felt her heart kicking at her ribs.

Deirdre flipped the tea towel she was holding over her shoulder. 'I'm sorry I didn't tell you I asked Sybil to come here today. But I felt I had to. Perhaps I should let her speak whilst I get that brew on.'

As Betsy listened, after slumping into a chair fearing her legs would give way under her, the shock of what Sybil was saying made it hard for her to make sense of it. Confusion, bewilderment and panic crashed through her head.

'This will make you believe me. It explains everything,' she said, thrusting a letter into Betsy's hand. Heart hammering against her chest, Betsy opened it tremulously. Straight away she recognized her mother's distinctive handwriting.

Feather Street tenements, Flat 18, Floor 4.

Dear Sister Cyril,
As we discussed when I brought the child to you from Fazakerley Hospital the day after the dreadful bombing, my daughter Betsy believed that her son had died and still does. I know that he will be well cared for by St Mary's and hope you find a good and loving home for him. What I want for Betsy is to now try to live without shame and to have a second chance to move forward in her life. Please, I hope you will help in enabling her to do this by keeping the secret from her. I know asking you to lie would be sinful, but I hope withholding the truth when it's her future happiness that is at stake is not. Only God will judge whether I have made the right decision.
Respectfully yours,
Hope Drew

PS I have included the birth certificate. Betsy wanted to call him Vernon, but that's a little silly, so I have recorded his name as George Vernon. I understand that his name may be changed when he is adopted. Thank you and God bless, and I will pray for this baby to have a better life, as well as my dear Betsy.

There was another sheet of paper tucked inside the cardboard binder. Written in columns were the child's weight – eight pounds. Colour of hair – fair. Distinguishing marks – birth-mark. Heart-shaped. Top right thigh. Name – George Vernon Drew.

Her hands shook. Could this be true? Trembling, she put the letter back into the envelope.

She thought back with despair to her mother's reluctance to have a funeral. And then the nurse at the door one day, a vague memory of indistinct voices and her mother not letting her in. But what a deliberately cruel thing for a mother to do to her daughter! Although . . . like the letter said, her mother only wanted her to have a chance to live her life free of shame. And hadn't the past year proved that? She had been happier than she could ever have imagined. And now she was getting married. If the child was alive . . . Of course, a year or so ago that would have been a good thing, a wonderful thing . . . But now . . .

'Your boy, Betsy. I know him. Georgie. He's the loveliest thing on earth,' said Sybil.

She frowned. Why wasn't Betsy falling into her arms thanking her and smothering her in grateful kisses? But she looked like someone had stepped over her grave and her hands were trembling. 'Aren't you happy?' asked Sybil.

Betsy flinched. 'Happy?' she said, desperately. All she could think of was that she was supposed to be getting married in three weeks' time. What was she supposed to do?

'I know it's a lot to take in . . . But your Georgie is a lovely lad. He's got a serious little face but when he breaks out into a smile . . . You should see him smile.'

'Georgie?' she said vaguely. 'I called him Vernon.'

'Your ma changed it. I think it would be confusing for him to go back to Vernon. Try to think of him as George from now on.'

'Betsy, I remember you said it would bring him luck,' said Deirdre gently. 'The name Vernon?'

'And it has, hasn't it?' pushed on Sybil. 'Why are you crying?'

Betsy wiped a finger under each eye. 'But how do I know for sure?' she whispered to Sybil, turning away from him.

'Know what?'

'That it's my baby?'

'He has blond hair and blue eyes. But since you ask, if that's not enough . . . He also has a little strange heart-shaped birthmark just at the bottom of his thigh.'

Betsy winced.

'It said that in the file. And I realized I knew that little boy. He was tumbling around with Belinda in the sunshine all last summer. You're lucky no one has adopted him. Yet.'

Betsy spoke to the floor, urgently. 'No. I'm sorry,

Sybil. Even if he was . . . is . . . my child. It's too late. Isn't it, Deirdre?'

Deirdre frowned.

'I thought he died. And back then my mother said he'd be adopted. Why wasn't he? He's nearly two. Is there something wrong with him? Like your daughter?'

Sybil put a protective arm around Belinda. 'Don't say that in front of Belinda. Belinda is perfect. Your George always had a rash around his mouth when he was little. A habit of licking his lips. He doesn't do it now, but it didn't look nice. They only take the pretty ones. He's bonny now, but he's too old. They all want a beautiful fresh baby. And there's plenty to choose from.'

'I don't understand why this is so important to you?' said Betsy.

Sybil leaned forward in the chair, grasped Betsy's hand and spoke in a low voice. 'The nuns want to send my daughter away . . .'

Belinda was now sitting on the peg rug engrossed in playing with coloured wooden balsa firelighter sticks that Deirdre had given her. 'If people knew what a terrible thing has been done to you, if that comes out, if you were to tell people, it might change the way everyone thinks of Sister Annunciata. It might mean I can keep my Belinda,' she said hopefully. 'If folks knew what's been going on at St Mary's, they might even close the place down. We should tell the world what they did to you. To us. We all know what that nun has allowed to happen under that roof, not only to you but to all the others: the boats to Australia, the lies about how lovely it is there and the oranges you can pick off trees.'

The little girl in her baggy brown tunic, with her unruly tuft of blonde hair sticking up from her head, glanced up wide-eyed and curious. Deirdre had a box of the twins' toys and a way with children, always one on her hip and another one crawling after her, and she produced a knitted dolly for her to play with.

'I brought Belinda to show you.'

'Show me what?'

'How being a ma is a wonderful thing . . .'

But Betsy just looked down at the floor worriedly, her eyes swelling with tears. 'I can't, though. My life has changed.'

'I think what Betsy wants to say is . . . she's getting married and . . .'

Betsy's lip wobbled.

'Deirdre, I can speak for myself. Sorry, Sybil. I know you mean well. It's just, how could I give him a better life . . . ?' Betsy's face screwed up. 'I can't give him any kind of life. If I could give him a better life, I would . . . Before he . . . before, I thought he had died . . . But I was always going to give him away . . .'

'But you said—'

'I didn't mean it. I'm sorry. Look at me . . .'

Sybil's expression hardened. 'You look dandy from where I'm standing. You're wearing stockings. They're real. You look healthy. You look like you could give him a better kind of life than most people I know.'

Betsy felt her cheeks smarting. It was true, and the life that she was going to be living, married to James, would no doubt be a hundred times better than any of the people's around here. There was a good man with money who was in love with her. A good man who would be horrified to find out that she had a child. But how could she tell this to Sybil?

'We are looked after in the RAF.'

'Is that all you've got to say?'

Betsy stared mournfully at Belinda. Deirdre had found her a cup and she was standing on a chair that she had pulled up at the sink, pouring water from one beaker to another. It was remarkable, Betsy thought, how content she looked with all this sadness going on around her, as her hands splashed about patting the water. 'Sybil, I'm sorry, how . . . what could I do to help? I just don't think—'

'You sound like one of the flaming nuns! I thought you'd be happy. The least you can do is be honest. You just want your fancy wedding to your toff gent. Bet you haven't even told him, your fiancé. Does he know, love? That you're a fallen girl? I don't expect so. A posh fella like that wouldn't put up with that. They want their lasses to be pure. Not like you and me.'

Betsy cast her eyes to the floor. She felt the walls crashing in on her.

'Stop!' yelled Betsy. She raised her hands to her ears but then dropped them and began twisting the hem of her sleeve and plucking at her skirt.

'Sybil!' cried Deirdre. 'That's enough!'

'I understand. There's plenty like her. Everyone feels sorry for us girls who get up the duff, but there were some who thought the nuns were their saviours. You one of them lasses then? Relieved the sisters meant you could hide your dirty secret? I thought I was doing you a favour. I risked a lot for this. Me and Belinda have an appointment with some ducks.'

Sybil turned and marched out of the door, dragging Belinda with her. Shocked, Betsy could feel herself shaking.

Deirdre hovered at the door. 'This is too much to take in . . . That Sybil is a wild thing . . . Let's calm down. Cup of tea will help.'

Deirdre and Betsy sipped at the sugary tea and nursed the mugs against their cheeks. 'But why would your mother do this?'

'Because she loved me,' replied Betsy sorrowfully. 'She thought it was a way to save me from the shame. What a mess.'

'Betsy, I've spoken to Ma about all this. She said we can have your boy here. Until this war is over. I could even take him to Wales. Fresh air and pigs and scrumping . . . She loved your ma and made a promise to take care of you when she got ill.'

'And what about after the war?'

'I can't answer that. Betsy, don't you think you should at least tell James?'

Betsy screwed up her eyes.

'Then there must be someone in your family . . .'

'No. This girl Sybil, she thinks it's easy. Of course I want to be with my baby. But that was my baby. He's a boy now. I'll never get those years back with him. And I've met someone. Do I tell James? Do I tell *Alvis*?'

'No, you certainly don't do that. Alvis wanted nothing to do with you when you found out you were in the club.'

'Deirdre, I can't tell James. Not ever. His mother

280

already hates me. Imagine if she knew I had a child and had kept that from him. Oh, God, I don't know what to do. I've been such a fool. Why did I let James think I was some kind of pure, innocent thing? I should have said right from the beginning, but I didn't have the courage to.'

'Betsy, he didn't fall in love with you because you're a pure, innocent girl. He fell in love with you because you made him laugh, and you're clever and pretty . . . and . . . and . . . Sod this cruel bloody world that makes this feel so shameful. One moment of weakness with Alvis. He caused all this. He did this to you.'

'I didn't say no.'

'Just because you didn't say no didn't mean he had a right to do what he wanted with you.'

'I can't be a mother to Vernon . . . George,' she said, correcting herself.

Was it wrong to think like this? thought Betsy, in turmoil. Not to want her son? And yet . . . Sybil had said he looked like her. He had straw-coloured hair and a sweet smile. She tried to picture him, but no, she wanted to slough off the thought.

'Betsy, you just called him by his name. Don't you think . . . maybe . . . with time . . . ? We can have him here.'

Sighing, she said in a low voice, 'Deirdre, I will never get to be his mother . . . It's just such a terrible mess. If I tell James, it will be over; there's no way he could marry me. And what's the alternative? Me, a single mother, no mother to help me, no home for me or the child. Nothing. How could I make a life for my son?

281

I'm doing this for him. His future with the nuns will be better than any future I would be able to give him.'

Ten minutes later, Betsy put aside her tea.

She went down the stairs, glancing up at Deirdre hanging over the balcony waving. She was planning to head towards the tram, but when she came out from the stairwell, there was Sybil, smoking a Woodbine and sitting on top of an old oil can whilst Belinda was chasing around waving a stick, dragging it along the railings and enjoying the clattering sound. For a moment she didn't know what to do. She hadn't expected to see them. Standing quietly, her heart thumping, she just watched as Belinda raced through the gate into the rec and started running around in dizzy circles, laughing and whooping, as Sybil sucked down on her cigarette.

'Betsy,' said Sybil, coming over after seeing her standing at the railings.

'Sybil . . .'

'What is it? You're crying again. Stop. I just wanted you to know about your little one. That's all.'

'I would have liked to be a mother to him. I hope you don't think of me as a bad person. I just don't know how,' she said, fighting tears. 'But please don't think this is because I don't love him. I always will.'

'I don't think badly of you. I know how difficult this is.' For a moment they just silently watched Belinda coming down the slide head first. 'Kiddies make you smile, though. Seeing them toddling around without a care in the world. Giggling away about something daft, putting a bucket on their head, wiggling their bottoms. When everything around us is just so . . .

awful . . . I don't know, it cheers you up. We don't all walk around crying, Betsy. You find happiness everywhere. Don't feel sorry for us. It's you I feel sorry for, believe it or not.'

A pang of something inside Sybil – sympathy? – meant she reached out, touched Betsy's arm. 'But if you change your mind, I can help you, Betsy, love. And Deirdre will. She even said that her ma has agreed for you and your boy to stop here. Will you let us help you? Don't shut the door on him yet . . . It's not fair on George. Please? And trust me, if you rescue him from the orphanage, it will mean freedom. For both of us. Your James will come round, I'm sure. Don't see this as choosing your son over your fiancé. No matter how bleak and desperate it feels.'

Betsy turned away and blinked against the watery sun, exhausted with the effort of just breathing.

Chapter 30

'Sister, the Patrons' Mass. I have the list . . .'

Sister Cyril thrust it into Sister David's hand. 'Most of the boys are so rumbustious. We need a few babies, preferably the docile ones, in the front pew. They always look lovely. I want them all in white. Frills where possible. Broderie anglaise socks. No brown uniforms. Monsignor is coming.'

'I see,' said Sister David, nervously. She felt a chill in her bones. Sometimes all this sadness they saw here took the edges off one's kindness, and even the most good-natured, compassionate of women ended up spiky and bitter and full of self-hatred when they had to face the very worst in people so often.

Lettice Swann was wearing a peacock-coloured suit and a wide-brimmed hat with a chiffon scarf tied around it. The pews at the small chapel of St Mary the Blessed Virgin were full, and she had to bustle past the sisters and patrons to find her seat. Everyone seemed to be showing off their best clothes. The men wore tweed jackets; a few were in uniform. Those with moustaches had waxed them and had their hair slicked back with Brylcreem and styled. A few faces nodded at her: the architect's wife, Mr Higgins from the

Corporation. In the front pews, the children wriggled and twisted to see what was going on behind them, to point and giggle at the beautiful frocks and the cravats. They knew the clothes they were wearing would be returned as soon as they were taken back to their dormitories, but for now they revelled in their lace gloves, neat socks and shining shoes.

'Stop fidgeting and face the altar,' muttered Sister Annunciata. But the dignitaries were enjoying the mischievous looks, and they returned their smiles and waved and winked. After the service they would be treated to scones and tea and shown charts and told stories of the good work they were doing, and how their money and enthusiasm were making a difference, but Lettice was hoping to slip off. The organ started to play 'Hail Redeemer', and a hush descended as the priest and two altar boys began to process down the aisle.

Lettice sang thin and reedy, but she tailed off when she noticed at the end of the pew Sister Annunciata leaning forward and hissing to the nun who was sitting with the children. Lettice looked over at the commotion. The nun was whispering something into the young sister's ear.

'Sister David, where's Sybil and Belinda? You said they were going to be here. They aren't in the nursery, and I have counted every single one of them. More than once.'

The young nun opened her mouth like a fish, but the words didn't come.

'Where are they?'

The nun was whispering hoarsely. Now the whole row was looking. 'Is the child back in the nursery? We counted before we left. That girl is up to something.'

The nun shook her head again quickly, frowning.

And then the priest's voice lifted to a crescendo. 'In the name of the Father and of the Son and of the Holy Spirit . . .'

At the end of the service, Lettice followed Sister out through the corridors and onto the chapel steps.

'Sister, who were you looking for?'

'I have to go, Mrs Swann. One of the girls . . . We try to help these people, but they don't help themselves.'

Lettice pushed her hands into her coat pockets. Looking back when she reached the steps, she saw the two nuns were still in heated discussion. She walked back towards them. Seeing her, they started.

'Is everything all right?' asked Lettice.

'Perfectly. Mrs Swann, please don't worry . . .' said Sister Annunciata as she took the young nun gently under her arm and they walked out of the side gate.

This place was full of secrets, thought Lettice. Secrets whispered down corridors and behind hands. She wondered what this one was.

Meanwhile, the two nuns had headed back inside. Sister Annunciata whisked a vase of flowers off a small table. 'These can go in my room now Monsignor has gone. Sybil will be back. And if she's not, to hell with her. Now, go and help Sister Cyril. The children need changing out of their white socks and ribbons. Get them back into their uniforms. And run the baths. Give them a good scrub and I'll be along to check them later.'

Chapter 31

Betsy arrived back at the camp before supper was served, numb and bewildered, still in shock from what had happened over the past six hours.

'Drew, you look awful. Why are you so pale? Well done for getting back, though. We're needed in the tower in half an hour. Practising night landings.'

Betsy nodded seriously. She made her way across the airfield, following Melanie.

'What happened?'

She started to reply in disjointed sentences. About Deirdre leaving the Wrens, the place being unrecognizable. She wanted to tell Melanie about Sybil. She had wanted to tell her about Vernon, who she was now thinking of as George. She had planned to. But she couldn't. It was too big, too sad, too shocking.

When they took their places in the tower and placed the headphones over their ears, the Spitfire was already waiting to take off. Melanie chatted brightly with the officers and Betsy sat at her station waiting, chewing the skin around the base of her thumbnail. Melanie, out of the corner of her eye, noticed she seemed distracted as she put on her headphones.

The plane began to roll forward. The announcements started. 'Prepare for take-off' crackled over the wireless.

In five minutes, the plane was up in the air. Two perimeter circles, out towards the coast, and then they would be back.

Betsy's mind wandered again to James. What was he doing right now? These young airmen faced death repeatedly, but like the one she had seen earlier limping, and the one with the scarred face, they had continued to fly. One terrifying mission after another. Duty. It was a powerful thing, she thought. Whatever happened in James's plane, he would always be the last to jump. How many times did she watch those brave men climb into their Lancasters? And yet when there was an empty chair at an empty table, the hush in the room, everyone fighting tears, the only possible answer as to why they would get in the air again was because it was their duty. Duty. She certainly wasn't doing her duty as a mother, walking away from her son with barely a backward glance. Was it that hard? Not to be selfish? How was it these lionhearted young men knew how to be so self-sacrificing? Putting their own needs aside, serving something bigger, something good and noble? So why couldn't she do that for her child? Her child, for heaven's sake. Even Deirdre had said she would take him in. And, yes, James needed her, and she needed him. But her child needed her more, didn't he? Sybil had told her with exaggerated gestures and dramatic words about adoptions that hadn't ended well, about children sent to Timbuktu, and asked her: what if they did that to George? Would she ever forgive herself? But really? Timbuktu? Was it even a real place?

And then she was aware that there was shouting.

'Drew! What are you doing?'

Blinking and glancing up, she saw that the plane was coming in to land, and within minutes it was swerving across the runway, knocking over the flares on the right side.

'Drew! Didn't you hear him?' cried the officer. 'Skipper was on the wireless! Move out of the way.'

He pushed her aside, grabbed the headphones.

Betsy stumbled back in shock. Melanie was glaring at her as if to ask her what on earth had just happened.

'I'll take over. ED 452. Can you hear me? Winco here. Can you hear me? Over,' said the officer, sternly.

The sergeant responsible for chalking up the return times leaned in and hissed to Betsy, 'Drew. Stand down. You've done enough damage as it is.'

Back in the hut, the crushing weight of so many things that were against her in this world made her want to die. She felt embarrassed by what had happened in the tower.

'What's the matter with you?' Winco had asked brusquely. 'We've noticed you're distracted. These things matter. Over the past week you haven't seemed yourself.'

Her eyes had filled with tears. 'I'm fine,' she stuttered.

He normally would have said a lot worse, but he could see she was in some kind of torment, twisting her sleeve, hands trembling. Instead, he spoke about how her actions could have had terrible consequences. 'Men, having seen the very worst of the war, come here for routine and recuperation, then face more danger because of some silly girl not concentrating. Daydreaming about some airman?' he asked pithily.

No, not an airman. My son, the one I so coldly abandoned, she had wanted to reply, darkly. It was George she had been thinking of when she had missed the skipper's calls and the plane had almost swerved off the runway.

Betsy sat on her bed, her back against the wall, hugging her knees to her chest. 'What am I doing? Running away from George?' she blurted to Melanie sitting on the stool beside her, having just told her the whole sorry story of her boy, going right back to Alvis and the Mill Road Hospital. 'I look at those posters – your country needs you. Doesn't my child need me? But would James see it that way?'

Melanie had listened in stunned silence.

After a short while she said, 'Could you be . . . a family? If you tell him?'

'How could I?' wailed Betsy. 'Imagine his mother.'

'I think you should tell him. Could you really carry that secret the rest of your married life? You would soon get sick of lying and pretending you are something you're not.'

'A slut?'

'Betsy . . .'

'I don't know if he could bear it.' She sighed. 'But maybe that's what I deserve? To lose him . . .'

To be punished for that horrible moment with Alvis behind the musty curtain, she thought. Not by God, as the nuns said she would be, but by James.

She turned to Melanie. 'I looked after a baby once. I wasn't very good at it. I could never get him to sleep. He cried all the time. I would be hopeless . . .' She faltered. 'What if I didn't love him? Couldn't love him?

290

And besides, I really don't know if James would forgive me. What if he were to find out the truth about me? Just how different we are? Perhaps it would come out not by words but by small things: the way I hold a fork, the things that he laughs at now – when I say *heck-as-like*. But how long will he laugh about them? If I tie a ribbon in my hair that's too gaudy. Or if, God forbid, he was to meet my brother, my cousins, who would search me out eventually. They'll already be looking for me.'

Melanie sighed and took her hand. 'I understand, love.'

Betsy raised her head and let out a long exhalation of breath, rubbed her temples, blinked back tears. 'No, you don't.' She winced. 'I've always had my way of coping: turning away quickly when I see a baby, blocking my ears when I hear a tin whistle, avoiding nuns and nurses. But none of that matters now. It's time for me to face it. Because all the worry of what James will say, or his mother, or how hopeless a mother I would be, doesn't mean I shouldn't *try* to do the right thing.' Her decision clarified and sharpened in her brain. 'Don't I have to at least try? For my son? He's my son, Melanie. My son . . .'

'Pregnant, is she?' said the medical officer. 'They so often are.'

Melanie shrugged. 'There's a child involved.'

'Very well. I'll sign her off for a week. We don't want a fuss. The RAF is not the place for hot baths, needles and gin. But she should have come and told me herself. Go and get her. And I don't know whether we will be able to have her back. But send her to me. I need to speak to her.'

'Thank you. She'll appreciate that.'

'Sit down, Drew.'

Betsy chewed the skin at the base of her thumbnail. The light bulb on a wire seemed to sway like it was a snake.

'Lightfoot has asked me to speak to you. She asked me not to be too harsh. Well, you wouldn't be the first. But if your work here is suffering . . . And I see you've had no extended leave for over six months. Why don't you take ten days? That should be enough.'

Betsy frowned.

'Be careful, Drew. These backstreet abortionists are not good. It often doesn't end well. Choose carefully. And the gin, hot baths. They don't work. And Drew, like I said, I've seen other WAAFs in this . . . unfortunate situation . . .'

'No,' she stuttered. 'It's not that.'

'Then what is it?'

'I have a son.'

The officer raised an eyebrow. 'And you didn't tell anyone when you signed up? The WAAF is not for mothers. Thank the Lord.'

'Ma'am, I didn't know until last week.'

She frowned. 'What do you mean?'

Through sniffles and sighs and twisting of handkerchiefs and hand wringing, she began to tell her story. Surprisingly, the officer listened without interrupting.

'He's in an orphanage,' Betsy finished, swallowing a sob.

The officer nodded. 'I'm sorry, Drew. I'm very sorry about that. Are you sure you're not lying to me? Are you sure you're not pregnant?'

Betsy blinked away tears. She waved away the accusation with a vague gesture, drawing something in the air, and gave up because there was nothing else to say.

'Whether you are or not, you can't stay here. I will have to discharge you. Unfitness for service. You'll have to leave at once.'

So that's it, thought Betsy. My life really is ruined.

'Well, if what you're saying is true, and because the child is under the age of fourteen . . . He's still yours, I'm afraid. Rules are rules, Drew. I'm so very sorry . . .'

Betsy, shocked and numb, packed a small bag and looked across over the airfield. 'Surely she can't do that?' a horrified Melanie had said. 'She seemed like she was on your side!'

Betsy shrugged sadly. Melanie's heart ached for her.

'You know you don't have to give up on being part of this war completely? You can still volunteer in the WRVS,' said Melanie sadly.

'I know.' She sighed. 'Perhaps it was never meant to be. The WAAF . . .' She shook her head and then her face went blank as she went hurtling back to another time, another place, to the little cramped kitchen with Deirdre and the gramophone. *Remember that September in the rain* . . .

'What's the matter?'

Betsy shrugged the question away. 'Nothing,' she said, smiling brightly. 'Except . . . James . . . an officer . . . Stupid of me to think I could have . . .'

Her mind turned to the wedding. Why had she never really thought beyond it? At some point James would have had to meet Jacky. With his rough hands and missing tooth and worn clothes and shoes. And what about Malcolm and her terrible wild cousins and Auntie Winnie sucking on a cigarette, always moaning, with her flaming this and sodding that? They were still family. Why had she never thought of that?

'Melanie, will you call the vicar and cancel the wedding? What about the dress? Will someone else have it?'

'I'll call and postpone it. I won't cancel. And I'll keep the dress. If there's one thing I'm sure of, it's that James loves you, so this story isn't over yet.'

'But does he love me enough to marry a fallen woman? And someone dismissed from the WAAF as unfit for service? Everyone knows what that means. It will follow me for ever. Does he love me enough to take on another man's child? I doubt it . . .'

'Don't say that. You're not a fallen woman.'

'What am I then?'

'A girl who made a mistake. Go and talk to the nuns as soon as you can about taking George back. We'll talk about cancelling the wedding later. You said there was a kind nun.'

'There are lots of kind nuns, Melanie. Most of them are good women. They're not all like Sister Annunciata. Now, can you leave me for a moment?' Betsy rubbed her temples tiredly.

'All right, petal. But I'll jump on the first train to Liverpool if you need me. It's not far.'

*

Betsy took up the pen from her shelf and the notepad. How could a pen feel so heavy? she thought as she sat down to write at the little desk in the hut.

Dear James,
    I don't know where to start, apart from to tell you I love you and ask for your forgive-ness. I'm afraid I shan't be returning to Dishforth to marry you. It's a long and difficult story and I will do my best to explain. But my shame should not be yours . . .

She hesitated, knowing she would probably regret this for her entire life. But Melanie was right: whatever happened next with George, she knew she couldn't walk down the aisle a liar. Deirdre had said the same – *If James loves you, he will forgive you and accept George.* What did she have to lose? Everything and nothing. But she would find out soon enough.

She picked up the pen again.

This breaks my heart to write and I am crying as I do so . . .

Chapter 32

Betsy was shocked at how normal everything seemed. Trains were running, cleaners came with mops and buckets, vans started their engines. Now, as the bus pulled away, she thought how different the camp always looked in the morning. The planes were lined up in front of the hangars, but they looked peaceful amongst the hedgerows and the meadows rolling out into the countryside towards the dunes. There was birdsong and someone far off was whistling. The bus drove out through the gates. She rested her head on the window as the glass rattled, trying to stop the din in her head. Half an hour later, driving through the grime of Liverpool, she was on her way to the tenements. When she arrived, dragging herself up the stairs, Deirdre was waiting.

'You said what?' said Deirdre, over tea and oatcakes, astonished at what Betsy had told her she had written to James.

'I told him I couldn't marry him.'

'Why? You haven't even given him the chance to think about it? You didn't ask me?'

Betsy sat with her knees hugged to her chest on Deirdre's sofa.

'Betsy,' said Deirdre. 'Do you have a copy of the letter?'

She shook her head sadly.

'What on earth did you say in it?'

'I told him about George and how I thought he had died, but then Sybil came to me with news he was alive. I told him I loved him . . .'

'But you called off the wedding?'

Betsy shrugged.

'In other words, you jilted him without even talking to him . . .'

'Stop!' said Betsy, crunching her fists into her temples. 'I love him. But how can he love me . . . knowing . . . knowing . . . ?'

'You didn't give him a chance. Betsy, not everyone is like your mother or the nuns, thinking you are an awful, disgusting person just because you had sex and you weren't married. That's what you think about yourself, but it doesn't mean to say he sees it that way . . . I certainly don't. Half this city doesn't. They just put on a show. We're all human, Bets.'

Betsy groaned. She had been so sure she was doing the right thing, writing that letter, but from the minute she had posted it, she was having doubts. She had heard from the vicar. She had a letter from Carol asking about the bridesmaids' dresses. But each new day without word from James had become a day of regret.

'What can I do?'

'Well, if you don't hear back from him, you can go and tell him you were too hasty. You can find him and tell him . . .'

'But what about George? I was going to get him. I told Sybil.'

'Do that when you've sorted James out. Betsy, you're such a noodle . . .'

Betsy's bottom lip trembled.

'You really think there's hope?'

'Call the camp at least.'

'You're only allowed if it's a justified emergency. Is it? Would they see it that way? Anyway, I can't have a conversation over the phone about this . . . You're right, I should have told him to his face. It would have been easier to explain.'

Two more days passed, the mornings and afternoons slowly, and then the long evenings. She was only made of flesh and bone, and she could feel her heart pumping every time the boy arrived with the post. She had heard nothing from Melanie and nothing from James, even though she hadn't really expected to. It was unimaginable that the same thing would happen the next day and the day after that. Could a person stand this?

Deirdre finished the dregs of her Bovril and got ready to leave for work. 'I suppose your friend Melanie will be in touch if there's any other news.'

'About what?'

Deirdre didn't want to say it. But she knew James was flying sorties.

The next morning, Betsy went down to the post office with a renewed vigour in her step. Shaking, she went into the small booth and dialled the number of Dishforth that James had given her. The person who answered was sharp and efficient but when Betsy said who she was, she softened.

'Drew? Is it a justified emergency?' said Maeve Devlin. 'You're lucky you got me. He's left. Left yesterday.'

'Norfolk?' asked Betsy, her voice quavering.

'I can't tell you that,' she said gently. 'Top secret, Drew. You know that better than anyone.'

'Please . . . I'm desperate . . .'

There was a silence on the line.

'I can tell you where Janice Rushton and Carol have been transferred. To Foulsham, Norfolk,' she said quietly.

'Thank you. Thank you,' whispered Betsy.

'I'm going to Norfolk,' Betsy said to Deirdre, bursting through the door. 'I've made a mistake. You were right. A terrible, *terrible* mistake . . .'

'What?'

'I need to see him. I need to explain. If I see him, he might understand. He's not at Dishforth, which only means one thing. A letter wasn't enough. I need to tell him I still want to be with him. I don't think I was clear. Or maybe he hates me . . . I've been so stupid, haven't I?'

'Have patience. It was a lot for him to take in. Wait a couple of days at least to see if he replies.'

'No, Deirdre. Don't just stand there, get a shovel. Isn't that what we northern lasses say?'

'Telephone for you, Swann. Urgent . . .' said the sergeant, trotting across the airfield.

James was smoking, watching one of the ground

crew painting another yellow bomb on the side of his Lancaster. The twelfth. Always a milestone to pass the eleventh. Psychiatrists who knew better than him had worked out why the odds of staying alive had increased after that number, and it made him feel confident about tonight.

James frowned. 'Betsy Drew?'

'No.'

'Group commander?'

'Your mother.'

Goodenough paused from watching the erk who was painting and grinned. 'Mrs Swann didn't read the pamphlets then? *Do not use the telephone except in a justified emergency.*'

They were constantly told about the dangers of jamming the lines and James frowned as he walked back to the office. He put the telephone to his ear warily. The operator's voice crackled down the line.

'Will you accept the call?'

'Definitely not,' he replied, and turned on his heel and left. He didn't need this drama, not now. Thoughts thundered around his brain. He needed to stay focused for that evening's sortie. He needed to stay clear-headed. Walking back out into the cool air, he tried to stay calm as he made his way to the ops buildings and into the briefing room.

'Hairy last week, I heard,' a sergeant was saying to the pilot huddled around a map.

'Spot of bother on the tail . . . but we made it,' replied the officer with the usual understatement. James knew a gunner had nearly died when flak had dented the side and zinged into the turret. He also knew on his last mission Mathers had messed up with the photograph, forgotten the flash, and the crew was sore about not being able to record it as a successful sortie, and he could hear Mathers talking about it.

'We know you scored a hit. Photograph's not all that . . .'

'Flaming Jocks,' said a voice from the back. It was Mathers and he was laughing.

'Being Scottish is not the problem. Mathers is seventeen.'

'Ma wee fat fingers,' said Mathers, to more laughter.

Officer Taylor shook his head. 'Next time, do better, shall we? Good work on the bomb aiming, though.'

After a conversation about targets and numbers and wind speeds and more Met reports, Winco told them to leave. 'Not you, Swann . . . Can I have a word?' James stood. 'Your crew are a tight-knit group. Family. But Mathers likes a drink. Keep an eye on that. Let me know if you need to swap him out. It's not going to be an easy mission, this one. But we have every faith in you, Swann. Good luck, Skipper.'

As they were driven out to the plane that evening, James felt an unusual shiver of fear. Usually he felt excited. But there was something off in the way the bomb aimer, Paddy Riordan, touched the mascot – a teddy bear with one eye and a flying jacket, wedged behind the fire extinguisher – before he slid down into the front turret. He understood why they had called him and his crew at such short notice from Dishforth to Norfolk. They were losing so many planes. But he had just been told about the most recent sortie from here. Seven planes crashed over the Ruhr whilst missing every target. It had been a mistake blamed first on the Met Office and then the plotters, which had meant three had flown off course and obliterated a small village eight miles north of the intended munitions factory.

He thought about his crew. Were they prepared for this? They hadn't flown together on a bombing mission in this plane, just test runs. Nevertheless, the group commander had told him that with three crews down, three pilots missing, twenty-one aircrew dead, he was one of the best and they were relying on him. 'Moral fibre: you have it, Swann,' were his words earlier when he had walked James across the airfield to the waiting vehicle and had patted his shoulder. 'Not like some here. And remember, if you miss the target, don't worry, you'll have another go the next week.' Apparently, a few had been taking chances; others had got scared and had been flying too high to let others below face the flak. It had been brutal losing so many Lancaster bombers. Bad for morale.

Mathers made a joke and they all laughed, and for a short time it relieved the tension. They knew tonight was serious. They would be going deep into the Ruhr Valley. Other squadrons would be joining them from all over the country – they didn't know how many, but enough.

'Sergeant Mathers? I hope you've not had a drink?'

'Yesh, shirr . . . rather, no, shirr . . .' he said, grinning.

James looked at the picture of Betsy that he had slipped in the frame of the window just like he always did.

The navigator climbed into position, and then flight

engineer Goodenough wriggled into the small seat beside James, took his flask out of his pocket and swigged from it. James didn't ask whether there was alcohol inside it, but assumed the commander had made sure there wasn't after the conversation they had had.

The lights flickered as the wireless operator, Toe Howman, was the last to climb in, heaving himself through the gap.

'Got your Bible?' asked Willis.

'Too right,' he laughed, tapping his top pocket.

'Toe always carries his Bible in his pocket, don't you? Just as long as he doesn't start quoting it.'

'Go on, Skip. Your turn to ask him tonight.' Mathers laughed, poking his head into the cockpit.

'What's that?' said James.

'Is he Goodenough to fly with us?'

They all chortled. They made the same joke every time. It had become a mantra.

'Are you serious?' said Goodenough, laughing.

'Skipper Swann is never more serious than when he's joking. Are we all looking forward to our trip to Happy Valley?'

'If Goodenough can keep those Jerry bullets from hitting my turret, that's good enough for me,' shouted Paddy.

James let out a long exhalation of breath. He needed to concentrate, and the weather was filthy. A bank of rain was sweeping down from Scotland. As long as Paddy got his precious photograph this time, he thought, as he switched on the engines and went through the procedure for take-off.

*

Ten minutes later, they were, thankfully, engulfed by the clouds. From the back he heard a cheer as they slowly lifted higher into the air. It always felt safer to be flying above the clouds as they crossed the Channel. He could feel the cold in his bones now. There was a frost beginning to form on the glass window of the cockpit.

'*Oh, we've a bloody big bomb,*' sang Toe Howman.

'*A bloody big bomb,*' chimed Goodenough, beside James.

He had taken out his pipe. James knew he never smoked it, just sucked on it intermittently to calm himself. He wondered if he thought it made him look older than his ridiculously young seventeen years.

'*Flying Avro Lancasters at zero zero feet . . . We've got sod all ammunition and a great big blooming bomb,*' sang Goodenough, as they flew on over the sea. Glancing up, James thought how bright the moon looked. It felt wrong. And then the clouds parted below them.

'Bloody Met boys,' murmured Paddy over the intercom. 'We're lit up like a flaming Christmas tree.'

'Skipper, did you hear about the Met boys who knew how to read a weather map? Neither did I.' Goodenough laughed throatily.

'Did you hear about the officer who paid for a round of drinks?'

'Neither did I,' chorused the reply.

It was an old joke and one which started a chain of more daft jokes, all ending with 'Neither did I' crackling over the wireless to ease the tension.

'Skip, did you hear about the gunner who remembered to clean his compartment after he was caught short?'

'Looking a bit dicey, still not much cloud cover,' said James, over the intercom. 'Howman. Coastline ahead. All clear?'

'Aye, Skip,' came the muted reply.

The singing and joking stopped abruptly. The sky felt treacherous suddenly, but then the red flares of the marker planes appeared just like James had wanted, cascading down, small bursts of flames like fireworks. It was beautiful in its own way. Apart from, with that came the flak. No one wanted to see that. It meant that Jerry had found them, the searchlights would be swinging into action and this mission could become deadly at any minute.

'Bugger's flying above us . . .'

'Too many of us . . .' said James.

The carbon and sulphur smelled strong tonight as it hit the back of his throat.

They continued, the moon breaking through wisps of cloud. James reached into his pocket for one of the mints he sucked on to relieve the pressure in his head.

And for an awful moment it was as if time had stood still.

The letter – his reply to Betsy's – it was in his pocket beside his cigarette case. Damn it! He hadn't left it on the shelf ready to post like he had thought! Blood thundered around his brain. So what if . . . what if . . . ? He didn't dare think about it. That if things didn't end well tonight, she would never read it. The idea that he might die without her ever knowing that he didn't care about the fact that she had a child, didn't care about the shame of it, or the damn stupid notion of what others might think. Nothing could taint his love for her. Why would it?

And the mood in the plane was becoming serious. Now more than ever, he *had* to get out of whatever lay ahead alive.

'Come on . . . come on . . .' said James, half an hour later, alarmed at the quivering needle.

The flak below was now like deadly confetti. But it was the explosion of the shell hitting the side of the plane and puncturing the metal that changed everything. 'Fighter starboard!' yelled Sergeant Goodenough as he was thrown off his seat and across the floor. It caused James to spin round, meaning the radio wire attached to his helmet ripped off, cutting off communication with Paddy. Worse, somehow, the direct hit had started a fire onboard. The plane jerked as James tried to wrestle control of it. The intense heat and the fire licked towards the box of ammunition. He knew what would happen next. And it was hot, getting hotter.

'Fire extinguisher!' Paddy cried, scrambling on his stomach. 'No!'

The red and green flares that continued to burst into flames below, combined with the deadly flak, made it feel as though they were entering hell. The noise of the one engine seemed to lower in pitch, becoming worryingly quiet. The blip on the radar had died away. The clouds separated again, and the moon shone sickeningly bright.

'You all right?' said James. 'Can anyone hear me?'

But there was only silence and the crackle of more small explosions and the noxious smell of more deadly fumes hitting the back of his throat. He thought about the horrible statistic that crews had a lower survival rate than infantry in the First World War.

He knew, even if they turned back and limped home, they might not have enough fuel to get there, but he pushed on.

'Toe's not moving. Bloody bad luck, Skip. Through the eye. Awful sticky back here . . . So bloody hot. Still burning . . . Langham . . . He's pretty shot . . .'

James felt his whole body tense. 'Give him morphia?'

'Aye, Skipper . . .'

'How bad in the turret?' asked James. 'Goodenough?'

'Not quite, not today, Skip. Pretty bad . . .'

James could feel the temperature rising, felt his skin burning. The plane was overheating, the lights danced on the controls, but he didn't know whether it was his eyes or a fault on the panel. The red glare of the sky taunted him.

'We've lost Willis,' someone said.

'Mathers?'

'All good,' came a small voice.

The plane kept its height and James used the throttle to let it drop gently.

'Crew, bail . . .' he said. 'We're sitting in a tinderbox.'

'Goodenough can't move . . . Mother of God . . .' he screamed.

'Then push him out and pull the cord.'

'We going down, Skip?'

'Yes. Bail . . . I'll be all right. But bail now. Good luck.'

'Tell me mother I love her!' cried Mathers as he jumped into the black and Goodenough and Paddy waited to follow.

'Steady . . . steady . . .' murmured James, still wrestling with the controls. But it was pointless, and the thought of Betsy, the letter she would never receive, came searing into his head, knowing that all was lost now.

Four hundred degrees and the first bullets hit the roof and bounced off the floor. Some burned through the metal. S for Sweetie began its descent, screaming to the ground. Below was the smudge of the dunes along the Dutch coast, and beyond the treacly slick of the North Sea awaited.

In the NAAFI the next morning, the atmosphere was strange and sad. It was as sad as the two empty tables and the fourteen empty chairs where yesterday young men had sat laughing, drinking tea and eating poached eggs. The happiness everyone had all felt knowing that the first of the two crews had come back had soon evaporated. They wouldn't be celebrating after all. They thought of the football match before they left. 'Mathers, in goal, was seventeen,' whispered a WAAF as she stirred sugar into her tea.

'It's a secret, but everyone knows Sergeant Goodenough and Janice were courting. Curless is crying too because it's her job to telephone his parents and tell them to expect the air marshal's call. The telegrams have already been sent.'

In the office, Janice's hand quivered as she took the sheet of paper.

'Here are the telephone numbers,' said Officer Minton.

'Can someone else?'

'You jumped at this job, Rushton. It was never going to be easy.'

'I can't. I'll start crying.'

'Oh, for heaven's sake.'

'I'll do it,' said a voice. She leaned in and whispered, 'Janice's fella was the flight engineer.'

'Ah,' Minton murmured. 'Rushton, go back to the hut and lie down. I'll do the phone call,' she said with a sigh. 'And what about Officer Swann? Who'll call his mother?'

The Bakelite telephone felt heavy in her hand. She dialled the number, heard it purr, wondered who could afford a telephone in their house. 'Mrs Swann?' she asked when Lettice picked up the receiver. 'Would you be free to speak to one of our officers in half an hour?' said the WAAF, slowly and clearly with only the slightest tremor in her voice.

Lettice's heart lurched. And the phone fell, bump, bump, to the floor.

Meanwhile, the typewriter clacked. A WAAF was handed a slip of paper with the words already written down. Though she knew them off by heart by now.

Dear Miss Drew,

I regret to inform you that a report has been received from the War Office that officer number 97633567, James Swann, was posted as missing on 6th February.

'Where's the priority stamp?' she called. PRIORITY. The blue stamp in the right-hand corner that everyone dreaded.

'Is Betsy Drew still at Woodvale? How quickly can we get a telegram to her?' said Carol.

The typewriters clacked and clattered more urgently. Beyond, someone murmured instructions to two sergeants. But then something made them all stop and turn around at the same time.

Silhouetted in the doorway, Betsy looked so small and so fragile.

'Carol, I'm here. What is it?' she asked, pale-faced and trembling, white with fear, feeling as if she had forgotten how to breathe. She tried to find the courage to ask the dreadful question but was terrified of the answer. 'Why is no one saying anything?'

Chapter 33

A week later, Liverpool

'Chin up, love,' said Deirdre, bringing her an oatcake. 'Do you think you could get up today?'

Betsy had been awake all night. Everything hurt: her head, her legs, her heart. She couldn't get that moment out of her head, the shock, her body convulsing violently, the disbelief. *Betsy, we just got word. I am so sorry. James never came back last night. Missing in action . . .* And her tragic reply . . . *But I've come all this way. I've come all this way . . .*

Deirdre handed her a cup of Bovril. 'Drink that to give you strength.'

Betsy had collapsed when she had fallen through the door that first day after Carol had borrowed a service motor car and driven her back to Liverpool. Deirdre had been bringing her smelling salts each day and tea but she still hadn't wanted to talk, sleep, eat, or do anything. She just wanted to die, she cried to Deirdre, hugging herself and curling into a ball. And nothing had changed since then. It hadn't got better, it had got worse.

'I can't stand it,' she whimpered, folding into herself, whining pitifully like a wounded animal.

Deirdre gently placed a hand on her shoulder. Betsy clutched it and she wanted to cry again, but she just felt numb. She couldn't even do that. She was so exhausted with the sadness of it. She frowned, bewildered, and turned away, trying to piece together the thoughts in her head.

'Did he read my letter, though? But why didn't he write a reply before he flew? That's when they write, don't they? I've seen them, sitting on walls outside, resting the notepads on their knees, or in the quiet corner of the NAAFI in the morning.'

'I have no idea,' said Deirdre.

'Oh, Deirdre. I can't bear it that he died hating me. Do you think he did?'

'Don't be daft, Bets. He loved you. And I keep telling you, missing in action is not dead.'

The following weekend Deirdre headed down to Paddy's Market, where she kept her mother's stall open on a Saturday. Just second-hand clothes – tat, Deirdre called it – but her mother always said those bits of tat would bring them another shilling for the meter, so what was wrong with that? Deirdre had told Sybil about the stall and so she was only half surprised to find her standing there that morning.

'Do you want the good news or the bad news?' sighed Deirdre. 'Or rather, the bad news and the worse news . . .'

Sybil frowned and dropped the lace bonnet she had just picked up and was feeling between her fingers.

'Betsy has told James about George.'

Sybil looked surprised. 'What did he say? I bet he

was fine. Happens all the time – fellas who are supposed to be plain bad come back to get their girls and babies, or turns out didn't even know they had a baby in the first place and start bellowing at the nuns.'

Deirdre frowned. 'That won't happen. Betsy wrote to him, but his plane crashed . . .'

'Oh no!' said Sybil. 'Did he die?'

'No word yet. Missing in action.'

Sybil tutted when someone jostled behind her.

'Let's go somewhere quieter,' said Deirdre, leading her by the arm. 'You can have that bonnet.'

Sybil stuffed it in her pocket. They found a low wall running behind the warehouse. They sat down on it and Deirdre told her in disjointed sentences about what had happened.

'And so she doesn't know what to do. The last thing she's thinking about right now is George.'

Sybil nodded. 'Georgie is the thing that will pull her through, though . . .'

'You think so?'

'I know so. Some people look at girls like me and think we're dozy but that's one thing I know better than most.'

'Mmm. Betsy might be able to multiply thirteen by forty-two, but sometimes she's dozy.'

'Ask anyone from St Mary's. We're all supposed to be stupid, getting up the duff, must be, but what we know is that your kiddies give you something to live for. Betsy might be good with her sums but she doesn't know one plus one equals happiness.'

'Be patient,' sighed Deirdre.

'I'll try. But Sister Annunciata is on to Betsy. She's

trying to get George adopted, I'm sure. And Belinda. After I went missing with her she's been watching me like a hawk. So she hasn't got much time.'

When they returned to the stall there was a woman flapping a pair of bloomers. 'How much?'

'Tuppenny with elastic, penny without . . .'

'You will tell Betsy that she hasn't got time on her side, won't you?' entreated Sybil.

The one question that kept Betsy awake at night and brought the dark circles under her hollow eyes in the morning was whether James had read her letter. She had asked Deirdre so many times that even kind-hearted Deirdre was getting sick of it, and had today answered with a sigh. 'What does it matter, Bets? Whether it was your letter that put him off his stroke? Whether he died thinking you were a virgin or a fallen girl or whether he cared? We just don't know.'

'I need to know. Did he die after reading it?'

'We don't know. There's still hope he might be alive, Betsy.'

'I think it's worse to hope. And even if he is alive, he must hate me.'

Deirdre shrugged.

Betsy had asked her this question every morning, every evening, every day. Perhaps soon she would realize she couldn't possibly answer it.

Deirdre touched her arm. 'Betsy, George . . . Maybe if you had someone to love, you wouldn't feel so alone . . . Sybil came to see me at the stall. Only she was asking . . .'

Betsy nodded and looked away vaguely.

'She wondered if this tragedy might have changed your mind?'

'Alone?' said Betsy. 'George won't change that . . .'

Deirdre bit her lip. *He might*, she wanted to say, resisting the urge to shake her.

At Mottram Hall, Lettice woke to begin another day and cursed that she hadn't died overnight. She had howled like a wolf so loudly when she had received the telegram that Gordon had had to put his fingers in his ears. She had spent weeks moving around the house and now it was April and the swallows had returned and windows were being quietly opened and shut. She was breathing through her mouth and a little bewildered why, with this much pain in her heart, each breath hadn't been her last. There was a vagueness about her, and she saw no point getting up in the morning. She was tired all the time. She no longer left the Hall. She didn't care that Hitler was battling Russia or that Churchill was celebrating success in the Ruhr. There were other changes too. Cobwebs didn't trouble her. A mouse scurrying across the rug to nibble at the food she had taken one mouthful of and discarded on a plate for days didn't bother her. Baby spiders hatched and scuttled across the threadbare carpet. It seemed curious to her how her body made strange smells. She wasn't troubled by it, and she didn't have the energy to do anything about it. Gordon would try to persuade her to bathe; he would fling open windows and make polite but pointed comments about odours and ask her if she was all right. She would only answer with a frown and a sigh.

'I have put a chair under the oak tree. It's a sunny day, Mrs Swann.'

'Under it? I only want to hang from it,' she had replied sadly.

A few more letters arrived. More effects. The most painful – a photograph of the seven crewmen leaning against the plane, smiling. They all looked so youthful. As though they believed they were immortal. James had survived eleven trips. Why not a twelfth? Had he been wearing his father's ring? she wondered, as she squinted at the picture, but it was a detail that she couldn't see. No one wanted to visit. Apart from Clementine, who had come once dressed in black with pungent-smelling lilies, but they had made Lettice sneeze. Someone needed to arrange a memorial service, Clementine suggested. 'I can sing "We'll Meet Again" if you want? I can make a decent stab at the high notes.'

'Can we try a cup of tea at least? Earl Grey?' sighed Gordon to Lettice, who was sitting in the armchair with a rug over her bony knees and her hair tangled in a clump of knots. She was like a skeleton, he thought.

'Missing in action. Why can't they just say it? Dead . . .'

He looked at her and moved quietly away. He wasn't sure why she often refused to have the curtains open now the bombing had stopped and blackouts weren't quite as necessary.

'Sister has been around with her prayer cards. She wants to have a mass said for James. Pray for his safe return.'

'She can say her mass, but I shan't go.'

Soon Gordon noticed how she kept the curtains drawn all day. How another letter came that she didn't open, and another phone call that she didn't answer. The priest sat at her bedside, urging her to let him take her to the chapel to pray for comfort. But no, she wouldn't do that either.

'Clementine is here again,' said Gordon.

'I don't want to see her . . . Please God she hasn't brought stupid flowers again.'

The voice was shrill and pierced the silence. 'Is she in the drawing room? Yoo-hoo! Lettice?' she said, as she swept in. She was wearing all black again but this time she looked even more ridiculous. A black stole, a black dress with a scalloped hem and a ridiculous huge black hat, and this time she had brought white roses. No doubt she had a notion that the absurd get-up made her look dramatic, thought Lettice.

'Lettice, Gordon says you still haven't got up. I'm so sorry that this is—'

'Are you? You jilted him . . .' she interrupted.

'Jilted him? We were never going to marry. From what you've told me, he must have loved that girl. Betsy. What chance did I have? Now, should I put these into a vase? This place needs brightening up a bit. It's so gloomy, Lettice. Let's see what we can do, shall we?'

Chapter 34

A week passed. And then another. The days started dully for Betsy and ended with her feeling exhausted. Today she had at least left the flat for an hour and was coming home from the wash-house a little disgruntled by Deirdre's insistence that she should help with the chores.

'Don't move. Don't say a word.'

Even in the dingy stairwell of the tenements, she knew it was Alvis. She could tell by the tone of his voice, the smell – of the oil he used in his hair, sweet and sticky, the cigarettes. Capstan Full Strength. She could smell it on his yellow-stained fingers over her mouth. She thought she might bite him but instead she twisted her head and snarled and glared at him.

He was grinning. 'Long time no see. I've come to say goodbye, Betsy. I've been called up to fight in Burma . . . And then when this war is over, I've decided I'm not coming back. It's Australia for me . . . With my fiancée. Julie. She's a grand lass.'

He took his hand away.

'Why are you telling me?' asked Betsy. 'I wrote to you over and over again and you didn't reply. I tried to find you and you disappeared. Why bother with me now?'

'Because I heard you've been sniffing around me ma again.'

'I haven't . . .'

'Your pal Deirdre has. Talking about the kid again. The one you had and didn't tell anyone about.'

'The one *we* had. He's your son and you know it. I told you in every letter I sent to you. And he's alive. I thought he'd died but he's alive and why won't you accept it, Alvis?' She wished that there was something more that she could say.

'Our little Betsy. Feisty. Always the same. This is our goodbye. You have to think of me as dead now. You have to, Betsy. I'm sorry, love. That's just the way it has to be.'

'Alvis, I wanted nothing from you.' She screwed up her face, pressed the bottom of her palms into her temples. 'Apart from you admitting my son is yours . . . It would give me . . . some . . . some . . .' What? she thought. Comfort? Peace?

'Why's it so important? I've heard that you have a fella in your life? Pilot? Can't he be the da? And anyway, where is the kid? I haven't seen him.'

Betsy felt her cheeks reddening.

'He's waiting to be adopted . . . Hopefully to a good home. Someone who will love him.'

He nodded and laughed. 'So, you'll tear a strip off me for not wanting the boy, but you won't have him either? What's the difference between you and me then? I might have walked away but you've done the same.'

'I'm in a mess. I'm not able to . . . to . . . look after him. And I didn't walk away from him, I was told he had died! You know all this. Deirdre must have told you!'

'Let me try to get this straight? You thought he was dead, but now turns out he's alive? But you haven't gone back for our lad, have you?'

'Shut up!' she said. 'And by the way, you just finally said he was yours!'

'Mebbe I did. But that still doesn't change what I'm thinking. You're so high and mighty with me, but why won't you do right by the nipper? I'm sorry, Bets. You and me. Peas in a pod we are. We're bad to the core.'

He thought he was being cruel. He thought he would make her cry. But in that moment, with startling clarity, she realized he had set her free. She almost thanked him. Men like this would never understand women. Never.

When she told Deirdre what Alvis had said, Deirdre nodded quietly. They were leaning over the balcony, Deirdre finishing a cigarette and listening intently.

'Selfish,' said Deirdre, quietly. 'He always was.'

Downstairs two girls were sitting on the swings in the rec. Deirdre smoothed down Betsy's hair. 'That's what we used to do, love. Remember?'

One of them had twisted the chains tight and she was laughing as it unspun. Betsy remembered the simple joy of that. That was what she needed to do now, she thought. Unspin. Untether. 'I'm only twenty. I'm still so sad. But I don't want my boy to think that I'm selfish. Like awful Alvis. What has my son done to deserve me abandoning him?' She sighed. 'I'm ready, Deirdre. I think I just needed time. Will you help me? Before it's too late?'

Sybil met Betsy in the little tea shop around the corner from the orphanage. Betsy shook when she reached a hand across the table and Sybil grasped it to calm her.

'Look at you. All shivery and sniffly amongst the sugar bowls and the teapots.'

'I'm a wreck. I'm sorry I was so awful to you. And George.'

Sybil smiled. 'Shush now. You're doing the right thing. I'm glad Deirdre got your note to Sister David.'

'I'm still not sure, Sybil. What if the sisters say no? What if they deny it?'

'We have your ma's letter. And they might think I'm nothing, but you . . . because of James . . . and that lady. His mother. Mrs Swann . . . that will make things different. For both of us.'

Betsy looked surprised. 'You know Lettice?'

'I know who she is. She wears an astrakhan coat with a fur collar. That's enough round here for people to think she's important. Come on.'

Standing in the small porch of St Mary's, Betsy practised what she was going to say. Just like Sybil had told her. *Sister, my child needs me. He needs a loving home. He's my son, and I want him back.*

'What do you mean, *your child*?' Sister Annunciata answered after Betsy nervously and haltingly delivered her lines that she had practised.

'Sister, I've read the letter that my mother wrote to you.' She thrust it in her direction, shaking slightly.

The nun glanced at it, then sneered. 'That could have been written by anyone.'

'No. I know my mother's handwriting. The way she does that strange looping thing with her Ys. And in any case, my son has got a birthmark. The nurses at Mill Road Hospital have a record.'

'Do you know how I know that this is not your child?' she hissed. 'Because he isn't. You do know what the police would think of this? Stealing a child.'

'I'm not stealing him! I'm his mother!'

'He's an *orphan of the living*. We don't give children back just because their parents are alive. You can't just come in here and say, I've changed my mind. Imagine what a mess that would be! These parents can't cope. Just like you. That's why our job is to find them new homes and families.'

Betsy drew herself up. 'I'm not afraid to stand up to you. I'm a different person to the girl you met that awful day with my mother in our parlour. So much has happened to me. I might still be small, but misfortune has made me full of rage.'

The nun sneered. 'Oh, really?'

Betsy batted aside the comment. 'If you want, we can pretend he's not mine and say I have adopted him. But I am taking him.'

'Don't be ridiculous . . .'

Betsy glared and leaned forward and banged her fist on the table. 'If you don't let me, I shall take that letter to the police.'

'The police wouldn't believe you.'

'Yes, they will. And by the way, Sybil Donaghue wants a promise from you that her child will not go to the Barneses. Or anywhere else.'

The nun snorted. 'Who are you to make these demands? You're nothing.' She narrowed her eyes and looked at Betsy sternly, but Betsy held her gaze.

'Yes, I am.' Her lip quivered but she gave the nun a hard, cold stare. 'I believe you know my fiancé, James Swann.'

'What?'

'Ask his mother if you'd like. Lettice can vouch for me.'

The nun paled. 'Lettice Swann? What? Your mother-in-law?' she replied, looking faintly disgusted. 'Are you sure?'

Betsy thrust out her hand and, trying not to shake, showed her the ring. 'You recognize the Swann crest?'

'Then you'll know that he's dead,' said the nun, coldly.

The words hit Betsy as though she had stabbed her in the heart and twisted.

'Missing in action doesn't mean he's dead,' she said, tears filling her eyes.

But the nun just tipped her head to one side. 'Very well, you can take the boy. If you're so determined, take him and keep him,' she snapped. 'One child in this godforsaken place won't be missed. But I'll leave you to consider this, Betsy Drew. Your poor mother came to me in the dead of night after rescuing that child on that terrible evening. She came here out of her mind with worry, and was only trying to do the best by you. You're ungrateful. You'll see in time. It's a cruel world out there. And you, with a dead fiancé and now a baby. You'll see, she was only trying to protect you.'

Betsy counted in her head to calm herself. One elephant, two elephants, three elephants. 'What my mother thought would be the best for me turned out to be the worst. But she only did it because people like you made her feel that my life would be full of shame and one not worth living. I don't blame her, I blame you. I wouldn't have cared. Do you know that? I never cared what people thought. I'm leaving now. But not without my son. I'll be waiting on the front steps.' She faltered. 'And you'll also let Sybil keep Belinda? You'll not send her away?'

The nun spluttered a hollow laugh. 'We're not a charity,' she replied flatly.

Ten minutes later, a flustered Sister David met Betsy standing in the porch with a small suitcase and George. He looked confused but he was smiling fiercely. For a second Betsy's heart stopped. This boy. Her boy. With his wild straw-coloured hair sticking up in a clump and his round blue eyes. He looked so small. So hopeful.

'Am I doing the right thing?' she asked Sister David in a low voice.

'Only time will tell, dear,' she said, patting her hand. 'I expect so. I'm sure you will be a good mother. Where will you go?'

'My friend Deirdre has a flat. We can stay there to start with.'

'If you need me, dear, just come to the back gate. Like before. And Betsy, good luck. May Jesus be with you. I have every faith he will guide you and George. Dress every day to meet God and everything will be fine.'

Betsy nodded tearfully. 'One more thing, Sister. Sybil. Please make sure the Barneses don't take Belinda. She's tried hard to keep her. When I'm on my feet, I'm sure me and my friend can help her. I've promised her. I don't know how. But I will.'

The nun pressed her hand. 'Don't worry, dear. I'll take care of them.'

Outside, beyond the walls, Betsy filled her lungs with air that smelled sweet, of roses and foxgloves.

'Can I have me gobstopper?' said George. 'Sister said you gived her me gobstopper.'

'*Gave* her *my* gobstopper,' she said, ruffling his hair. 'Of course you can, lovey.'

His serious face broke into a smile. 'Are we going to have a grand time?'

'Yes, we are, Georgie . . . You're going to stay with me and my friend, Deirdre.'

He frowned and tilted his head. 'Why are you crying, Betsy?'

She wiped a tear under each moist eye. 'Don't worry, love. They're happy tears. And if you want, you can call me Mummy. Would you like that?'

'Yes, Mummy,' he said, slipping his hand in hers, pressing his sticky palm against hers as if the sweetness would glue them together for ever.

Later, back at Deirdre's, Betsy picked up George who had fallen asleep on the battered sofa and held him tight to her and buried her head in his hair. She looked

at him, and irrationally, just as Deirdre had said, something began to stir inside her. Was it hope? A future?
Maybe it was, she thought, as the days passed, and it
was George who miraculously got her out of bed, sometimes before dawn or before the knocker-upper, who
still did the rounds. Without him she would be lost.

She started with small things – taking him to feed
the ducks at Sefton Park, or to stand on the wobbly
bridge and watch the steam trains rushing under them,
or for a walk to the Pier Head to hear the seagulls and
see the boats slipping out into the estuary. It felt like
he was her life raft amongst the wreckage of this
dreadful war. She marvelled how he seemed to grow
another inch every day, reached out instinctively to slip
his hand in hers, and crawled into her bed in the night
to spoon and snuffle. Moving around wordlessly, she
picked up discarded items of George's clothing, pressed
them to her face and breathed in the smell of him
whilst he was still sleeping, and thought it was remarkable how quickly she had got used to being a mother.

'You're a natural, Betsy. And why wouldn't you be?'
said Deirdre.

It was a crisp, sunny morning. George was pestering
around her skirts, and she was glad Deirdre had offered
to take him out. He skipped over to Betsy and snuffled
his head between her breasts. Sliding off the sofa, she
sat cross-legged on the floor with him.

'Kiss Mummy,' said Betsy.

He raised his face to hers and, beaming, kissed her
on the cheek.

Later that day Jacky was coming to visit. She had

sewn and ironed the gingham curtains, climbed up a ladder and dusted the picture rails.

'Bye,' said George as he left for the pram club with Deirdre.

She smiled and climbed off the chair and ruffled the top of his head.

When Jacky arrived, he threw his kit bag on the floor with a thud and scooped her up in his arms. As they nursed cups of tea, Betsy started at the very beginning, forgetting crucial details . . . No, Sybil didn't tell the nuns at first, she did. And how she had also told James. She looped back and forth, described James, how kind he was, how he could even play the piano backwards, but said dolefully that with no photo, she dreaded one day she might forget those blue eyes and cheekbones and his laugh and whistling. At least she had kept his ring. The ring that said they would love each other for ever.

'And so here we are. Just me and George. And everyone knows about my dead airman, and the irony is they all think George is his son. Malcolm is away at sea, thank God, and Alvis is still refusing to say George is his and threatening to go to Australia after Burma.'

Jacky shrugged. 'I didn't look after you, Bets,' he said sorrowfully.

'You couldn't have done anything. Besides, it was hard for you as well. The things they said about me to you in the pub. I'll always remember you bringing me cinder toffee. That was kind. And George . . . well, Ma thought the bombing was God's plan for me to start again. But James didn't trust God, and neither did I. This, though . . . you . . .' she said wistfully, taking his hands, caressing his fingers. 'I've missed you. I've never felt so alone without you and Ma . . . And I want you, me and Georgie to be some kind of family.'

'You've not given up hope that James might be found? In a POW camp? Or hiding?'

'That's all I thought about at first. But time goes on. It's been nearly four months now and nothing. I do the maths in my head every night, the possibilities, the odds of survival. How that decreases after the number of days, weeks, months, with no word. If you keep hoping things will turn out different when it's so unlikely they will, then don't you stop your future in its tracks?'

An hour later, George returned home with Deirdre. He tugged at the hem of Jacky's jacket. 'Uncle Jacky. Read to me,' he said.

'He likes Biggles. He likes looking at the pictures of the planes . . . It was in *The Boy's Own Paper*,' said Betsy. 'Wasn't it, son?'

George beamed and nodded.

'Does he? Come and sit on Uncle Jacky's knee then . . . Ready? *Biggles*,' he began, turning over the page. '*Our chaps are taking a hammering across the Channel . . .*'

The next day, after Betsy had kissed Jacky goodbye and George had hugged him so tightly she thought he would never let him go, Betsy was on her way back from the wash-house. It was heavy work and her hands were chilblained but she enjoyed the women's chatter and they didn't judge her. Strangely, their approval had given her some kind of respectability. There was confusion over the dates as to when George was born, they all knew. Like so many others, she had lost her sweetheart and they assumed the father was James and no one asked any questions about a wedding. They had stopped asking questions anyway when the Blitz arrived. Everyone was too busy with their own losses, their own secrets, the daily grind, to bother much. Especially when George kept them all entertained clapping his hands as he made bubbles and clutched the air to pop them. And amongst all this pain, it was also George who each morning when she would fling open the curtains lifted her out of the blackness that still sometimes crept in during the night. It had been the right decision. Imagine, she thought with a shudder, if she had turned her back on George. He might be halfway across the world now, or worse. It was the one thing she held on to: the thought that if she had walked away from her child, she would have nothing and nobody now. There had been talk of charges being brought by the RAF, but when pregnancy was involved, they didn't like to ask. It was not worth the trouble. They were quick to get rid of those with a 'lack of moral fibre' who showed 'unfitness for service' and had this stamped on their file, and it was the same for pregnant WAAFs. Despite the fact that victory over an increasingly desperate Hitler was beginning to feel as if it was in reach, the war trudged on endlessly.

She was good at her new job at the wash-house, organized by a friend of Hope's, and she had already been asked to help out in the office. She put the receipts on a spike and was able to total them up in her head, much to the amazement of everyone. When she got home, George was leaning out of the upstairs window.

'Mama! Five add three is eight!' She smiled. As well as his planes, he enjoyed counting and they played together doing simple sums, which he loved as much as she did. She remembered Jacky once saying that things were meant to happen. Maybe this was where everything had been leading to. Her sweet boy. The child. He deserved to be loved.

Deirdre was washing the pots at the sink.

'I've come to a decision,' Betsy said. 'Jacky made me feel that I still have a contribution to make to this war. I'm not going to continue at the wash-house. I'm going to see about going back to Cunard's. Would you help me?'

'Of course. Attagirl. Betsy, you won't let this defeat you. Besides, your country needs you and your maths. You're an absolute whizz . . . All that coding and those wiggly graphs you love . . .'

Betsy looked at her through moist eyes. 'Sister Bernadette used to say maths gives us hope because every problem has a solution . . .' The sentence tailed off. She couldn't think of anything else to say.

Chapter 35

'What's the point?' Lettice asked when, once again, Gordon urged her to eat some toast. It was late afternoon, almost five o'clock, and she had slept all day.

'You have a letter. OHMS.'

Lettice sat bolt upright and snatched the letter from the silver tray, tucked into a small package wrapped in brown paper and tied with string. She fumbled as she opened it.

'I took the liberty of opening it,' said Gordon quickly. 'Still no news, but they found some of James's things in a drawer. They've returned them.'

'Go on, read it then,' said Lettice, slumping again, turning vaguely towards him.

Gordon cleared his throat.

Dear Mrs Swann,
The remainder of your son's effects have now been collected and so we are forwarding them to you. Any others will in due course go through Air Ministry channels. Once again, please accept the deepest sympathy of us all, and we hope that we may soon have some good news regarding the safety of Officer Swann.

331

Gordon coughed again and pulled out James's tie, his book about birds and a letter, all contained in the bulging envelope. He handed them to her.

'What's this?' asked Lettice, holding the letter addressed to James written in childish writing. She frowned. It piqued her curiosity and sharpened her focus. But then her expression darkened.

'What's the matter, Mrs Swann?' asked Gordon.

Her voice when she answered was bitter and twisted, sharp-edged. 'No! It's from *her*!'

She felt the blood pulsing behind her eyeballs as she scanned it, gobbling the words in a fury. All this time she had been shouting at the sky and at God and at Hitler. But it was this girl she should have been screaming at. Betsy, who made the blood run cold in her veins and her hands quiver.

Dear James,

I don't know where to start, apart from to tell you I love you and ask for your forgiveness. I'm afraid I shan't be returning to Dishforth to marry you. It's a long and difficult story and I will do my best to explain. But my shame should not be yours. This breaks my heart to write. I am crying as I do so. I never dared I could feel joy like I have with you and our wedding plans sealed my happiness. But I haven't been entirely truthful. I'm ashamed to say that I'm not the girl you think I am. I will be as brief as I can, and it's so very difficult. When I was seventeen, I had a child. I thought this child – my son – was a

*secret that I could keep buried, and in doing
so, I could begin a new life with you. You
might be thinking where is he, why did I
abandon him? How was I able to keep him a
secret? I believed that he had died. This is
what I was told. But if someone can come
back from the dead, it's what has happened.
He wasn't dead, he was at St Mary's
orphanage with other children, a good many
like my boy – orphans of the living; a horrible
phrase. Left to choose between a life with you
or my son, well, it's impossible and I am so
sad about this and so very sorry. But I hope
this letter explains why I can't marry you –
not because I do not love you or because I
think we are too different, as I often worried
about. It's because I can no longer carry this
dreadful secret. The least I can do is to be
truthful.*

*I was able to be a different person with
you, 'pure, innocent little Betsy', but I'm not
that and we would be embarking on a future
built on a lie, which would only create bitterness and resentment. I love you so much, but
my bad name and guilt should not be yours. It
hurts to breathe knowing that I have deceived
you. I don't know what's next for me. Maybe,
maybe you could find it in your heart not to
hate me? I hold out such little hope for the
future. Were we ever meant for each other?
Were we doomed from the beginning? It's
with a heavy heart I write this, despairing of*

*the stupid mistake I made. Know that I love
you always.*

In anticipation, but also dread, of your reply.
Betsy

'Gordon!' stuttered Lettice, staggering to her feet. 'I
need you to drive me to town. I need to find her! She
said St Mary's orphanage! They will tell me about her.
I shall wash and change. Meet me on the steps in an
hour.'

He was shocked to see her spring out of the chair
nimbly and move across the room with the energy and
the determinedness of a girl. He wondered what she
hoped to achieve but knew holding her back would
mean retreat, and she would never agree to that.

Chapter 36

The sky had threatened rain earlier and sure enough it had been pelting down for an hour, but now the sun had burst through, and the pavement slabs were steaming. Betsy noticed that the railings where blimps had been tied a few years before had rusted into the pavement. She looked around her at the grime and the soot. This is my life, she thought. Ridiculous for me to think it could ever have been anything else. She came out of Cunard's and checked the clock in the foyer. Deirdre was on a late shift at the factory, so she needed to hurry to get back to George before she left. Passing the woman from the architect's offices, Mint Imperial Maguire was what they called her, she nodded a hello. Dodging her way through the crowds, she headed towards the Pier Head, where she would get the tram home. It was busy today. There were still so many in uniform. A pang of jealousy hit her. But then she thought of George. She loved that child so much. She was officially classed as a reservist, and finally at Cunard's she felt she was a useful person, doing a useful job. Ahead, she could see the tram. Damn, she thought. Missed it. The voices that she heard behind her jostling to queue for the next tram were bad-tempered and gruff.

'Move . . .' said a man with a white face who had come from the docks unloading flour.

'Move yourself . . .' came the shrill response of a woman in Tate and Lyle overalls and with her hair in a turban.

Betsy turned around to see the commotion. And then she realized someone was calling her name. 'Betsy Drew! *Betsy Drew.* You stop right there!'

Squinting above the sea of heads, she stopped in her tracks and frowned.

The crowd parted. And that was when she saw her: Lettice Swann. There was rage in her eyes and bitterness and fury twisted her mouth into an ugly sneer.

'You devil!' Lettice cried, rushing forward, shoving people out of the way and pushing Betsy in the chest with her flat palm.

Betsy reeled and gasped.

'You killed him. You killed my Jum!' She was screeching now.

Betsy stuttered and fell backwards. Lettice lunged at her again and grabbed her arm, shaking something in her hand, thrusting it in her face. 'My Jum! Jum!!' she wailed.

'Mrs Swann,' she stuttered. 'Everyone's looking . . .'

By now, a small crowd had gathered. Some were laughing, others just looked on in shock.

'You guttersnipe!'

'What? What did I do?'

'You tricked him. You lied. This letter . . .' Lettice snarled, shaking it in her face. 'You sent it to him the night before one of his most dangerous missions. How could he fly a plane when you put all these terrible

336

thoughts in his head? He wasn't thinking straight. Because of that wretched letter. You said you didn't want to be with him!'

Betsy's jaw clenched. 'Well, you would be happy about that at least.'

Lettice scrunched up the letter. 'You killed my son! You dirty, lying . . .' And then she stumbled and gasped in horror, one hand flying to her mouth, the other pointing at Betsy's hand.

'My husband's ring!'

'James gave it to me . . .' stuttered Betsy, instinctively drawing her hand to her body. 'We were getting married . . .' She knit her brows together, but Lettice grasped her arm. Betsy twisted herself free and, eyes brimming with tears, pulled the ring off her finger. 'Have it. I don't need a ring to remember him by . . .' she said, throwing the ring to the ground.

'You sly harlot!' Lettice spat out the words, raised her hand to strike her.

Betsy ducked, but then she drew herself up. 'Go ahead, hit me. If you think you can hurt me with your pathetic blows . . .'

The slap was stinging and sharp. Betsy's eyes filled with tears. She looked out towards the silver Mersey, her chin trembling. And then she slowly turned her cheek.

'Do it again, Mrs Swann . . . Please, do it again . . .' she said.

Chapter 37

The sun was throwing long shadows across the grass. George was weaving through the tall grass around the base of the tree on the patch of land beside the scaldies. Six months before, she had barely seen the top of his head, but now it was the end of summer, she could see his shoulders. She sighed and stood and brushed down her legs. She looked out towards the jumble of small houses squatting in the shadow of the docks, with their sloping rooftops, and out towards the river. Beyond were the majestic buildings, the Three Graces, on top of which were the beautiful outstretched-winged Liver Birds and golden domes. She thought of Mottram Hall and took some comfort in the fact that she now knew that not everything was as grand as it looked on the outside. Before she had met James, she might have stared at the spires and gargoyles of the Hall with awe, but she knew there were buckets under the eaves and on the stairs just like at the tenements.

She looked at George; at his round cheeks and his eyelashes like brushes. This was her boy. He was her future now. And it didn't matter that she was doing long, difficult hours at Cunard's, because if it meant she could buy him a tin drum or toy aeroplane or a

Biggles comic, she was happy to do so. She now found pleasure in the smallest of things. Stones skimming off the surface of a pond, his face when she took him to Bertorelli's ice cream parlour. He loved steam engines, and he would happily stand on the bridge for hours watching the trains rush underneath. When he beamed at her through clouds of steam, how could you not smile back, whatever you were feeling? Moving quickly amongst the crowds, dodging the Mary Ellen selling sprigs of heather, she thought ahead about Christmas and George. The rocking horse at Blacklers was gone, but it would come back when this war was over. And there was Lewis's grotto and a wooden reindeer to look forward to. They stood to head back home, following the sound of the rag and bone man and his horse clopping along the cobbles. Taking George's hand, she felt his fingers curl around her fist and his thumb slip inside her palm as they stepped off the kerb, gently pulling him to safety as a taxi unexpectedly appeared from around the corner.

'They should look where they're going. We managed to get around in the Blitz in the blackout without hitting anyone, but these days people step out in front of you in broad daylight,' said the driver of the taxi.

The passenger nodded in reply as they hurtled on, driving out of the city to the suburbs and then into the surrounding countryside, finally passing the three-penny-bit house and swinging off the road into Ince Woods.

'Nice day for it,' said the driver.

Nice day for what? The passenger didn't reply.

*

Inside Mottram Hall, Sister David was sitting beside Lettice's bed.

'It's the Feast day of Saint Bartholomew,' she said, fiddling with Lettice's plaid blanket, rearranging it over her knees. 'We're saying mass at St Mary's chapel. Would you like me to say a novena for you? You might want to come to mass there soon. It's peaceful.'

'I have lost two children, a husband and a brother. I cannot face a God that could be so cruel to me.' The world felt dead to her, and she couldn't understand why the nun couldn't see it.

'But Lettice . . . the Lord works in mysterious ways . . . He didn't take your loved ones away deliberately. There was no plan.'

Lettice groaned. 'I'm sick of this nonsense talk, Sister. You're only here for my money. I have none.'

'Mrs Swann, that's not fair. We care about you.'

'No, you don't.'

The nun faltered. She glanced over at Gordon, who was standing at the door. 'Would you think the same of your God if James were alive? What if I were to say that to you?'

'I would say that it was a cruel joke. You wouldn't do that to me.'

'No, I wouldn't.'

Lettice turned slowly. The figure was slightly stooped, leaning on a stick, one arm in a sling, and was blurred around the edges, backlit and oscillating.

'What's this?' she whispered. 'Am I dreaming?'

'No, Mother, it's me.'

Lettice gasped. 'Jum!'

'Lettice, yes, it's James. We were worried about the shock. That's why I'm here . . . Are you all right?' said Sister David.

James walked across the room unsteadily, using the stick. He bent towards Lettice and grasped her hand, noticing her veins were like knotted ropes underneath skin like paper.

'Jum . . . Jum . . .' she said in his ear. With a bony finger she traced over the line of his nose and his cheekbone as if checking to make sure he was alive. For one second, she squeezed her eyes shut. How often had she seen this in a dream? When she opened them, she saw something glinting, metal. Wheels? A wheelchair?

'Jum? Your legs?' she said in a quivering voice.

'Yes. They work. But not all the time. And I get headaches.'

He sank into the chair that Gordon had pushed towards him.

'You're so thin . . .' said Lettice.

'I could say the same of you, Mother.'

'Oh, my darling boy. Tell me everything . . . Tell me what happened, so that I know you're real . . .'

He began to talk. His voice sounded different, shaky, and in parts he stopped and rubbed his temples, or squinted up as if trying to remember. But soon all around him became quiet as he tried to recount each moment, hurtling back to the cockpit of the Lancaster.

Lettice tried to make sense of what he was saying. He was speaking slowly but it sounded as if his voice died right away at the end of the sentences. She had been losing her hearing months ago and could make

341

out very little. Dinner became dimmer, sunshine became some sign. He was shaking violently as he spoke. Did he even know he was doing that? And she looked at him fearful that he had gone a little mad; or was it she who had gone mad? Whatever it was, it was kinder, gentler to pretend she was following what he was saying. Finally, her hand slowly crept to his lips and touched his hair as if to tell him to stop, because despite her efforts it was unbearable to hear his story about fires on a plane and French girls with baskets of warm bread rolls.

'So that was it, Mother. I think all my crew died.'

'Oh, Jum . . . What can I do to make it better, darling?'

'Nothing. Apart from . . . Betsy. Where's my Betsy, Mother?'

How quickly it went from intense joy to bickering. The following morning, after a good night's sleep and a breakfast of kippers, he asked again.

'You can't want to see that girl? Not after everything she's done!'

'Why not? I love her.'

'But Jum!' She hesitated. 'I'm sorry to be the one to tell you this, but you do know she's a fallen girl? Do you know that? The sisters told me. And, my dear, she jilted you. She wrote you a letter. Did you read it? She didn't want to marry you. She turned you down.'

He shrugged. 'Mother, that's a conversation between Betsy and me, not you . . .'

'You're not thinking straight. If it hadn't been for that girl . . . Gordon, find the letter!'

342

'She saved me. It was Betsy that willed me to push on and live. I love her . . . Mother, I'm tired. I don't care about any letter.'

Sister David, who had just arrived, moved forward. 'He's still very weak, Lettice. Please stop . . .'

'He should stop saying he loves her! What about me?' she said, her voice steadily rising.

'What about you?'

'James, she has the illegitimate child living with her. Sister, tell him!'

Sister David dropped her eyes to the floor. 'She's a good mother, I think.'

Lettice whimpered. 'Jum, what about Clementine?'

'Mother, I've walked in this door, alive, barely, after months missing, and this is what you say?'

'I'll cut you off to make you see sense,' she said bitterly. 'I will, Jum. You'll see.'

'Cut me off? From what? This place? Go on, do it. I'd rather live free with Betsy than rattle around in this draughty hole for the rest of my life . . . Gordon, you said you have Betsy's address?'

Furious, she stood and scrabbled in the drawer and reached for the screwed-up letter. 'Here, read this if you don't believe me!' She thrust it into his hands. 'Read it if you want to see what I've been through!'

He glanced tiredly at them.

'Nothing here could change my mind about Betsy.'

And then she turned to the nun. 'What did I do?' she whimpered. 'I'm dreaming, am I? This is a nightmare . . . Is it?' she murmured, ticcing and blinking wildly.

James winced. He turned, dragging his bad leg, his

head hurting. Gordon was waiting for him with the wheelchair.

'Take me to the kitchens,' he said. 'There's something I need to do.'

After being wheeled through the back kitchens of Mottram Hall to the old garage and jumble of outhouses across the courtyard and behind the stables, he got out and, with the help of his stick, he pushed open the wooden door of the small, squat brick barn, bending to stoop inside. 'Leave me for a moment, Gordon,' he said. 'Go back and see if Mother has calmed down. She will do soon.'

The familiar smell of old coats, diesel and straw hit the back of his throat. The battered wardrobe propped up against the far wall had its door slightly ajar. He limped across the stone-flagged floor and opened it further, the door creaking on the rusting hinges. His father's uniform hung stiffly on a battered coat hanger. His pipe sat on a shelf above it. Disgusting habit, his mother always said. She hated him spitting into the fire and picking tobacco from between his teeth. But that was his father, and the smell of him came back to James in a rush of memories as he held the pipe under his nose and breathed in. Steeling himself, he walked over and opened the side door, then went awkwardly down another step to the garage. There it was. What was left of the little Tiger Moth. He pulled at the tarpaulin covering it, peeped under it and then yanked harder at it. This plane had sat untouched for years and clouds of dust rose from it. Running his flat hand over its side as tenderly as some would stroke the flank of a favourite horse, he sighed. He let it rest on the metal, thinking again of the last time his father had taken him up in this little plane, when James was frightened that they might lose power as they thrummed and bumped and wobbled in the air, scared that at any moment they might hurtle down into the trees just like that fateful day. The sky had seemed so big and the little plane so fragile. He should never have let his brother go up in it after him. His mother had tried to get rid of it after the accident, but Dick the housekeeper had said that they should keep it. James span the propeller and was amazed that it turned, squealing like a stuck pig, but it was nothing a squirt of oil couldn't remedy.

'Gordon! Can you take me to my study?'

Betsy was standing at the sink washing pots when she heard whistling outside the front door. The postman was reaching into his sack of letters, though the buff envelope he pulled out with URGENT scrawled on the outside made him pause. He took a breath as he slipped it through the letter box and moved quickly away.

Deirdre got up off the sofa and walked across the room to pick it up.

Miss Betsy Drew, she read on the envelope. Her heart galloped. 'Betsy! A letter for you,' she said, coming into the bedroom.

'I can't . . .' said Betsy, fear clutching her. 'Open it and read it to me.'

Deirdre opened it warily, then scanned the note on

thin paper inside. 'Betsy, it's James's final note,' said Deirdre, quietly. 'He did write one to you . . .'

'Oh, God,' said Betsy, sitting up, her eyes squinting. 'Why has it only arrived now?'

'I don't know.'

Betsy gulped air as tears spilled over onto her cheeks. 'Deirdre, please, will you read it?'

'Of course,' Deirdre replied.

'*My Dearest Betsy*,' she began falteringly, her voice shaking a little. '*This is the letter we all dread writing, though the bigger dread is that someone one day might be reading it. My sweetheart, if that's you, it means something gloomy has happened to me. It means I will never see your smile again, or carry you over the threshold after we are married, but I can't bear to think about that. So, dear, if that's the sad outcome, know in another, kinder place I'm waiting for my hand to brush over yours or my eyes to rest on your face, and I'm longing for the time when I can put my lips on yours. You don't need to read this letter to know that I love you. But you do need to know I don't care a jot about you having a child. You should feel no shame or sorrow because of it. I would have hoped, when we were to marry, if the child is alone with no father in the world, you would let me have the privilege of being a papa to him. So maybe I just need to write and thank you. For showing me that true love exists. We flew so close to the sun, touched heaven on earth, you and I. Stay safe, my beautiful girl, and I hope you will be reunited with your son and tell him how proud I was of you, my darling girl. Your one true love, Jimmy.*'

Betsy felt her whole body shaking. There were no words, just overwhelming grief and shock.

'He was a good man, Betsy. He didn't mind about George. I told you he loved you. Will you rest now?'

Betsy pressed her heart. It felt like it might explode outside of her body. But then, just as she was about to collapse into a mess of tears, Deirdre picked up the envelope again.

She frowned. 'Wait. Bets. The envelope. D'you see? Different ink. And shakier writing, but the same nevertheless . . . The date. It was two days ago.'

Betsy took it, squinted at it.

'The postmark. Look, the postmark. Liverpool. This was sent from Liverpool. Crosby. What does it mean?'

Betsy's eyebrows knitted together, and then she stood, grabbed her coat. 'I don't know. Why has it only arrived now? Someone has had this for months and chosen not to send it. Is Lettice behind it? Did she post it? I'm going to Mottram Hall to find out.'

'Betsy, no . . .' cried Deirdre after her.

But she had gone. And Deirdre was left wondering if it would lead to more upset and drama, and if so, whether this time Betsy might never recover.

Chapter 38

Betsy ran as quickly as she could to the Overhead Railway. People were jostling onto the platform. The 'Pneumonia Express', many called it, because of how many were tightly packed into the carriages. As she waited for the train to arrive to take her out of the city, she worked out that she had half an hour to get from the end of the Overhead Railway to the threepenny-bit house, and then the long walk up the drive. The letter, pressed between tissue paper and pocket, was burning a hole in her linen shift dress. Repeatedly she turned it over, compared the writing on the envelope to the writing on the note.

A guard blew on a shrill whistle and told everyone pushing forward to move back. Betsy craned her neck to see if the train was coming.

'Stand back!' he yelled. 'Coal engine coming through to Aintree!' The train belched clouds of white steam, whistled and chuffed noisily.

Betsy watched and waited. On the other side of the tracks, at the same time, a second train arrived coming from the opposite direction. People got off and slammed the doors and spilled onto the platform. Some began to walk over the bridge but as they did so they all became enveloped in the fog of billowing steam clouds. Gradually the few figures hurried down the iron stairs, but there was one – a man – walking slowly and stiffly, stopping for breath. A slightly stooped, silhouetted figure, he was just standing there on the bridge; a curious sight, thought Betsy as she approached and the mist disappeared and he began to sharpen into focus.

She tipped her head to one side. The uniform, the buttons glinting, the man's jawline, perfectly proportioned limbs . . . and then . . . his face, his eyes. Every part of her began to shake.

'Is it you, Jimmy?' she murmured, hardly daring to breathe, touching him on the shoulder after walking up the steps and onto the bridge to meet him.

There was a loud whistle, then the chuffing, and the creaking and clanking of metal.

He moved towards her, and she fell into his arms. He kissed her but then held her slightly away, touched her face.

'Betsy, I was coming to find you. And you're here. You look so beautiful. God, that little dimple in your chin . . . it's still there. I thought I'd never see that again. And those eyes . . . You read my letter then?'

Betsy faltered. She could feel herself swaying, like the ground was moving underneath her. 'Oh, my Betsy,' said James, his legs buckling. Betsy steadied him with her arm. Grasping his hand, it felt warm and alive, and she knew she wasn't dreaming. He bowed his head, and she cradled him as they both cried rivers of tears and his hand gradually crept to her face and his thumb caressed her cheekbone. 'I love you. I never stopped.'

He kissed her tenderly and she had never felt joy like it.

'Would you still marry me? I have your pin. Do you have my ring?' he asked.

She was about to explain that his mother probably had it, but then her mouth fell open. He was getting down on one knee. She noticed a few on the platform below beginning to stare up at them.

'Will you?'

Tears swelled in her eyes. 'Of course . . . Oh, Jimmy . . .'

'You'll have to help me up get up,' he said, beginning to rise unsteadily. 'So I can kiss you.'

She smiled as she pulled him to his feet and put an arm out for him to lean on. When he was standing, he kissed her tenderly.

People began to clap, and a boy whistled.

'I'm the happiest man in the world,' he said, and turned and waved at the small crowd that had gathered.

As he walked her towards the tram, where they sat down on a bench – words spilling out about how he had moved from safehouse to safehouse until he reached Spain – a ship was slipping into the Mersey Estuary. A cloud moved away from the sun and the ship shone a glittering white. 'A Liverpool wedding. Glorious,' he said. 'I'm sorry I put you through this. But I'm here for you now, my love. And your boy?'

'You have no idea how many times I regretted not telling you. I wanted to tell you . . .' she said in a rush of words, tears spilling onto her cheeks.

'Shush,' said James gently, putting a finger on her lips.

'I thought somehow the horrible truth of my world would never touch ours. I thought it would destroy us. But then I realized it wasn't a horrible truth I was hiding. It was my son. He's joyous and good and . . . my boy. Only you had gone before I understood that. And it was too late.' Her voice died away. 'But your mother. She can't get past it, Jimmy. She says I'm . . . well, you know all the names. A fallen woman . . . That you would never stand the shame of being married to someone like me . . .'

'You are the miracle that saved me in that plane. Why would a baby put me off? I'm sure your son is terrific. I can't wait to meet him. Betsy, tell me . . . who is the child's father?'

She looked vaguely away. 'His name is Alvis Dooley.'

'Does he not want him?'

She shrugged. 'God knows I've tried, written so many letters, banged on his door. Even your mother probably tried,' she said with a bitter smile. 'But when he last saw me he told me he and his new wife were going to live in Australia when he's finished fighting in Burma. So that's it. And George will probably be the better for it. I've told George the truth about him. I'm done with lying.'

She sighed. He wasn't saying anything, and she couldn't tell what he was thinking.

'Then I'm looking forward to getting to know your son. *Our* son, if you'll let me be George's father.'

'Even though I'm damaged goods?' She couldn't bring herself to say it was his mother who had called her that.

'We're all damaged, dear. Me more than anyone.

351

You're my life raft and I'm clinging on by my finger-tips. We're both wounded, Betsy. Look at me. Busted leg. My hearing comes and goes. And this scar . . . Not pretty . . .'

'You're beautiful. Don't say that . . . Your mother thinks that it was my fault you crashed. Because of that stupid letter I wrote to you.'

'No, darling. It's war that kills people and the mad people who start it.'

She threaded her fingers through his. 'What happened on that mission?' asked Betsy, softly.

James sighed. And wondered why it was that as he began to tell her, finally he could remember every second, every moment with astonishing clarity.

One minute Mathers and Goodenough had been singing that song again, 'This one's a bloody big bomb', and James had glanced at Betsy's photograph in the window frame. But the next they had been hit and there seemed no hope of survival. Goodenough had muttered darkly, 'I know a fellow who's a betting man. Someone will be getting a pint on us . . . Cheers to him . . .'

The plane climbed higher and fire was licking the tail, slipping through the hole and the open door where gunner Paddy was struggling with his parachute, and James knew that he would have to crawl through there too.

'Crew, bail! Now!' James shouted.

He could feel the plane losing power. He knew soon it would begin to drop like a stone, and it was keening starboard badly. He had to decide whether to jump or try to steer her out of the tailspin.

Sergeant Goodenough began to cry. 'My leg,' he whimpered.

'Hold on to me and Paddy,' said Mathers. 'We'll go together.'

'I can't,' he murmured.

James could feel the cold now despite the fire spreading through the back of the plane. The glycol tank had exploded and the windows were icing up. Pretty soon the fire would reach the bullets and they would go off like firecrackers. If he wasn't dead from the crash, they would explode and ricochet around the plane and kill them all that way. But he knew what he had to do. He could carry on, but they would never have enough fuel to get across the Channel. If he could reach Holland. If he could only reach Holland.

He squinted ahead. He could see the mushroom shape of the parachutes drifting gently below and he knew there was nothing he could do now. No more time. There was only one choice now. Death and never see Betsy again, or jump. As he floated to the ground, he lost consciousness almost immediately.

When the snowflakes, wet against his cheek, stirred him, he thought there was something vaguely comical about finding himself tangled up in a fir tree. Clambering down, miraculously it was the tiny compass, the one he and Betsy had laughed at, and the little handkerchief with the map printed on it, that would save him. Finding his way out of the trees, he collapsed exhausted onto a grassy bank amid a small copse. Three hours later, after walking north towards a village, he heard a voice.

353

'Monsieur? Monsieur! *Come!' He could vaguely see that the girl parting the branches who was calling him was smiling. 'S'il vous plaît. We have safehouse.'*

It was three months before he recovered. Spain beckoned. Weeks passed in which he was helped by brave people – some who were the resistance, some just ordinary Dutch people. He slept in a farmhouse, in an outhouse, a cellar, an attic; a week in a pipe that was to be used for a tunnel. A month in a cowshed, but all the time getting closer to the border. Longing for clean sheets, a hospital bed, a wheelchair and splints to straighten his shattered leg. And sleep. A restful sleep. Before a nurse leading him gently into the day room, and the news that he had been waiting for.

'Home now, Señor James. Home.'

'Shut your eyes again, Deirdre!' George said. 'Start counting . . .'

Deirdre laughed. George raced around the small sunny kitchen as they played hide-and-seek. Opening and shutting cupboards to find somewhere to crawl inside, finally he scrambled up onto the work surface and hid behind the pretty gingham curtains, drawing them shut and giggling.

'I can hear you. Coming, ready or not! Where's my George?' Deirdre opened her eyes, grinning as she heard him trying not to make a noise with his giggles. But then his giggling stopped abruptly.

'Look!' said George. He had drawn the curtain aside.

'What is it? You've given it away!'

'A pilot! With Ma! *A real one!* Come and see!'

Deirdre froze. Then her hands went to her mouth. No . . . it couldn't be . . .

George was scrambling off the work surface, barging past her, racing to the door.

An airman . . . coming here? Or was it just someone to tell them that James had been found dead? How could Betsy stand this? But wait, they were holding hands . . .

George twisted the door handle and flung it open. 'George?'

'Mister, is you real?' said George, enthralled, staring up at him. 'Is you Biggles?'

James and Betsy's eyes remained fixed on one another as if time had stopped. George gasped. As Betsy led James inside it was as if some kind of unreal presence was stepping into the room. And seeing him through George's eyes, he looked like a god.

'Ma? Why's you crying? And him,' he said, thrusting a stubby finger at James.

'Because we're happy, son. Because we're very, very happy,' Betsy replied, her fingers slowly creeping up to James's lips and then his hollow cheek, where she tenderly placed her palm flat against it.

'I'm George, mister. When I was a baby Ma called me Vernon. Like the Pools. But that was a long time ago. I'm George now.'

Betsy blushed. She wanted to say to James she was young, daft.

'Here, sonny, take my cap. You can wear it if you want.'

George's face shone. He put it on his head. He could barely see as it slipped over his eyes, but he beamed.

'Skipper . . . Our chaps is taking a hammering across the Channel . . .' he said with a salute. 'But fings are looking up at last!'

'Aren't you going to introduce me?' said Deirdre, with a shy smile.

Chapter 39

A month had passed. James had tried with Lettice, but the more he insisted that Betsy and George would be in his life for ever, the worse Lettice had become. She had even suggested Betsy should ask Sister Annunciata to send George to Australia. Every time he saw her, she would hurl more insults. He had now spent more time with Betsy on the sofa at Deirdre's than at Mottram Hall. Lettice soon began to stubbornly refuse to talk to him whilst he was living there. In sin! Under the same roof! The dingy tenements! More comfortable than Mottram, James had replied. Finally, he announced what Lettice had been dreading. He was marrying Betsy. And that was the end of it.

'What would that mean? If she cut you off?' Betsy had asked.

'It would mean no Mottram Hall. But that's a relief.'

Six weeks later, Betsy rose with the first morning light and put on the dress made from parachute silk that Carol had sent over from Dishforth. Deirdre gasped with the sheer beauty of her – her blonde mane of hair and honey-coloured limbs and full lips – as the winter sun rose over the tenements and flooded into their little kitchen.

357

The lofty church down by the docks was already full. No Lettice, of course. James had asked Jacky, who was on leave, to invite Betsy's father, but no one expected him to come, and he didn't, and it was Jacky who would walk her down the aisle. No Malcolm, thankfully. But everyone else. Even Aunt Winnie and all the boys bunched up and were having a good look. No Alvis, but Joyce Dooley arrived and had the nerve to complain glumly that Alvis didn't even bother to write her letters now. A few of the boys James had met during rehab made it, and Melanie drove from Woodvale. The city was beginning to recover; the war was still not over, plenty of James's friends were still flying, plenty were still losing their lives, but Hitler had turned his head away from Liverpool. The bombing of Hamburg had been brutal and Zygmunt Kanski had lost his life in that one, but miraculously Sergeant Goodenough had survived the crash – was still in a hospital with his one arm, still telling his one joke. Barely alive but feeling just about good enough to keep breathing through his scarred lungs, he said in a telegram.

Sybil, who was living in rooms with Belinda in Kirkby – the nuns had had enough of her at St Mary's, shouting her mouth off about Betsy and Timbuktu – and had taken a job at the munitions factory where no one cared what an old nun might say, was beautiful in hot pink. Belinda was the perfect flower girl, clutching George's hand, who was a page boy – both scattering rose petals and confetti and laughing when it got it up their noses and made them sneeze.

As Betsy walked down the aisle on James's arm, a

pretty, white winter rose in her hair and the blush of love on her cheeks, she wondered if Lettice might still arrive at the church, late, flustered and apologetic. She didn't. But apart from that, it was a perfect day.

'Mother will come round in time,' said James as he drew back the curtains of the small farmhouse in Anglesey the following morning. They had left for their honeymoon quietly and without much fuss, arrived on the small island in the evening at the same time as the sun was setting, pale pink and then fiery gold. James unbuttoned her dress, then pushed one strap of her slip off her shoulder, and then the other. And with her underclothes falling away, he gasped at her golden skin, her blushing cheeks, her reddening lips. They made love with the window open in the softly fading light to the sound of a trickling river and cows gently mooing outside the bedroom window and a chicken pecking about in the yard. Betsy had never felt such peace, had never believed love could be so calm and so gentle, that a man so heroic, so brave, could also be so soft and kind-hearted. Afterwards they sat in bed overlooking the tranquil sea, gazing towards Liverpool. He kissed her gently on the nape of her neck and her fingers slipped to his cheek. She could feel his arms tight around her. She turned to face him, and her lips met his.

'Betsy, is this real?' he asked. He traced his fingers down the slope of her jawline, then placed his hand on her breast. 'It must be. Your heart. I can hear it: bu-bum, bu-bum. I love you, Betsy.'

'And I love you too. You saved me,' she murmured.

'No, you saved me, dearest. I wonder . . .' he said,

lolling his head on her shoulder. 'Maybe you can only truly know happiness when you know what it's like to have real pain . . . We both know about that, don't we? But maybe this war will do that for others? Devastation leads you to freedom.'

'So much devastation, though. Jimmy . . .' She took a deep breath. 'That night at the hospital . . .'

They had talked so much: about St Mary's, Cunard's, Deirdre, Sybil and Sister Annunciata. But this was the first time Betsy allowed herself, in halting sentences, to say out loud to him the words 'the Mill Road bombing'. And it was like a great weight lifting from her, as she spoke about Malcolm turning up, of her mother's worry, and of the girls and women on the ward who had lost their lives, the flames, the noise, the terrible heat. The pain of being separated from George. Of being told by her mother that he had died. He frowned as he listened, remembering the night when he held a baby in his arms, choking in dust and heat and fire. 'Betsy, I was there. And this might be strange, but I think I met George that night.'

They could hardly get through another sentence without crying, but finally his head fell back on the pillow, and she nestled into his chest.

'We've turned our wounds into victory,' he said, drawing back the sheets, marvelling at her naked body, the rises of her breasts and the smoothness of her thighs, her graceful sloping neck, the tiny scars across her belly – like silver eels under her skin – the mark of motherhood, and those private sacred parts of her. 'I love you, Betsy. Can I show you again just how much?'

Epilogue

1951

Lettice stared out at Mottram Hall's ornamental lake. Bone dry now, it only filled up when the rain came, and even then it was always laced with the green slime that floated to the surface. Her eyesight was failing her, so what did it matter? Gordon had let Mr Worboys in through the conservatory and, silhouetted and backlit by the sun, for a moment she thought it was James. How could it be?

'Thank you for seeing me. You know I'm a trustee of St Mary's like you, Mrs Swann? We have met. I wanted to talk about our plans for the orphanage.'

She shrank into her chair and sighed. 'Surely you know I have nothing to do with the nuns? Is it my son you need to speak to? I'm afraid I'm estranged from him. Have been for years.'

She could see him frowning. *Why?* his expression said.

'I cut him off. I'm a foolish old lady. I have not been involved with St Mary's for some time.' She shrugged and looked at him with dull eyes.

'That may be, but I'm not here to talk about your son. Though I hear he's doing marvellous work at RAF

Woodvale. These new jet propulsions he's working on are wonderful. No, the orphanage . . . Surprisingly it was one of the nuns there, Sister David, who came to us wanting change. Since the end of the war, with Mr Atlee and his National Health Service, everything is so very different. No, I was hoping I'd find Betsy here. We would like to talk to her.'

'They live in Ainsdale, I believe.'

'Oh. I see. Sister David must have it wrong. But can I ask you? Orphans of the living? Have you heard of that phrase?'

Lettice squinted. She thought back to that wretched letter. 'I believe I have.'

'We are beginning to gather stories of girls who found themselves at the orphanage in unfortunate circumstances. Some of them are difficult to hear. It began with two sisters, Marcia and Cynthia, and then another girl, Ellie. And there's a plucky lass called Alice. Many of these "orphans of the living" have found a home in a house that my architect's business helped build. We are interviewing as many of the girls as we can. Betsy's name is on my list.'

She winced.

'We began to hear stories of the orphans of the living – of the Corporation sending them to St Mary's, taking children from their mothers without proper permission. But without writing them down, there's a danger people will forget, or they will get lost or misremembered. We hope that one day when people say "orphans of the living" – that terrible phrase – they will say that they have never heard of it, perhaps when we're in kinder times. But we must never forget. Rather like the men we lost in the war. So, Mrs Swann, I know a little of your daughter-in-law already, and what happened to her and her son, and I wouldn't want you to be embarrassed. But I would like to meet her and talk to her, if I may.'

She nodded.

'Would you give me her address?'

Lettice was silent. Her lips pressed together in a thin line.

'Gordon?' she called, waveringly.

The sturdy Edwardian terraced house that James and Betsy had rented in Ainsdale was small, but it was clean. This was their family home and would be for a while, and despite James's leg moving stiffly, Betsy still felt her heart flutter with excitement when he walked into a room. He had shown great courage, and his expertise, said the RAF, was not to be wasted, and it had led to his job at Woodvale. He had never been so busy. And neither had she. Sister Bernadette had invited her back to her convent school earlier that week to talk to the girls about maths and her work at Cunard's and in the RAF. She looked at them and wondered if sitting out there was another Betsy, and was grateful the school seemed to be changing. St Mary's, however, was still grim, still foreboding. She shuddered when she sometimes went past it on her way to Liverpool. It was a place that seemed dark and dingy. Thankfully Sybil was out of there, but she often thought of the girls who were still shut up inside and wondered each day what she could do to help them. Betsy wondered about Lettice from time to time, but

James always just sighed. The new baby on the way had kept them distracted and busy, decorating the upstairs room, buying furniture. His mother hadn't wanted to see him. Betsy had tried.

But one morning, looking out to the river and cradling her bump as she listened to James play his favourite Cole Porter song, 'At Long Last Love', on the piano they had recently bought, she said, 'I think I should go and see your mother.'

James took his hands away from the keys and looked at her, aghast. 'Shouldn't I go and visit her before you do? Are you sure?'

He had seen Lettice from time to time, but it felt each visit had been worse than the last, and still she had refused to see Betsy.

'I lost my mother and I still miss her. Mothers matter. Even difficult ones,' she said one morning. 'And the older she gets . . . well, time is running out. I want to tell her about the baby. Maybe that will change things.'

'I'll bet my good leg it won't. She's stubborn, my dear mother.'

'I shall take George with me when he comes home from the Boys' Brigade. Who knows, he might soften her.'

An hour later she was walking with George down Mottram Hall's gone-to-seed drive, edged with blue cornflowers and daisies and bright red poppies, and then a frail Gordon was opening the door to them. George, who was clutching her hand, stared open-mouthed at the brass knocker and the ornate carvings. Steeling herself, Betsy took a deep breath.

*

The light was flooding in through the bay window. On the table sat a vase of slightly wilting pungent-smelling chrysanthemums. George threaded his fingers nervously through Betsy's.

'Lettice. Thank you for seeing me,' Betsy said, thinking how old she looked, how sad, and yet, bewilderingly still alive.

Lettice nodded and then her gaze dropped to George. 'So, you are . . . ?'

'George. My middle name is Vernon,' he answered brightly.

Betsy blushed. The name Vernon would always be a reminder of the sad start to his life, but George never tired of happily telling everyone.

Lettice paused. How could she not return this ten-year-old's sweet smile? Suddenly she felt lonelier than she had ever been.

'Vernon. Unusual name. I knew a Vernon once,' she said.

'The man from the Pools?'

She smiled and leaned forward. 'No. The Vernon I knew was very serious, very clever and very important, something in the Sri Lankan government. He had a smart uniform with gold tassels on his shoulders. Would you like a pear drop?'

George nodded.

Betsy took a deep breath. 'Darn, I think I've dropped a glove.' She stood. 'Maybe when I put my handbag down on the steps? I'll just go and see . . .'

'Gordon!' said Lettice, tinkling the bell.

'No need. I'll find it.'

Taking her chance, she slipped outside, leaving

George sitting on the chaise longue swinging his legs crossed at the ankles, sucking on the pear drop.

'That's a splendid uniform that you're wearing,' Lettice said after a pause.

'I had the Boys' Brigade this morning. We do marching. I want to be in the RAF. Daddy says one day he'll take me up in a plane . . . He got a medal.' He squinted at her. 'Are you my nan? Everyone in my class has at least one nan. I don't have even one.'

She stopped and thought about the question, shrugged and patted her thighs. 'I can be your nan if you want me to. But I'd rather be your granny, dear. Grannies are the same as nans. I don't think I should want to be a nan. Might you call me Granny?'

He nodded and smiled, took the pear drop out, regarded it. Put it back in. 'Granny is fine. Wait till I tell my daddy and my pals I've got a granny.' He leaned forward and smiled again.

Betsy watched the exchange from the door. Her heart stopped as she listened to the conversation.

'Found it! Thank goodness. We have news, Lettice,' she said. 'That's why I'm here.'

She let her coat swing open. Smoothed her hand over the rise in her belly. Lettice's eyes widened.

'You're . . . ?'

'Due at the end of the summer.'

'We have to call Lettice Granny,' George chirped.

'Yes, Granny. Always Granny . . .' Tears were swelling in Lettice's eyes. She dropped her gaze to the floor. 'I'm so sorry,' she said. 'For everything . . .'

'You don't need to say sorry,' murmured Betsy.

'But you need to get knitting. Like what grannies do,'

George said cheekily. 'And bake shortbread and get cross about the trams being late . . . and . . . other things.'

'Shush, George. Some grannies do knitting,' smiled Betsy, taking Lettice's hands. 'But not all grannies,' she said.

'I can't wait,' said Lettice. 'Clickety clack. Now, where's Gordon? Do you like cherryade, George?'

The girl, Ellie she was called, sat chewing the end of a pencil sitting in one of the booths at the Kardomah Café in Liverpool. She was rosy-cheeked with freckles sprinkling her nose. She had taken her seat, Betsy and Mr Worboys had taken theirs, and for a short time Ellie had been unable to meet their eyes. But now Betsy had given her a piece of paper and she had started to try to write in shaky letters about what had happened to her. Mr Worboys had told her to write about how the nuns had taken her in after her mother had died, and her grandmother's house had been destroyed by a bomb, and then about Australia.

'I'd rather tell you my story out loud than write it down. I'm not so good at writing,' she said, chewing the end of the pencil. 'It's hard to know where to start. It's ended happily, thanks be to God. I went to live in Alice's house and now I have a job at Lewis's and I've met someone . . . He's called Trevor . . . The beginning of my story was not so bad . . . but the middle . . . Is it the middle you want to hear about?' She faltered. 'It's not so nice. They told me Australia would be lovely and we would be picking oranges off the trees . . .'

'Ellie . . .' Betsy reached out a hand tentatively. 'Once you tell your story, there will be others. Marcia and her sister Cynthia, who you remember from St Mary's? They have already written theirs down, and Alice, who took you in. She has written about her brothers and sister, who were also orphans of the living for a short time. Just like you. But there are others, girls like Angela, and June, Matilda, some who went to St Sylvester's mother and baby home, Peggy and Evie. Thankfully Mr Cherry here has worked hard, and the orphanage has finally shut down, but we just want people to remember the girls who went there and read about them if they need to. Remember *us*, I mean. I have my story to tell as well, Ellie. There are also plenty with sad, unfinished stories, but perhaps hearing others speak . . . Well, if they feel they are not alone, it would help them as well.'

'All right. I'll start again. But can we start with cake?'

Henry Cherry, who had just joined them with his wife, Marcia, smiled. 'We can, Ellie. Surely the best place to begin,' he said, nodding towards the waitress threading her way through the tables of the cafe. 'Victoria sponge or rhubarb and custard cake?'

A month later, Betsy sat in her front room with a mound of papers on her lap. It was early evening and the room was bathed in a soft rose glow. Her stomach was getting larger and rounder. The cherry tree in the garden was dripping with blossom and the front lawn was spotted with pink. George, with flushed cheeks, chased around the room pulling a toy racing car on a string. The house had a feeling of beautifully organized chaos.

'Shush, dear,' said Betsy.

He rested his head on her lap, yawning as she pushed fingerfuls of hair off his face. Outside she could hear a buzzing. It was a plane swooping low across the river.

'Daddy?'

'Maybe . . .'

It had been a miracle that James was flying again. Mostly his work at Woodvale airbase had been teaching the young men doing their National Service. But the new jet-propulsion engines were making great strides and his expertise in flying the planes had been invaluable, so he had soon been moved to a more challenging and exciting job, helping design the interior of the cockpits and test flying the new commercial planes.

The suitcases were lined up in the hall. George was now running around playing hopscotch with the numbers chalked onto the path. How had her life brought her to this place of joy? She was older, wiser, but at still only twenty-seven she had so much yet to experience. And today was to be another one of those days.

'Taxi's here, Ma!' cried George, wheeling around in circles.

They were soon on their way out of the city, Betsy clutching the plane tickets in her hand.

'Will there be tigers in Spain?' asked George. 'Will we be in the clouds? How does an aeroplane stay in the air if it's made of metal?'

They arrived at Speke airport early.

'Granny!' cried George, when they went into the departures hall.

Lettice was waving, coming towards them dragging

a suitcase. 'We're going on a two-week holiday but she's brought the kitchen sink! I told her not to!' laughed Betsy. An hour later the plane took off, rattling and shaking. Betsy gripped George's hand. The voice came over the tannoy.

'Ladies and gentlemen, this is your captain speaking. We have a smooth flight ahead . . .'

'Don't worry, George. We're in safe hands. Daddy knows what he's doing. He's flown planes hundreds, thousands of times before.'

Gently resting her forehead on the Perspex window, the countryside below stretched out in a beautiful green patchwork quilt. All was calm. Peace now. No dodging enemy aircraft, no flares or flak or guns. The sound of the engines that had once been so terrifying it had always threatened to overwhelm her now seemed a gentle growl. And the air was bluer than blue, with James's beloved clouds wispy and white. She thought of Mr Cherry's file, of the stories that were now neatly typed up and bound waiting to be told as they were passed to men and women to be read quietly in rooms and corridors. Of the girls who, like her, had already spoken of what had happened to them. Marcia and Cynthia, Alice . . . Ellie, Sybil, so many others, and hopefully more.

Who could have imagined, amongst so many heart-breaking stories, that they would all have been lucky enough to finally find such happy endings? She sighed contentedly as the plane rose higher in the endless sky, as they pushed on to warmer places, pushed on to the bright.

Author's Note

Between 1949 and 1976, there were 185,000 forced adoptions in England and Wales. In 1946, 21,000 children were adopted compared to 2,980 in 2024. More than 100,000 children were sent abroad from the United Kingdom to Canada, Australia, New Zealand and South Africa – many from Liverpool, which was one of the main departure cities. During the Blitz 70,000 in Liverpool were made homeless. And 4,000 lost their lives. Families were fractured and struggled to cope. The children of these families, who often turned to religious institutions, were known as 'orphans of the living'. Young single mothers, like Betsy, felt that they had no choice but to give their babies away for adoption. The shame of being an unmarried mother has disappeared, and the expression orphans of the living is rarely heard today. But this book is dedicated to all of those who found themselves in this unbearable situation – including my own grandmother, who after she was widowed with nine young children sent my father and his siblings to St Joseph's orphanage nestling in the sand dunes of Freshfield. I walked with my father many times over those same dunes, and yet he held that secret of his time in the orphanage with the nuns close to his heart until he died, and I only discovered it whilst writing this trilogy. This was a generation who after the trauma of war rarely talked about it. Instead, they often looked forward and didn't dwell on the past. I would like to thank all those who have shared similar stories and helped me bring them into the light so we can remember the heartbreaking yet resilient and inspiring lives that have gone before us. This final book in the trilogy is also dedicated to the incredible bravery of more than 55,000 men – nearly half of Bomber Command – who lost their lives in the Second World War, and to the memory of the 76, including mothers and their babies on the maternity wards, who tragically died in the bombing of Liverpool's Mill Road Hospital on 3rd May 1941.

Acknowledgements

Thanks to my brilliant editor, Gillian Green. This is my seventh book that Gillian has edited. Her insights and experience, without fail, have always helped my storylines and characters become the very best versions of themselves. Thanks also to the wonderful team at Pan Macmillan for such care and detailed work. Thank you to my agent, Judith Murdoch. Thank you to Perryair for the experience of flying a Tiger Moth so I could feel something of what it was like for Betsy and James. Thank you, as always, to Louis, Joel and Peter. Especially for understanding how important me taking to the skies was for this book, and for holding your nerve! And a final mention to Fletcher, Tina and Nelly. When I was a young actress, we were in a musical called *Girlfriends*. We were playing WAAFs and I hope I've captured the spirit of those happy times in this book.

The People's Friend
The Home of Great Reading

If you enjoy quality fiction, you'll love
The People's Friend magazine.
Every weekly issue contains seven original short
stories and two exclusively written serial instalments.

On sale every Wednesday, the *Friend* also includes travel,
puzzles, health advice, knitting and craft projects
and recipes.

It's the magazine for women who love reading!

Angel of Liverpool

*Her mother called her Angel, but now she's
a fallen woman . . .*

There are different opinions as to what happened to
Evangeline O'Leary's mother. Her younger sisters
believe the story that she's in heaven. But Evie has
heard the gossip – that her ma upped and left with
the man she had an affair with whilst Evie's dad
was fighting in the war.

As the eldest, Evie has become 'mum' to her three
siblings, all whilst holding down a job at the
Tate & Lyle sugar factory. But when her childhood
sweetheart leaves for Canada, he leaves Evie with
more than just a broken heart. Her father agrees to
keep the pregnancy a secret but is determined to
marry her off to the first hapless fellow who'll have
her. Evie doesn't want a loveless marriage like her
parents', but how long can she keep her baby a
secret from her neighbours and the nuns who run
the local home for unmarried mothers . . . ?

**Set in the aftermath of the Second World War,
Angel of Liverpool is a gritty and emotionally
compelling historical saga.**

OUT NOW

The Girl from Liverpool

Will the coming war divide them?

For as long as she can remember, Peggy O'Shea has been expected to work at the family dairy, look after her younger siblings and eventually marry cow-keeper Martin Gallagher. And that's the way it has predictably gone, apart from one glorious summer when, at the age of eight, she met handsome Anthony Giardano.

But there's bad blood between the Irish O'Sheas and the Italian Giardanos, so perhaps for the sake of both of their families, it's a good thing when Anthony suddenly disappears.

Ten years later, at the start of the war, Peggy bumps into Anthony again. But as they begin to rekindle their friendship, Italy joins forces with Germany, and Liverpool turns on its Italian residents overnight, making any relationship between Peggy and Anthony impossible . . .

OUT NOW

The Orphans from Liverpool Lane

All she wants is to go home . . .

1944, Liverpool

Marcia is only twelve years old the first time she is sent to the orphanage with her older sister, Cynthia. With their father in a POW camp in Singapore, her mother is struggling to cope and hands them over to the nuns to be 'orphans of the living' – a harsh term for those children with living parents whose families have abandoned them.

Things are looking up when their father finally returns and the girls are allowed home, but it's clear the years in the camp have taken their toll on the sweet man Marcia barely remembers – and the family disintegrates.

Cynthia finds an escape with an aunt and through her ambitions to be a dancer. But Marcia is sent back to the orphanage. And, whilst she finds friends amongst her fellow 'orphans', it is no substitute for the family she so desperately craves . . .

OUT NOW

The Children Left Behind

Will she be able to find hope again?

1940, Liverpool

When Alice Lacey was seven, she and her two best friends, Bob and Matty, watched as the sky was set on fire. Ten years later, the three remain friends and Bob is now Alice's sweetheart. He would marry her tomorrow, but Alice has ambitions to better herself. She finally leaves her factory job to work as an architect's secretary, dreaming of a brighter future and of playing some small part in rebuilding Liverpool.

But will the hope last? The war has ripped families apart and many children are left with nowhere to go but the orphanage. When tragedy strikes and Alice's mother struggles to cope, Alice is horrified to see her brothers and sister facing the same fate. And, to make matters worse, both Bob and Matty seem to be harbouring secrets . . .

OUT NOW